The Opening Sky

The
Opening
Sky

Joan Thomas

McCLELLAND & STEWART

CIP DATA IS AVAILABLE UPON REQUEST

ISBN: 978-0-7710-8392-1
ebook ISBN: 978-0-7710-8393-8

The epigraph is from the poem "River Edge:" from the collection *Torch River*. © Elizabeth Philips 2007. Used by permission of Brick Books.

Typeset in Fairfield
Printed and bound in the United States of America

McClelland & Stewart,
a division of Random House of Canada Limited,
a Penguin Random House Company
www.randomhouse.ca

1 2 3 4 5   18 17 16 15 14

In memory, with love
Joy

Nothing is more beautiful
than anything else: this is how April warns us
and breaks us down.

ELIZABETH PHILIPS, *"River Edge:"*

FOUR CHILDREN WERE LOST THAT NIGHT, THAT'S what they thought at first. And at first this reassured them – how could anything terrible happen to four kids at once? Then an open Jeep drove into the clearing with two little boys in the back, the white-blond brothers from Wisconsin. Someone from a nearby cottage had picked them up on the highway. Their mother, a pretty woman with platinum hair cut as short as theirs, ran across the clearing and fell on them, hugging them, cuffing at them ("You brats, you stupid little jerk-offs," she cried), and their father, who had spent the afternoon drinking cider and sleeping in a hammock tied between two trees, strode around the Jeep to shake the driver's hand.

So then it was just Sylvie missing, and the dark-haired boy with the sick mother, Liam.

From where she crouched at a corner of the woodpile, Sylvie could hear most of what they said. She was thirsty, and light-headed from hunger, and her feet were cold and hurting. She'd run barefoot up from the lake, avoiding the paths where the adults hurried back and forth, calling the kids' names. The tops of the trees were bright, catching the last of the light, but darkness had settled onto the forest floor. The nameless trees were wide enough to hide her, and in the dusk she'd scrambled from one to the next, stifling her yelps of pain when the twigs and roots hiding under the leafy carpet bit at her. Not a child, she was not a child. She was a dark forest creature, lost by her own hand.

At the edge of the clearing, she squatted in fragrant shreds of bark. Above her the forest canopy opened to a dome of brilliant evening sky; a minuscule jet from a different world lifted silently into it. She saw a police car roll up the lane, and then they were all around it, the blond boys and their parents, the driver of the Jeep, the filmmaker, the babysitter, and Sylvie's mom. The faun was led forward. She was the fifth child, the one kid who had not been lost. Two policemen in Smokey the Bear hats (sheriffs, they were sheriffs) bent over her. She was wearing jeans now, and her hair had been taken out of its elastics and straggled down her back. She was talking now too, though Sylvie couldn't make out what she was saying for her crying.

Then Sylvie heard her own name ring out. She shifted on her heels and pressed her face to a gap between the logs. Her mother was standing with her back to the woodpile. "Eleven," she said to the officers. "Quite tall for her age. Her hair's about to here, sort of reddish blond. She's wearing a bathing suit."

"No," sobbed the faun, shaking her head.

"No," said the mother of the blond boys. "She's not wearing the swimsuit."

So Liz tossed her head and began to describe Sylvie's clothes in detail: her jeans, her sandals, her glittery belt, her white T-shirt with the turtle design.

"Yellow," interrupted the faun. "It's yellow."

"White, yellow," Liz cried. "I doubt you'll mistake her either way."

"Did you think of searching your own vehicles?" asked one of the sheriffs. Everyone started eagerly across the clearing in the direction of the cars.

In her yellow T-shirt Sylvie sprang from her crouch and slipped towards the house. There was a side door that opened to the kitchen. The house was quiet and full of warm light. She ran quickly up the stairs, heading for the front bedroom – and a man was standing there. She gave a little prance of fear. But no, it wasn't a man at all, it was a shirt hanging on the back of the closet door. She was alone, in the room with the braid rug and the iron bed and the big wooden desk, where a family photo stood in its cardboard frame, and the boy with the falconer's sleeve gazed out at her with neutral brown eyes.

She went to the desk and opened the drawer. In a tray of pens and paperclips lay a retractable knife, the sort of blade people use to cut open a cardboard box or hijack a plane. She fished it out and slid back its casing. The point of the blade bit boldly into the photograph, slicing through it and through the cardboard backing. *More,* the blade ordered, *deeper,* so when she was done excising the boy from his family, she went to the bedside table and picked up the book she had looked through earlier, a beautiful gilt-edged book. First she slashed its cover with jagged lines, and then she turned to the colour plates inside and took the blade to them. It was a furious relief, this slashing and gouging; it felt natural, like a language she used to speak when she was little.

When she'd had enough, she slipped the picture of the boy into the pocket of her jeans and went to the window. Night had fully fallen. She could hear the squawk and stutter of police radios. A revolving light revealed and then erased the trees at the edge of the forest. Car doors slammed and strangers stepped into the clearing; they sprang up in brilliant detail and vanished. The faun, wearing a jean jacket now, stood with the parents of the blond boys. The father reached for her, and in spite of her size (she was almost as tall as Sylvie), he picked her up. She clung to him, drooping over him. Then headlights caught Sylvie's mother. Alone, perched on the edge of the picnic table, her white capris gleaming. Standing in a fold of the dust-smelling curtain, Sylvie pressed her forehead against the cold glass and peered down, through hot tears willing her mother to turn and look up.

ONE

In the Deep Midwinter

SIX O'CLOCK, AND IN THEIR ATTIC BEDROOM THEY open their eyes wordlessly to each other, roll in opposite directions, and lie on their backs dozing. Aiden hears the traffic start rumbling up Portage Avenue, but he's still his night-time incarnation, and when his eyes open again, he catches sight of *meaning* darting across the skylight like a bird. Then he's awake, looking up at a curved square of Plexiglas dotted with snow. Still dark out, but they're prey to decaying light from ten thousand sodium-vapour street lamps. Liz has dipped back into real sleep, breathing deeply, her mouth slightly open as though she's about to say something. She's angled in the bed, crowding him. He turns onto his side to give her another inch or two. Sleep's over for him anyway, it's moving on to the nocturnals.

To the cats and coyotes and paramedics, and to his daughter, who's a mile away in her dorm room, propped up in a nest of photocopies and muffin papers. Celebrating the solstice by pulling an all-nighter, dozing now in the light of her laptop . . . and in her dream, a girl says, *Loser,* and she opens her eyes. 6:23. *God.* She stretches her legs and feels a Red Bull can under the duvet.

She's been working since yesterday afternoon, since four-thirty to be exact, which is when the sun went down. Sixteen hours of darkness last night, courtesy of the tilt of the earth. Oh, astronomy – if only she could have fitted it in.

Her eyes slide back to her screen and she tries to pull her botany project into focus. Around three she was totally in the zone, ideas coming so fast she could hardly get them down. But now her words have morphed into something she can't read – Cyrillic maybe, or Cree syllabics. With a sigh she saves the file, drops the lid of her laptop, and turns her cheek towards her pillow. Instantly she's back on the fast chute to sleep, falling heavily into it, greedy for it, roaming through its tangled garden, a hungry scavenger gobbling sleep up.

It's ten-thirty by the time Sylvie makes it to the Notion, the new café where she's meeting her friends to work on their Fringe show. They're all standing out on the street.

"We're not going in," Nathan says. "It's a stealth Starbucks." He just read this on Twitter and they've been texting her. She was rushing, she didn't check her messages.

As they cut across to the cafeteria in Lockhart Hall, she glances at their faces. No one's sulking. Sylvie can get away with almost anything.

They take a table along the side, leaving a trail of salt and sand from the mucky sidewalks, and spread out their gear. Emily buys a bottle of green tea from a machine and passes it around, but Sylvie's desperate to eat. She pulls her mug out of her backpack.

The usual guy is working the counter. Bacteria have colonized the pores on his forehead since Sylvie saw him last. She gives him a nice hello. "Brown toast," she says. "Peach yogurt. And I'll have an Americano – make it a triple." She slides her mug across the counter. Tea tree oil, she thinks, that's what he should try. It's counterintuitive because it's an oil, but it works.

While he makes her toast, she turns and looks back at her friends, sitting there like the undead, waiting for her:

Emily, their Fringe director, in a blue MEC anorak that no doubt belongs to her mother.

Thea, Sylvie's friend from Wolseley. Who hasn't brushed her pale hair in two years. They're proto-dreads, she keeps insisting, she's using the neglect method.

Nathan, their only guy. Sylvie can still picture him back in grade six, standing sweetly under a trellis with a plastic rose pinned to the lapel of his Value Village suit jacket. They would stage weddings in someone's backyard on Saturday mornings. They had bouquets, a veil, and Celine Dion on the ghetto blaster, because Nathan was in charge of the music. He had zero sense of irony then and he has zero now. But he's all theirs – the guys have no claim on him.

And Kajri, her beautiful roommate for three semesters now, turning a warm and funny look in Sylvie's direction.

Sylvie smiles back. *Kajri, Kajri,* she says in her mind, savouring the sound. She has her precious mother to thank for Kajri. When Sylvie won the argument about moving to Laurence Hall, she really wanted a private room and her dad was willing to pay for it. But Liz was being a cow – not because she wanted Sylvie at home, and not even because of the money, but because it bugged her that Sylvie was getting what she wanted. The argument she came up with was "It's not a bad experience, when you're young, to have to live with someone who doesn't love you." And then Liz must have been totally, totally burned, because the minute Sylvie walked into their room in Laurence Hall and her new roommate looked up from the box she was unpacking, she and Kajri *loved* each other.

The guy with the bad skin is back with her toast. He hands her the coffee in a Styrofoam cup. "I gave you my mug," she says. So he reaches for her mug and pours the coffee into it and drops the Styrofoam cup into the garbage. Without a second thought!

"Wait," Sylvie says. "Why do you think I'm carrying a mug?" But he's turned away. She wants to make a fuss but she's no better than he is. All night she was *aching* for a Starbucks latte. She can't help it, she's been socialized like everybody else, she was born the year the Starbucks mermaid lost her nipples.

Emily has her laptop out when Sylvie gets back to the table. Sylvie sits down beside her and starts to eat her toast, keeping her eyes on the screen.

Adieu, Les Isles Maldives, Emily types. She frowns briefly over the font, picks Tahoma and then switches to Shruti. She takes the title up to seventy-two points and swivels her laptop around so the others can see.

"*Adieu, Les Isles Maldives*," Kajri reads out. "That's the name of our show?"

"Why is it French?" says Nathan.

"It makes it more pitiful," Emily says. Less banal, she must mean. Words are not Emily's strong point. On the lid of her laptop is a sticker: Earth as a ball of ice cream melting over its cone.

They sit in silence. Emily is waiting to hear from Sylvie and Thea. But Thea has zoned out; she's gazing down at something. Sylvie leans over to see. It's her tights. They're lime green and purple, an intricate pattern that may actually be tessellation. Where did you get them? Sylvie mouths. Pico's, Thea mouths back, batting her eyes.

"Also," says Emily loudly and firmly, "*adieu* means 'to God.' These islands are being given back to god, for eternity. Not *God*-god – you know what I mean. Anyway, forget the name. The name doesn't matter for now. What did you all bring?"

"I found a piece about the Maldives government," says Kajri. She got up around five and went to work in the common room, but still she found time to put on gel eyeliner, perfectly, top and bottom. "The cabinet of the Maldives government actually held a meeting *underwater*. They were wearing oxygen tanks and wetsuits, to dramatize what rising sea levels will mean to their country."

"No shit!" says Sylvie in admiration. She sips her coffee. She's finished her toast and yogurt and she's still ravenous.

"Well," says Emily to Kajri, "so that's been done. And for real. Good for them." She produces a tense, insincere smile. She's their director because she did the Fringe application; they're all grateful to her for that, and Sylvie is *not* going to undermine her. She's not, although it's stupid and unnecessary to be working on this during Christmas week. Emily is testing her power and they're letting her.

Sylvie is waking up now, she is tuning in to the fact that this day has actually started, the shortest day of the year. Think of all the other things she should be doing! *Noah*: She should be getting ready for Thursday, when he's arriving from Guelph (doing her laundry, shaving her legs, finding her only tube of lip gloss). *Christmas*: She has to make her gifts (the little cactus gardens). *School*: Her Evo-Devo take-home; her Human Impact on the Environment paper, currently overdue; the permaculture project she worked on last night. All these jobs are flashing in her mind like icons on a task bar, yet here she sits, staring at Emily with her frizzy hair and her dorky jacket and that look of parental anxiety – a monster they've created themselves.

Thea finally comes to life. She lifts her eyes from her tessellated tights and reaches for her backpack. "Observe," she says. "I went to the trouble and expense of printing this in colour. At Staples. It was in a magazine at my oma's, and she wouldn't let me tear it out because it belonged to someone else." She spreads a two-page article on the table.

It's about a restaurant at a resort in the Maldives. An underwater restaurant – an acrylic dome five metres below sea level. In the picture, tourists seem to be sitting in a slice of aqua water filtered with light. Silver fish dart around them, hundreds of fish, moving together like a lithe comet. This restaurant is so exclusive it seats only twelve diners. Flat rate US$250 per person, before drinks.

Sylvie and her friends stare in awe. "Lamb," says Nathan, reading upside down. "They copter in *lamb* for a restaurant with twelve customers. *Fuck*, that's obscene."

Thea sits with her big head tilted, soaking up their amazement. "So," she says, "I thought we could do a scene in the restaurant. The customers order all these imported things, they sit with fish swimming around them, they're all like, 'Awesome! Wow!' and then gradually the fish disappear and the walls are smeared with tar balls."

"How would we do that? The fish, the tar balls."

"Black light."

"Is there even offshore drilling in the Maldives? Does anybody know?"

"Or is it on a tanker route?"

"That's not the point," says Sylvie. "We're totally missing the point."

Thea throws a dark look in Sylvie's direction.

"Okay," Emily says. "Before we get too obsessed with the restaurant, let's finish going around."

It's Nathan's turn. "All right," he says. "Get this. I found an article where the journalist is like, 'These beautiful islands are being destroyed by the excesses of the Western world.' And at the end he goes, 'This is a paradise. Go and see it, jump on a carbon-spewing plane today, because it won't be there tomorrow.'"

Silence settles over them. This is their problem: reality always tops them. Behind them the espresso machine roars on. Nathan's eyes dart eagerly from one of his friends to another. And our other problem . . . thinks Sylvie, but then she can't think. Her mind goes back to high school grad night, a year and a half ago, when they went to the Pancake House in the grey light of dawn. Over a platter of French toast Nathan suddenly teared up and asked them not to call him "The Groom" anymore. And so they don't. Now they call him "Ken," behind his back.

"Sylvie?" says Emily.

"I didn't bring anything on the Maldives," Sylvie says. "I don't know if I'm sold on it, as our subject. There are other places being ruined by climate change, like Bangladesh and Pakistan, where millions and millions of people live. Or the Horn of Africa. Or our own Arctic. Why did we choose the Maldives? It's sexier, I guess. Or we think it's sexier because there is more tourism there."

They stare at her. Across their faces flash two signals Sylvie is used to seeing. *You're so smart, Sylvie. Why don't you piss off, Sylvie?*

"I'm not trying to slow us down," she says. "Honestly. I'm not being a bitch about this. It's just that . . . I don't feel well. In fact, I have to go right now."

Someone's in the bathroom, looking at her from behind the sinks. What a hot girl, is her split-second thought when she glimpses herself (grungy, sleepless, sick) in the mirror. Noah's responsible for this, even though he's still in Guelph. Sex, sex, sex – this run-down tiled bathroom throbs with it. That's what her dream was about just before her phone woke her up. Not Noah coming home, just sex. Something secret and delicious tugs at her from it. It was like being deep in a colour, or a texture like velvet. It was just a mood. Not a *drama*, which is what most dreams are.

She sits on the toilet with her jeans still on, folds herself over with her head hanging down – a private bit of theatre to justify leaving the meeting. She's in no danger of puking. She's not sick, she just feels weird. She straightens up and leans into a corner of the tiny stall, and exhaustion crashes down on her like bricks. In a flash her eyes are closed and she's dreaming again. She's skimming through a stand of massive trees, a dark, enchanted forest, trees with jocular patches of red hung here and there in their upper branches, trees crammed so close she can hardly slip between them. "Roots to shoots," she mutters. She pushes her way through the forest and hears a snore, and shakes herself awake. Oh god, how could she fall asleep on a toilet?

She stands, picks up her backpack, and pushes open the door of the stall. It's not just that she's tired, it's the fucking pill. She should never have started it, and the longer she stays on it the worse she feels. She did it to please Noah. Not that he'd asked her to (he'd probably be against it if he stopped to think it through), but he told her his penis-wearing-a-condom riddle (What is happy and sad at the same time?) and just because of that she ignored her own principles and went to the doctor and asked for the pill. She did it to make Noah happy. And that is wrong in every way – her body is telling her how wrong it is.

She moves to the sink and turns the tap and watches water run silver over her fingers. What is bad for the planet is bad for the body. And vice versa, she tells herself. She'll go to the walk-in clinic, she'll go now. She doesn't have time. But she needs to get some different birth control before Noah gets home. Go now, she orders herself, banging on the chrome bar of the hand-dryer. Go right now.

On his noon break, Aiden heads for the footbridge to the park. Across the bridge he swerves onto the river trail, plodding like a pony. He reaches up and sticks in his earbuds (they're new, he loves them, they fit like a charm) and Tom Waits is growling in his ear. He hits Forward and lands on a guitar riff he knows to his bones.

Below him the river is clotting into ice. Or is it melting? It's melting, and the snow that fell in the night is softening, each little origami of a snowflake losing its hold on itself and turning to water. And then everything will freeze, and the city will be a mess of frozen ruts until March.

Another freak December. A dog turd on the path – Aiden sees it and then, Aw shit, he nails it. Almost Christmas and not cold enough to freeze dog shit. He does his midday mood check, gives himself a seven, but a knot of shame catches when he breathes.

He thuds along the trail and forces himself back to it, back to his fractious morning, to nine o'clock, nine-fifteen. He was sitting by the desk with his mug of coffee in hand and his first client, Norman Orlikow, dapper as a badger on the pleather couch, was telling a long story about his neighbour dying the week before, during routine elective surgery.

Aiden listened conscientiously, taking note of Norman's grasp of medical detail and how much satisfaction he took in displaying it. But finally he gave his chair a cut-to-the-chase swivel. "You were really close to this neighbour?" he said, or words to that effect. That's when he registered the light in Norman's eyes. It was triumph.

Turns out that one day last summer, the neighbour's dog, a possibly illegal pit bull cross, had lunged at Norman as he innocently walked by on a public sidewalk. So Norman called the police. Two officers came but they wouldn't take the incident seriously. There was a scene on the street, people gathered. The dog made nice, rotating its ugly stump of tail, and the neighbour cracked jokes and rolled his eyes in a private signal to the cops that what they were dealing with here was the local nutbar. And now the neighbour has died.

Norman paused, shiny eyed. "You know what's really strange?" he said. "Since the summer, three people I know have . . . passed. Tom Spokes – you might have heard of him, the guy who was killed in that freak accident on the Osborne Bridge? His SUV jumped the guardrail, d'you remember? And Nancy Sylvester, my old piano teacher – she had an embolism. And now this gentleman. And you know, it's kind of bizarre, but a few weeks before each of them passed, we had what you might call a run-in." His face was thoughtful, almost reverent. "It's true, you know. I only just realized it last night. At one time or another, every one of those three people treated me like dirt."

Man has no greater happiness in life than watching his neighbour fall off a roof. But Aiden knew this was something else. "You believe the deaths of these people are connected to the way they treated you," he said.

Embarrassment rejigged the lines of Norman's face. "Ha! Like I have that kind of power. Ha ha, I wish! Of course I don't think that, Doctor Phimister." He's been in therapy a long time, Norman has, with other people.

Aiden said, not for the first time, "I'm not a doctor." He let a beat go by, put down his coffee. "I wonder if you haven't felt humiliated at one time or another by pretty much every person you know. Then when somebody dies, you see this sort of cause and effect. You feel vindicated, as if they were being paid back for how they treated you."

NORMAN (*gone very still*): That would be sick. It would be. Really sick. Is that the way you see me?

AIDEN: You're the one who linked the three of them. I'm just trying to make sense of what I'm hearing.

NORMAN (*eyes round and black, as if he were summoning up the furies*): Are you trying to humiliate me, Doctor Phimister?

AIDEN: No, I'm trying to help you understand yourself.

NORMAN: I don't think so, Doctor Phimister. I think you're trying to humiliate me.

AIDEN (*grinning like an ass*): Maybe *I* should start watching my back. I might be the next to die. From no real cause.

That's when the histrionic bastard jumped to his feet and started kicking. First at Aiden's wire wastebasket, then at the weeping fig, knocking it over. Then he stomped out into the waiting room and kicked in the privacy glass by the door, putting his boot through the middle pane.

Can't you joke? Aiden asks himself, shifting his weight to the balls of his feet as the trail rises. No, you can't joke, at least not with Norman Orlikow. Who's got his precious diagnosis from the DSM – he waved it like a diploma the first time he came to the office. Social Anxiety Disorder. Who did actually say he wished he had the power to kill people who offended him. He did! Aiden should work with a tape recorder for instant playback, the way the police do.

No, Aiden should watch his own reactivity.

Steve Earle in his earbuds now, and Aiden's by the English Garden, the flowers are mounds under the snow, and he turns his mind to the most troubling hour of this troubling morning, to Odette Zimmerman. Who appeared in the doorway annoyingly early, while Aiden was still picking glass out of the carpet in the waiting room. "Don't ask," he said.

She lowered herself into a chair and watched him, amused in her haughty way. She looks like the woman who walks into the private eye's office at the beginning of a film noir: she's got the widow's peak, and the scary eyebrows, and the severe, dramatic way of dressing, and you know without a doubt that what you're about to hear has bugger all to do with the real story. She's a cultural historian,

Odette, though she doesn't have a position at the moment, she's reduced to displaying her erudition to bus drivers and the paper boy and, of course, to Aiden. She was caught shoplifting – that's why she's in therapy. A filet of Arctic char, then a lava lamp from a second-hand store. As acting-out behaviour, none of this interested her much. She tried to intellectualize it: wasn't the lava lamp about something called *thing theory*?

This morning she launched into one of her pontifications as soon as they'd moved to the office, holding her gaze aloft as though she were reading the words off the ceiling. One minute Aiden was listening for the vital thread, then the next minute he was completely at sea. "Anyway, last night it came to me, crystal clear," he surfaced to hear her say. "And I don't know why it took me this long to see it. I need to tell him. We'd both be so much better off if I just spoke my truth."

"Come again?" Aiden said.

"Dante," Odette said, lowering her gaze to the altitude of Aiden's forehead. "I just need to tell him how I feel. The way we are with each other right now, it's always there. It's the elephant in the room. It's not good for either of us."

Dante. It was her son she was talking about, her eighteen-year-old son. A month into therapy she'd announced, "I'm very tuned in to my sexual attraction to Dante. Very. He walks into the room and I am instantly aroused."

The shock and revulsion Aiden felt, it wasn't just for what she'd said. It was the exhilaration in her eyes, the level of self-involvement that would let her reveal something like that with no inhibition. He knew she read psychoanalytic theory for fun; in her mind, she and Aiden were consulting, peer with peer, over a fascinating patient. This lust for her son she seemed to regard as her Freudian bona fides. "You can't control what you don't own," she was fond of musing, a sentiment Aiden could hardly dispute. Since she dropped that bombshell, he's worked hard to keep the focus on her, on how she can deal with her sexuality in healthy ways, but she's always been more interested in parsing the strands of this anarchic attraction, as though there might be a treasure at the end, some big psychoanalytic payoff.

So, this morning. "Better it should be clear between us," she said.

"Odette," Aiden said. He leaned forward and took her hand, something he never did – in six or eight years of counselling he had never before touched a client. But he held her wrist hard to get her attention. She finally met his eyes, already resentful.

"Listen to me," he said. "That would be a huge mistake. It would be extremely damaging to your son. It would deprive him of his mother. These feelings of yours have nothing to do with him." He could feel his anger in his nostrils. "Tell me this," he said. "You chose your last appointment before a two-week break to drop this. Why?"

"It just came to me."

"I don't believe that. You've set your mind on this. You don't want to give us a chance to work it through. You're asking me to ratify a decision you've made to act destructively."

"So feelings are bad? That's what you're telling me?"

"Acting on them can be. You're an adult. It's infantile to think we're entitled to act on every feeling."

Finally she promised not to talk to Dante about it over the holidays. That was the most Aiden could extract from her.

As soon as the door closed behind Odette, Aiden picked up the phone, punched in Edith Wong's number, and left a message. She's a good colleague; they do a lot of consulting. Don't obsess, he tells himself now, plodding between stands of red dogwood poking through the snow. Have a little trust. She brought it to therapy first.

He overtakes two women, passes them in a show of strength. He jogs by the shack – the homeless shack hidden in the trees on the riverbank. Simple living. His thoughts jump to his daughter, to Sylvie at Lower Fort Garry, the job she had as a kid. As a historical re-enactor – what a great job – it was 1832 the whole summer. He was away a lot, doing the intensive for his counselling program, but when he could, he got up in the morning and drove her there. She'd sit in the car braiding her hair with nimble fingers, holding each pigtail in her mouth while she fixed it with a white ribbon. No elastic bands back then.

"Was that in your handbook?"

"Nope," Sylvie said. "I figured it out." She was about eleven at the time, she was under some sort of child-labour contract.

The path curves into the forest and the city falls away – just him in the bush. Twelve trees per person in this city. He reaches up and squelches his iPod. Sometimes you hear chickadees along this path. Today all he hears is his Adidas on the gravel, plod, plod, plod, plod. His feet *have trod, have trod, have trod, and all is seared with trade, bleared, smeared with toil, and wears man's smudge and shares man's smell.* Ah, fuck Hopkins, you can't run to Hopkins, all those sprung rhythms. Running, you gotta have the old iambic. Ta-*da*, ta-*da*, ta-*da*, ta-*da. With tears he fights and wins the field, his naked breast stands for a shield, his camp is pitchèd in a stall, his bulwark but a broken wall.*

Then he's back in traffic, he's jogging on the spot at the stoplight, and then he's at his building. Sweat worms down his face and his runners are sopping. Somebody's plastered cheap Christmas crap all over the elevator; tinsel droops like cobweb onto his head. He's riding up with an MBA in a tailored suit. Sixteen floors of tax lawyers and marketers and accountants and real estate tycoons in this building – the whole block hums with mercantile intrigue.

And there at the centre of it, in a cloister of secrets and tears, sits Aiden Phimister, Bachelor of Arts (Psych./Eng.), Master of Arts (Eng.), Master of Family and Individual Therapy. The MBA sharing the elevator doesn't look at him, but no doubt he smells him, he feels Aiden's heat. They're two different species, sensing each other in the woods and veering in opposite directions.

The winter sun is a white disk behind the clouds when Sylvie slings her backpack over one shoulder and starts down Ellice Avenue. Christmas wreaths hang from the light poles, shreds of limp plastic, the colour of camouflage gear. Who thinks that sort of thing is a good idea? *Pine boughs*, Sylvie thinks as she walks swiftly along the slushy street, refreshed by her tiny nap on the toilet, and her mind veers to her botany project, her brilliant permaculture design – the globe artichokes and borage and Swiss chard and kale growing in free and happy collaboration, the strawberries for groundcover and the flowers to attract predator insects to keep the pests down, and no wasteful rigid rows like the garden she planted when she was young. A warm light fills her mind, the light of Dr. Hillsborough standing in his office doorway, saying, "I think you have a gift for this." And then an ugly image snaps its jaws, a flash of recall from just before sleep swamped her this morning. The words "Replace Existing File," and *herself clicking on them.* She'd opened a new window with her rough draft – her lame, pathetic rough draft – looking for a paragraph she'd deleted. Had she ever, once in the night, saved all the new work she had done?

She's just past Lockhart Hall. She wheels around, runs back, and dashes up the steps. On a bench in the wide, empty common area she yanks her laptop out of her pack, boots it, taps frantically on the control pad. *Neglected_garden.doc*. She scans the first paragraph. "Oh god!" she gasps. UNDO, UNDO.

Benedictor is where she hoped he'd be, working in a study carrel just outside the library.

"Oh god, Benedictor," Sylvie cries. "I'm so glad you're here! I did something so, so stupid!" Her laptop is still on; she's been running through Lockhart Hall with it open in front of her like an accident victim. She sets it on his desk. "Look. My botany paper. It's due tomorrow. But look." She scrolls down. "Oh my god, it should be twelve pages! My tables – where are my tables?"

He gets it instantly. "You saved an old version on top of your new one."

"Oh god!" She weaves her fingers through her bangs, clenches them. Now she does feel like puking. "I did so much great work yesterday and in the night. Oh god. Oh, I'm so stupid! It's like, I saw Replace and my brain was on drugs or something."

"That's bad, Sylvie. That's really bad." He looks at her gravely.

"I know, but it was six o'clock in the morning. I haven't slept since, like, last week. Oh, Benedictor, can you get it back?"

"I don't know. I can try. Can you leave it here?"

"Yes. Yes!"

There's a half-eaten egg sandwich on plastic wrap in front of him. He was probably up all night too. She can see his kindness in his face. She can see him wanting to reassure her, but he's so honest he can't. Instead he raises a hand to give her a high-five. When their two hands touch, they could be an Olympic symbol, his so black, hers so white. She loves him. She should date him. If she hadn't found Noah, she would.

At the clinic she asks for Dr. Rodham. He's away, but she can see someone named Dr. Valdez if she's prepared to wait an hour.

She's prepared – she can study anywhere. She finds a chair in the crowded waiting room and pulls out her Evolutionary Development handouts. *Evo-Devo, Evo-Devo,* her mind chants. It would make a great name. Or, like, Eva Diva.

Dr. Roadster, she calls Dr. Rodham. *Of course* he's away. He'll be driving along the California coast in a convertible with a blond beside him. Sylvie's seen him twice. The first time, last August, when she came to ask about going on the pill, the nurse put her in an examination room to wait. Through the wall she could hear a guy talking on the phone. He was trying to rent a car at LAX. "Honda Fit?" he said in a disgusted tone. "What do you have in the Porsche line? What about a BMW? A Z4? You don't have a single bloody roadster?" Finally he hung up and then the door opened, and he came in flashing a smile that had nothing to do with happiness or friendliness. His teeth were over-whitened.

She told him she wanted to start on a contraceptive pill and he gave her a sales talk about a pill you took for three months straight without having a period.

"Is that natural?" she asked. "For your body?"

"Natural?" he said. "Cave women didn't menstruate. They were either malnourished or they were pregnant or they were lactating."

It felt like a trick. Normally people in a doctor's position want to make things harder for you. But the next thing she knew he had printed the prescription and was holding it out to her. "Fun, fun, fun," he said.

Or possibly she added that when she told her friends that night, when they were having a big conversation on Jenn's deck.

"Wouldn't your mother know all about this?" a girl named Ella asked. "Isn't this, like, her thing?"

"My . . . *mother?*" Sylvie said, as if it were a word she'd never heard before.

"Yeah, doesn't she run a birth control clinic or something?"

Thea started laughing like a maniac. "PMS! Think about the PMS you're going to have!"

"I saw an SNL bit," Jenn said, suddenly remembering. "About a *twelve*-month pill. Tina Fey was in it – she was crazy with PMS, she was swinging an axe around."

But that actually reassured Sylvie. In the afternoon she'd googled the drug. Somebody had posted a comment: *I would wait till its been on the market longer and not let yourself be a ginny pig.* But this pill had been around a long time – since when Tina Fey was on *Saturday Night Live*. The more they talked, the more Sylvie could see that it was absolutely the most responsible thing to do. Tampons every month made a lot of garbage. And then there was the land given over to growing cotton, which is a terrible crop for the soil. Of course, Dr. Roadster was likely being bribed by the drug company. That's not something she thought about then, though she thinks about it now.

She reads her Evo-Devo handouts for half an hour and then takes a break and goes out to a machine in the hall to buy some pseudo-food. It's now afternoon, only four more hours until sunset. When she was a kid, she'd made a model of the solar system, with a beach ball as the sun and a dried cranberry stuck on a crooked silver pin as Earth. THE AXIS OF THE EARTH IS JUST AN IMAGINARY LINE BETWEEN THE POLES, she wrote on the legend. But all the same, she used a protractor when she bent the silver pin, careful to get the angle right. Because Earth is a *slave* to that imaginary line: it spins at a tilt around it, which is why, minute by minute, everybody's being carried deeper into the cold and the dark, whether they like it or not.

Everybody. That is so North-centric, as Noah would point out right away. *Noah is coming.* She stands in the hall chewing sugary glued-together oatmeal and thinks of them wedged together on her narrow bed. How cool would it be if they could evade their parents for a few days, hide out at Laurence Hall after Kajri leaves for the holidays. They'll do it. Sylvie will *kidnap* him. She sees him riding down the escalator at the airport, everyone but him carrying huge shopping bags spilling over with wrapped gifts, his alert eyes scanning the crowd of families hugging hello, and here it's *her* leaning against the back wall of the arrivals area.

She turns back into the clinic, but before she can sit down, the receptionist calls her name and leads her into one of the examination rooms. A mirror's been hung behind the door and she raises her upper lip and checks for bits of granola caught in her front teeth. Sleepy, scruffy, silly Sylvie, she hums, neatening her eyebrows with a finger.

She sits down and checks her cell again. Nothing. She's been at the clinic almost an hour. Benedictor will be done. He'll have found it, she knows in her heart. But it's crazy to be waiting here while she has so much work to do. I'll just leave, she's saying to herself when the door opens and Dr. Valdez comes in.

A woman, young. Hard to guess her age – she's wearing a plastic hair band, and Sylvie knows instinctively that she looks exactly the way she did when she was a fourteen-year-old sitting in the front row of science class with her hand up. Dr. Valdez is a nerd. They will be able to talk through the whole contraception dilemma.

"I'm on the pill but I want to talk to you about going off it," Sylvie begins. "My boyfriend's away for months at a time, so it's a stupid method of birth control for us. It's kind of complicated why I agreed to it in the first place. I know there's a big issue with hormones entering the water table. I knew this all along, but I just saw a documentary about the fish in the Great Lakes, and I kind of *got* it in a different way. So, I need something else. Also it's making me feel weird. And it didn't work the way it was supposed to."

25

"What do you mean?" Dr. Valdez asks.

Sylvie tells her how she stopped after the first three months but she didn't have a period like they said she would. And how Dr. Rodham, when she came to see him again, said this was not uncommon and she should just restart anyway after a week.

The doctor is reading Sylvie's chart, and Sylvie realizes with disappointment that she's not really interested in her concerns about the pill. She may be a smart woman but she's not looking at the big picture. She sends Sylvie into a little room to pee into a bottle, telling her to put on a paper gown afterwards and get up on the examining table. When she comes back she sets about doing a complete physical. She checks Sylvie's blood pressure, she hits her knees with a little hammer to test her reflexes, she makes her stick out her tongue and say "Ahh." She is thorough just for the sake of being thorough. She's the sort of person you always want in your group for projects – picky and annoying, someone the whole group subtly resists, but in the end, when Little Ms. Perfect pulls out a spreadsheet with all the data no one else bothered to keep, you *worship* her.

Sylvie lies down as requested and sticks her heels into the stirrups on each side of the examination table. She endures the insertion of a freezing cold clamp thing. There is something reassuring about being handled and examined in this neutral way, having all your orifices inspected. I am going to be a doctor, she thinks. I'll be a doctor who looks at the big picture. She tries to merge the image of herself in a white coat and stethoscope with the picture that took hold in her heart during the fall: herself standing in a terraced field backed by blue mountains, clasping hands with grateful subsistence farmers.

"You still have a few tags," Dr. Valdez says.

"Tags?" Sylvie asks.

"From your hymen," the doctor says. Then she presses hard all over Sylvie's abdomen, asking question after question. You're nineteen? Are you living at home? How much alcohol do you drink? Are you in a steady relationship? Your boyfriend's also a student? Did you ever miss a pill? When is the last time you were intimate with your boyfriend? It's like she's trying to develop a profile of young adult sexual behaviour. Her voice is pleasant but expressionless. Sylvie feels an overwhelming curiosity about her, about *her* sex life. Just for a clue about what she'll be in for if she becomes a doctor. Dr. Valdez has clean, smooth skin. She is pretty in the way of serious women who have absolutely no interest in their looks. A lot of people disregard that kind of beauty. Her hazel eyes drift to Sylvie's face and Sylvie smiles encouragingly.

Aiden's desk phone is blinking when he comes in from his run. The first message is from Jake Peloquin, terse, cancelling his four o'clock appointment. The second is Sylvie.

"Dad? I'm going to come by your office. Five o'clock, okay? Don't go home before I get there." She's crying.

Aiden tries her cell but she doesn't pick up. While he's still at the desk, the phone rings.

"Hey!" Liz says.

"Hi. I was just going to call you."

"Well, I got in first! So guess what? *We got the apartment!*"

"The apartment."

"In Sarlat? The flat in Sarlat?"

"Oh."

"We got it! That New York couple cancelled. Somebody *died*. I got an email from the agency. I can't believe it! We've got it for the last week of April. That's perfect, don't you think?"

27

Aiden produces a sound about halfway between *wow* and *well*. He reaches for the venetian blind rod and twiddles it, peering down into the street, as though Sylvie might already be out there, walking up to the entrance with her backpack over one shoulder.

"So I'll put the deposit through on my card?"

"I guess that's the plan."

"And I'm thinking maybe I should just book our flight this afternoon. Fares are going way up in January. Cheryl Ogilvie told me – her husband works for Air Canada. What do you think?"

"Makes sense. Listen, Sylvie called, she's coming by the office later. Do we have anything planned for supper? In case she wants to come home?"

"I took something out of the freezer this morning."

"Any eyes floating in it?"

"Oh, quite possibly. It's lamb stew. But that lamb ate grass until they killed it."

"We'll stop for something. We'll go to DeLuca's on the way home."

"Aiden," Liz says, "if Sylvie wants to come for dinner, she can pick a few slivers of lamb out of her stew."

"You're a hard woman," Aiden says.

He steps into the shower, a narrow stall he had retrofitted into what used to be a closet. Drop your soap and you have to open the door to bend for it. The water hits and the morning's anxiety lifts a little. The endorphins are humming from his run, and Liz is in his mind, her excitement about April in the Dordogne. She'll dress up every night and they'll prowl the cobblestones for an hour, scrutinizing menus at thirty euros a pop. He can see it all, extrapolating from Provence where apparently no one goes anymore, he can see the amber carriage lights, the awnings, and the candles in their little jars, the maitre d' in his white jacket, staring at them with avarice and contempt. *Cassoulet au canard, confit de canard, canard à l'orange.* We're the offspring of labourers, Aiden thinks, reaching for his shampoo. We're totally broke end of the month and we live like potentates.

Dry and dressed, he fishes his lunch out of the bar fridge, drops down on the couch, and sets into it, a piece of leftover grilled salmon with mayo on that seedy bread from Gunn's Bakery. A can of V8, that's his veg. "O Holy Night" is labouring its way to a dreary climax in the waiting room as he chomps on his sandwich, shaking the crumbs off the front of his shirt onto his lunch bag; the radio's always on, so a client who shows up early can't make out what's being said in the office. When Norman Orlikow flipped out this morning, flinging his boot like a Cossack dancer, some sort of rousing symphony was playing, Rimsky-Korsakov maybe.

Normally Aiden can tune out the music, though a client called him on it once. Carol Feldman was sitting there itemizing her husband's faults and Aiden had one ear tuned to the waiting room, trying to figure out which movement of *The Four Seasons* he was hearing. Carol finally said, "Am I boring you?" Well, he paid her the respect of a frank response. "Yes," he said. "You've been saying the same thing for almost a year. It's time to listen to yourself." An important moment for both of them.

He shoves the last corner of the sandwich into his mouth and drains his juice. As he tosses his sandwich bag towards the garbage can, worry stirs in his chest. For Sylvie, who rarely cries. She's got a fierceness about her, her mother's fierceness, though (and this is not like Liz), Sylvie doesn't care a lot what other people think. Even when she was tiny, riding around on Aiden's shoulders with her hands in his hair, she was absolutely clear about what she wanted; it was like she took her counsel from a white bird perched in a pear tree. And now, though they live a twenty-minute walk from the university, she's on her own, in student housing. He hates it, he loathes that fucking co-ed dorm with its dust balls the size of rats, and holes in the walls, and crates of empties stacked outside the doors, and bad rap blaring day and night, and in the morning, testosterone-crazed nogoodniks dragging themselves into the toilets bare-chested, their pyjama bottoms sliding down their butts (just snagged up by their morning boners), while his daughter with her sleepy face like a flower walks past them in her pink bathrobe to take her morning pee.

He shifts, recrosses his legs. They don't actually have communal toilets in Sylvie's dorm.

But she's got a boyfriend now, and a guy will do it: he'll steal away a young woman's poise and independence. This boy's been out of town all fall, in grad school – apparently he's a bright light in science – but they seem to have lasted. Sylvie has never brought him home, and Aiden and Liz might not have known he existed except that, last August, Aiden ran into them in Osborne Village. They were standing outside the Gas Station Theatre eating roasted corn from a cart. "Busted!" he said, sliding up beside Sylvie. She swung around, and he could see that she did feel caught out.

Noah Oliphant, that was the guy's name. "Sorry," he said, gesturing with his corncob that he couldn't shake hands.

"Noah just got off a boat," Sylvie said. "The *Namao*." It was a social smile she gave Aiden, but he forgave her – she was trying to compose herself.

Aiden knew what the *Namao* was, a research boat on the big lake. "What was your job?" he asked.

"Benthos," Noah said. "I'm the benthos guy. I'm spending my summer screening mud from the bottom." He pushed his shades up on the bridge of his nose with the back of his wrist.

"What's in the mud?"

"Tiny invertebrates mostly. Mayflies — what we call fish flies. We're monitoring how the eutrophication of the lake affects their growth."

"How big are the little buggers at the moment?" Aiden asked.

"Practically microscopic," Noah said, not missing a beat, though Aiden knew he'd been talking about population growth.

"But he saw bald eagles! And moose. And bears! Three different times, on the shore." Sylvie was wearing a miniskirt and a bright green T-shirt, and her lips shone with butter. "He's still walking like he's drunk. Show Dad, Noah."

Aiden could see their eyes sharing a joke behind their sunglasses. He felt a little stab; he couldn't help it. "They're dating," he told Liz when he got home. "He isn't just a friend. It was obvious."

She was pissed off that he'd had the luck to run into them. "I'm the one with the powers of observation," she pointed out.

"I took careful note." But Aiden was at a loss to describe the kid. What could you say? He looked fine — tall, tanned, wearing the right sort of cap. "There's something funny about his face," he finally said. "His features are good, separately, but they don't cohere. He looks like a police sketch." That got a smile out of her.

Noah came home for Thanksgiving and Aiden and Liz didn't see Sylvie all weekend. And now he's due back for Christmas and she's in tears. Aiden knows it in his gut: the boyfriend is being a dick.

He's got an hour at the end of the day to wait for Sylvie — Jake Peloquin's hour — and he stands for a long time looking out into the twilight. Below him Portage Avenue glistens, a long furrow opening the city all the way to the prairie, where the sun scored a red gash in the horizon when it sank. The park's vanished; all you can see is cars idling their way to the mall, bumper to bumper, exhaust rising. Three more days of work and then Christmas, and then, with any luck, the cold will finally come and they'll get a decent snowfall and he'll make it up to the cabin. You have to drive partway in from Minaki on the ice – they plow a winter road. And then you ski across to the island, pulling your grub on a toboggan. Just when you're about to perish, you see the solitary lost cabin hove into sight against horizontal lines of white and blue and the rock faces thrusting up through the snow, everything transfixed by winter.

He moves to his desk and turns on the lamp. The cabin makes him think of Jake – Defrag, as he calls him privately – a guy who likes the wilderness as much as Aiden does. He picks up the phone and punches in his number, lets it ring a long time. Defrag doesn't have an answer function.

Okay, the notes. He boots up the computer, gets comfortable, and turns his mind back to the morning. To Norman Orlikow, slim and neat and intense, like a bit player in a Shakespearean tragedy. *Vengeful fantasies,* Aiden types. *Grandiose ideation, resistance to insight.* Suddenly he can't be bothered to go into their little drama. *Invoice for broken window,* he instructs himself.

Odette Zimmerman – he'll write her up after he talks to Edith.

Christine Tolefson, a new client today. Forty-three. She gave her age as if Aiden was forcing her to admit to a criminal record. She'd been referred by her GP for anxiety. She wore a fake animal-hide jacket and fake lashes that clung to her eyelids like insects, and her square-ended claws were a jumbled heap of plastic in her lap. Only her eyes were real, and sad. He told Christine how they would work, what he expected of her. She sat for a minute without speaking, and then she said, the words wrenched out of her in pain and fear, "I don't know if I can say anything honest. I don't really know what that would be."

Thank you, Christine, he thinks as he types. You could spend all night at a party, standing by a bay window with a glass of wine

32

in your hand, and you would count the evening special if you had just one moment like that, one moment of true connection with another human being.

It's ten to five. He closes his files and turns off the computer. He rinses the mugs and cleans the grounds out of the coffeemaker and sets it up for the morning, and then he takes his V8 can out to the recycling bin. The hall is silent and empty, ceiling lights blazing.

Down at the end, the elevator opens to reveal Sylvie, standing alone among the loops of tinsel. She's wearing her second-hand Cowichan sweater, her bright hair hanging to her shoulders. Not crying – she looks drained of emotion. Her face is filling out, he thinks in surprise. There's an almost matronly look about her, all her exuberance dialled down. There she stands in a cage of yellow light, her backpack slung on one shoulder, motionless as in a diorama: a future Sylvie.

2

Never Explain, Never Apologize

TWO CHRISTMAS GIFT BAGS SIT ON LIZ'S OFFICE chair. She lifts them to the desk, not bothering to peek inside, and switches on the monitor to check her calendar. A private appointment at noon – that's her yoga class – otherwise, the day is wide open.

Will she tell the staff today? She unwinds her scarf and sits down to think. It would be great to have one less thing to fret about through Christmas. But she's got to be calm about it, and matter-of-fact. A touch of wry wit. She's not there yet. *Are you taking this as a personal failure?* Aiden asked last night. *Failure?* Liz said. *When have I ever pretended to have any influence over Sylvie?* But the whole thing is bound to reflect badly on her. It's just a fact – even people who like her and respect her will have a little laugh at her expense. So who in Liz's shoes wouldn't be anxious?

Two nights ago, when Aiden brought Sylvie home with him from the office, her eyes were swollen from crying. He wouldn't say what it was – he wanted Sylvie to say it – while meanwhile dread was building in Liz's chest and she was getting more and more frantic.

They were standing in the kitchen and Sylvie still had her big sweater on. Finally she burst out, "I'm pregnant!" and Liz felt a brutal twist in her gut at this fresh evidence of Sylvie's ability to surprise and subvert, and then fury at herself. Of course she was pregnant. One glance at her silhouette, at the new plumpness in her throat, and it was as plain as the nose on your face.

They ended up not eating the lamb stew Liz had thawed. They sat in the living room for a long time with the lights dimmed, no fire in the fireplace but the Christmas tree glowing and twinkling. Sylvie sat on the sofa beside Aiden, Liz close by on the hassock, and she sobbed and sobbed. It was years since Liz had seen Sylvie cry. It gave her the face she'd had as a baby. Five months? Liz thought. "We need to wait for the ultrasound," she said several times. The doctor *had* to be wrong. "You will be astonished, the love you will feel for this baby," Aiden said at one point. "In no time at all you will not be able to imagine your life without her . . . or him." Which was not a direction to take, in Liz's view. Surely, surely, if the ultrasound came back saying *too late*, Sylvie should be encouraged to consider adoption?

In any case, Sylvie took the conversation in a direction no one could have predicted. "You don't get it."

"What don't we get?"

"He would *never* have children, at any time. He's into vehement."

"He's vehement about it?"

"*No!* He's into VHEMT – the Voluntary Human Extinction Movement. He signed the pledge."

They stared at her in confusion. Liz was the one who understood first. "Oh, Sylvie," she said. "One little baby is not going to change things for the whole planet."

"It's not 'one little baby.'" She directed this at Aiden, as though he was the one who'd said it. "This baby will have a carbon footprint equal to fifty kids in Bangladesh. This baby might go on to have kids of its own!" And then she turned that rage on Liz: "Stop looking at me!"

Oh, Sylvie. Eventually Liz said, "You should have something to eat. We should all eat." So they went back to the kitchen and she made a pot of tea and they had bowls of cereal, because that was all Sylvie wanted. They stood in the warmth of the under-cabinet lighting and Sylvie leaned against the counter eating Cheerios, telling them how hungry she had been for the past few months.

"I knew I was gaining weight," she said. "But I was trying to listen to my body. You know, trying not to listen to all the media shit about being thin. *Eat! Eat!* my body was screaming. And so I just kept eating."

"Your baby will be better off for it," Liz said.

"But let us see, honey," Aiden said, and she opened her sweater and smoothed her T-shirt over her belly. They all stood close, and Liz felt a lift, the honey-sweet thought that maybe this would be a new time for her and Sylvie.

But five months along! Their family already sounds completely out of control, and the longer she waits, the more she'll have to explain. Liz sits with her eyes on her calendar and tries to think. We've had a bit of a surprise on the family front, she'll say. She'll start with Genevieve, her deputy, and work her way down. As soon as she's had a word with the mail clerk, she'll wish them all a merry Christmas and send them home. They're expecting a three o'clock closing; if she lets them go at two-thirty, they'll rush away with gratitude at the top of their minds.

She hangs up her coat and sets into the job she's decided on: tidying her computer files, something mindless to fill the morning. Chris and Maggie Oliphant, she thinks as she clicks and drags. They're coming over at seven-thirty – Sylvie set it up. Liz will finally meet Noah. Please, God, let him be a nice guy, let them be reasonable people. Sylvie's promised to be home for dinner and they'll have a chance for a good talk before the others arrive. Just to make sure they're on the same page about everything. A good talk, Liz thinks hopelessly as she clicks and drags.

At eleven-thirty she puts on her coat, says to Megan, "I'll be back around one," and heads for the elevator. The yoga studio is a ten-minute walk up Bannatyne. You won't be able to operate the way you've been operating, Liz is saying to Sylvie as she strides along under a pale sky. Your life will change more than you can imagine.

The class is overcrowded and the teacher is aggravating, but being there quiets her mind somewhat. When she comes out afterwards, snow is falling in sticky clumps. Karen Kemelmen, the accounts clerk, is standing outside their building having a cigarette. "Get your shopping done?" she asks.

"I had a meeting, actually," Liz says. She's carrying a laptop case with her yoga gear in it. You have to get up early in the morning to outfox Liz Glasgow.

She eats at her desk. Just before two she makes a cup of mint tea and sits composing herself. Then Karen appears in the doorway with Genevieve and Marietta, the new receptionist. They're making Christmas rounds, passing out chocolate truffles.

With a flourish, Karen presents a gift bag to Liz. Nestled in red tissue paper is a heavy lump, about the size of a goose egg, made of plasticized clay. Liz sets it upright on her desk. It's a fertility symbol – that headless, armless goddess you see in women's studies textbooks, all boobs and belly.

"My goodness," Liz says.

"I know, isn't it amazing?" Karen says. "I saw it and right away I thought of you."

"Karen, I'm guessing you've never read SERC's mission statement," Genevieve says.

Megan, the administrative assistant, hears them laughing and drifts in, followed by a couple of staff from the cubicles. They discover the truffles and set into them.

Liz stands by her desk chatting reflexively. It's hard to keep her eyes off Karen's gift. It's a monstrosity, but also eerily apt. Karen Kemelmen has a crude sort of intuition, Liz has noted it before. "Let's see what else Santa brought me," she says, reaching for the gift bags she found on her chair when she came in.

The first is a big slab of soap, from Cynthia. "Smells good enough to eat," she says, passing it around. Glances are exchanged. Cynthia's been selling homemade cosmetics from her desk for several months now, and they all wonder if Liz knows and how long she'll let it go on. She can read them like a book.

The other is a lovely bottle of port covered, as it should be, with fine dust. A gift from Genevieve. "Oh!" Liz says, truly touched. "I've been longing for port. I was so sorry I didn't bring any home from Portugal last year."

"I bought it in Coimbra," Genevieve says. "I know you loved Coimbra."

"You are such a sweetheart," Liz says. She catches her assistant's eye. "Megan, do we have any plastic cups?"

By the time they've moved on, Liz's cheeks are warm and the weight of her worry has lifted a little. And, she sees with dismay and relief, it's almost three o'clock. She waters her Christmas cactus and her weeping fig, then sits down to the computer and pulls up the template for an all-staff bulletin. *The Sexuality Education Resource Centre will close at 15:00 today and reopen 8:30 December 27. Wishing everyone a safe and happy holiday,* etc.

———

The first thing Liz notices when she walks into the house is the reek of fake-lemon cleaning fluid, drowning out the woodsy smell of the Christmas tree. She opens a few windows and gets the rice started (brown rice – it takes forever). While it simmers, she walks the house, checking ledges for dust, trying to scuff the vacuum tracks out of the rugs. This cleaner is new. Liz has met her only once, but her resentful presence hovers in the hall. Her mission statement, according to Aiden, is *If you really gave a shit, would I be cleaning your house?*

The dog sticks close to Liz, assisting in the inspection. They pause in the entrance to the living room, where they'll sit tonight. It's a gorgeous space, their living room, entered through what they call "the archway," which is really a square opening for double pocket doors between the front sitting room and the back. The back sitting room, with its bay windows and fireplace, is the space they use most – their whole life together is in this room. And now this gathering, a meeting that no one in their wildest dreams could ever have foreseen.

Liz stoops to pick a piece of tinsel from the rug. She stands for a minute looking out into the backyard. All three of their beautiful elms have fluorescent orange dots painted on their trunks. The spots of death – they mean the city will be taking them out. Those trees are 120 years old; you'd lie on the ground under the largest one and its height would make you dizzy. It doesn't bear thinking about. Why couldn't the city have marked them on the other side so they didn't have to look out at those orange dots all winter?

She turns back to the room and her eyes seek out the jar of bittersweet she gathered herself in the Pembina Valley, and the Day of the Dead figure on the mantel. She's momentarily consoled by them, by the subtle way they pick up the Christmas aesthetic. Liz has a playful style but she respects the rules of colour and proportion, which is where many people go wrong with an eclectic decor. It might not be right out of *House Beautiful*, but their home is crammed with personality, unlike, say, Carmela Soprano's bleak nouveau riche mansion. Where, as a matter of fact, Liz has begun to picture the Oliphants, lounging on recliners in front of their mammoth plasma TV.

Back in the kitchen, she opens a can of lentils and drains them. She'll make that rice and lentil dish that Sylvie considers comfort food – rentils, they call it. She grates the Parmesan and snips a pile of oily sun-dried tomatoes with the kitchen shears.

The front door opens and the dog patters up the hall. It's not Sylvie, it's Aiden; she can hear him talking to the dog. She reaches into the freezer for her homemade pesto, breaks a chunk out of the Ziploc bag. They just have to get through tonight. Tomorrow she'll bring her paperwhites out of the cold storage room and put them on the kitchen window ledge, and they'll have the miracle of delicate spring flowers blooming at Christmas. Everything will be better tomorrow.

The pesto melts greenly in the frying pan and Liz stands with spatula in hand, wondering what the hell that crazy hope was based on.

At 6:45, Liz and Aiden finally sit down to dinner.

Aiden helps himself to spinach salad, picking through it to avoid the mandarin oranges. "Did you check to see if she texted you?"

Liz nods, she sighs. "I could kill that girl. We need to talk. We know *nothing* about these people. And it's such an emotional thing to have to discuss with total strangers."

"I keep picturing them as real Tory types. I don't know where I got that, given their son's politics."

"I do too! I wonder why."

"Well, they live in River Heights. And they own a clothing store. Do you know many pinko entrepreneurs in River Heights?"

A clothing store. Liz serves herself a tiny portion of rentils, and while she eats, her eyes wander the kitchen, lingering on the fretwork half-doors where a pantry used to be. She's startled on Maggie Oliphant's behalf by the sight of a toilet just visible behind those half-doors. One day she was at an auction in the little village of Saint Clements when the Catholic church was being demolished, and she came home with the confessional booth disassembled in her hatchback. At the time they were trying to figure out how to retrofit a bathroom into the main floor. It was perfect in every way.

"You know," Liz says, "it's an awful thing to say, but this makes me glad my mother is gone. I can't help it. She'd see someone who'd been happily married for twenty-five years, and she'd drop her voice and get that awful smug expression on her face and say, 'She got into trouble. They had to get married.'"

Aiden picks up the wine bottle and Liz slides over her glass. "And then there was us," he says.

"Yeah, then there was us." Well, they did have that hand-fasting ceremony in the living room – their neighbour Wendy's idea, some sort of Scandinavian tradition. Liz was wearing an empire-waist frock that showed off her pregnant tummy. Her mother arrived in a pink mother-of-the-bride suit and hat, trying gamely to turn the occasion into something it wasn't.

"I keep wondering how the Oliphants are feeling," Liz says. "But that's crazy. It used to be the boy who was blamed when this happened. For ruining your daughter. Now it's the other way around. They'll be thinking she's stupid, or she trapped him on purpose."

"They'll be fine once they meet Sylvie," he says.

She wants to grab his ears and give them a sharp twist. A *force of nature*, he always calls Sylvie, as if she can do no wrong. Since the news broke two days ago, not a word has been uttered about the trip to France, the fact that Liz paid a deposit of two hundred euros on the apartment in Sarlat, the fact that just that day she'd bought their airline tickets. For the very week this baby is allegedly due. Liz is no more selfish than the average individual. She grasps the scale of things. She doesn't need much, just, *Liz, I know you had your heart set on that trip.* That's all.

"Great supper," he says.

"Umm."

"You went to a lot of trouble."

"Well, what else can I do?"

"What indeed." He changed before supper, while they waited. He's wearing his best jeans and a soft white cotton shirt Liz bought for him at a kiosk in a market. You can see how worried he is in the set of his mouth. His hair is a colour no one could name: sandy hair turning grey. It looks poignant to Liz, old age creeping up on boyishness. At this moment it's hard to hold anything against him.

"I'm trying to keep calm," she says. "I forced myself to go to yoga, but it was so bloody crowded. The woman beside me wouldn't use a proper mat. She was working on a little cotton towel and she kept slipping. She toppled into me twice during the standing poses."

"You should have said something."

"I did. I said, 'You know, the studio provides yoga mats.' And here she's one of those chemical sensitivity types, she says, 'I can't use synthetics because of the off-gassing.' Oh, whatever, it was just too crowded. On the way out I said to the teacher, 'You need to put a cap on class size,' and of course she gets all self-righteous and says, 'You've obviously never done yoga in India.'"

"You'd think everybody would be out shopping."

"Christmas drives them to yoga. It's the shtress of the season."

"Oh, Jade was teaching."

Poor Aiden, he knows her rants by heart. *Feel the shtrength as you shtretch.* Liz used to think this annoying speech affectation was just yoga teacher Jade (it's her *shtick*, as Aiden put it), but now she's hearing it everywhere from a certain age and class of woman. There's always something in yoga.

Well, there's always something in everything. When she was in high school, in synchronized swimming, her coach would stand on the edge of the pool in a tangerine Speedo and chant, "Synch or swim, synch or swim," which made no sense whatsoever. And again, she notes, savouring the taste of a sun-dried tomato on her tongue, she is thinking about synchro in the same breath as yoga, when actually it's different in every way possible – the fact that in yoga you are constantly reminded to breathe while in synchro it's the reverse, and the fact that yoga is from a realm so foreign to her mother that even from the grave she can have no opinion about it, whereas her mother was in love with Esther Williams and the aqua-musicals. Her mother's enthusiasms always involved things that eventually mortified Liz, in this case the rubbery bathing caps with lurid lime-green flowers, the grotesque nose plugs, and figures like the kip split: head down in the pool and frantically sculling, Liz and the other girls would slowly, slowly spread their legs in synchronized display, presenting a pornographic row of slashes sheathed in Lycra to the dads and boyfriends drooling from the bleachers.

Yoga, it seems, is not about displaying anything. It's about – well, she really couldn't tell you what it's about. But today, for a moment, she got it. At the end, in Savasana, when her petty irritations suddenly fell away and she lay quietly feeling her stomach move up and down. The thought of all those people breathing in the dark, that was what calmed her. All their ragged thoughts floating above them. She didn't sink very deeply into her own self, but she tuned into them: thirty women and a few men lying vulnerable, side by side on the studio's tiled floor. That in itself was helpful. Who knew the pains and troubles being borne by the brave strangers in that windowless room? How tragic was her situation in comparison to theirs?

Liz puts down her fork and surveys the kitchen again. Her beautiful kitchen with the warm cork floor in a checkerboard pattern of charcoal and cream, the craftsman cupboards, the high ceiling with its schoolhouse lights (real, not reproduction). If she were in the Oliphants' shoes, if she had walked into this home for this sort of meeting, what she saw would run contrary to all her expectations. She'd know at a glance that it would not be simple to work out the whole story. She'd figure there had to be something a bit off, but it wouldn't be easy to spot. Nothing like . . . her eyes catch the mark on the granite countertop, a stain in the perfect shape of Newfoundland, where vinegar was spilled and lay undetected overnight. Nothing as obvious as that.

They finish their dinner. Aiden goes to set up the fire and Liz feeds the dog. If the past is anything to go by, Sylvie will show up ten minutes late for the meeting and she won't say a word about missing supper. *Never explain, never apologize.* Isn't that what we all aspire to?

Liz loads the dishwasher and gets a plate microwave-ready for Sylvie, just in case. Just as she's putting it in the fridge, the side door opens and Sylvie slips in. She goes straight down to the basement without so much as a hello. Liz's emotions coalesce into a familiar helpless rage and she backs out of the fridge and tips the contents of Sylvie's plate into the compost pail.

Straight down to the basement. Like a rude finger raised in Liz's direction. She's got a gorgeous second-floor bedroom with huge windows, but by choice she'll hide in a cave favoured by a certain loathsome brown beetle you never see anywhere else in the house. Sleep on a musty futon where the damp of Red River clay sweats coldly through the floor and the walls. Shower in a thundering tin stall where the previous owner kept his cat litter. Screw you, she's prepared to say to her mother, even now. *Screw you and your so-called life.*

Liz stands for a minute with the plate in her hand. She opens the freezer door and cold, stale-food air wafts out. She hears the basement shower start up and she turns her eyes to the tumble of plastic and tinfoil packages that make up her frozen stash. Stollen, she'll serve the stollen she made for Christmas. She gets out the log and unwraps it. Breathe, she says to herself, leaning on the big butcher knife, feeling it sink in evenly. Not everything is about you. The basement suits Sylvie; down there she can believe she's being subjected to Third World deprivations. Consider the Oliphants. No doubt true Chamber of Commerce types, and they've raised a kid who wants to wipe humans off the planet. Though apparently this doesn't involve keeping it in his pants.

Liz wraps up the remaining stollen and stows it back in the freezer. She reaches into the fridge for the jar of homemade tapenade, calculating. There's still Christmas and New Year's.

Aiden is in the doorway. "Did I hear Sylvie come in?" he asks.

Liz tips her head towards the basement door. "Is this too much?" she asks, gesturing at the tapenade. "I don't want to go overboard."

"Looks okay to me," he says. "But I'm not quite ready. I can't seem to find the shotgun."

"Oh, babe," she says, and reaches for him. He lays his head on her shoulder and she says, "This is a kick in the gut, eh?" and he says, "It's a kick in the balls, babe," and they hug until she feels his warmth seeping into her. She's afraid she'll start crying and she lets him go.

When she's alone again, she runs her fingers through her hair, looking at herself in the window of the microwave. Her reflection lifts its chin in the black glass. She knows how to run a meeting – it's one of the things she's best at. Aiden doesn't do groups. It will be her; she'll be the one who takes the lead.

They'll offer wine first, but she'll set up the coffeemaker just in case. She's at the sink filling the carafe when headlights turn off the street and a grey minivan rolls up the driveway. There's a fitting hesitation in the way the van drives up and stops, and in the slowness of the simultaneous opening of the front doors, and the gravity with which two people get out, in the manner of a gangster film or a funeral. Just two. The woman was driving. She's wearing a red coat, Linda Lundström or a knock-off. She has a tangle of grey hair, but otherwise she's a dead ringer for a legendary figure from Liz's past, Mary Magdalene Calhoun. And then they're moving towards the house and the mop of hair lifts, and Mary Magdalene herself looks up towards the window. She sees Liz peering out at her and produces a mournful smile.

Sylvie is just climbing the stairs from the basement, her fingers working her towel-dried hair up into an elastic. "Sylvie," Liz says, "didn't you say Chris and Maggie Oliphant? Isn't that what you said?"

The front doorbell rings. "No," Sylvie says, standing in the kitchen, her eyes averted. "I have no idea where you got that," and Liz sees in her flushed face and the set of her shoulders that she's known perfectly well all along.

3

Glad Tidings

SEVEN PEOPLE IN THE GLASGOW-PHIMISTER LIVing room for a meeting of the Montagues and the Capulets. The dog lies smugly on the rug, as though he's just succeeded in rounding them all up. On the hearth a little fire dances. The Christmas tree is a seven-foot balsam from New Brunswick – not the most graceful tree in the supermarket parking lot, a balsam, but it is fragrant, and beautifully decorated, because Liz has a knack for that sort of thing. From her perch a red-cheeked, yellow-haired angel surveys the living room, the prickly bifurcated tip of the Christmas tree up the back of her papier-mâché skirt.

Sylvie's in the swivel chair below, one leg tucked under her and one bare foot on the rug so she can give herself a shove whenever her terror threatens to reach up pudgy hands and choke her. She darts a glance at her mother, who's sitting with her legs and arms crossed, and then she turns her eyes back to the man who's talking. Someone she's never met before – George Oliphant, Noah's real father, one of those sad old hippies. He's staring at her; they all are. Five parents in this room focused on her like hungry ghouls, gawking at her stomach and her boobs, suddenly swollen and voluptuous. Humiliation sears her throat like heartburn. For being Bristol Palin. Worse – for not knowing, for being the sort of girl who gives birth in a toilet at Walmart and says, I had no idea.

Aiden, on a corner of the couch, notes them all staring at Sylvie. But really, he thinks, who can blame them? His daughter, who always has a bloom about her, is incandescent tonight. Her jeans have a frank three-cornered tear on the thigh. She's wearing her SORRY FOR WHAT'S ABOUT TO HAPPEN T-shirt, and the tender swelling of her tummy is plain as day. For a second this pregnancy seems a natural climax to all her adolescent transformations, which have taken him by surprise day after day. Then she gives her chair a little swivel and he sees how scared she is, and his own sadness laps at his rib cage. For all she's losing, poor kid, for the cruel lesson she's facing in the narrowing of things. He enjoyed twenty years of adult idylls before he had to deal with parenthood.

Five loving parents assembled now, but to be frank, the only ray of hope Aiden can see is Noah's mother. When she stepped through the front door with Noah, sober-faced, behind her, he could have wept with relief at the sight. Not one of those toned, tanned, brittle, cruise-going Tory types – no, thank Christ, she was a comely, comfortable woman dressed in a loose tunic thing in rich colours, a woman with a warm smile and a confident voice and the calm light of self-knowledge in her eyes. And then Liz came down the hall and they were greeting each other – she was someone Liz knew!

MAGGIE: I was thinking about calling you. In the fall, when Noah
    first told me he was seeing Sylvie. And then he was gone,
    back to school, and it slipped away from me. Well, now we do
    connect. Whoever would have dreamt it!

LIZ: Mary Magdalene and I know each other through GAP.

AIDEN: GAP?

MAGGIE: The Group for Alternative Parenting.

AIDEN: Oh, yeah. Whatever that meant.

Maggie laughed politely and possibly reprovingly. Then they rose in Aiden's mind, the GAP women who used to hang around this house, a clowder of back-to-the-earth types wearing striped leotards under woollen skirts, their kids exuding an unfamiliar body odour from the chickpeas and tofu they were forced to subsist on.

"It's just Maggie," she said. "It's been Maggie for a while. And this is Noah, of course. My big son, all grown up. Noah, go find Sylvie, honey. It's fine, go on. Listen, I am *so* sorry Krzysztof can't be here. He's doing a seminar at the Banff Centre and we're going to meet up in Calgary for Christmas."

Taking Aiden's arm familiarly, she bent down to unzip her boots and slip into the shoes she'd brought in a drawstring bag, all the while outlining the complications already plaguing their Christmas – the flying and driving in various directions across the country, and Krzysztof's mother, who'd just moved in with them, and her own mother in Calgary, showing signs of dementia. And then suddenly she caught sight of the dog and bent over again, to pat him. "What a big head!" she laughed. "And look at his little hind legs! He's like something out of a *New Yorker* cartoon."

"He was sired by a warthog," Aiden said. "That's what we figure."

"What's his name?"

"Max."

All the while, Liz stood there clutching Maggie's red coat. "Maggie's partner is Krzysztof Nowak," she explained when she managed to catch Aiden's eye.

"Oh gosh," Aiden said. "Well. I didn't put that together at all." Krzysztof Nowak. A minor national celebrity whose Prairie Gothic films Aiden is vaguely familiar with, though he registers the guy largely for the overweening display of consonants in his name.

MAGGIE: But you never met Krzysztof, did you, Liz? Wasn't he after your time?

LIZ: No, we met. He was at that party on the river. On Palmerston.

MAGGIE: Oh yeah, at Esme Gwynn's. I remember.

AIDEN: Sorry, I'm not quite with the program here. You didn't realize you knew Noah's mom? All this time, since Noah and Sylvie started dating?

LIZ (*heat gathering visibly around her eyes*): Mary Magdalene's little boy was always called Sparky. I'd totally forgotten his name was Noah. You met him in the summer, but I didn't, remember? And I was thinking Maggie Oliphant. I could swear that's what Sylvie said. (*finally turning to Maggie*) Why *is* Noah's name Oliphant? Isn't George Stonechild his father?

"George Stonechild," Maggie said, as though she were telling a long, sad story just by saying his name. "George is his dad, all right. George's real name was always Oliphant. He dropped the Stonechild thing a long time ago. Anyway, Krzysztof is the one who more or less raised Noah. And he and I have a little girl, Natalie. She's just turned six. So she's a Calhoun-Nowak. We've got four different surnames in the house – it makes the letter carrier crazy."

She offered Aiden a tender, regretful smile and poked the tips of her fingers into her hair, elevating the silver cloud a half-inch. This is all good, he thought. (One of us, he couldn't help but think.) Although Liz and the woman were stiff as hell with each other. And when they stepped into the living room, he saw to his surprise that Noah and Sylvie were sitting on separate chairs, not holding hands on the love seat as you might have expected. Noah had the hood of his fleece up monkishly.

"Noah," Maggie said softly, and he looked at her and slid it back. Then the doorbell rang again and Noah said, "That will be my dad," and Aiden saw Maggie's equanimity slip. "He called me. He's leaving for the States tomorrow, so I told him."

"He's got the right to know," Sylvie added primly.

Aiden went back to the door. "Weren't sure we could fit it in," a tall man cried, springing into the hall with every assumption of intimacy. "Flying down to Texas first thing in the morning. George Oliphant."

And this guy with his hand stuck out, greying hair hanging to his shoulders in some misguided homage to his youth, was also not entirely a stranger. Not that Aiden knew him by name, but it was a small city they lived in. Aiden would have seen him in lineups at the Folk Festival or buying bread at the Forks, could even vaguely picture him at younger stages. And here he stood in their own front hall, wiping his boots assiduously on the Afghan prayer rug, he and his tiny wife handing Aiden their jackets as he cried to the assembly at large, "Great to have a thaw this time of year."

"Yeah, the polar bears are loving it!" Sylvie swivelled her chair impatiently.

"Leaving for Texas in the morning," George repeated from the archway, rubbing his hands. "Going to stay through January. It's always been a dream of mine to be part of the studio audience of *Austin City Limits*. It's on my bucket list. Or what the hell is it they say now? You only live once. YOLO!" He was almost yodelling. "It's on my YOLO list, *Austin City Limits*. Not as easy as it sounds – you can't just go online and order tickets. Those Texas buggers want to keep the tourists out. They post the location a week before, and you got to know the city blind to find it. But I got a buddy in Austin. We're going to get in – my buddy is confident."

"They keep changing the concert venue?" Aiden asked stupidly.

"No, no, dude, the ticket wicket."

George shook Liz's hand and ogled Sylvie with avuncular appreciation. "Congratulations, kiddo! Noah is one lucky guy!" Then he turned to his son. "So, big guy! What's all this?" and Noah got up with the courtesy Aiden had noticed when they met in the summer (though he kept his head down as if he was afraid a high-five might be coming his way) and offered his chair to his stepmother. Then he sat cross-legged at Sylvie's feet and the dog wandered over and curled up beside him. George Oliphant arranged himself expansively in the leather armchair and turned his winsome face from one to the other with eagerness and satisfaction.

Turned his face a second time to Liz, who was just sitting down again. She looked away quickly. George Stonechild! With a wife like a miniature aged teenager, a wife named Patti, and his long, tapered braids gone, his dark hair shoulder-length now and showing some grey, but otherwise as good-looking and as absurd as ever. Her mind cast up a memory of carrying a sleeping Sylvie across a field, George Stonechild's arm around her waist in ostentatious chivalry. But there was not a flicker of recognition in George's eyes.

And Mary Magdalene Calhoun. Liz's hands had been actually shaking when she took Noah's mother's coat. Maggie, Maggie Calhoun. She still has that gentle, precise way of speaking that asks you to drop what you're doing, surrender to her tender gaze, and soak in every word. She's still undeniably beautiful, though sporting a rough-woven anthropological ensemble that says everything about how stuck she is in the past. Resolutely, Liz drew courage from her own sleek outfit with its artful combination of neutrals, and from her lovely front hall with its one-of-a-kind prayer rug and the antique boot chest, from her knowledge that this house, which had been good when Mary Magdalene used to hold court from the Mission chair, was even better now, that it testified to Liz's gradual transformation into a mature woman worthy of respect.

And sure enough, "What a great house" was the first thing Maggie said as she walked into the living room. Instantly Liz's confidence sagged, because she remembered that after Mary Magdalene moved away from Wolseley, she lived in an absolutely unique property in Point Douglas – one of the original farmhouses, tucked into the middle of the city in a pod of green, at least 150 years old and with all the cachet of a funky, fabulous house in a marginal neighbourhood.

"You're still in that amazing house in Point Douglas?"

"Did you visit me there?"

"No, but everybody in the city knows that house."

"I guess they do. It's true, it is kind of special. Well, we sold it. It was impossible to heat. We're in River Heights now."

And this young man was Sparky, a tall version of his younger self. He was five or six or seven when Mary Magdalene used to come to this house, a serious little boy, and Mary Magdalene was a single mom, moving on to the matriculation level of full-time motherhood: home schooling. Her boy was called Sparky because he had a fixation with electrical circuits. At his birthday party he was the happy recipient of a heap of extension cords in different colours and lengths and he worked intently all afternoon while the children played around him, arranging a circuit to some precise template in his mind. When he was done, Mary Magdalene supervised the insertion of a plug into a wall outlet. A lamp came on and they all clapped.

Would Liz have known him if he'd come to the house without his mother? Yes. He's got the even-featured face he had as a kid, and the same dark, straight eyebrows, and that way of really listening, but from a distance. And there he sits, all six feet of him, with Sylvie in a half-lotus in the chair above him. Sylvie, who *never said a word* – that's what truly knocks the breath out of Liz. Her wine's on the end table, she's longing for it, but she doesn't trust herself; she just sits with arms tightly crossed in her cashmere sweater, digging her fingers viciously into the slippery tenderloin of her forearm, pressing right down to the bone.

The Christmas tree lights twinkle on the windows and the fire crackles into perfection. The angel leans in to hear George Stonechild/Oliphant talk. No one has the will to wrest the meeting back from him.

"Sure would love to jump in the car and drive down. That's on my bucket list too. Anybody here ever do the Will Rogers Highway?"

"Never heard of it."

"Sure you have – it's the old Route 66. You pick it up at Chicago. You can stay in the room where Elvis used to crash on his way to Vegas. The Trade Winds Inn, Clinton, Oklahoma. They haven't changed a thing. Still got the same toilet seat. Can you believe it? You can sit on the can where the King took his dump."

"You'd never get that room, sweetie."

"Aw, I'd talk them into it. They love Canadians down there."

Shut up, shut up, Sylvie breathes. She untucks one leg, willing Noah to lean back against her.

"Course, peace-loving folks can't actually drive into the southern U.S. these days."

"What do you mean?"

"You got to cross states where carrying a gun is mandatory."

"I don't think that's strictly true."

"Oh, buddy, it's true." George casts Aiden a glance of pity for his naïveté. "And I've got no intention of packing heat."

"George doesn't have the greatest eye-hand coordination." Patti's eyes are gleaming as if there's a story she's dying to tell.

The colour in Sylvie's face has gathered into a perfect crimson circle on each cheek and Noah is expressionlessly flexing his hands. Aiden gives up on any help from Liz. "You know," he says, leaning forward, "maybe we should move on to the topic that's brought us all together. Sylvie, Noah, this is a big thing you kids are facing and we'd like to sort out what we can do to give you some support."

He gets to his feet and moves to lay another log on the fire. "Nobody expects the Spanish Inquisition," he says in his Monty Python voice as he passes Sylvie's chair.

Oh, Dad, what would I do without you? she thinks. But it's Noah's face she's yearning to see. Sparky, who last summer, when they were wading in the lake in the moonlight, fell recklessly backwards and pulled Sylvie onto him so they lay tangled up in the cold-warm water on a sandbar, one of his thighs angled across her stomach, and her joy oscillated out into the vast lake, and she said to herself, pressing her heels deeper in the dense sand and inventing a perfect word for it, This is *love*. She lays her hand on his shoulder and he hunches up his muscle. He's trying to reassure her. Or maybe he's going, *Don't touch me!* Frightened, she pulls back her hand.

They ask all the things you'd expect them to ask. They are gentle and respectful and insistent. Or Maggie is – Maggie's the one who does most of the talking. "Can I ask, Sylvie, when exactly you found out?" she begins.

SYLVIE: On Tuesday. You know – I talked to you right after.

MAGGIE: But you're five months along? And you didn't feel sick?

SYLVIE: No, I felt fine.

MAGGIE: You had no idea? When I was pregnant, I pretty much knew within a day or two. I just felt it. I felt my whole body gearing up in a really special way.

SYLVIE: Well, I didn't. Not until this week.

GEORGE: I guess a quick trip to Doctor Morgenstern is out of the question?

SYLVIE: Morgentaler. Yes.

PATTI: He's passed away, dear.

MAGGIE: Did your doctor say as much, Sylvie? Did you ask him?

NOAH: Her. Doctor Valdez is a woman.

SYLVIE: I can feel the baby moving. Now that I know what it is.

MAGGIE: Well, I guess it's a faint hope, although maybe we should all try to keep the option open until after the ultrasound. But naturally we're worried about the health of the baby under these circumstances. I hate to ask, Sylvie, but did you drink alcohol during the past five months?

GEORGE: We've all been there, kiddo. We all have a pretty good idea what goes on!

SYLVIE: I drank a little, but not too much. I was studying like crazy, because I want to get into botany field school this summer – it's a third-year course. And I worked weekends at Stella's. So I wasn't partying. Plus Noah was away.

MAGGIE: Sylvie, do you have any idea how it happened? Noah tells me you were on the pill almost from the time you started seeing each other, and that you used other protection before that. What is the effectiveness rate supposed to be?

SYLVIE: The failure rate is between three and eight percent. I looked it up.

MAGGIE (*frowning*): I'm surprised it's that high.

AIDEN: Liz, you probably know what that's about.

LIZ: There's a perfect use rate and a typical use rate. The perfect use rate is based on an actual failure of the pill. It's extremely low – point three percent, actually – with most oral contraceptives. The typical use rate takes human error into account, such as times when the user forgets to take a pill. It can be as high as eight percent.

MAGGIE: And where would your use have fallen, Sylvie, between typical and perfect?

SYLVIE: Perfect.

She's motionless now in the swivel chair. This baby has been bombarded with hormones every day, she wants to scream. Every day from the beginning. The way the mist thing in Safeway comes on and sprays the helpless vegetables. She's started to imagine the baby's dark eggplant shape, although really it's only the size of a large pear. Liz could not resist showing her, that first night. About Liz's contribution to this interrogation, her eagerness to talk about human error, Sylvie has nothing to say but "Typical."

Sylvie is not fooled either by Maggie's gentle tone. The way she says *Sylvie* in every single sentence is patronizing. When she was a little girl, she loved Mary Magdalene, who once gave her a candle shaped like a pink flamingo and who used to make Jell-O cut-outs for the kids. Just before Noah left for Guelph she'd bugged him to take her to see his mom, so they stopped in at her shop on Corydon. Sylvie decided then that Maggie was not interesting or funny or especially smart, but she seemed honest and warm. She likely had good politics.

When Sylvie left the doctor's on Evil Tuesday, Maggie was the first person she called. Not to tell her – not with the least intention of telling her – but to ask what flight Noah was coming in on, because it was desperately important for her to meet him. *And Maggie wouldn't tell her.* She just said no. She said it was part of their Christmas ritual to pick up Noah (how could that be true when it was his first year away from home?) and that they were driving straight out of town afterwards to visit his grandmother in Calgary. Sylvie was in shock. She was standing at the corner of

Ellice and Maryland and passing cars were throwing fans of muddy water at her. "I don't know if Noah has given you a clear picture of how busy his Christmas will be," Maggie was saying in her placid voice. "But I hope you two will have a chance to get together closer to New Year's."

That's when Sylvie hung up on her and called Noah in Guelph. By then she was crying. He was in a car with a friend, taking their bottles to the Beer Store to get some cash for Christmas. It was stupid, stupid to call him at that point. Telling him over the phone would be so shitty they would never get over it, but of course when he heard her crying, he freaked out. So she told him about losing her botany paper on the computer and he suggested things she might do to get it back. She told him she'd try and that she had to hang up. She was so panicky that she didn't ask him his flight time and number. Then she called Maggie back and said, "I have to meet Noah at the airport," sobbing so hard she could hardly talk. Finally she just blurted out, "I'm pregnant," and in a shocked and subdued voice Maggie gave her the flight information. And now Sylvie *hates* Maggie for the fact that she knew before Noah did, and for piling on all that extra shit.

They've lapsed into silence. Noah seems so much younger now than when I ran into him in August, Aiden thinks, watching him from his corner of the couch. Although there's something meticulous about the guy – meticulous and inward – in the clean and pressed quality of his jeans and the Harry Potterish fall of his dark hair. Vehement about the whole situation, no doubt – you can see it in the tight way he moves and sits – but he's got his mother's composure, if not her expansive warmth. And Sylvie . . . Aiden has never felt prouder of his daughter. Tonight Sylvie isn't crying. And in spite of her distress, she's not tailoring what she says to what they want to hear. She's poised, with her straight, perfect white teeth and her confident voice. She has an old-fashioned wave-of-the-future look about her, like the girls in Communist Youth League murals.

George heaps a cracker with tapenade and eats it with gusto. "What would that be?" he asks. "The black stuff." No one answers. Caviar? he mouths to Patti. She shakes her head furtively.

Maggie sits with her face turned to the fire, its light picking up the rosy tones of her skin. She looks expectant, as though the poignant resolution of this dilemma is just around the corner. But it's obvious to Aiden that the meeting is foundering. Something concrete has to be put in place, promises made, a plan hammered out. No doubt if they were the kind of people things like this happen to, they'd know what that was.

It's the tiny stepmother, with her thin blond ponytail, who rises to the occasion, murmuring a hope that Noah and Sylvie will go for a June wedding, by which time Sylvie will be able to fit into a lovely gown. Their disdain rises and washes over her. She feels it, tries to get a purchase on the rug with her dangling feet, then scrambles out of her chair, setting her wineglass on the coffee table, and turns fiercely on Noah. "I'm not exactly a stranger to this situation, you know. I was seventeen when I got pregnant with my son Troy. My boyfriend was just seventeen too, and he did the right thing by me. He dropped out of school and got a job pumping gas. We lived in a basement apartment on Arlington and it was bloody hard. We didn't last forever, but that boy made sure my baby had a father. That boy did the right thing by me."

She's about four foot ten, one of Santa's ancient elves, and she's standing right over Noah, scolding him. He pulls himself to his feet. Then he's looming over her, and looking just as uncomfortable with that. "You knew what the right thing was," he says when she pauses for breath. It's not aggressive, the way he says it; it's just a thoughtful observation.

"We did," she protests, thrusting her wrinkled little face up at him. "Of course we did. And so do you."

Maggie gets up and steps around the coffee table. "Listen, Patti, I know you mean well, but Noah is not seventeen and he will not be pumping gas — not now, not ever." She turns to Liz and Aiden and says confidingly, "I should let you know the dilemma we're facing with all this happening right now. Noah has been hoping to become part of a research team on Lake Malawi this summer. It's a fabulous opportunity. One of his profs, Doctor Anish Chandak, is the lead, and Noah has every reason to believe he'll be accepted into the project. This is not an experience we want to see him miss. He is a strong candidate for a doctoral fellowship to Stanford or UCB, and the Lake Malawi project would be a huge asset."

"He is *going*," Sylvie says. "He's still going to Malawi. There's no reason for him to change his plans. I'm not changing mine. I'm staying in school. I won't know the exact due date until the ultrasound, but the doctor thinks the end of April, when exams are over, which is perfect. I still want to go to field school in the summer. It's just an hour or so out of the city."

"Field school?" Liz says. She gets to her feet too, for a better sightline into Sylvie's mind. What she sees there is the baby swinging in a shawl from the low branch of a tree while Sylvie scrabbles in the dirt below.

Sylvie looks back at her mother defiantly. "There's a daycare at the university. A good one."

"But you're going to move home."

"No."

"Oh god, darling, you have no idea."

Maggie turns the full melting beauty of her eyes on Sylvie. "I know you're really struggling right now to come to terms with this news. We all are. And it might be a few weeks before you and Noah are able to reach a decision. But we're hoping you will explore the many options for adoption. You know, hundreds of families wait years for a baby. Families that would provide a dream home for this child. The timing is *so* bad for the two of you. It's not just Noah's education and future we're thinking of. We're thinking of yours too."

Sylvie's on her feet now too, and she rounds on Maggie. "There are lots of childless families all right. And there are *millions* of starving children in the world. Anyone who really wants a child can adopt one. Even here – there are lots and lots of homeless kids right here in Canada. They're stuck in foster homes for their entire growing up, *like dogs at the pound*. People who say they want a baby and have been waiting years for one make me want to puke. I have no sympathy for them, none. They can't get a baby because all they will accept is a perfect little newborn." She pauses for breath. "*Perfect*," she says, raking quotation marks around the word. "*White*."

No one's prepared to take this on. The two dads finally hoist themselves out of their chairs like the holdouts in a standing ovation. Standing momentarily in a silent circle, they hear the click of ice pellets against the black windows. Liz fixes her eyes on the Christmas tree, on the angel at the top – a tarty angel from the art gallery gift shop that says, Christmas is all just shtick to us, and Aiden, following the direction of her gaze, thinks of a book of Annunciation paintings he looked through once, left in a carrel at the library. The sky opening and the angel with its glorious, muscular wings dropping into a sunlit room where the Virgin sat reading or weaving or embroidering and seldom welcomed the interruption. And then a sort of horror seizes him, a sense of hope snatched away.

The dog's had enough. He shakes himself, bones and collar tags rattling, and revolves once to wind things up. Sylvie drops back into her chair, her face sorrowful, and puts Aiden's dark epiphany into words. "I really thought it could all end with me."

4

There All Along

WHILE SYLVIE SLEEPS CHRISTMAS MORNING away, Aiden and Liz poke through the gifts under the tree. Liz decrees that Aiden can open one, and designates which. It's a great little stovetop espresso maker. She froths milk with a handheld battery-powered device that looks like a sex toy and they drink lattes. It's sunny out, and icicles drip from the eaves. The sun shows up how badly the windows need washing and how faded the loveseat is, makes plain the shameful amount of dog hair on the cushions and the slapdash ways of their new cleaner.

"I'm sacking her," Liz says. "I didn't want to tell her just before Christmas, but that woman is *gone*."

"And then what?"

"Do you think I'm stupid? I've got a line on somebody else."

The Christmas lights are cold and wan; there's a dry, minuscule rustle of needles falling when the dog brushes against the tree. You're supposed to feel *wonder*, having a living tree in the house, but really it's a dead tree, after ten days on the road and three weeks wrapped in netting and stacked in a lot. Some of these trees are spray-painted green.

Maybe some music would help, Aiden thinks. A madrigal, or something baroque. No "Silent Night" in this house, it's a rule. He gets up and pokes his starter wand under the split logs in the fireplace, which are set up as a classic tepee. Earlier he tucked two blocks of sawdust and paraffin wax inside the tepee. Because he's a lazy sonofabitch. He wouldn't do that on the island. On the island he does it right. Except when he skis in, of course, and a fire feels like a matter of life or death.

Ten o'clock and Sylvie's still sleeping. He's hardly had a chance to talk to her since the Calhoun/Oliphants were over. After they left, she headed straight for the basement. "Cripes!" Aiden called after her. "Nobody expects the Spanish Inquisition!" She was not drawn back by the pathetic repetition of his little witticism, and he had to get up and go to the head of the stairs and call her.

When she dragged herself back to stand in the archway, he told her how proud he'd been of her throughout the meeting, the way she'd held her own.

But she turned on him in fury. "I'm not taking money," she said (just at the end they had talked in general terms about finances). "I'm not letting Noah give me money. It's not his fault."

"Honey," Aiden said, "we're not talking fault here. You have to take it. He has to give it. It's what he has to do." He tried to lead her over to the couch but she stood adamantly in the archway, her face fierce.

"It's not his money. He has no money. It's his mother's money."

"Well, that's his situation right now," Aiden said. "He has to deal with that. God knows, you'll have enough to deal with."

She'd already turned away when Liz spoke. "Sylvie, you knew Noah's mother was Mary Magdalene. Why didn't you tell me?"

"Because," she called from halfway down the stairs, "this is not about you."

Aiden didn't dare look in Liz's direction. "She doesn't give an inch, that girl," he said. "You know, daughters have to work hard to separate from their mothers. You were probably just the same."

"Who knows?" she said. Not giving an inch.

This morning she's got her hair pulled loosely into a ponytail. You can see the grey it's shot with for a quarter-inch along her hairline. She's been in a state for two days, since the meeting with Noah's family. He recalls her standing by the mantel, poised to go for drinks – they were exchanging basic biographical details at the time, acknowledging each other's right to know – and he figured she was dreading the planned parenthood conversation, so he said, hoping it would be the last word on the subject, "Lucky Liz works downtown, in the Exchange District. But I'm way out on Portage Avenue, close to Assiniboine Park."

But in a voice you could only describe as savage, Liz spurned the gesture. "We may as well have our little joke and get it over with," she said. "I'm the executive director of the Sexuality Education Resource Centre – SERC. We call it the circus. You probably know it as Planned Parenthood." Then she turned a dreadful parody of a smile on Maggie: "So! What can I get you to drink?"

Technically they've had lots of time to talk in the past two days, but he's an experienced husband; he's biding his time. He gets up again, pulls open the CD drawer, and picks out a Telemann, Tafelmusik. It was a standard in Christmases past, when there were wolves in Wales and Sylvie was up at five o'clock in the muffling silence of the eternal snows to check that Santa's glass of milk had been drained and his cookie eaten. When out-of-town cousins slept over and a row of striped stockings hung from the mantel. There's just one now, and it's a silky cowboy boot, purple.

"That's her stocking?" He stands by the music system with the silver disc in his fingers. "Where the hell did it come from?"

"Osborne Village. A chic Santa stocking for a chic young woman."
Liz makes a rueful face.

Aiden drops the disk onto the CD tray and the machine swallows it smartly. Something bulges like a bunion in the narrow toe of the purple cowboy boot – a chocolate orange, no doubt. He fishes an iTunes card out of his shirt pocket and drops it in. Sylvie will hate this stocking and most of what's in it.

The music starts up, the delicate display of baroque instruments courting each other.

"Is Noah coming over?"

"No. They're still driving to Calgary for the grandparent thing. They're leaving today."

"God. Poor guy." He drains his latte, tries to snag the last grimy snowdrift of foam with his tongue. "So you knew them fifteen years ago. Why didn't we catch on?"

"I don't think I ever knew his name back then. He was just Sparky."

"Sparky. He wasn't the kid with the Band-Aid fetish, was he?"

"No, Aiden, he was the kid with the extension cords."

"The extension cords. I remember that."

"Yup. He was good at fitting the male and female parts together even then."

Oh, she is a beauty! "Come here," he says, reaching out a hand for her, beckoning her over to the couch. "Come and sit with me." She comes, she curls up against him with her legs on the couch. He slips his hand inside her silky blue kimono and lays it on her warm belly. She shivers, grabs at his hand, and then surrenders, leaning back into him. Their fit is still perfect, though their bodies are not.

Liz had her hair tied back the day he met her. She had (he would learn) just suffered the humiliation of being dumped by a guy she looked down on, but at the time he didn't know the signs of her moods. They met on a cross-country ski foursome to the Sandilands. Aiden's friend Roger was dating Liz's friend Charlotte, whom he eventually married. Aiden didn't get a good look at Liz until they stopped for breakfast at a gas station on the Trans-Canada. She wasn't exceptionally pretty, but the character in her angular face drew him. She talked very little over her scrambled eggs and hash browns, but he formed the impression of a smart and irreverent habit of mind. She had that contained way of using her eyes: you'd say something and those eyes would travel over to you in wry appraisal before she turned her head, before her face registered any expression. He liked that. He was working at a group home at the time, and he had no patience with nicey-nice women. He'd pick salty over sweet anytime.

When they got to the trailhead, he discovered that she was one of those rare individuals who knew how to wax their skis properly – she had checked the temperature, she had a full kit with her, and she used a softer wax on the kick zone. He made a point of skiing behind her, admiring her herringbone technique and the tidy ass below her red jacket. It was a cold day and Charlotte was a lousy skier. They couldn't maintain the pace they needed to keep their feet warm. By the far end of the loop Charlotte was bleating and carrying on, almost in tears. Aiden had caught a glimpse of some buildings along a road on the other side of a bluff, so he veered off the trail and skied over to check them out. It was a little row of cottages. He got lucky – three or four of them hadn't been boarded up, and one had a window unhooked. By the time the others arrived, he had the front door open and was crouched by the stove, arranging kindling.

"Seriously?" he heard Liz say. He looked over his shoulder. She was standing in the doorway, looking shocked and disapproving.

"Oh, it's a time-honoured tradition," he said, aiming (who knows why?) for a Scottish accent.

"Snowmobilers break into a cabin every time they go out," Roger said. "Just for the hell of it. They shit in the chamber pot. Or on the kitchen floor."

They found a mickey of rye on a shelf. There was an old Victrola and some seventy-eights; he remembers dancing to ragtime and to Elvis, to "Hound Dog." Liz seemed to get over her snit. She was a neat dancer, flashing her eyes at him and expertly imitating his moves, which – given that his own style on the dance floor was pretty much self-parody – really broke him up. When they left, they locked everything up tight. Back in the city, in Liz's apartment, he discovered (well, she discovered) bruises on his torso from his shimmy through the window, which had been four feet off the ground. He was well over thirty at the time, a little old for that sort of courtship display. "You idiot," she said, not indulging him with the least bit of sympathy.

Below them the dog lies on the rug with his nose on his front paws. They listen to the Telemann and watch the fire, and he can feel her tension ease.

"Noah sure is a quiet guy," Aiden says.

"Quiet! He hardly said a bloody word."

"I wonder how the two of them are doing."

"Well, I watched them after the meeting, when they went outside." She describes Sylvie shivering by the step, talking in her usual passionate fashion. Noah opened his mouth just once. He was facing Liz (who was looking out the hall window) and his face was lit up by the fairy lights in the spirea bush. But in spite of being a celebrated lip-reader, Liz was unable to make out what he said. All she can report is that they kissed before he turned to leave. "Lovingly," Liz says. "It was a loving kiss."

"I'll be there for you," Aiden says.

"What?"

"That's what he said. I'd lay money. That's their standard line, kids. *He was always there for me.*"

"Well, I hope he is. That's what matters, isn't it, when a girl is knocked up."

Suddenly Aiden has to stop talking. He has to listen to the minor-key meandering of the harmonium. Just when it seems the whole notion of the piece might be lost, the strings jump in, rein the harmonium back, and order is restored.

"How are things looking for dinner?"

"Good. But I'm hoping she'll set the table and do the potatoes."

"Leave her alone. I'll do it."

"I have you down for the gravy."

"I'm not making the gravy."

The tepee has caught now, and it's burning merrily. He builds these fires as homage to his real life, on the island, evenings sitting out on the rocky shelf with a firepit at his feet, watching sparks rise against the fringe of black spruce across the narrows. There's a rock in the narrows that looks like the head and shoulders of a swimmer doing a front crawl – face buried, one arm powerfully lifted and just plunging into the water. The Australian, they call him. When there's wave action on the lake, it adds a splash to the plunging arm. But usually the Australian's got an easy crossing. Otter Lake is so calm that a motorboat can tear across it early in the morning and at noon you'll still see a trace of bubbles on the water. It's so calm that on clear nights you can see the stars baffled on the surface.

"You know," Liz says, "I've been sitting here thinking about a doll we bought for Sylvie one year, that doll that was supposed to eat and poop and was constantly bunged up with rotting food. And

I just remembered something: Mary Magdalene had anatomically correct dolls. She got them from a clinic somewhere."

Liz pulls away from Aiden, sits up, and swivels to face him. "They were dolls the counsellors used for interviewing abused children. They were *so* ugly, those dolls." Suddenly her eyes fill with tears and he can't make out whether she's laughing or crying. He reaches for her hand. "Oh, they were ugly! Their faces were flat and the eyes were drawn too high on their foreheads. The boy's penis was sewn square at the end. The girl had a little cotton pocket between her legs, with crude flannelette lips sewn on the outside. *Yuck*, we hated those dolls. But nobody was allowed to criticize Mary Magdalene. The kids would play with them – not playing sex, or not that I noticed. Just putting things into the girl's vagina. Marshmallows. Playskool figures. Or, I don't know, a battery. Oh, oh, Aiden!" She's gasping for breath. "There was some sort of scene, with the mother of those androgynous twins. She finally threw a fit about the dolls. I think it might have been what broke up the group."

By now they're both helpless with laughter.

"Well, well," Aiden says when they've recovered. "An old friend from GAP. You didn't exactly fall on each other's necks."

"We were never close." She pulls back from him again. "*I know what it's like to be a single mom.* Did you hear her say that?"

"No."

"She said it, I'm sure she did. I couldn't believe my ears. Like, she's already deciding her son will be out of the picture? In fact, she *adored* being a single mom. She made a cult of it. She was living on welfare – to devote herself to her son. She could have got a job, but she wanted to make some sort of statement about society's obligation to mothers."

How tired she looks; she has dark smears under her eyes. "You didn't say much all night," he says.

"Yeah, well, it pisses me off that Sylvie didn't tell us she was going out with Sparky. So we had to be broadsided like that in front of everyone. On top of everything else."

He lets his mind go slack and a question surfaces. Does Liz *enjoy* their daughter? And then swiftly the answer: no. And that makes all this so much harder.

He moves Liz over gently, gets up, and goes to the window. It's like a defaced mural, this scene: their dead elms spray-painted orange. Skeletons against a curdled grey sky, and they're still full of squirrels. He watches a big one with its tail flicking erratically, as if it's on an intermittent power source. The neighbour to the north feeds them, doing his conscientious bit to upset the balance of nature. Aiden looks at squirrels in a new light since the day one of them chewed through the attic eaves and dropped onto their bed like a demon commando from another civilization.

Liz stands up and tightens the belt of her kimono. "Sylvie should be getting up now. And you should go pick up your dad. I'm going to get dressed."

That's her dad walking across the living room. She can recognize his tread, slower and heavier than Liz's. She's sitting cross-legged by the wooden Coke cases, right under his path. Her dad used these cases when he was a bachelor. They're full of her books now, the books she loved when she was young. She's halfway through the first case, pulling out each book, shaking it by the spine, fanning the pages. *Sleeping Beauty. Charlotte's Web. The Secret Garden.* The dust of her small self clings to them all. *Princess Furball.* Oh, Princess Furball. She opens it to the picture she loved best as a kid: the princess curled up in a hollow tree in her coat of furs, just like an animal hibernating. And under *Princess Furball* is *Sabriel* – Sylvie feels a throb of joy just at the sight of its cover. She leans back against the cement wall and reads the first chapter, whispering the lines she knows by heart, the part where the old man chants a list of all the things that live or grow, "or once lived, or would live again, and the bonds that held them together."

She puts down *Sabriel* and goes back to looking. She finally finds it, tucked inside the front cover of *Alice in Wonderland*. Noah – Sparky – at thirteen, posing in the laced leather vest of a Renaissance falconer, wearing his silver sleeve. She looks closely at his young face, which is not so different from now. She runs her finger along the edge of the picture. When she cut it out with the box cutter, she made a long, curved slash on each side of Sparky, so he seems to be the figure in the central pane of a stained-glass window. The background is blue and brown. Mary Magdalene's blue gown and Krzysztof Nowak's brown shirt.

It's a souvenir. Of a day filled with tests and lessons, most of which she failed. Alone in a house in the Minnesota forest, she cut out that picture and then took the blade to a beautiful book. A few days later, the owner of the book left an angry message on the Glasgow-Phimister answering machine: "Hey, what is this? Your fucking kid defaced my *Golden Bough*." Sylvie listened to the message first and then she went to get her dad and played it for him. She was confused in those days about whether she wanted him to know or not. He made a baffled face. "Must be a wrong number," he said, and she understood then how stupid-on-purpose he was. Who leaves a message for a wrong number?

Sylvie props up Sparky on the trunk where she keeps her things. No one will notice this picture of him at thirteen, or ask. She's in sole possession of the events of that day, because Liz never gives a sign that it affected her in the least. She lies back on the futon and looks up at the ceiling, resting her eyes on the brown wooden planks with their crisscrossed little braces. How rough the wood is, how bare and real and unimproved – a ceiling that is revealed to be the hardworking floor of the storey above. When she's down here, her eyes are drawn to it constantly.

Her mom is back in the living room. She can hear their murmuring voices above her but not what they're saying. She should go upstairs, but she has too much to do down here. Too much thinking to do. She needs to scrutinize the fall, the golden, deceitful fall that seemed to be about certain things but was really about something entirely different. She rolls over, untwists her pyjama shorts, and nestles deeper into the futon. It's like watching the trailer for a movie called *Sylvie Is Happy*. But all fall, she thinks, another film was being furtively shot deep inside her, using fibre optics. A film of a curled-up zygote with ET eyes. She jerks at her pillow, angles an elbow over her eyes – and then she hears the back door slam, her dad going outside. She crawls out of bed and reaches for her bathrobe.

When Sylvie finally climbs the stairs, her grandfather is standing in the hall in his parka and an old red cap with an Esso logo on it. He sticks out his hand and says, "Rupert Phimister. Pleased to meet you."

She kisses him and says, "I'm pleased to meet you too, Grandpa."

She helps him take off his parka. He's wearing a red plaid shirt and the measuring-tape suspenders they once bought him as a joke. The sacks under his eyes look as if tears have leaked between the thin layers of his skin. He doesn't have his glasses on; maybe that's why he doesn't know her.

"What happened to his glasses?" Liz asks.

"I guess he forgot them," Aiden says. "And I didn't notice. Sorry."

"Why say sorry to me?" Liz says. "It's got nothing to do with me." She's like a snake with bright yellow don't-mess-with-me stripes.

She hands Sylvie a glass of booze-free eggnog. "Let's get this show on the road."

In the living room they distribute the gifts slowly, trying to drag it out. Nobody mentions the baby. Sylvie doesn't have the heart to tell her grandpa. She'd have to say it over and over, and it still wouldn't register. They all shout at him as though he's deaf. Well, he is deaf as well. He never talks to her but she knows he loves her. One day when she had her garden, he rolled up in his big old car and sat with his elbow out the window, watching her hack away at the hard clay with the new hoe she had bought with babysitting money. Then he got out and came over, took the hoe out of her hands, and drove away with it. An hour later he brought it back, all shiny-edged. Nobody had told her that hoes have to be sharpened.

Most of the gifts under the tree are for Sylvie. Sadly, there are no hand-planted cactus gardens for the members of her family. For her father Sylvie bought a pair of goats for a family in India. "That's in honour of your being an old goat," she says. For her grandpa she bought a beehive for a family in Ethiopia. He studies the card for ages, though he can't read it and doesn't get the concept. For her mother she bought a satchel of school supplies for a girl in Kenya. "A very worthy cause," Liz says.

From her dad Sylvie gets a new iPod, loaded with his own top-fifty playlist. "This is a pity gift," Sylvie explains to her grandpa. "Dad feels sorry for me because he thinks his music is so awesome compared to mine."

"Sylvie's got that exactly right," Aiden says. "The harmony bands, the Beatles, the Byrds – there's a sweetness to them. Even though they were stoned for decades. Even though they were fighting like beasts in the studio. And the lyrics. Those dudes could write. Dylan – what a poet!"

"I never really got Bob Dylan," Liz says.

"Well, that's the brilliant thing about him," Aiden says. "He's always just on the edge of meaning."

When they're finished with the gifts, Liz goes out to work on the dinner and Sylvie manages to slip downstairs. But her dad won't let her go. He follows her, shaking the bead curtain she's hung at the entrance to her cave, as a way of knocking.

"Got a minute?" he asks.

"I guess." She turns her back on him and dumps all the consumerist beauty crap her mother bought her on the old trunk she uses as a dresser. "What do you want?"

"I want to know what lover-boy got you for Christmas."

"None of your business."

"Aw, come on." He leans against the pillar and looks around her cave. He's wearing the sweater he got from Liz. "I'm not trying to pry. But I've been wondering, how are things going with the two of you? How did Noah react when he heard the news?"

"You're not trying to pry?" she says. "You're insatiable." But he looks so pathetic that finally she gives in. She tells him that Noah was just really quiet.

Her dad keeps watching her. "Well, it's a good thing, isn't it?" Sylvie says. "If he doesn't know what to say, he doesn't say anything. You don't have to pick through a lot of bullshit. Noah is a cat." This is her dad's own theory: some people are cats and some people are dogs. Sylvie herself is a dog. Her tail wags and her tongue hangs out; everything she feels is obvious as soon as you look at her.

He's still watching her. The other day she could not get the crying stopped once it had started, and she's determined not to start again. In fact, she and Noah are still not over the taxi ride from the airport, when he wouldn't talk. He just kept glancing warningly at the back of the driver's head, as if the guy could hear them through the Plexiglas, as if it *mattered*.

"This vehement thing," her dad finally asks. "Is that bothering him?"

"He's not a freak, Dad," she says. "He's just committed to other species surviving on Earth. There are far too many of us, you say – I'm going to stop breeding. But what are you supposed to do? Condoms sit in landfill for a thousand years. So I started that fucking pill. But every time I peed, a bit of it went into the river. And now the fish are growing two heads. And it didn't work anyway."

The tears are coming now, and he sees it. "Hormones are natural, you know," he says. They're sitting on the futon and he's holding her hand. "And this is partly hormones. They make you more emotional."

He reaches over to the old trunk, trying to find a Kleenex. She's got a pile of handkerchiefs and she digs one out.

"Come upstairs," he says. "We can play Chinese checkers. Or Risk. You love Risk."

"We don't have enough people."

"Parcheesi, then. Grandpa could handle Parcheesi."

"Maybe later." She wipes her eyes and her nose. The handkerchief is useless – she made it from an old pillowcase and it just moves the snot around.

"And talk things over with your mother, eh? This is exactly the sort of situation your mother knows about."

She tosses the handkerchief in the direction of her dirty clothes pile and wipes her nose on her sleeve. She squeezes his arm to say, I'm fine, thanks. It's over. "If this was only a computer game," she says, "I could reboot. I would have saved it when I was on a roll and I could start again from there."

"Where would you have saved it?"

"I don't know . . . After I met Noah at the lake last summer. I wouldn't want to have missed that." He smiles, and so much love shines in his eyes that she wants to keep talking. "You know, Dad, it's really weird, but I think I knew I was pregnant before the doctor told me."

"What do you mean?"

So she tells him about meeting her friends to plan the Fringe play, and how they talked about a restaurant deep in the ocean and she pictured fish tapping on the glass. And then later, sitting bent over on the toilet, she felt a *tap, tap, tap* against the wall of her stomach, *from the inside.*

"You're probably right," he says. "No doubt you knew on some unconscious level. It was too big for you to let yourself think about it openly. But something took you to the doctor that day."

"I know – that's what I was thinking! And something made me wait to see her, even though my own doctor was away. Even though I had so much work to do."

"You know, Sylvie," he says, kissing her tenderly, "you have all sorts of wisdom. Far more than you know. You can count on it in the next few months. You're going to be all right."

He goes back upstairs. He meant what he said to reassure her, but actually it makes her feel worse. Because it's not just her body that has a secret life, her mind does too. The way it sent her scurrying to the clinic, totally oblivious to what she was doing.

Once when she was little and slept upstairs, her mother was reading her a bedtime story and they were distracted by the sight of a silver moon out the window. A crescent moon tipped on its back, a moon like a sly smile. "It's growing a little bit every day," her mother said. "Just like you are." Then she kissed Sylvie goodnight and closed the blind and left. When she was gone, Sylvie got out of bed, dragged her chair over to the window, and knelt on it, looking out into the night, the window blind draped over her back like a turtle shell. That was when she saw it, for the first time ever: the dark, stony, gloating round of the whole moon. *There all the time.*

"Why don't you boys play cards?" Liz suggests. She serves them each a glass of red wine and some crackers and tapenade and cheese. Aiden pulls out the cribbage board and sets up, but Rupert just looks suspiciously at his cards. His eyes are strangely bright; he looks like Buster Keaton. "Try him with your reading glasses," Liz says. Aiden does, but it's hopeless.

The monster turkey fills the oven as though it has expanded in the heat. Liz slides it out and bastes it. It's glistening with real fat and juices, not that cheap hydrogenated oil they inject under the skin of supermarket turkeys. She ordered it at the butcher shop in early December, back before Charlotte and her kids had pulled out, when she thought they were having ten people for Christmas dinner. Up till Wednesday, they were still six. Wendy's son and his wife are in Hawaii, so Wendy was planning to come and bring her Somalian refugee. But she's got the flu, she's been sick all week. And after the Blessed Annunciation, as Aiden's taken to calling it, Liz cancelled the Somalian refugee. "We don't even know him," she said to Aiden. "Wendy hardly knows him herself."

"Mary Magdalene Calhoun," she whispers, rinsing the baster under the tap. Maggie Calhoun, into the "alternative fabric movement," running a hemp and bamboo store in a strip mall on Corydon. Liz sets about crimping foil over the wings and drumsticks so they won't brown too fast. It's a fiddly job and she feels strangely worked up doing it. It's the memory of those anatomically correct dolls, which brings with it a thought – a welcome thought – that in some perverse but deep way this situation is Maggie's fault.

Why? Because those dolls speak of a dangerous ideological purity, and ideology so often trumps sensible action.

Maggie's ideology was not so evident at the meeting. What was striking was her perfection: the perfect, serene bow of her upper lip; her gentle, even voice; her Mona Lisa smile. None of which can be real, given what she must be feeling, and which therefore reveal her as a perfect fraud. This is a woman who had a child with George Stonechild, a white guy from East Kildonan who braided his hair with rawhide and said *meegwetch* at every opportunity. He fooled no one.

They'll need a leaf in the table, there are a lot of side dishes. She glances into the dining room to see if the candleholders need fresh candles, and she's caught off guard by the sight of a window with curtains blowing in a summer breeze. The *trompe l'oeil* fresco on the north wall, with its painted curtains perfectly matching the real curtains – it actually tricks her eye. It's brilliant; nobody believes she painted it. The blue for the sky is three shades brighter than most amateurs would have dared. She and Aiden were at each other's throats that summer, and she was trying to keep herself busy. She can see herself in the dining room with cans of paint on a drop sheet at her feet, a redhead in shorts and a halter top (she was a redhead that long-ago summer).

Oh, that summer. Thanks to Sylvie, the house feels crammed with people from that summer, or an even earlier one. Sparky, a brave little boy with two state-of-the-art shiners, and the self-righteous, bleating GAP mothers. The beauteous Mary Magdalene and her evil ex. Liz sees her old self, a restless, reckless woman she never expected to meet again, stopping in at George Stonechild's one night when he lived on Dominion with a fallen-down maple in his front yard. Everybody knew that house, for the tree that had been growing sideways for decades and for George's incessant drumming.

Liz was walking home from an evening drinking wine at Mary Magdalene's when she heard the drumming and George Stonechild drummed her into his yard. Swiftly he popped a beer for her. Somehow he knew where she'd been, at the house on Greenwood with the purple steps.

"So what were you lovely ladies nattering about?" he said.

"Terminology," Liz said, taking a long drink. "We were arguing about what to call a certain neighbourhood ex. Whether he's a prick or just an asshole."

"And what am I?"

"Sadly, just an asshole. According to Mary Magdalene." She went so far as to explain: "You're not smart enough to be a prick." She could see him trying to find some way to take this as a compliment.

How extremely drunk she must have been to say such a thing to his face – it's unbelievable. As she pulls down serving dishes from the cupboard, she peers into a yard where the yellow light of a street lamp is falling through the boulevard trees and watches George crowd her up against the fallen-down maple, leaning in for a kiss, sees herself shove him away, sees him laugh. But still she stayed, long into the night, avoiding going back to the house on Augusta Street she was suddenly allergic to, the kitchen smelling of mouldy leftovers and the upstairs hall eerie from the little fish nightlight Sylvie loved. Sylvie muttering in a bed rocky with disassembled toys. Aiden lying on his back snoring, on a sheet that hadn't been washed in two weeks. She had another beer and another and lounged against the tree, soaking up George's gaze, taking in his puerile flattery, not enjoying George so much as she was enjoying herself, her fast-talking, careless self.

When Rupert has fallen into a doze with his head against the cushions, Aiden comes out to help. He's quiet and gentle, which is always his way when he's troubled. He peels the potatoes and sets the table and then drifts off for a while. When he comes back, he mashes the potatoes. Liz works on the gravy and the side dishes, a butternut squash gratin and braised red cabbage with apple. She glances at the turkey resting on a warming stone. It has browned perfectly, as if varnished for the cover of a culinary magazine.

Aiden calls Sylvie and she wanders up from the cave. Liz asks her to light the candles and she does, and then she leads in her grandpa. They all sit down and look at each other in that little moment of recognition that stands in for grace. Sylvie has her vivid hair up in a knot on the top of her head and her bangs pinned back with a tiny silver bluebird clip. She's a Renaissance beauty. She called Mary Magdalene right after she found out. This fact still burns in Liz, with such pain that she can't look at her daughter for longer than a second.

"Isn't this a feast!" Aiden says. He pours the wine. It's a Montravel Sec they bought in celebration of their anticipated trip. He glances at the label but doesn't comment.

"Your father loves Christmas," Liz says to Sylvie. She picks up the carving knife. "When he was young, it was always winter and never Christmas."

"Because you belonged to a cult, Dad?" Sylvie asks.

"Something like that."

Liz carves because she's better at it. She passes Rupert a plate with all dark meat, as per his preference when he was still able to voice one. She passes her daughter stuffing only – since she was twelve or so, Sylvie has declined to eat her friends. She passes Aiden two slices of thigh, two slices of breast. She follows this with the pear-and-ginger chutney.

"When did chutney enter the Western diet?" Aiden asks.

"Your father always references prehistory when he's trying to decide whether he likes something," Liz says. "It's all 'What would

Cro-Magnon man do?'" Sitting in the soft light of the antler chandelier, she feels the full weight of her anxiety again, pressing on her like one of those lead vests you wear for dental X-rays. She flattens her potatoes for gravy; then the gravy comes to her and she passes it on without taking any. If only Charlotte had come.

"So why was your mother so religious?" Sylvie is asking.

"My mother was never religious," Aiden says. "She just hung out with the Jehovah's Witnesses because they were always prepared to fight with her."

"But you never got a Christmas present?"

"In those years? No." He turns to Rupert, who is stalwartly eating his way through his mashed potatoes. "Although, Dad, I do recall you coming in off the line one Christmas morning and tossing some bags of candy at us kids. You were my hero – do you remember?"

Rupert doesn't even look up.

Leonard Cohen broods from the speakers over the sideboard – Aiden's notion of sacred music – and Liz notes the fresh sage in the dressing, musty and subtle. I got it just right, she thinks. But would it have killed me to open a can of cranberry sauce for Aiden? She watches him in his Christmas sweater, methodically portioning turkey and potatoes onto his fork, this lanky, warm-faced man who's always ready to talk about himself, though his stories never shed much light on what he's really about. When they first met, she could never mesh his easy confidence and clever talk with his working-class clothes and the startling gaps in his manners. Liz and Charlotte would joke about Aiden's mysterious past, but all she ever heard about was aimless years and career changes and the girlfriends he'd broken up with for no particular reason – the usual male commitment phobia. She's going to die waiting for the big reveal.

Sylvie's eyes are drawn to her dad too. "You know, Dad, you look like a hipster in that sweater."

"Thank you."

"It's not a compliment. Sorry."

"What I really should have bought your dad," Liz says, trying to summon up a bit of gaiety, "is a wired sweater. Did you read about them in the *Globe*? They're called hug sweaters. They're lined with copper wire, and when someone who loves you wants to send you a hug, they press a button on a remote and the wires heat up."

"Oh god," Sylvie says. "That is just gross. Women are walking three miles every morning for contaminated drinking water, with their babies strapped to their backs, and we're engineering self-hugging sweaters."

This from a girl who could not be bothered to buy a single Christmas present for a single person in the house. "You're a puritan. We didn't raise you to be moralistic, but that's what you are. That sweater is just a whimsical way of staying in touch. Using technology to send a warm, human message."

"Exactly. That's what else is gross. The child thinks he's on his own at last. He's out there, a big kid feeling cool with his friends, playing hockey on the road. He misses a shot. 'Fuck!' he yells – and just then his sweater starts heating up. *Your mother is thinking about you. Don't think you can escape!*"

Grandpa catches at least one of Sylvie's words and looks at her with interest. Then he turns back to his crusty roll, which he is endeavouring to eat with his knife and fork. He's lost the concept of the bread bun and he never really had the concept of conversation; he always seemed dazed by the way they talk at this table.

"You know, Sylvie," Liz hears herself saying, "you will really enjoy getting to know Noah's mom. When I was hanging out with Mary Magdalene and her friends, they were true back-to-the-earth types. They didn't just make soup – they made broth first, from herbs and vegetables they grew themselves. They didn't make

82

bread from yeast you buy at the store – they kept sourdough starter in their fridges. If there was a hard way to do something, they found it."

She's warming up to something and she can't seem to stop. "I think it was to justify staying home. I was the only one in the whole group with a semblance of paid work. I could never get the hang of how they thought. If someone broke a rule, they'd all talk about it in these shocked, grieving voices: 'Susan handed out *Oreos* at the playground.' Or 'Elaine feeds her kids *Kraft dinner*.' Or 'Liz lets her daughter watch *Sesame Street!*'"

"What's wrong with *Sesame Street*?"

"It destroys the attention span. There wasn't any handbook for this, no – what would you call it? – scripture. Only leadership . . . i.e., Mary Magdalene." The venom in her voice startles even her. She shoves aside her red cabbage and squash and wipes her fingers on her napkin.

"On this festive occasion," Aiden says, "in this intimate and loving company, I would like to propose a toast." They raise their glasses. Sylvie has a real Shirley Temple that Liz went to the trouble of making. Aiden looks to his right, to Sylvie. "To new life," he says. Bravely they drink to it, except for Rupert.

Then Aiden looks down the table at Liz. He raises his glass again. "And to the old one."

"To the old one?"

"To you, Liz. To my darling Liz. A cook who's not afraid to lick her fingers."

The faux candles on the antler chandelier burn steadily and the beeswax candles on the table flicker. Liz looks around the dining room, trying hard to take everything in, the beautiful home she's made for all of them, as if this is the last time she'll see it. "Thank God we didn't plan a party for New Year's," she says.

5

Begin as You Mean to Go On

THEY'VE DECIDED THAT WE'RE PARALYZED WHILE we sleep. This is an evolutionary adaptation to stop us from acting out our dreams and our nightmares. Scientists claim to have found the paralyzing switch; they turned it off in a cat that had the bad luck to fall into their hands. Aiden saw it on TV. He saw the cat, an ordinary domestic tabby with an electronic device the size of an old-fashioned alarm clock screwed into her brain. She was sound asleep and hunting: crouching, staring, pouncing, doing her predatory thing to a dream mouse that only she could see.

But Aiden already knew this. You're too hot, he says to himself as he drifts towards sleep. Take off your T-shirt. But his arms lie inert, too heavy to be moved by an act of his puny will.

In the post–Boxing Day morning he's overheated and tetchy by the time Liz gets up and leaves the house. When he finally pries himself out of bed, Sylvie's gone as well. To the library, she said last night – she's in some sort of fix with her plant science paper. He putters around the kitchen, cleaning up the mess she made creating her smoothie, relieved not to see her, not to have to do the chipper optimism thing.

He stands with his coffee in the living room, looking out at the doomed elms in the yard, where the squirrels are chasing each other in a mating frenzy. It's a bloody Carry On movie. Their babies are going to freeze when winter kicks in, if they can in fact breed off-season. He knows nothing about squirrels. He should study them, chart the population. Figure out if they're monogamous. How many offspring they have and how long they live. Two years? Ten years? He has no idea. Orange roughy live to be one hundred. He and Liz ate a lot of orange roughy at one time. It was flown in from New Zealand and it was bloody expensive, but it was their favourite company dinner. And now the orange roughy with its turned-down mouth is gone, because they were eating fish as old as they were and no one knew.

He touches the heel of his hand to the triple-pane window and judges the temperature to be about minus two. Yesterday a blanket of snow lay over the yard and Liz went out and swept the patio clear. Now, all around the patio, the snow is retreating, pale and springlike, shrinking away from the dark bricks so fast you can almost see it melt. The albedo effect – that's what you call it, isn't it? – that feedback loop where the less ice you have, the less ice you have. When he first read about it, he came away saying to himself, How extremely stupid not to have thought of that.

Don't start thinking about arctic ice. What about the ice on Otter Lake? No hope of a ski-in to the cabin this week. He should have scheduled some clients between Christmas and New Year's; two or three really wanted an hour. But when he was setting his schedule in November, he was counting on being up at Otter Lake.

Aiden was a kid when Rupert built the cabin in north-western Ontario, on land made available to CN employees. They went in every summer weekend on a train called the Campers' Special, two or three passenger cars full of railway families, hitched to an eastbound freight train. Rupert had scored a prime lot, a tiny, rocky island in a tiny lake, a five-minute boat ride from the train stop. Aiden's parents were matter-of-fact about the property, almost gruff: they'd both grown up in the country. But an *island* – this amazed and thrilled Aiden. He still remembers the first time he saw it, a ten-year-old in too-small runners who had thought the city's north end was the whole world. And then there was this island, with its continuous rocky margin, its resident turtle and visiting eagle. The private, intricate beauty of its lichens and mosses. He was the only one in the family the island really spoke to – that's what he believed from the beginning – except that at certain times it seemed to take them all in. In the evenings especially, as the sun slid behind the spruce trees on the mainland and their parents sat out on the rocks, the embers of their cigarettes glowing red, and he and Carl and Ken dove off the end of the new dock, over and over, their shoulders felted with sunburn and their arms goosefleshed with the cold. Sloughing off the city, sloughing off their enmity, they'd be slotted into the night, merged into one black shape shouting over the shining water. He never lost it, what he felt about the island that first summer.

One day eight or ten years ago, Aiden was over at his dad's, rebuilding his back fence, and Rupert let drop that he'd been talking to a realtor at Minaki about selling the cottage. Back in the eighties CN had stopped the Campers' Special, and without the train, you had to be a diehard outdoorsman to get in. Aiden set down the picket he was fitting and straightened up. "I thought you might sign it over to your kids, Dad," he said, aiming for a lightness of tone.

"Aw, they're not interested," Rupert muttered around the home-rolled cigarette dangling from his lower lip. Aiden's mind cried out for witnesses: he wanted somebody from the Cosmic Tribunal on

Parental Malfeasance to note how unconsciously Rupert's mind leapt to the two sons he considered his real progeny, totally blind to the existence of the chump who'd just spent two days in this yard breaking his back with a posthole digger. But on the facts, Rupert was right; they weren't interested. Aiden's older brother, Carl, had moved to Fort McMurray and hadn't been in touch in two or three years. And Ken, the last time they'd seen him, had a mob of creditors waving tire irons on his tail.

That was the summer Aiden entered the master's program in counselling. His pension from the group home was just about to vest, so he started the paperwork to pull it out and he bought the property. For the price his dad was asking, as a point of pride. Obviously he and Liz could have spent that money ten different ways, but he made what at the time he called a unilateral decision. Well, maybe every marriage has its black holes – differences so fundamental you just have to back away from them – and they did, they did back away. She was beyond angry for about a month and then she dropped it. The issue's still alive somewhere, no doubt, but she's packed it away in some storage facility for undetonated resentments. It's still there for Aiden, for sure: the island's always on the rim of his consciousness, gleaming with his knowledge of how much he was prepared to pay for it.

Anyway, there's no hope of a winter road out of Minaki for weeks now. Aiden lowers himself into the Mission chair and contemplates the mess in the fireplace, three charred logs that failed to burn last night because he failed to stoke the fire. Liz was pissed off with him that entire summer, and it wasn't just the Otter Lake thing. He'd gone back to university with her full and generous support after fifteen years of working in group homes, and he was almost at the end of the long road to a Ph.D. in English. But he was hating it, finding it hard to breathe the rarefied air of the semioticians, and fed up with departmental politics. If he's honest, he stopped believing in his dissertation about a year into it. You can make decisions based on an outdated understanding of yourself and the world, and that's how you get trapped. Then one day at the library he ran into the director of the counselling program and she encouraged him to apply for a master's of individual and family therapy (the deadline was just a few days away), and that's what he did.

This eleventh-hour career change surprised everybody, and it broadsided Liz. But she was finally on solid professional footing herself, and he couldn't see any practical reason why not. God knows, he never had much hope of a tenure-track position in English. So he followed his instincts and applied for the MIFT program and he got in, and discovered to his surprise that psychotherapy picked up what you might call the bright thread of his interior life in much the same way as reading did. Literature was always more a private delight for him than an academic vocation, a furtive pleasure after the belligerent redneckism he grew up with. He still remembers the moment he understood that poetry is not bullshit, that it is maybe the antithesis of bullshit. He was in first-year English, standing in the stacks reading an assigned poem (Yeats? Or maybe earlier – George Herbert?), when a light rose up off the page and cast something essential he'd been feeling into high relief, something he had never tried to articulate. When he started the MIFT program, he sensed right away that therapy drew from the same well. It was rigorous in ways he hadn't expected. The human psyche, like the poem, tends to tell things slant (is how he came to think of it). Readers of both have to keep their wits about them.

One of the program's premises was that therapists in training needed to do personal work on their own issues. Aiden arrived at his first group therapy session uneasy and suspicious, but by the end of the day he was completely disarmed. It was a gift in your middle years, he saw, this chance to probe your experiences with astute listeners. He was moved by his group's struggles to disclose themselves honestly, by the risks they took, and by how forthright they were in their responses to each other. He felt as though he were reading a brave and original text and the even braver gloss on it (it was a fact that, in his previous studies, a piece of intelligent criticism often lit him up more than the literary text itself). He was the only man in his group, but his colleagues let it be known there'd be no hiding behind some ideal of male reticence. Like a woman learning heavy-duty mechanics in a class of men, he'd be held to an even higher standard: he had to make up for the privilege that no doubt had gotten him into the program in the first place.

In a workshop held in an old convent, in a stale-smelling room with a crucifix and dried reeds over the door, they talked about their primary relationships. Aiden told the group about an incident with Liz from the early days, before Sylvie was born. He owned a motorcycle, a Honda Interstate, and one day he and his buddy Glen went out for a highway ride. The big Harley-Davidson rally was happening that week in Sturgis, South Dakota, and when they stopped to grab a bite to eat, Glen suggested going, just for a laugh. Aiden had a chunk of time off, so he said, "Sure." He called Liz from a payphone at the gas station and ended up leaving a cryptic message, intending to call again later. Somehow it didn't happen that first day, and then it didn't happen at all. When he got home, every muscle shaken to mush after four days on the road and sporting a WHAT WOULD JESUS RIDE? T-shirt, Liz's sister Maureen, who lived in Toronto, was at the house. She and her husband both came to meet him at the door, as though they lived there and Aiden didn't. It turned out that Liz's father had suffered a heart attack the night Aiden left for Sturgis, and he'd passed away just that morning. He was sixty, an insurance salesman, about to retire.

Possibly the crucifix over the door had encouraged Aiden to mistake his therapy group for a confessional, but that's the first story he told them. Edith Wong was the one who spoke into the silence when he was done. "How did your wife react when she saw you?"

"She said, 'I'd throw you out if I had the energy.' She got over it eventually. But I felt like a true piece of shit."

"And why didn't you call her?"

"Well, obviously, if I'd had any idea what was happening—"

Edith cut him off. "Come on," she said. "This isn't about your father-in-law's death. This is about the disrespect you show your wife when you take off for four days and don't even let her know where you are."

"I had every intention of calling again the first day. And then when I realized I'd forgotten . . . I guess the idea of not calling began to take hold." This was more than he had ever admitted to Liz.

"So it made you feel good to think of her in distress?"

Well, all right, this was the sort of ballsy response he came to value in that group. With all those thoughtful female eyes on him, he acknowledged something he'd never seen before: how afraid he was of being sucked into something that would drain the life out of him. But he also took a stand for a high degree of autonomy in relationships, as a matter of principle, as a counterbalance to all the compromises you have to make. His own quasi-marriage was better off for a bit of breathing room, he insisted, though he didn't go so far as to mention the great sex he and Liz sometimes had after a nasty standoff.

But the women in his group got the picture. "Woo-hoo, Aiden," somebody called. "Treat her mean, keep her keen."

Okay. He came out of that group understanding that few rela- tionships would have survived what he put Liz through in their early days. But he never cheated on her and he never lied, not about any-thing big. And she was feisty as well. If he didn't come home when she expected, she never whined, she never said, I was terrified. I thought you were dead in an alley somewhere. She got what it was about and she met it square on.

And as provocative as his behaviour might sometimes look from the outside, as unlucky as the timing of that Sturgis trip turned out to be, somebody had to draw a line in the sand with Liz. When he first met her, she had him over for an amazing meal — Moroccan-style lamb cooked in an authentic tagine dish. Sitting in an arm-chair afterwards, finishing off the Beaujolais and soaking up the quirky charm of her apartment, he said to himself, It could be like this every day. But of course that sort of comfort comes with a pile of domestic expectations. Liz came by it honestly — you spent an evening with her mother and by eight o'clock you were ready to stick pins in your eyes.

And there was this: if Liz had had power of veto over his entry into the MIFT program, she would have used it, and she'd have been wrong. His move to counselling made no external sense but it had a deep internal logic. He was doing something hopeful and he was better at the work than he would have predicted. He'd found a pro-fession that asked him to bring to it everything he was. You didn't need to have worked through all your own issues — well, you did, to the point that your ego needs didn't intrude in the relationship with the client — but beyond that it was a matter of listening intel-ligently and being real.

He swallows the last of his coffee. It's stone cold. He feels weighed down by sadness. For his lovely daughter and for himself as well, because her energy and spirit have buoyed him up for two decades. He can trace his funk right back to the Grandparents' Summit, to that moment at the end, the Annunciation. All night he brooded on the angel's terrible message: *Business as usual, over the brink.*

He glances at the clock on the mantel. It's after eleven. He's got to muster his energy, get into some reading, start a project of some kind. Be the sort of person who charts the squirrel population in his spare time. Work would have helped him today. Every tiny step a client takes, negligible in itself, helps to build the dike that holds back the deluge. Or maybe it's just that work lifts him out of himself. Is out of himself where he wants to be?

To forestall getting sucked into that particular loop, he leans over, picks up the phone, and calls his message function. He can hardly recall who he saw just before Christmas, what with all the chaos at home. Odette Zimmerman. And there's fallout, a message left on Christmas Day.

"Mr. Phimister," she says (already he knows she's in a rage), "I need a therapist who understands that feelings are honest and need to be affirmed. Not a *moralist* who thinks in black and white. On Thursday I paid you a hundred dollars to be told what a bad person I am. I've been sitting here wondering why I would keep doing that. This message is to cancel my standing appointment." An intake of breath. *Click.*

Oh shit. Aiden sinks his fingers into Max's ruff and stares at the ashes in the fireplace. He has to talk to Edith Wong.

And then worry for a different client starts up – for Jake Peloquin, a.k.a. Defrag, who is never far from Aiden's thoughts, especially when he cancels so abruptly. He's been a client off and on since Aiden started his practice. He takes a break when he's maxed out his benefits package, and then when he's eligible again or has enough cash, he phones Aiden and says, "Can you fit me in for a defrag?"

Jake makes it sound like a discretionary thing, but Aiden has been his lifeline for years. He's alone. His long-time girlfriend was someone Aiden knew by reputation, a woman named Jessie Alwin who had started a terrific transition-to-employment program for youth in the North End. She was very highly regarded in the city. But she had one of those diseases where your body turns against itself, and it eventually killed her. Her death was the tipping point for Defrag. When he first came to see Aiden, he had serious slashes crosshatching the insides of both arms. For a while he was also seeing a psychiatrist, who had him on antidepressants, and Aiden and the psychiatrist consulted. But now it's just him and Aiden.

Defrag has a job at the university, some arcane singular position related to data flow, but he's always got an art project on the go. He's into the sort of work where the artist surrenders any role in shaping the image. Lately he's been taping pinhole cameras to trees. They're 35-millimetre film canisters with a hole pierced in them using the finest needle available, an acupuncture needle. The little bit of light leaking through that tiny hole is enough to leave a ghostly impression on the film or paper or whatever's inside. Defrag's hidden these cameras all over the city. He's going to leave them up for six months and see what they have to show him.

Defrag has a project. A little gust of hope and energy accompanies this thought. Seizing on it, Aiden climbs the stairs to the loft and gets dressed. When he comes downstairs in his running gear, the dog is thrilled. "Sorry, buddy," Aiden says, pushing past him out the door.

It's a relief to be outside. He walks up to Portage Avenue, catches a westbound bus, and gets off at the park. Standing by a bench, he bends over his extended femur, counts to thirty. Lifts his head, looks up through the trees into space, at garbage from satellites falling into the ether. Straightens, gives himself a shake. Does a little prance, impersonating a runner, just to get his blood up. Picks his gravel path and sets off. One of Defrag's cameras is along this trail. He first located it about a month ago – Defrag told him how to triangulate to find it.

It's still there, duct-taped to the trunk of a native basswood almost bereft of branches, about eight feet up. It looks undisturbed. As Aiden runs by he can't resist lifting a hand in a two-finger wave.

When he gets home, Liz is in the kitchen, just hanging up the phone. "So that's that," she says, aggrieved, which is always her way when she's fighting tears. "I guess I was hoping Sylvie got it wrong."

"Sylvie's doctor? You tracked her down?"

Liz nods.

"What did she say?"

"She wouldn't talk to me about it, as I'm not the patient. But she said, 'I can't refer for an emergency ultrasound unless the case is urgent. Like, if the pregnant woman is in the first trimester and termination is still an option.'"

So. They stand and look at each other for a long minute.

"She sounds about twelve," Liz says. "But I can only assume she's qualified."

"Are you going to tell Sylvie you called?"

"Of course not. I'm going to go upstairs and email the child support guidelines to Maggie. Then I'm going to break the news to Vacances françaises and *beg* them to refund the deposit for Sarlat. After that I'm going to cancel our airline tickets and get a voucher from Air Canada. Then I'm going to check out the private adoption websites."

They turn down two invitations and they even bow out of the New Year's Eve party on the next street. Noah's still in Calgary and Sylvie is working on her take-home exams and her botany paper. Her friends come calling – the big-haired little troll and others he doesn't know. They crowd into the hall with suppressed excitement on their faces, never mentioning the baby, as though Sylvie is pulling a fast one on her parents. Sylvie comes up from the basement wearing a big sweater that hides what her friends likely call her bump. She looks as though she's run out of nerve.

On a day when hoarfrost blossoms over the city, Aiden walks up to the little house north of Portage where he was raised. He chips the ice off Rupert's sidewalk and then he starts up Rupert's old Chevy and takes him grocery shopping. It's been five years since Rupert lost his licence but he's stubbornly hung on to the Chevy Caprice Brougham he bought new in 1986 and considered the fulfillment of all his earthly ambitions. His wife died in that car, and he just kept on driving it.

After the groceries are hauled in and unpacked, Aiden collects the garbage and takes it out, in the process locating the source of the stench in the kitchen, a hamburger patty rotting on a saucer in the cereal cupboard. He cleans the bathroom, scrubbing at the dried piss spackling the floor. How long can this go on? Nobody else is going to step up. Carl is three thousand miles away and apparently doesn't own a phone, and Ken – who knows? A few years back he did time for boosting merchandise off the loading dock at Home Depot, and then he dropped out of sight altogether.

All afternoon Rupert sits in his recliner watching game shows. Once in a while Aiden throws a jocular comment in his direction, but he never gets anything back. It's characterized by aphasia, Rupert's dementia, but it's of a piece with how he's always been. He's shrinking, he's stooped, his stomach is rising towards his armpits, forcing all his fundamental qualities to the surface: his disgust for everything outside his narrow ken, his contempt for words. "Feet" is the one cogent thing he's said to Aiden all day, as in *Wipe them*. ("Aw, suck it up," Aiden said under his breath.)

He tramps down to the basement and then he's pulled back to a savage fight he had there with Ken, in which he resorted to scoring Ken's ribs with a pick comb. A girl's defence – no wonder they despised him. A lifetime ago, but it still hangs in the air in this house, the ugly fear that wracked him for years: that, unlike his brothers, he would fail at being a thug. "Where are ya now, ya losers?" Aiden calls, flicking on the basement light.

Three cheap vacuum cleaners are snarled under the basement stairs. None of them work. Aiden messes with them for a while and then he gives up, goes back upstairs to the kitchen and runs a rag mop over the linoleum floor. He picks up two bread crusts and a Bran Buds box from under the table. He shoves a footbath up onto the hat shelf in the closet to get it out of the way.

"Couldn't walk out of Canadian Tire empty-handed, could you, Dad," he says. In fact, that's the entire reason Rupert owned wilderness property – it was an excuse to buy stuff. To talk about stuff with other men, to source it cheap, to transport it and install it and tinker with it. Diesel engines and generators, fish locators, buoys. Log splitters, chainsaws, power winches, gas tanks. After Aiden took possession of the cottage, he had the guy from the marina bring over the construction barge and they loaded it up with all that dreck, as well as an old TV and rabbit ears (which had never remotely worked), two lawn mowers, two large animal traps, a hooded hairdryer, plastic fish, a plastic lettuce spinner, and a fucking plastic swimming pool. Aiden paid a fortune to have it all hauled away and dumped on some other patch of the Canadian Shield.

He sticks the mop back into the crack beside the fridge and glances over to the chair, where Rupert is asleep now, his chin on his chest. "And it'll be me who shovels this shithole into landfill," Aiden says. He raises his voice. "As if I don't have enough of my own crap." Rupert doesn't stir.

Midafternoon, he closes the door and steps outside. The frosted branches and telephone wires are still extravagantly beautiful against a blue sky, but they're starting to drop white petals in the sun. He stands on the back step for a minute, breathing out his rancour into the humid air, before he sets out for home.

Evenings, he and Liz drink mulled wine and sometimes Scotch. They watch pirated movies (nothing noteworthy) and they eat a heap of the mashed olive appetizer Liz likes so much, shovelling it onto crackers, sometimes with soft cheese. She's in a better mood because she got a refund from Vacances françaises. It took fifteen minutes of charming persistence in her dreadful French, but she hung in. They can't do much to plan for the baby until some decisions are made. But they can talk; they can surf the same conversation over and over, sometimes taking a short ride on an exhilarating wave when they think about what it would mean to have an infant in the house again. Details from the past come to him – baby Sylvie's callus-free little heels, and the way she would nuzzle blindly for the nipple.

Then Noah's back in town. He comes to collect Sylvie for New Year's Eve. He stands in the hall in a parka while Sylvie rummages for her boots.

"You two will have so much to talk about," Liz says hintingly, though it looks to Aiden as if Noah is already three sheets to the wind. There's a Ford minivan full of kids at the curb, driven by a forty-year-old designated driver wearing a plaid cap with ear flaps. A hockey stick pokes out of a window like a periscope.

"Not a drop, eh, Sylvie," Aiden says as she goes out the door. She rotates a shoulder in his direction, irritated.

When they're gone, Aiden puts on Lyle Lovett and opens a bottle of Bergerac Rouge (to say, France is not going anywhere). He gets his little film canister out of the freezer and rolls a couple of joints. Thirty-five-millimetre film canisters are getting harder to find than the weed.

"So, you met your dealer?" Liz says.

"Looks that way."

They lie feet to feet on the couch, a fine fire crackling. Within three minutes Liz is back to the Grandparents' Summit, rooting around for little pockets of scorn she hasn't unpacked yet. "You know what really got to me?" she says, louder than necessary. "In her mind, in Mary Magdalene's mind, the main meaning of this pregnancy is its impact on her brilliant son and his fabulous career. Isn't that the impression you got? As though the three of us got together and planned this and failed to consult. Like, once I gave her the phrase 'planned parenthood' she couldn't get it out of her mind."

"No," Aiden says. "I didn't pick that up at all. I thought she was great. You notice she didn't question paternity, even though Noah's been away most of the fall? And she was the one who said, 'If they decide to keep the baby, we'll have to get together to talk about maintenance.' That was decent, especially since she is so set on adoption."

Liz shrugs.

"And I think Noah's okay. I'm assuming George was a really shitty dad, but Noah doesn't seem to have lacked for parenting. Well, I guess he's had that other guy, that Nowak character, as his stepdad for quite a while."

Liz stretches out her hand for the joint. "What's Stonechild doing now? I didn't hear that part."

"He makes those long-necked birds out of stones and iron that people stick in their gardens."

"You're kidding me."

"No. He makes a living selling high-end pink flamingos at craft shows."

"You know, he looks exactly like he did fifteen years ago."

"You knew him?"

"He was the good Samaritan who drove me home from the Folk Festival that time. Remember? When I lost the car in the parking lot and I was wandering around at midnight carrying our big lug of a daughter, being bitten to death by mosquitoes?"

He remembers. He remembers driving her out the next day, to the sight of their Datsun sitting alone in the middle of a huge, empty field. "Did he hit on you?" he asks.

"Of course." She looks directly, brownly at him. Her eyes are not that melting tropical brown. They're Celtic eyes, with a lot of amber in them.

"You never told me."

"Yeah, well. Maybe if Aiden went places with his wife she'd be protected from schmucks like George Stonechild." She's holding the smoke, talking out of the corner of her mouth. He loves it; it's worth the effort it takes to get her to this state.

"I'd never met him before," he says, "but I've seen him around town. Didn't he used to hang around the Bella Vista? Wearing a cape – remember that guy we called Zorro? Anyway, you're right, he hasn't changed. Maybe the music keeps him young. Music is his *bag*."

"He said that?"

"Yup. 'I'm a stone-and-iron artisan, but music is my bag.'" They gaze at each other in wonder. "Is he good-looking?" Aiden asks.

"Of course. He looks like Jesus. It's the most annoying thing about him, the way he's always sticking his face at you, pleading, *Admire me*."

"Noah's not like that."

"Full of himself? No, he doesn't seem to be."

"Although he's . . . hot?"

"Hot? Hot-ish. Sylvie must think so. He could use a proper haircut." Fireworks start banging in the distance like popcorn in a tin pan. "What's your impression?" she asks suddenly. "Is he a nice guy or just well-trained? Like, super-polite."

"I think he's a nice guy."

"Smart, or just a nerd?"

"Probably both."

She's pensive again. "You know," she says, "Noah would have been just one of the stories of Sylvie's life, a fun summer she'd think about from time to time when she was stuck in a rut. But now he will be *the* story, at least for a long time." She leans forward to toss the roach into the fire. "And now, as we speak, our genes are all duking it out in the cells of that poor little fetus. Yours and mine and Mary Magdalene's and George Stonechild's. Oh my god!"

"What grade was it you dropped biology?" He reaches for the ankle nestled against his ribs, squeezes it. How long they've been together! One night, just after they met, he happened to see her on the street, on Broadway, waiting for a bus. It was late, dark, and she was standing under a streetlight, holding a magazine up to her nose, reading. She wants everything and she wants it now. If he were a foreign correspondent needing a man on the ground, he'd hire her every time. His fixer – that's what she is, the one who knows the right words for things, who slips dash to the authorities, who forces you to drink a foul-tasting tincture to kill the local amoebae. The one who hustles you out a back door into the alley when things get hot.

To Liz, he thinks, enjoying the high arch of her bare foot with the back of his fingers. She sits back and flashes him a rueful smile and slides her hand along his thigh. A new year. Begin as you mean to go on.

6

Transition Species

NOAH HAD TO GO BACK TO GUELPH BEFORE
the ultrasound. Well, he could have stayed, but his mom
had paid for his airline ticket and he didn't yet have
Sylvie's insight into what a total waste of time the first week of
semester is. So in the end it's her parents who walk with her down
the long hall of the hospital and sit with her for an hour while she
pretends to be absorbed in a *People* magazine so they'll leave her
alone. And Noah misses it all, he misses a big lesson in the secret
inside strangeness of things.

Afterwards Sylvie's parents wait by Liz's car in the parking lot
while Sylvie stands in the litter of butts at the hospital entrance
and calls him. He picks up on the second ring. "It's a girl," she says.
Though really, this is the unnerving thing: it's a baby. An actual
baby, lying grey and remote and unconscious of being spied on.

"That's great," Noah says. His voice sounds weird and phony,
and so does hers.

In the car, she sits in the back seat and watches the narrow
houses of Maryland Street slide by. Her parents were quiet in the
ultrasound room, but now they talk on and on about how amazing

the picture quality was. When Liz was pregnant with her, they say, ultrasound technology was much cruder. Every once in a while you got a flash of a limb or an organ, but the image was so gibbled you started having nightmares that your baby was misshapen or maybe in pieces. Whereas this baby is evidently intact, as the technician confirmed by her bored manner.

She tapes the image over her bed at the dorm. It's hard to put it up where everyone can see it, but she knows it's part of getting used to the idea. It looks like a big-headed doll seen through wind-shield wipers on a dark night in a heavy rain.

Late in the afternoon, Sylvie's friends from the Fringe troupe come to her room bearing various drinks based on soy milk, cow's milk, yogurt, and ice cream.

"First pick for Sylvie," Thea says.

"I'll take the banana smoothie," Sylvie says. "I'm starving."

"One banana smoothie," Thea says, handing it over, "for the miracle mama." Somebody (maybe Sylvie herself) told them about the point three percent failure rate of the pill, and they are turning her pregnancy into some sort of victory of nature over pharmacology.

They spy the ultrasound picture. While they're all still raving about it, Benedictor comes to the door to wish Sylvie a happy new year. He's never been to her room before. "I wanted to see if you got your botany paper finished," he says. He makes a sad face, as though the loss of her brilliant paper was his fault. Her friends draw him over to see the ultrasound.

"Meet the seven billionth human baby," Thea announces.

"That's over," says Jenna. "Isn't that over?"

Benedictor stares at the image and then looks at Sylvie in confusion and surprise. She has so enjoyed his fascination with her, she is so used to sipping it like a hummingbird and then darting away, that she feels embarrassed as she smiles to say, Yes, it's true. He comes over and squeezes her hand and says courteously, "I congratulate you."

Kajri passes around a Tupperware container of veggie samosas her auntie from Windsor Park just delivered. Once they're all settled into eating, Sylvie grabs the moment of distraction from her ultrasound to ask, "Where are we at with the play? You guys met without me, didn't you? Last week?"

"You knew we were meeting."

"I know. I'm not mad, I'm just asking."

Well, they did meet. They've dropped the Maldives. They spent the whole meeting talking about the news from the U.N. climate summit. Then they were so depressed they walked up the skating trail as far as the Norwood Bridge, where they found two old packing crates buried in the snow on the bank, dragged them out onto the ice, and built a symbolic fire to say goodbye to the human race.

"Oh, come *on*," Sylvie says.

They drink their smoothies and munch on their samosas. She gets the impression no one wants to meet her eyes.

"We have no ideas," Kajri says finally. "It's too big. And too scary. No one wants to hear about it."

"Well, let's do something smaller then," Sylvie says. "Like, who was that environmentalist who walked into the oil and gas auction in the States and bought up a whole bunch of wilderness leases and ended up in jail? Maybe we could tell his story."

"Tim DeChristopher," Nathan says. "He's out now. He's turned religious."

"Or," Sylvie says, "maybe there's some sort of allegory we could do. Like, I don't know, that play we read in grade ten, Arthur Miller and the Salem witches."

"Or let's do something futuristic," says Thea. "When we really get into a global burn and can't grow food anymore, and everyone is starving. Scare the shit out of people."

Benedictor is leaning against the closet door. "Ask people in the Horn of Africa if that is the future," he says.

They sit and stand in silence, well rebuked.

"Benedictor, you have to join us," Sylvie says. "You totally have to!"

She's leaning against her desk beside Nathan. His sleeve is rolled up; he's got a fresh tattoo along the inside of his left forearm. She picks up his arm, feeling an upswell of tenderness. He's one of her oldest friends. So full of need, so gentle and delicate, as though it's hard for him to be exposed to the elements. He makes her think of a trembling whippet. She bends her head closer to the wound. The tattoo is text, a plain font, but it's tiny and hard to make out because his skin is still swollen. Four words: NO WATER, NO MOON. What does it mean? she asks with her eyes, and she feels his gratefulness flicker up like a little flame. He takes back his arm and taps on his smartphone.

> In this way and that I tried to save the old pail
> Since the bamboo strip was weakening and about to break
> Until at last the bottom fell out.
> No more water in the pail!
> No more moon in the water!

She passes back his phone and they look at each other in understanding.

Sylvie finishes her samosa and presses some crumbs off the desk with her fingertips. She turns back to her friends, looking from one anxious face to another. "You know what I think about?"

she says finally. "The hot summer nights when this show will be running. It'll be about thirty degrees out."

"All the venues have AC now," says Emily. When she's nervous, she has a deeply annoying way of talking, with her eyelids flickering.

"That's right, they do. And our audience lives out in Fort Richmond or Charleswood. And they'll start their SUVs – which also have AC, of course – and drive across the city, and then they'll walk into our cool, comfortable theatre. And we'll hand them a program printed on paper made from a clear-cut logging operation, which they'll drop on the floor a minute later. It'll be dark outside, but our stage will be blazing with light."

Another long silence. Nobody looks at Sylvie. She picks up her smoothie from the desk and takes a last drink, sucking air with a rude slurp.

"Emily knows a guy who will rent us a sound system powered by a stationary bicycle," Kajri says. "Don't you, Emily."

Emily herself doesn't say anything. She turns a look that could kill on Sylvie. I am so, so, so, so done with this, thinks Sylvie.

"She needs to move home *now*," Liz says when Aiden comes into the kitchen that night. Rolling chicken fillets in a Dijon paste and then in finely chopped pecans, Liz goes through the obvious advantages of this plan. Aiden is leaning against the counter watching her, doing the reverent-listening thing that most women would appreciate but Liz has come to resent, actually, because it's all about holding his cards close to his chest.

"And you know," Liz goes on, "if they are at all considering adoption, she needs to be exploring her options. These things aren't arranged overnight." She goes to the sink to rinse her sticky fingers. From the living room she hears the *boom-boom-boom* of the nightly news theme. "I wish you'd talk to her about it, Aiden. It doesn't do any good for me to go after her."

"Okay," he says. "Will do."

The oven pings that it's up to temperature. "It's that damn ultrasound," she says. "They're the kiss of death to adoption programs. Once a girl sees the baby's face, she's smitten. This is something we talk about all the time at work." She reaches for a towel and dries her hands. "And if Sylvie thinks she's going to keep the baby . . . Well, there are a thousand things we should be doing."

"If I could give you a piece of advice," Aiden says finally. She turns in his direction, letting her face show how stony she suddenly feels. "Speak your heart with Sylvie. Instead of always telling her what you think she needs to hear."

"Speak your heart?" Liz says. "*Speak your heart?*" She picks up the tray of chicken and slides it into the oven. "Well, seeing we're turning this into a character issue, seeing that this problem is suddenly about *me*, Aiden, let me just make a small observation of my own: I doubt that Sylvie appreciates her father diving in to touch her belly for luck the instant she sets foot in the door."

Liz's quilting group meets that night and Aiden's in bed when she comes in afterwards. She can tell from the way he's lying that he's not asleep. She strips off her clothes, drops them on the wicker chair, and crawls in. She's washed her face and moisturized but she gave herself a holiday from flossing. The dog followed her upstairs. She lies for a minute listening to him settle down, his tags clicking. Aiden doesn't move. You can share a bed when you're fighting; you just have to maintain a scrupulous decorum. But why fight this one with Aiden? She rolls over and curls herself against his back. He has a T-shirt on to keep his shoulders warm, but his butt is bare and his cheeks feel cold.

"I get it," she says. "You're trying to make this seem normal."

He reaches for her hand, pulls her arm tighter around him, weaves his fingers through hers. It's a gesture she loves, like tying twine around the cocoon of their curled-up bodies. "Yup," he says. "Like it was happening ten years from now."

"I know, I know."

The baseboard heater comes on with its electric hum. He turns a few degrees, resettles himself, and pulls her back into their lock. "It seems like just last year we were lying here and you were pregnant with Sylvie."

"Not here. It was downstairs. We still had the waterbed." So lovely, the waterbed, so *amniotic*. Night after night she floated on it, astonished by the thought of the baby floating inside her. She was the first person it had ever happened to. That's what they say about women who make a drama out of being pregnant, but that's how it felt. They'd set out to make a baby but they'd never really thought they were signing on for the whole marriage-and-family thing. It was as if they'd embarked on something unique to them. Why did they think they were so different? She presses on the question, and all she can see is them – the way they were in those years, blithe and brash and scoffing, as though they alone, out of the whole world, could hang on to that beautiful freedom forever.

"I'm not ready for this," she says to Aiden. "I never really got the hang of the mom thing."

"Come on, that's not true. You were great. Look how you stayed home all that time with Sylvie."

"I was working, Aiden." The years she spent freelancing out of the house, writing grant applications and strat plans for non-profits – she'll never forget what it was like, scrambling to get packages together for inflexible federal deadlines, files spilling from every surface in the house, the phone ringing every two minutes, and a restless, curious, wilful child pawing at her knees. Sylvie would be up before dawn every morning without fail, sitting on the kitchen floor making an amulet out of alligator clips and twist ties and Cheerios and Scotch tape, singing, "The wise man rode a coconut, the sad man rode a horse" or some other bit of nonsense. Liz would take a sip of her coffee and lift her eyes to the microwave and see that it wasn't even seven yet, and know that everything the day would offer her was already there in those untidy rooms.

Which must be why she fell in with the GAP mothers, that strange collection of throwbacks who sat by the hour in each other's houses, drinking tea made from mint and chamomile they grew in their own borders, and trading lore – all the things counter-culture women just knew, the insider tips about fenugreek and blessed thistle (*You haven't ingested enough if you can't smell it on your skin*). If Liz thought her paid employment would give her any cachet with that crew, or her witticisms regarding the things they were so earnest about, she was badly mistaken.

One very hot day she invited them to sit outside, where there was a breeze and her pale pink monkshood was in bloom along the fence. She opened the back door to the beautiful deck she and Aiden had just put in, and in a flash someone named Ariel had scooped up her toddler. "Is that, uh, pressure-treated pine?" Ariel asked delicately. "I'd rather not sit out there with the kids, if you don't mind. It's known to contain arsenic."

So they met in the living room with the blinds down, the kids fretful and bored because their mothers (tactfully, while Liz was in the kitchen making the tea) had gone through the toy box and set out of reach everything interesting – the painted toys (for fear of lead) and the plastic toys (PVCs). There was Victoria, swollen and miserable and a week overdue, panting like a dog in the heat.

"My doctor wants me to come in tomorrow," she said. "He wants to induce."

A male doctor trying to fit her baby's birth around his golf schedule! So Mary Magdalene, sitting like a queen in the Mission chair with someone else's toddler contented on her lap, told the moving story of Sparky's birth, how at thirty-seven weeks Sparky was breech, a complication for which every doctor in the city will sentence you to a Caesarean. But on the advice of her midwife, Mary Magdalene pressed ice to her solar plexus, where Sparky's head was, and at the same time shone a thin but powerful flashlight up her vagina. Within a day Sparky had swum around to follow the light. Three weeks later he emerged in a victorious home birth.

Liz presses her forehead against Aiden's shoulder. "Ask Maggie what kind of a mother I was," she says. "I almost killed her kid once."

"What are you talking about?"

So she finally tells him. About the time she looked after Sparky because he had a cold and Mary Magdalene had to go to the welfare office. "I pushed her to leave him with me. I was in a panic about a deadline and I figured he'd keep Sylvie occupied. But he was sick and he just wanted Sylvie to piss off and let him play with Lego. So she was at me, at me to take them outside. You know how she is – resisting her always costs more time and energy than giving in. So we ended up going to Vimy Ridge Park. They had those old swings with thick, heavy slabs of wood dangling from industrial chains. I pushed the kids for a while, and then I'm sitting on a bench, working through a set of notes with a highlighter, because I'm truly in a jam with that job, and they're swinging high, pumping themselves. They're facing in opposite directions so they can see each other, and then I look up and I see Sparky jump off his swing, and Sylvie's swing comes up and clunks him right in the face. Oh, it was awful! It just happened in a second. By the time I got him home he looked like a space alien – you could hardly see his eyes. When Maggie gets there, I'm icing his face like crazy. Of course she makes a *huge* deal of it." Liz can still see her walking quickly up the polished hall of Urgent Care with Sparky riding on her hip, without a thank-you or a backward glance.

"Was his nose broken?"

"Well, yes. And he had a mild concussion, as well as two spectacular shiners. So of course it caused a sensation on the street. Mary Magdalene moved away right after. I think she was trying to get away from me."

Aiden lets her hand go and reaches up to rearrange his pillow. "Is this why you were so freaked when you saw Maggie again? I doubt she even remembers."

Liz rolls onto her back. He follows her, lays an arm across her breasts. She can smell his breath – toothpaste and garlic and something from a different register. Old age, possibly.

"Aiden," she says. "Darling. You should be put on display in a glass case."

"What do you mean?"

"For being such a naïf. A man could say, Very sorry, accidents happen. But a woman – oh my god!"

After he's asleep, Liz lies gazing at the square of night sky framed by the skylight. It's never blue or black. It's the colour of bruises, Aiden always says. Or bile. It's chartreuse, Liz insists. *Puce.* Although she doesn't really know what colour puce is. She rolls to her side of the bed and then Mary Magdalene is standing on the street with her hand on Sparky's shoulder, her hair long and full, like Cher's. Sparky's swelling has gone down but his face is still lurid. It's Halloween. Exhausted by a round of contrite apologies, Liz attempts a joke. "Hey, Sparky, you could be a Ninja Turtle." Mary Magdalene looks hard at Liz and says something absolutely savage. Liz hears the words in her mind and they make her gasp, they flip her right out of bed. She sits on the edge, cradling her pillow. She hasn't thought about that moment in years. Not because she forgot, no. Because she buried it deep, the way you bury radioactive waste.

She stands up and pulls her robe off its hook and goes downstairs. The dog follows. In the living room she turns on the shell lamp. Let's face it, she was floundering in those days, going slowly around the twist. They were on the cusp of making it, she and Aiden, but things were taking a long time to come together. He was always amused that she put up with that group. "But I get it," he said. "People with a seamless view of the world are intimidating, even when they're full of shit."

Why *didn't* she laugh in their faces? Because the GAP women had something she didn't have. She remembers Mary Magdalene crouched on the kitchen floor beside Sparky, her warm face totally absorbed by what her son was saying. It was never hard for them. They were never frantic and bored. They were like women in love.

She pulls a quilt out of the press in the corner and curls up on the sofa. Aiden had a fire while she was out. Embers glow on the hearth, under the ash, like veins deep in the Earth. Just a few tiny nuggets of orange fire and soon (she knows from experience) the whole room will be rosy with their light. She fusses with the cushion under her cheek and then drops a hand down to dangle it in Max's ruff. He's happy to have a friend in the night, she can sense his doggy satisfaction. She nestles deeper into the couch and covers her face with her arm. Sleep, she orders, but nothing resembling sleep responds. After a few minutes she lowers her arm and looks into the room. In the dim light she makes out the curve of the Frank Lloyd Wright vase on the mantel and the art deco figurine standing up gracefully beside it.

Where do I go wrong? she asks the house.

It takes the house a minute to respond. In your haste, it says at last. You, Liz (the meticulous, painstaking craftsperson who made this quilt), you grab for things. Sometimes what you want is not what is best.

The edge of the quilt is tickling her face; she folds it over and readjusts the cushion. She stretches out her legs, measuring the luxurious length of the leather sofa with her body. Sirens race up Portage Avenue, screaming thinly in the distance, and then the furnace murmurs to life.

What do I do right? she asks the house.

You're hasty, the house replies. Nobody can make a cake without breaking eggs.

Sylvie gives herself a day off from classes and spends most of it in bed. She's not sick but she has some strange physical symptoms, including a metallic taste in her mouth. When the building falls quiet, she falls back to sleep. Around noon she wakes up and fishes Kajri's human physiology text out of the bed. It's got a long chapter on the development of the *Homo sapiens* fetus, full of fibre-optic photos of babies in the womb. Through the fall, unaware, Sylvie harboured a tadpole, a fish, and a lizard. But now her baby is a mammal. It has lost its tail. It's covered with hair. It has an alien's face, with raspberry-coloured veins twining over its bulging forehead. It's already equipped for its evolutionary task of over-populating the planet – those little olive-shaped ovaries have fifty thousand eggs in them.

Sylvie can take this only in small doses. She drops the book to the floor, gets up, and eats two things of raspberry yogurt and a morning glory muffin from the windowsill. Her phone beeps. HAPPY

MOUTH NOON TOMORROW? Her dad is trying to lure her to his office with sushi. He's done this before. She texts him back: MAYBE. He's so sweet, although his wife is a witch and he's completely under her thrall. There's a word for him that few people know: *uxorious*. Sylvie learned it in first-year English when they read *Paradise Lost*. Adam the First Man was uxorious, and look what came of that.

She pulls her laptop over to the bed. She doesn't check Facebook but she reads her Twitter feed and the usual blogs. They're all about the climate summit, at which greedy nations showed their true values and less than nothing was accomplished. She drops the lid of her laptop, feeling sorry for all the activists who anguished for years about whether to get on a plane and fly halfway around the world to attend.

Then she gets up and tries on a bunch of clothes. Because suddenly, now that she knows what's going on, none of them fit. Around the middle of the afternoon she calls in sick at Stella's. It's the evening manager who picks up and he's pissy about it. "Believe me, you don't want me there," she says, trying to sound contagious or at the point of vomiting.

She straightens up her bed and crawls back in. At Thanksgiving they lay curled in this bed for a whole afternoon, she and Noah, when Kajri had gone home and all the jocks from the dorm were out at some sporting event. Sylvie drew Noah an awesome sleeve tattoo with Sharpies and wouldn't let him shower before he went home for turkey dinner. She expected to have a whole new stash of memories to draw from after Christmas, but the Christmas holiday was totally stolen from them. She saw him twice, not counting the airport run. Just twice – it's unbelievable. And on New Year's Eve, after she'd said no to three house parties so they could be alone, he invited Zach along, and they were both totally wasted by the time they picked Sylvie up. The whole night was a bust.

She hugs her pillow, trying to call him up. It's the parts of his body that have nothing to do with sex that move her most – his neat ears, his bony ankles, and the slight widening of his nose where it was broken when he was little (something she never comments on, because she doesn't want to remind him that it was her fault). Last summer, when they met after twelve or thirteen years of not seeing each other, he was naked. It was night out on Lake Winnipeg, and he was caught in a spotlight, balancing on the gunnels of a canoe with his arms out. He dove into the water the instant the light hit him, but not before a vivid picture had etched itself permanently in Sylvie's mind.

They were out at a diving rock at Zach's cabin, which was close to the research station at Presley Point. They – five girls counting Sylvie and Thea – had driven out late and found an empty A-frame cabin all lit up. They could hear the guys out at the rock. Jenn wanted to swim out. "Don't be stupid," Thea said. "You'll drown and take us down with you." In the boathouse they found an old rowboat with oars in its locks. They waded in and drew it out and stepped into it off the dock. Creaking their way across the lake, they were laughing softly because they knew the guys would be skinny-dipping. Sylvie had a very special feeling that night, because she had just broken up with her Neanderthal boyfriend Seth. She was herself again, but more than herself: her new, experienced, single self.

Thea was carrying a great big flashlight. When they got close, she shone it at the rock and spotlighted this new guy. Up on the gunnels of his canoe, he looked like Leonardo da Vinci's man in a wheel. Not perfect in some muscle-bound way, just neat (neater and younger than the Da Vinci man), well-proportioned, his penis drooping from the hair on his abdomen in the normal, beautiful way. Like a representation of *Homo sapiens* (masc.) at this stage of evolutionary history. The light hit him, and everybody shouted and laughed and he dove neatly into the water. In a flash, Sylvie pulled off her T-shirt and shorts and bra and panties and rolled out of the rowboat. She was clumsy rolling out – she almost tipped the boat – and she heard Thea and Jenn scream as she fell sideways into the cool water. When she surfaced, she lay on her back and looked up at the Big Dipper pouring stars into the lake, aware of the new guy treading water close by in the darkness.

Eventually everybody stripped and jumped in, and they fooled around in the water for a long time. The guy with the canoe was the only actual stranger, but they were all shy with each other. They'd been friends since junior high but most of them had never seen each other naked. Zach's golden lab was there, and they threw an orange ball and he swam after it like a fool. They started to play keep-away. Sylvie caught the ball deftly in one hand – and it wasn't a ball at all, it was a little stuffed animal, wet and yucky, a cheap Kmart toy a kid had left in the bottom of the boat.

She threw it at the new guy (Canoe, they called him), high, so he had to jump out of the water up to his waist to catch it. He caught it easily and threw it back at her and she tried to puzzle out the mystery of where she had seen and loved him before. He looked like an actor she knew (that's what she figured at first), so crazy familiar, the straight, dark line of his eyebrows, the way he tossed his hair back as he levitated in the water to throw the orange toy, as if this were a moment on a DVD she had watched over and over.

He'd beached his canoe on the rock. Later, when she had her shorts and T-shirt on and her damp panties and bra scrunched into a pocket, she went up to him and said, "I'll be your bowsman."

"I've only got one paddle," he said, but she stepped in anyway as he slid the canoe into the water. Two of her friends tried to clamber in and he pried their hands off the gunnels. He wasn't laughing; he was deadly serious. Sylvie knelt in the bow and they slid silently towards the empty cabin with its blazing lights. He paddled on the left the whole way – he had a perfect J-stroke – and she sat like a queen on a barge, the water slipping coolly past her dangling fingers. There was no moon, only the darkness spangled above them and the water brooding below. She can't pinpoint the moment she realized. It was just a knowing that grew in her, like the trees materializing from the dark as the canoe glided closer to shore.

Dawn was streaking the sky when they carried the canoe to the boathouse. They took it in the back door, walking up the rickety steps and onto a narrow ledge of rotting timbers, shuffling along carefully in the perfect darkness. Halfway in he stopped and fed the canoe forward, crouching to lay it gently on the black water. She couldn't see him, she could only sense his movements. Then he stood up and she felt his hand around her wrist.

"Sylvie," he said, "listen," and his voice echoed. They stood still and she heard the dry whir of bats. Then she sensed him take a step closer, felt his hand on her waist, felt the recognition and welcome in the kiss that landed first beside her mouth and then slid over.

"Hey, Sparky!" she said when she got her mouth back.

At supper Kajri tries to get Sylvie to go down to the caf. "You're turning into an agoraphobe," she says. But in the end she carries dinner up to their room. It's the green and purple casserole Sylvie hates, but it's the only vegetarian option and she manages to eat it. Afterwards they work in silence at their separate desks, their computer screens the only lights in the room.

Somebody's smoking a cigar in the lounge – Sylvie can smell it. The fire door at the end of the hall slams and Adam Moffat walks by laughing his crazy laugh, and in the next room Amy Winehouse starts to sing. Kajri turns her face, lit with pale blue light from her screen, and they share a sad smile. Oh, Kajri. She is as kind and lovely as her name.

When they're ready for bed they watch the news but there's no mention of the climate summit. Mostly it's hockey. "Hockey ice is the only ice the media cares about," Sylvie says. She surfs for a minute, pausing on the nature channel at footage of two big turtles lumbering along a narrow path. One's ahead, the female, moving as if she wants to be alone. The male is chasing her, going ten percent faster than normal turtle speed. When he catches up with her, he just keeps on walking. Sylvie and Kajri watch in fascination as he climbs her back and the two shells start to clack together. The male's mouth is wide open in an idiotic smile and you can see the red triangle of his tongue. Then the female pulls forward and he topples to the side and lies with his feet in the air.

"Reminds me of Seth," Sylvie says, turning the TV off.

"He'd lie with his feet in the air?"

"No, but the minute it was over, he'd reach down to the floor for his shorts and then he'd get out of bed – well, not bed, we'd be on the couch in his parents' basement with a blue plastic swordfish over our heads – and he'd go get a beer from the bar fridge and change the track on his iPod. Once he picked up this hair-zapper thing he ordered off TV and started running it over his pecs. I guess what I mean is he always wanted to have sex no matter how we were feeling with each other."

For a year and a half Sylvie has been unable to resist acting like a wise older sister, taking every chance to enlighten Kajri. Kajri's parents, who are both doctors and live in a town a hundred miles away, have asked her not to date until she has entirely finished her education. And she's going along with it – truly complying, not just lying to them. So far virginity is still working for her, as you can see by her flawless, glowing skin and her perfect GPA. "I can date through you," she used to say to Sylvie, although obviously she's stopped saying that now.

She makes a pitying noise and Sylvie wishes she'd kept her mouth shut about Seth. It's embarrassing to have people feeling sorry for her, although if she can take it from anyone, she can take it from Kajri.

"Noah was more sensitive?"

"He was shyer. But I mean, he didn't have any experience."

"Yeah, you said. That's weird, because he's older than you, and so hot. Well, except for his hair."

"What's wrong with his hair?"

"It's not exactly even. It's like shingles."

"That's 'cause he cuts it himself."

"Why? Is he that poor?"

"No, he just wants to be self-sufficient. I think it's very cool. The thing about Noah is he totally lacks the flirtation gene. Girls talk to him and they assume he's married or something. Or gay. I might not have had the nerve, except that we were best friends when we were little. And he was the one who kissed me first, last summer when we met up again."

"It's so romantic. It could never happen to me. I never had boys as friends, for one thing."

"Well, his mother was home-schooling, and when all the kids his age started school, he was alone on the street, so he had to play with me. I loved him then. He was such a neat kid. He taught me all kinds of stuff."

"Like what?"

Sylvie sees them lying on the floor at Mary Magdalene's, drawing an intricate city with tunnels and tepees in it. She sees them in the sun-baked back lane, the anthills they messed with, the dandelions exploding through cracks in the pavement. She was tiny then. All she has is still shots: she and Noah squatting in the thistles by Wendy's garage, or hiding in the dark, spidery shed, peering out through a narrow crack as the kid who was It wandered around the yard calling their names. Memories like little slits into a dazzling world where everything is big and distinct, shining with light. She wants to protect it from scrutiny.

"I don't know," she says to Kajri. "Just stuff." She lies back and pulls the duvet over her. "You know what's making me feel really shitty now? Can I tell you, Kajri?"

"Sure, of course."

"It's my own fault I got pregnant. I told all the parents that I fell into the perfect use category, but it's not true. I never missed a pill, but I didn't wait long enough when I started. I was going up to Presley Point for the weekend, so I went to Shoppers and filled the prescription and I took the first pill that Friday. Like, just a few hours before we made love. I was stupid. I was so fucking stupid." She'd been willing to be stupid because it was so sweet being able to say to Noah, We're fine, I'm on the pill.

"Did the doctor tell you how long you had to wait for the pill to kick in?"

"I don't think so. There was a sheet in tiny print in the box, but I didn't read it. All he said was that it might make me feel a bit sick at first. 'Your body will think it is pregnant' — that's what he said."

Kajri's face is tilted sympathetically. You don't even have to ask Kajri to keep things confidential — that's the sort of friend she is. "Have you told Noah?"

"No, I didn't really have a chance. His mother made him go to Calgary."

"She *made* him? Isn't he, like, twenty-two?"

"Well, his grandmother lives there, and who knows – she's really old and they think it might be her last Christmas. He's a nice guy, what can I say."

Kajri looks unconvinced. "But will you tell him," she persists, "when you get a chance?"

"I don't know."

"Are you afraid he'll be mad?"

"It's more that . . . Well, Noah is more or less perfect as he is."

"What do you mean?"

"He's so . . . I don't know . . . he has, like, perfect focus and concentration. He lives by his values. He doesn't screw up. He's happy in himself. He's going to do good work in the world. I don't want this to change things for him. It was my fault, and I don't want his life to be trashed because of it." She hasn't answered the question, but she can tell from the look on Kajri's face that she's already thinking of something else.

"You know, you sound like Mileva Marić."

"Who's she?"

"Einstein's girlfriend. Well, his wife, eventually. She had a baby when they were both students, and they were so afraid it would interrupt his brilliant career that they gave it away. Or maybe it died. No one knows for sure." She leans over, picks up an emery board from her bedside table, and starts to work on a perfect nail. "So," she says, "is that what you're going to do? Put the baby up for adoption?"

For the first time ever, Sylvie senses something less than respectful in Kajri, and it hurts her. "If I put the baby up for adoption, it will be because it's best for me," she says. "And *my* brilliant career. And for the baby, of course."

Kajri gives a little smile and goes to the bathroom to brush her teeth. When she comes back out, she flicks off the light. Sylvie watches her move through the dark in her white T-shirt and shorts. "Adoption would be pretty scary," she says as she crawls into bed. "Like, you'd never know what sort of people your kid would end up with. Whether she would be abused or something."

"It's not that," Sylvie says. "I'm pretty sure she would be loved. People who want a baby that badly would probably love it. It's just . . . It's a girl. So *how* will they love her? I mean, there's ordinary consumerism, but with girls there's the whole princess thing."

"I know what you mean. The pink canopy bed, the plastic tiara."

"Right! They'll take her to Disneyland. And they'll put her in beauty pageants. She might end up a cheerleader."

Kajri doesn't respond.

"Did you ever play *The Sims*?" Sylvie asks after a minute of lying in the dark.

"My parents wouldn't let me play computer games."

"Well, I played it a lot in high school. I had an amazing house and two kids. We all played it, all my friends. But we were all kind of getting into the environment and then suddenly we started thinking about *The Sims* – what it really was, the way it taught you to be a consumer. So then we all quit playing."

Kajri doesn't reply. The dorm quiets and Sylvie rolls to her side and watches the tangle of clothes she left on the floor gradually emerge from the darkness, lit up by the line of yellow light seeping in under the door. We thought we could decide who we were going to be, she thinks. We thought we could resist all that. And now, the thing is, she's not a parent. Since she found out she's pregnant she's been feeling younger than she did before, as if the child she used to be is overtaking her. Thoughts she can't quite lay hold of flicker on the edge of her mind, images just outside her memory, like outtakes of the real story. The faun crouching in the dim light of the forest, her golden eyes glowing. He's not my brother, the faun says.

My mother found him in a Dumpster. He's a filthy little beast. She lifts a thin arm and wipes her nose. He only has one ball, you know, she says. Sylvie leans closer to listen, sinking into a carpet of leaves.

What a relief to be back in the office. No silky toss cushions here. No Mexican cut-tin figures, no chili-pepper Christmas lights, no Afghan prayer rugs made by the slender fingers of unschooled, war-traumatized children, no ornamental vases or dried flowers or alligator suitcases stacked up in urbane imitation of a side table. There is a freedom in having only what you need.

By the time Aiden set up this practice, he had a pretty good idea of how he wanted to conduct his life. The address by the park so he has a green space to run in, the two-hour break in the middle of the day. His shower and his little fridge. Purcell and Haydn and Erik Satie hanging a spotless curtain between him and the dens of commerce all around. His brave and questing clients. And his casual clinical style, with its streak of mordant humour (*mordant* from the French word for "biting," because people in a state of unawareness need a sharp nip now and then).

Tuesday, nine o'clock. It's Norman Orlikow's hour, but no sign of the Badger. Aiden moves over to the couch, swings his legs up, and reads an article on self-harm and suicide among teenagers in Tonga after the introduction of television. Then he digs his nail clippers out of a tin in the bathroom cupboard and trims his fingernails, catching the clippings in a Kleenex.

Ten o'clock, Odette's hour. He waits until 10:15, then calls her answering machine again. "Hope you got my message last week. I got yours. I heard you loud and clear. I'd like to encourage you to come in next week so we can work this out. I'll keep your hour open until I hear back." Then he tries Edith Wong again, still hoping for a consult. This time she's got an out-of-office message on. Away until January 22.

Eleven o'clock, Christine Tolefson arrives. She's a true holiday confection, Christine, grotesque and (he would guess) very expensive, although her hair is like the hair on a cheap doll.

"I typically ask patients for a history in the second session," Aiden says when she's settled on the couch, legs crossed in a silver miniskirt just adequate to requirements. "So, just like you'd tell a medical doctor about the illnesses and conditions your parents and grandparents had, I'd like to know about the emotional dynamics in your family."

She's staring at him blankly, so he talks a little more about what this might entail. He can't read a thing in her face. She looks different today, as if her features have been subtly rearranged. "A history," she says finally, as though she's prepared to deny having such a thing. Her parents were "okay" (i.e., they left her alone); she was married at eighteen. No children – her husband never wanted children. She doesn't have a job and never really has. "My husband has money coming out his ass-end," she says. "Well, my ex."

"Why did the marriage end?"

"What do you think? Somebody hotter came along. Younger."

"You met somebody younger?"

She doesn't bother to respond, just stares out of those elaborate eyes. Over Christmas he told Liz how strangely plastic his new client's face seemed (or how *not* plastic, in the true sense of the word) and Liz said she must be using Botox. Maybe he'll publish a paper: "The Clinical Implications of Cosmetic Nerve Paralyzers in Assessing Emotional Affect."

"Tell me about your relationship with your ex."

"He's my bank machine. He's paying for this. He wants you to fix me up so I'll leave him alone."

"And what do you think needs fixing?"

She shrugs. She won't speculate. After a while they get to Christmas, which she spent with a single girlfriend who introduced her to a computer role-playing game. She's happy to talk about her new cyberspace incarnation. "My name is Zara Foxtrot," she says, telling him at length how you pick a name and build your avatar. "You have to know a lot about computers. Like, even to fly properly. Because you don't walk there, you fly. I still haven't made it off Help Island. A lot of guys hang around Help Island cruising the newbies. There's one guy online every time I go on. He acts like he's really into me. Although, how do you know who he really is?"

"You're hoping to meet a real man through this game?"

Duh! the eyes in her frozen face say. She's got a line of dark red drawn a few millimetres outside her natural lips. You keep this up, he wants to warn her, you're going to look like Tammy Faye Bakker in no time.

"You know," he says, "the end of a marriage can be a great chance to be on your own for a while. Get to know yourself better."

She dismisses this with a little moue of her stretched-out-heart-shaped mouth.

"Christine, we all want love. We all need it. But romantic love can't carry all the demands of life. It can't be the only source of your happiness." He's back in the groove. Sort of. That last bit is word-for-word from Virginia Satir.

It's mucky out but he dresses for his run at noon. He's standing at a bench doing his stretches when the Badger appears on the asphalt path. Walks along turning his head from side to side with an impassive expression, as if he's a foreman doing a routine factory inspection. As he approaches the bench he acknowledges Aiden with an unconvincing display of surprise.

Aiden wishes him a happy new year. "I was just about to drop you a line," he says. "The window hasn't been fixed yet because of the holiday, but the super shoved an estimate under my door. It's $245."

"Two hundred and forty-five dollars? That's bullshit."

"There's a privacy glaze on the glass, so it's more than it would be otherwise. I won't bill you for this morning because I didn't really expect you, but I think it would be fair for you to pay for the window as a condition of coming back."

"Who says I want to come back?" Norman says sulkily.

"Just a guess," Aiden says. "Based on your following me to the park. But suit yourself. You know where I am."

His run is slippery and fractious. His iPod is full of melancholy crap. There's a stink in the air – somewhere a heap of rotting factory waste is thawing. By the zoo, Aiden's sweating like a pig. How do you dress for a temperate zone winter? He runs by the riverbank shack. Without snow on its roof, it sticks out like a sore thumb. The cops are going to notice and tear it down. The stink he's been smelling gets worse as he goes along. The minute he gets into the narrow stretch through the trees, he realizes it's him. It's his shoes. It's the fish emulsion fertilizer he spilled in the garage when he was putting the Christmas tree stand away.

He's relieved to get back to the bridge. To see the iceberg on the other side of the river, a spectacular piece of public art sticking out of the ground like a tooth from a gum. Not that crazy iceberg blue – it's some sort of metal, like dental amalgam. One day Defrag pointed out the obvious. "It's a monument. For after the real icebergs are gone."

Defrag came to Aiden with the psychiatric diagnosis of "eco-anxiety." This is not a DSM-recognized diagnosis, at least not yet. It's treated as GAD: generalized anxiety disorder. Defrag's psychiatrist explained it as under-activation of the serotonergic system and over-activation of the noradrenergic system, for which they prescribe SSRIS. The psychiatrist was Peter Saurette, a man Aiden likes and admires. He first encountered Saurette at a professional conference, early in his training. A small man, homely and very attractive. He had a natural gravitas, a considered way of speaking that made Aiden want to listen to every word. Aiden used to fantasize about being his patient, opening up the murky depths to that revealing and judicious gaze. Of course, when they started consulting on a professional basis, Aiden discovered that the fifty-minute appointment was a thing of the past for Saurette; his patients dropped in at the rate of four an hour to get their prescriptions tweaked, and their counselling, if they got any, happened somewhere else.

"I'm struck by how aware and engaged with the world Jake is," Aiden said to Saurette on the phone. "He's one of the most conscious individuals in my acquaintance. And let's be frank – what informed person isn't anxious these days?"

"Suicidal ideation is not the hallmark of a healthy individual."

"No, of course. But still," Aiden couldn't resist adding, "I don't suppose we'd diagnose tornado anxiety in someone watching a funnel cloud move in his direction."

"Well, that's the standard line of the so-called green bloggers," Saurette said.

Aiden deserved that. He had actually lifted the tornado argument from a blog. He tries not to hold his embarrassment in that moment against Peter Saurette. He can only assume that, for his part, the guy feels diminished. At one time he led people along the path to self-knowledge; he watched with knowing eyes while they confronted their terror and loss and the spectres of their parents. He was once a shaman of the underworld. And then, Aiden thinks as he rides the elevator up to his office, Doctor Peter Saurette became an agent for Big Pharma.

Defrag, when he comes in, does not look well. Aiden can read the signs: his cautious movements, as if he's trying to fend off nausea. "Sorry about the last session," he says. "Bill me anyway."

"I intend to," Aiden says. "So, what was up?"

"I was a little under the weather." Defrag sits with his hands dangling between his knees. "Under the weather." He repeats the phrase thoughtfully. He looks thinner than ever. He lives on air.

"Are you eating?" Aiden asks.

"I'm eating."

"What did you eat this morning?"

"I ate a bowl of oats." He looks like Gerard Manley Hopkins, Aiden always thinks: a long, keen face and dark eyes, a hank of dark hair. *Counter, original, spare, strange.*

"Not bad," Aiden says. "Tell me about the day you missed your session. What happened?"

"I went to work," Defrag says. "But I couldn't work. And then I went home."

"Some days it's not even worth chewing through the restraints," Aiden says, and Defrag grins, recognizing the reference. When he first came to therapy, he'd have these bad days periodically, like waking up with the flu, and he could never pinpoint a cause. For weeks he'd live an ordinary, productive, middle-class life, and then suddenly he'd be too sick to move. He'd lie curled up in bed, dizzy, panicked, disoriented, as though his inner ear was out of whack. For no reason at all. They don't bother with that narrative anymore.

"What did you read that morning?" Aiden asks.

"I guess it was reports on the UN climate summit," Defrag says.

"I missed them," Aiden says.

"Yeah, well, they were on page eight." Defrag laughs.

"So what went down?"

Defrag tells him. He outlines the whole thing passionately and efficiently – he's clearly gone over it a thousand times in his mind. Aiden, listening, is ashamed. Unevolved people in power, he thinks. *We're all bozos on this bus.* He deals with it himself by not staying up on the news, but Defrag has never cultivated the protective layers that most people count on.

Defrag's previous counsellor (an MSW Saurette referred Defrag to) gave him a relaxation CD of birdsong. Brain-imaging technology has shown that birdsong promotes a sense of well-being, she explained. It's evolutionary: if the birds are singing, no predators are prowling the forest. Defrag lay on his bed and identified the silvery scraps of song in his headphones. The Acadian flycatcher – endangered. The black-capped vireo – endangered. Kirtland's warbler – only two hundred left. "Maybe you'd do better with whale music," the counsellor said when he brought back the CD. Laughter shook Defrag when he told Aiden. His chest is a cage full of unruly laughs just dying to get out.

"Who do you talk to about the things that worry you?" Aiden asked at the time. "Among your friends. Your colleagues at work."

"Nobody wants to talk about it. Why would they?"

"I have this sort of issue with my wife," Aiden said. "When I mention climate change, she says, 'Please. You think the gods are punishing you personally?'"

He rarely mentions his family in this office, but with Defrag, establishing trust was huge. Aiden found himself encouraging a kind of double thinking that would let Defrag acknowledge and process his fears while still finding ways to live a reasonably contented life. "As if" thinking, you might call it: live as if catastrophe is not just around the corner. Most people are extremely good at this. He also encouraged Defrag to join a group of like-minded individuals, an environmental lobby group, but it was all kids and he couldn't deal with it.

Frankly, Aiden is as close to a like-minded individual as Jake Peloquin is likely to find. "One organism, one vote," Aiden said during a session early on, and Defrag's expression sharpened. A couple of minutes later, Defrag dropped in "Clone me, Doctor Memory." Aiden hadn't run into anyone who knew Firesign Theatre since his buddy Glen died – it was like a Masonic handshake. They've never acknowledged it; they just drop a line now and then. It's the sort of humour you need headphones and a thousand wasted nights to get into.

Defrag wraps up his report on the UN climate summit. They sit without speaking while a string quartet drifts in from the waiting room. "You know," Defrag says, "I used to think the waiting was the hard part, back in the seventies, when we were all first getting the picture. I used to think it was worse when you knew this was coming but nobody else could see it. I figured an abstract horror was worse than a real horror."

"Only in the movies, I guess," Aiden says.

Defrag shifts in his chair as if his bones are hurting. "How was *your* Christmas?" he asks.

"Complicated," Aiden says. The kettle is boiling and he gets up to make coffee. He wants badly to tell Defrag about Sylvie – it would be a relief to talk about it with someone who gets what it means to him – and while he waits for the French press to do its thing, he arms himself against the impulse. He pours the coffee and hands Defrag a mug. "We were planning a trip to France for this spring, but it's off. I wasn't that keen anyway. I think my flying days are over. I just don't know how to break that to my wife."

"Oh, come on," Defrag says. "Jumbo jets are mass transit." He opens the trapdoor and lets a few peals of laughter escape.

Aiden's about to shift back to the bout of anxiety Defrag had before Christmas when Defrag asks, with genuine interest, "So why did you cancel?"

And he tells him. "We found out our daughter is pregnant. She's due in April. She's nineteen. Nothing planned about it – she's in a new relationship, they're both students." Defrag, about to take a sip of his coffee, holds the mug still. "You know, it's interesting," Aiden says. "I was turning into a bit of a misanthrope, but it looks as though I'm invested for another generation. Suddenly I find myself having to believe in the future."

"Didn't your daughter already do that for you?"

Aiden has to think for a minute. "I wasn't so afraid for Sylvie. I guess because I thought she would live in a world I knew. I knew it was liveable, at least for people like us. I don't know that for this baby."

Defrag drops his eyes, but not before Aiden sees the consternation in them. Freud had his reasons for putting his patients on a couch, with the therapist well out of sight behind them.

At SERC they're developing guidelines for implementing a new HPV program. The whole administrative staff is involved, so at the end of the meeting, while they're packing up, Liz sees her chance and asks for a personal moment. The instant their heads swivel curiously towards her, she's unnerved. Oh, how tense she sounds, how brittle. But she gets out the news and then launches into a little discourse about women trapped by oral contraceptives that mask the signs of pregnancy. "The best-laid plans . . ." she says flatly in conclusion.

She can tell they're taken aback – by her manner, no doubt, as much as by the news. All the same, they're lovely. This is all in a day's work for them, after all. They make kind suggestions, they joke about bringing their knitting to staff meetings. "And how are *you*, Liz?" they ask. Then everybody settles back into the routine of the morning, and Liz walks to her office, replaying the scene in her mind, scanning it for telltale exchanges of private glances. They can't all be entirely devoid of *schadenfreude*, can they?

A portrait of Margaret Sanger hangs on the exposed brick wall across from Liz's desk, posed with one finger pressed to her carotid artery as though she's checking her own pulse. When Liz was named director, she redid the office and took down the portrait. Didn't Sanger once speak at a Ku Klux Klan rally? Didn't she talk about "human weeds"? But everybody in the office flipped out. So muttering, "Choose your battles," Liz hung the picture back up. It's true that when she first learned about Sanger, while she was doing her public admin. degree, she was galvanized. "A woman's duty is to look the whole world in the face with a go-to-hell look in her eyes" – that was her motto. Liz thought of those words often during her early days at SERC, when she was so out of her depth. During that long uphill climb to confidence, which involved a very expensive business wardrobe.

She stands for a minute eye to eye with the Sanger, and then she goes to her computer and pulls up the forms for the annual staff performance assessments. By the end of the day she has a schedule posted, not something she usually manages this early in the year. It's a way of having an in-depth conversation with each of her staff, she explains to Aiden over supper. Building relationships. "And of course," he says, finishing the thought, "there is no better way to remind people, *I am your boss*."

But during these private meetings that take up a big chunk of January, Liz can't help but wonder if she's overplayed her hand. It strikes her that some staff members are nicer than usual, which of course indicates pity. And one or two are terribly passive-aggressive – Karen Kemelmen, for instance. The session starts off genially enough, Karen dressed up for the occasion in a new teal shift and leaping in to finish Liz's sentences with eager little laughs. But when Liz moves on to Karen's lateness and all the unauthorized time off she's taken, Karen immediately launches into long confidences about the trials of living with a bipolar husband. "You know what I mean?" she asks three times a minute in her ridiculous Marilyn Monroe voice. Then she assumes an expression of innocence and concern and goes in for the kill. "Once your grandchild is born, Liz, and your daughter is struggling to look after a tiny baby, you will see how hard it is to keep regular hours. Especially if, God forbid, there are complications. With either of them. You know what I mean?"

"Thankfully, you don't have to manage my work performance," Liz says. "It's the board that does that."

After Karen leaves, she sits at her desk with her chin in her hand. The phone rings and she ignores it. No doubt Karen deserves sympathy, but on the other hand she's an aggravating and ignorant woman who will exploit every advantage. What does she see when she turns her pale eyes (eerie eyes, like a husky's) on Liz? She sees something she can get at. She doesn't know what it is, but she's discovered that it's there.

Liz rouses herself and reaches into her bag for her lunch pack. She can feel a tension headache gathering at the base of her skull. She is going to have to make yoga work for her.

There's an afternoon class she likes. It's small, and the teacher, a guy named Cam, has a mild, humorous manner and ordinary articulation. That afternoon will be devoted to "breath work." Even the words are strange, Liz thinks, sitting cross-legged on her mat, although her breathing has never been totally unconscious since synchro.

They breathe in downward dog, they breathe with their legs up the wall. They feather their breath to the rhythm of Cam's voice. "Be fully in the moment," a gentle, toneless reminder. Liz closes her eyes against the fluorescent lights. Sylvie will have to learn controlled breathing for the delivery, she thinks. Not that she herself found it a big help. She can still see Sylvie on the ultrasound table, her face scared and intent. "Acknowledge your thoughts and let them go, a bird flying across the sky." She pulls the air into her hands as instructed; she pulls the air into her feet; she tries to tune in to which is her dominant nostril.

Then the lights are turned low and they're in savasana. "Close your eyes. You don't need your eyes to look inward." And she's standing in a doorway with Krzysztof's hand on the small of her back. In a beautiful old kitchen a woman with platinum hair is making coq au vin with organic rabbit, slicing carrots with the precision of a French chef. She lifts a face full of thoughtless high spirits towards Liz. Pink chunks of rabbit spit in the skillet, and Liz feels the hand – brash, cold, relentless – slipping under her waistband, below the elastic of her panties.

"Use your inhalation to pull back your rogue thoughts." Liz is prone in a dim room where twenty strangers lie in a posture that simulates their deaths. Her breath lifts her and drops her back, lifts her and drops her, and Cam's voice grows faint. She is only her breath. And then his voice is gone, and she's gone, just a frail shell abandoned on the mat.

She may have been hyperventilating, she may have had one of those highs people have when they choke themselves on purpose. But when the lights come up and she surfaces again into the dim room, she understands that yoga is the answer to everything.

On Skype Noah is familiar but different, like the digitally aged kids on posters at the bus depot. "Thanks for the email," Sylvie says. What he sent her was a Charles Darwin quote. She printed it in a big font and hung it on her wall, and she angles her laptop to show him. WHAT A WONDROUS PROBLEM IT IS, WHAT A PLAY OF FORCES, DETERMINING THE KINDS AND PROPORTIONS OF EACH PLANT IN A SQUARE YARD OF TURF. "I love it! He's talking about permaculture, the way all the plants support each other, and what he says – it's exactly what botany field school is. You are assigned one square metre of ground and you identify every single organism in it."

"I know," Noah says.

They used to play in Mary Magdalene's garden. Sylvie showed him how to pinch the throat of a snapdragon and make it open its jaws. And then he showed her something even cooler: a plant that curled its little leaves up over your finger when you touched it. Mimosa, it was called, and it moved like that to shake off insects or to freak out grazing herbivores. Even as a kid he knew the evolutionary reason.

"I never paid any attention to plants until I started playing with you," Sylvie says.

"Well, what were you – five? You used to play outside in your pyjamas."

"I did?"

"Yeah. They had owls on them."

He's got an eidetic memory, this guy. "Stop showing off," she says.

He shrugs. "Anyway, I hope you can still do field school."

"Yeah, so do I."

They stare at each other a minute. "Show me your room," she says.

He picks up his laptop and gives her a tour. It is sickeningly neat. "What's that? Hanging from the bookshelf."

He turns his head to look. "Oh. It's armour, scale armour. I brought it from home. I guess I just wanted something to make my room feel familiar." He swivels his laptop around and moves it closer. She sees the beautiful sleeve he wore in the picture, its over-lapping silver leaves.

"It's not for falconry?"

"No, it's battle gear. Falconers wear leather gauntlets."

"Where'd you get it?"

"Krzysztof gave it to me," he says off camera. "It was from a movie. It was when he and my mom first got together, and I really liked it. I wore it a lot when I was a kid. You have to wear a thick shirt under it, or a jacket. It'll scratch your arm to hell."

The room revolves and Noah is back. Tears sting Sylvie's eyes. There *are* forces at play in the world that she knows nothing about.

"So, how are you feeling?" he asks.

"I'm okay."

"Like, how are things changing for you? Do you feel like you used to feel?"

This is why she likes him: when he finally gets around to talking, he asks questions. Many guys do not.

"I feel tired. And sort of fired up at the same time. It's weird. I'll be falling asleep in class and I'll feel the baby kicking me in the kidneys – like, *pay attention!* Anyway. When is the deadline for the Lake Malawi program?"

"End of February."

"You're still going to apply, aren't you?"

"I don't know. I'd like to, but it doesn't seem right." In the Skype shadows she sees a reminder of his face when his eyes were black from the playground swing, back when he was Sparky.

"Noah," she says, "I didn't get to say this when you were here at Christmas, but I want to tell you how sorry I am. I know this doesn't fit with your plans or your values. It doesn't fit with mine either. But for you it was a clearer thing not to have children – you signed the VHEMT pledge and everything."

Strong feelings pass over his face but she can't quite make out what they are. "Well, I guess any time a guy goes off without a condom, he's responsible for what happens," he says at last.

She feels tears stinging again, because this is an insult to her trustworthiness. But what can she say? She did let him down.

After a minute he says, "There's nothing we can do about it now."

"Maybe it was meant to be."

"No, I don't think you can say that about anything. Meant to be, in what deity's mind? It's just a natural thing. It's just a biological consequence of the way we are, and we have to find the best way to live with it. The least damaging way. VHEMT is one way to live out your values, but there are other ways. Like, there's a guy in my building who's taken a vow to own only one hundred things for the rest of his life. So he really thinks about it before he takes on anything new."

It's awesome that there might be a right way to do this! Sylvie looks at his serious, shadowy face with gratitude. She's been looking after him for years – in a certain way she has – and he has proved himself to be the kind of person it was worthwhile to protect.

The next day she goes to her dad's office. She sets out at eleven and walks all the way. It is still ridiculously warm and the sky is blue, and at Vimy Ridge Park she passes a big bush full of sparrows, twittering like crazy as though it's spring. The door to the inner office is closed when she arrives, and she has to sit in the waiting room for ten minutes. The client who comes out, a professional-looking woman, is totally casual and composed, as if she's just been having her nails done. Sylvie is not really curious about what goes on in that office: she has had a lot of conversations with her dad.

They sit on his red couch and break open the sushi trays Aiden picked up that morning and stashed in his little fridge. He tells her about his client who is putting camera obscuras up in public places and leaving them for six months.

"Does he put them up in malls?" Sylvie asks.

"I don't think so," her dad says, in a way that appreciates the question. "Only on trees."

She catches him up on the news about her friends. "You should see Nathan," she says. "He's having his bones tattooed, one by one. With cool sayings. And he's bleached his hair. Not blond or platinum – it's grey! It looks awesome. He's so slim and graceful. He looks just like a fairy – like the fairies that used to live at the end of the garden in children's books. In England, I guess."

"When I was young, *fairy* was a homophobic slur."

"It still is," she says, suddenly feeling sad. "And all the real fairies are gone. People talk about angels now, but they never talk about fairies. It's like fairies have gone extinct." She pulls a piece of crunchy tempeh out of a roll and nibbles on it. "Although sometimes I dream that extinction is just a myth. Maybe the dinosaurs are living in the mountains of Siberia. And the Tasmanian tiger and the black rhino and the golden toad."

"You got that from Pee-wee Herman," Aiden says. "There were dinos living in the walls of his house, with a door in the baseboard, like cartoon mice. Tiny, shrunken-down dinos living a middle-class life with kitchen cupboards and table lamps."

She's forgotten all about that. What weird things he remembers from her childhood! "Of course," she says, "some of the dinosaurs did shrink down – the ones that evolved into birds. Have you ever seen a drawing of the transition species? There's one in my

Evo-Devo textbook. It's *so* funny-looking. It had feathers on its legs, like leg warmers, like it's from the disco era."

Her dad bends over his sushi tray. She's afraid, judging from the attention he's giving to mixing soy sauce into his wasabi, that he's warming up to give her a lecture. "So," he says, "what else is new in your life? Besides Nathan's grey hair."

She tells him she's dropped out of the Fringe show.

"Well, the timing would have been tough for you."

"It's not just that," Sylvie says. "We were having a really hard time coming up with an idea. We wanted to take on something *so* big, but you know, whatever we ended up doing would just make it seem small, or cheesy."

"Your dramatic skills were not up to your subject?"

"Well, are anybody's? Up to this subject, I mean. My friends actually think they can change things through a Fringe play. And I thought the same thing for a while. Art is bad that way. It gives you the illusion that you've been active. It's better to put your energy into actually *doing* something."

"You know, your mother is an activist. In a very practical way, in her work with SERC."

So he *has* lured her here to preach at her. "You're saying I should make Liz my role model?" she asks coldly.

"Something like that."

"Please. I want to point out, Dad, that the way I behave has nothing to do with her. The fact that she works at SERC – in her twisted mind that makes my problem about *her* in some way. Like I got pregnant to try to get back at her."

"What would you be trying to get back at her for?"

Sylvie can feel her cheeks warming. "I didn't say I was. I said that's what she was likely thinking."

He looks at her thoughtfully for a long time, and then he says,

"I wonder if you'd like me to help you find someone you can talk things through with. A counsellor who's not invested in the situation the way your parents are."

"I don't need a counsellor. Noah and I are talking it all through. We Skype. We were just talking about how we could raise our child so it's part of the solution. You know, not part of the problem."

"Well, that's a very important conversation. But Sylvie, you're not saying you've decided to raise this baby yourselves?"

"Yeah, that's what I'm saying."

"You've decided? You won't be looking into adoption?"

"No, we won't be looking into adoption."

"And is Noah totally on board with this?"

"Of course." She manages to hold his eyes without wavering, for what feels like forever.

"Well, then," he says finally. "I'm going to ask you to come home so we can have a proper conversation with your mother."

"All right," Sylvie says. "I'll come home." Suddenly she's terrified. "On Thursday. But Dad, will you tell her first?"

Two days later she walks home for supper. They're quiet and trying to act normal. Her mother has made vegetarian lasagna and a Greek salad. She's using the chafing dish with the candle under it to keep the lasagna warm. Her father has put Feist on the stereo – his idea of the sort of music Sylvie likes – and the table is set with a yellow tablecloth they bought on one of their trips. The room is like a movie set, Sylvie thinks. It's for one of those films where each actor gets only his or her lines during the shoot and has no idea where the story is heading or what the other actors think is happening.

Her father eats his salad first and then his lasagna, cutting a careful, identical forkful for each bite. She tries to catch his eye to tease him about this, but he won't look. He's wearing his Christmas cardigan. He is going to be absolutely silent through this dinner. He's done this before at other important times, leaving her entirely to her mother's mercy. Sylvie is almost twenty and has every right to make up her own mind. She doesn't have to justify her decision to them. But as they eat she shares a bit of the vision that's been growing in her for the past two days. She tells them that she's quit her job at Stella's so she can focus on getting ready.

Her mother interrupts. "What are you going to do for money?"

"I don't really need anything at the moment."

"Your phone?" Liz says nastily. "Well, we won't dwell on that. It's not the moment I'm talking about."

So Sylvie tells them that she and Noah have discussed how they will raise their child, about the movement Noah mentioned – people who make a vow to own only one hundred things. She has a lot of passion for the subject, she discovers, but there is something so bogus about the way she is talking. She can hear it and she loathes it. It's Liz, it's having to deal with Liz that forces her into positions like this. If only she and Noah could face this problem on their own, without her parents spying on her every move, and jumping up to point an accusing finger the very second she hesitates, and throwing huge roadblocks in her way. She would manage, the way she managed through her entire teenage years; she would be *fine*.

Liz has stopped eating. She's listening with a stunned expression. "Have you talked this over with Noah's parents?" she asks. "With Maggie?"

"No."

There's a long silence.

"Well, if you really are sure, Sylvie," Liz says then, "we have a lot of planning to do. Talking about the realities of the next eighteen years. How you'll support yourself and your baby. How you'll manage with child care and finish your education and so on. How involved Noah will be. What role you expect us to play."

She has the sort of voice you can *see* – it always reminds Sylvie of plastic rope snaking through the air. What a stupid mistake Sylvie's made, coming over here today. She helps herself to more salad and points out that very few families today are the white-picket-fence kind with two hetero parents.

"I'm aware of that," her mother says.

"And there are social programs to help single moms."

"Yes. Well," Liz says. Then she tells a long story about Noah's mother, who spent years on welfare. In those days you had to go to an office every month to pick up your cheque, and Mary Magdalene would bring back terrible stories of the callousness she endured, the interrogations and the efforts to humiliate. But Liz soon drifts from how badly single mothers are treated to slagging off Noah's mother. "We would have been happy to babysit," Liz says, "but she always took Sparky with her. I suppose to maximize the drama."

"You did babysit," Sylvie says. "I remember the whole thing, and I doubt Noah's forgotten."

"I did on one occasion," Liz says. "But in general Mary Magdalene made a point of taking her son to the welfare office. She would pass around homemade crackers to the other clients. Crackers, not cookies – spelt crackers, which are good for people with allergies. She set up activity centres in the corners of the waiting room for the kids. She wanted to be a lesson to the bureaucrats about people on welfare. How resourceful they are, how *noble*."

By the end of this rant her voice is shaking with emotion. Sylvie feels a deep revulsion at the sight of her: her upper lip puckered like a drawstring bag, her thin, dyed hair, the taupe eyeshadow seeping into creases in her eyelids. She's looking down into a forest clearing where her mother leans against a picnic table in white capris – Liz, who lied and lied again to take them to that clearing, to spend the day with those strangers.

"Are you doing this on purpose?" Sylvie cries. "Trying to poison me against Mary Magdalene? Or are you just trying to make me feel shitty?"

Liz doesn't answer. Sylvie can see her struggling to keep back tears, and her own chest is squeezed so tight she can hardly breathe. It's like the day she went down the basement and found her mom there crying. Because she'd found Sylvie's tampons and she had no idea Sylvie had started her period. "Oh, last summer I think it was," Sylvie said. She said it airily, though her arms and legs were suddenly heavy as cement. From the victory she was feeling, the terror of victory – that one day she would take it too far.

TWO

7

Rogue Thoughts

EARLY IN FEBRUARY, WINTER FINALLY WHEELS in, two months late and defiant about it. It's been touring the eastern U.S. seaboard, freaking out the Everglades and putting the kibosh on next year's orange crop. Then off to Ontario, where it dropped sheets of black ice on the old streets of Kingston and flash-froze the tender roots of rhododendrons in Burlington. Now it's hunkered down in its natural home, and on the eyebrow window of 385 Augusta, frost etchings sparkle in the sunlight.

Aiden's in the basement, bundled up and hunched over the computer he uses as a BitTorrent box, and Liz is at the kitchen table, listening to the wind howl around the corners of the house. She's thinking about Sylvie, who's just made a quick trip home to pick up her scarf and mittens and a heap of Aiden's plaid shirts as maternity wear. No time to talk, she said, opening the door to a wall of cold, black air and dashing out. Liz went back to the kitchen and made herself a mug of red tea, and there she's been sitting since, her hands wrapped around the mug, brooding about the note she slipped into Sylvie's backpack along with a Ziploc bag of homemade biscotti: *If you're looking for a birth coach, I would consider it an honour.* Let it go, she says to herself, turning the backs of her fingers to the warm ceramic wall of her mug. You asked, now let it go.

Then, as if an evil genie is taking her by the hand, she's seeing her old boyfriend Denis Fontaine. She's back to the cold winter day when she drove to the liquor store to pick him up after the whisky-tasting she'd given him as a Christmas present. He got into the car exuding alcohol from every pore, leaned his head against the passenger window, and said, "I have to tell you, I'm not in love with you." This was before Aiden – just before. She'd lived for three years with Denis, a middle manager at Autopac, a good-looking guy but entirely without wit, and so anal he washed the dishes in the sink before he put them in the dishwasher. She'd spent those years trying to decide if she could squish herself down small enough to spend her life with him. And then that moment in the car.

Liz pulls the sleeves of her sweater over her hands. She takes a sip of tea and hitches her chair a few more inches from the cold kitchen wall. It's Sunday night. Just three more performance assessments to go this week . . . and instantly she's fretting about work. About Thursday, when she discovered that Cheryl Ogilvie had hidden out in a spare office during the strat-plan meeting ("I had work to do," Cheryl said tartly). And Friday: the gust of laughter Liz heard in the hall on Friday, bitten off the instant she stepped around the corner.

The bottle of port Genevieve gave her at Christmas – I should have saved it, she thinks, I could use it tonight. Maybe I'll bake something, just to warm the kitchen up.

By seven o'clock she has the dough for a big batch of chocolate hearts chilled and ready to go. She rolls a ball deftly between two pieces of waxed paper and starts to hand-cut the cookies, working fast, keeping her knife hand loose. A perfect symmetrical heart of the cupid variety. One with a long, pointy bottom. Tasty valentines, each one unique. Maybe she'll take them to work; no one else has this recipe. Mom would approve, she thinks. Although Mom would have used a cookie cutter: she'd want them all to be the same.

She was the last of a dying breed, Liz's mom. Such a perfect cliché – mention the three-tier Royal Doulton cake stand stacked with pinwheel sandwiches and onion pickles, and people get the picture. As a twelve-year-old, Liz learned how to roll sponge cake on a linen tea towel to make a jelly roll. At seventeen she sewed her own winter coat, a houndstooth number with fabric-bound button-holes – who knows how to make those anymore? All this prepared Liz for something, though not exactly the life she ended up having.

She pauses, blowing a stray hair off her face. Cuts a cookie with a fat left ventricle and thinks about hearts. Like your fist, they always say – that's what your heart looks like. Years ago, when things were so bad with Sylvie (until they settled into it, you might say), she contemplated going to a counsellor. What stopped her was knowing the way therapists operate. A therapist would set out to tear down the beautiful structure she had managed to build of her life, though given less than ideal materials. That's what they do; it's their modus operandi. They strip away your ways of managing, ways that might be flawed and even duplicitous but are better than not managing at all. Things like baking cookies when office morale needs a little boost. You're trying to get your staff to like you? a shrink would ask spitefully. With homemade cookies? Is that wise for a woman in management? In answer Liz points to the recipe, which, along with chocolate, includes three kinds of pepper – black, white, and cayenne. Sweetness with a bite, she says.

She transfers the cookies onto the parchment-lined baking sheet with immaculate care. When the timer pings, she reaches into the oven with her hand-felted oven mitts to rotate the sheet so the cookies will brown evenly. She punches another three minutes into the timer and sits on a stool where she can keep her eyes on the double row of dark hearts in the lit-up oven. There are people who believe that all successful lives are just a front, she says to the shrink. Don't confuse me with one of them.

She could be fixing up a nursery tonight, but does it make sense to do that without Sylvie? And Sylvie so rarely comes home. How round her face is getting! Every time Liz sees her, she looks more like her prepubescent self. "A comely wench," someone called her once. Liz feels a flush of heat at the thought of Krzysztof sitting with the laddered back of a Wynn chair between his knees. A brilliant day in early autumn: they were lounging around a harvest table under the trees, early-fallen yellow leaves dotting the ground. *A comely wench?* Nothing could have been farther from the truth. At eleven Sylvie was Miss Piggy, her features the wrong proportions for her face and her breasts comic little bumps under her T-shirt. When Liz tried to picture her as a woman, her heart sank; all she could see was that whole graceless collection of parts scaled up.

But Liz herself – some days back then she felt so sexy it was unthinkable she would ever lose it. They're walking under the trees at an artists' retreat in Minnesota, she and Krzysztof; they've just been to the Renaissance Festival, although not together. "No claymores, maces, pikes, or halberds," Liz says. She's laughing and she puts her hand innocently on his arm. He pulls her to him and gives her a kiss that more or less takes her apart. Later they're in the studio and he has her pinned against his desk. "Swords, dirks, and daggers must be sheathed," she says. It's her wit that is her undoing. Or the swiftness of the way he grabbed her under the trees, which spoke of a kind of anarchy. She tried not to let on, but that one kiss was more stupefying than the whole deal sometimes was.

And then, on impulse, she picks up the phone and punches in the number stuck to the fridge on a yellow sticky note. While it rings, she decides to propose a supper together to do some planning.

He's the one who picks up. Well, it was bound to happen.

"Hi, Krzysztof. It's Liz Glasgow."

"Liz," he says neutrally. "How are you? Listen, let me grab Maggie for you. She's just going out the door but I'll try to catch her."

A long pause, then Maggie. Even her hello sounds straight from the heart. So Liz launches into her spiel – that's how it comes out, she's rattled to the point that it comes out as a spiel.

"They've decided to keep the baby?" Maggie says with surprise. "I was just talking to Noah and he said they hadn't made a decision at all."

"That wasn't my impression," Liz says. She gropes for some way to bat the embarrassment back to Maggie, but Maggie's already talking.

"If Sylvie has made up her mind, she's entirely within her rights, of course. But it would have got things off on a better footing if Noah had been involved in that conversation. Listen, Liz, I don't mean to cut you off, but I've got to run. I'm late for something."

Liz sticks the phone into its base and sits down. Scorching blossoms open in her chest, their heat licking up into her face. She bends over the table and rests her forehead on the linen placemat. Cold seeps through the wall beside her, but she's got her own crackling fire to keep her warm.

Late February, and light starts to creep across the kitchen floor at breakfast. The longer days are nice. The cold is normal. It will cheer Sylvie up, Aiden thinks. She can imagine the polar bears waking up happy with frost on their snouts. But the only recent word from Sylvie is a text to Aiden: TELL LIZ TO FK OUT OF MY LIFE. Apparently Noah is not entirely on board with the notion of keeping the baby. Apparently he only learned about this plan through his mother, who heard it from Liz.

Making coffee, buttering toast, they snipe about their next move. "You need to let them sort it out," is Aiden's position.

"I gather that's your standard professional line. 'Sort it out yourself.' How do your clients feel about paying a hundred bucks an hour for that?"

"Listen, there are two anxious kids and two distraught mothers already involved. I'm not jumping in."

She pries the lid off the yogurt, peers into it. "Somebody's been eating this yogurt directly from the tub."

"What are you talking about?"

"Look at it. Look how runny it is. It's been predigested – by your saliva."

She's wearing some sort of straight-cut grey dress that is meant to look sophisticated. She's shrill these days or she's silent. Liz is a samurai with silence, he thinks while she moves around the kitchen, hastily assembling her lunch. The year he pissed her off by withdrawing from the Ph.D. program, he was subjected to a deep freeze that lasted for weeks. No doubt it was high-handed, buying the Otter Lake property the way he did, but he always comes back to that: you suffer the silent treatment long enough, you start to feel that you've been cut loose. And then, when his summer counselling course was finished and he wanted some time alone at the lake, she actually gave him an ultimatum: don't go, or else. He has never responded well to ultimatums.

It was their worst time, he thinks as she races up the stairs. Maybe it gouged a permanent trench in their conjugal goodwill; when things are rough now, he has a sense that they're sliding into it. How seriously was she thinking of leaving him that summer? It was brinkmanship, on both sides. But brinksmanship can strike at the moorings of even a good relationship. It's staggering, actually, the risks you're prepared to take when you're provoked. For what? To gain the upper hand?

She's out in the hall now getting her things together. He goes to the doorway and leans, watching. She's got on a cloche hat, pulled low. A deep orangy colour, it suits her. We're past that, he thinks, watching her knot her scarf. Past the stage where we believe there's another life out there, that we could just throw this whole thing away and take up something else.

"You look like a *Vogue* cover."

"Oh god, Aiden, you don't know what *Vogue* is."

He goes over and kisses her. "I'm sorry Sylvie was so mean to you."

"Yeah? Well, me too." Her face under the hat is wry and plucky. A waif's face.

It's too cold for Aiden to run outside, though there are maniacs who do it. The river has finally frozen but it's too cold to skate, too cold even to think of skiing in to the cabin. They've invested in triple-pane windows but cold leaks in around the doors (or the heat leaks out). Aiden never hears the furnace muttering on because it never turns off. Mornings he battles the north wind on his walk to Portage Avenue. Freezing your face walking to the bus – it's expiation for every sin.

When he comes home one night, men in orange parkas with fluorescent hazard X's are swarming the backyard. They're wielding chainsaws. They've already lopped the limbs off all three elms. The massive columns of the trunks are still standing. Through the failing light Aiden spies the spruce, their only remaining tree. One side of it is sheared off. "Yeah, sorry," says the foreman in a yellow safety helmet. "Dropped a big limb on it. Coulda sworn we had the angle right. You can contact the city, make a claim for damages."

By the end of the next afternoon, two of the columns have been felled and they're just launching into the big cut on the third. Most men would stay and watch this operation. Aiden goes upstairs and lies obliquely across the bed, face down. A few minutes later the house shakes, a crash of three on the Richter scale.

He's still lying there when Liz comes in at suppertime. She stands by the wicker chair, taking off her skirt and jacket. "What's with the drama?" she says. "You knew this was going to happen."

He turns his face to the side. "I miss the winters when I was young."

"Oh, I know, everything was so nice then." She's at the wardrobe; he hears the rustle of clothes being arranged on hangers. "May I remind you, it's Dutch elm disease that got your trees. It's got nothing to do with the end of the world. You're a catastrophe slut, Aiden."

They go to bed early. In the middle of the night, a bunch of people visit Aiden. It starts with Meryl Streep as the hard-faced preacher's wife whose baby was eaten by a dingo. Aiden is in her house in Australia, they have a very friendly relationship. Then his client Christine Tolefson appears, although (he comes to realize) it's not Christine he's talking to but her avatar. His daughter is also there, sadly pregnant, swollen in every aspect. Her hands, where a ring is cutting into her flesh. She spreads her fingers to show Aiden. She is grieving, enfeebled by a terrible knowledge. I'll find something to cut it off, he says. But he wanders the bare concrete streets, stymied and distracted at every turn. The night gets darker and more threatening. He's waiting for it all to come down on them.

It's a wearisome, looping dream, and he's lucid through parts of it but can't seem to pull himself out. Eventually he manages to open his eyes. Liz is a long ridge lying motionless on her side of the bed. He turns his head cautiously and looks at the digital clock on the alligator suitcases. 3:59 . . . 4:00. He swings out his legs and sits up. His jeans and padded shirt are on the chair. He grabs them and heads down the stairs, stopping on the second-floor landing to pull them on.

Downstairs he and the dog greet each other. He pauses by the liquor cabinet and then walks into the living room and sits down, not bothering with the lights.

What a shitty day. In the morning he got a call from a ward clerk at the Health Sciences Centre to say that the police had brought Rupert in. He was wandering in a Safeway parking lot in his bedroom slippers. Aiden went at noon and found him hooked up to an IV, looking, with his frostbitten ears bandaged, more than ever like a nasty elf. Automotive booster cables lay tangled on the bedside stand – Rupert was apparently carrying them when the police spotted him at four a.m. Aiden knows he starts the car once in a while and backs it out of the garage. In the summer he gives it a wax job or just sits in the driver's seat, listening to right-wing rants on CJOB.

"Going to jump-start the Caprice?" Aiden asked, taking a chair by the bed. Rupert looked at him dismissively and turned his head away. Aiden glanced over at the other bed, where an octogenarian lay wrapped in a sheet as though it were the white shroud of his years, and then he leaned towards his dad and gave it another try. "You've got to watch it," he said genially. "Jump-starting your car in this cold. The battery could explode."

Rupert rotated his head on the pillow and stared at Aiden with open contempt. He reached up his thumb and forefinger to pinch his nostrils, and with that absent-minded gesture Aiden was hit by a tsunami of rage. *You little piece of shit*, he hears his dad say, as he did say more than once, though he never needed to. Day after day his coldness said it, his sneer said it, and there the cocksucker lay, a stubby beer bottle full of piss and old prejudice, still sucking back oxygen. It was a fucking travesty. Aiden felt it with a sort of horror – that there could be people like Rupert in the world, sheltered forever by ignorance of who they are.

"Okay, Dad," he said, getting up and reaching for the booster cables. "This bullshit is over. You like silence, you've got it." He coiled up the cables and went out the door with a pitiless swing of his shoulders.

Aiden leans his head back and trains his eyes on the window. In the greenish light of the night sky, the backyard is a clear-cut logging site. He's just old, Rupert, old and daft. It's not really that he hates me, Aiden thinks with some surprise. Not anymore. It's that I hate him. And what would I do without that hatred, where would the two of us be? Without that energy, without my compulsion to drag myself up to the old man's house and demonstrate, through gentle deeds of charity, the victorious knowledge that I am so much better than the nasty old fart?

He reaches up and pulls the chain on the floor lamp. His reflection leaps onto the window, a stuttering image: the pale face with startled eyes creased (and creased and creased in the layers of triple-pane glass), a plaid-shirted aging man in blue jeans clutching at his little shards of self-knowledge, while in the dark behind him, the bent world and his darling daughter hurtle past, at the mercy of an entirely different wind.

Charlotte comes to town, Liz's dear friend Charlotte, running out of Arrivals with her hair flying and her carry-on bouncing over the curb. In the kitchen, in the soft under-cabinet lighting, her beautiful face is long and lined, longer and more lined and more beautiful than the last time Liz saw her. She's got a new hair colour and a sweater of natural silk and linen – she's all gold and tarnished silver. Liz opens a Sauv Blanc and puts out olives and a great chèvre and bread. She sears prawns and does a flambé with pastis – it's the most delectable treat she can think of.

When the show is over, Charlotte peels a prawn and then breaks off a chunk of bread with her knobby fingers and plasters it thick with the chèvre. She eats it with great appreciation, and Liz is happy because she drove all the way to St. Boniface to get that baguette, for its authenticity and its perfection.

"I thought you'd have a bedroom decorated with duckies by now," Charlotte says.

"Oh, the nursery – don't even go there." Liz takes a sip of her wine. Her anxiety has hardened around her chest; she feels it chafe like a plaster cast.

"But Sylvie's decided to keep her baby?"

"Who gives up babies these days?"

"And how is she seeing the future?"

"I suspect she's blocking it out entirely." Liz crumbles off a bit of cheese with her fingers and eats it. "If you can block out a watermelon under your T-shirt. No doubt she's still just fretting about the oil sands and watching Jon Stewart. She has this goal that for the rest of her life she will buy nothing new. It's some Internet coven she's joined."

"Wow."

"Well, it's easy enough, isn't it, when you have all the comforts of your parents' home to fall back on."

"Liz, you have raised an idealist. I drink to you." Charlotte empties her glass. "Sylvie is not saving for a boob job or defacing her lovely body with tattoos. She's not starving herself to get into a made-for-TV movie about bulimic fashion models." This last is a reference to her own daughter, Lucy. "Your Sylvie is devoted to changing the world. And this year she's had a really bad break."

"You think?" Liz says, feeling the heat rise. The dog is under the table, trying to lie on her feet. She shoves him off savagely and refills Charlotte's glass. "You know what I think? I think it's grandiose for one teenage girl to believe she can do anything about the fate of the entire planet. And it's kind of sad to watch Sylvie obsess about it. Yes, she's in a fix at the moment, but in the broader scheme of things, she has every advantage. And she insists on being unhappy on behalf of Africa."

"What does Aiden say?"

"He thinks she's ahead of us. He says our entire civilization is in denial, whereas Sylvie's already at the anger stage. Or acceptance. I forget which."

"That's interesting, sweetie." Charlotte sops up butter and pastis from the pan. "Because, as a guru of the grieving process, Elisabeth Kübler-Ross has been totally debunked. Aiden should know that. Apparently the stages are bullshit." She leans forward to protect her sweater and pops the dripping bread into her mouth.

Liz sits in silence. She watches Charlotte attack another prawn, sucking sweet juice out of the tail. She drops the little husk of shell onto her plate and gropes for a napkin, which Liz hands to her. Their eyes meet. They go back a long way. They were once in love with the same guy, a Turkish exchange student named Doruk Aksoy, and here they are, still best friends. Well, neither of them landed him.

The door opens and Aiden comes up the hall, bringing the cold with him. He kisses Charlotte and she reaches up and hugs him, lingeringly. He's looking over her head at the spread on the table. Liz gives him a *bugger off* stare. "Love to join you," he says smoothly, extracting himself from Charlotte, "but I've got some calls to make."

"He's looking a little strained," Charlotte says when he's gone.

"No doubt."

"Maybe he needs to go up to the lake for a few days. You should go with him. Chill out for a while."

"Yeah, right."

"You don't like the cabin?"

"Not in winter. Anyway, he never wants me there. He wants to do the monastic thing. That cabin is his, not ours."

"Well, I'm not a big fan of peeing in a freezing outhouse myself. It's okay for men. They can stand." Charlotte extends her glass. "So, how's work going?"

"Work," Liz says as she pours. "Is it going to be all Liz all night?"

"Yup, it's Liz's turn all weekend. But speaking of peeing, I need a loo break first."

She jumps up and runs into the confessional. Liz takes a swallow of wine and sits back in her chair. What a surprising shape Charlotte's life has taken. When they met in university, she was so gauche and naive; she looked like Alice in Wonderland with her wavy hair and Mary Jane shoes and her baffled expression. And she stayed that way for a long time. Once when Aiden's friends threw a party, Liz and Aiden invited Charlotte because her boyfriend was out of town. It was at an infamous party house with no furniture and a disassembled motorcycle on the porch, and Char showed up with a chocolate cake. Word raced through the party that someone had baked a hash cake, and sweet Charlotte, straight as an arrow, had no idea why they fell on it so eagerly.

When she got married, she had the poofy white gown followed by a brocade going-away outfit with hat and corsage. But then she shook off her marriage and moved out west. She got a job as director of a great little jazz festival – all about drinking Scotch with saxophonists in fedoras – and she bought an apartment just up from the beach in White Rock and raised her girls alone. And now she smokes. How strange that Liz and Aiden are the ones who ended up looking conservative.

The toilet flushes and water runs in the tiny sink. "So tell me," Charlotte says, sliding back into her chair. "How are things at the circus?"

"I don't want to talk about work," Liz says. "Except to say I can't get no respect and I'm sick of it."

"I can't believe that's true. How could they not respect you? You are the most competent person I know."

This is the way they talk to each other. When Lucy was going through a shoplifting stage, all Liz ever said was "You're an amazing mom. You are! Amazing." But Charlotte is looking at her with genuine concern, so she rallies herself to tell the story of spiteful Karen Kemelmen, how she tried to put a hex on Sylvie's baby. *If, God forbid, there should be something wrong with the baby. You know what I mean?*

Charlotte sets down her glass. "What a witch! She'd never *dare* say something like that to a male boss. It's outright sexism."

"No," Liz says. "It's not sexism. It's just . . . This thing with Sylvie has completely undermined me at work."

"Oh, honey. Well, maybe. I guess they have to have their little joke. It's the revenge of the underclass. They'll get over it." She pulls out an empty chair and swings her stockinged feet up onto it.

"It's women, isn't it," Liz says. "They see an opening and they're ruthless." And then she is into it, well in. "Remember that accident I had with Mary Magdalene's son? When he was hit by a swing? Well, after that, Mary Magdalene escalated things to shitting on my whole way of parenting. It was just before they moved away. We're out on the street, and she looks at me in that I'm-too-pure-for-this-world way she has and she says, 'You know, Liz, if you blow it raising your kids, it doesn't much matter what else you're good at.'

She actually said that. I've never forgotten it. And now Sylvie has proved her right."

"Liz!" Charlotte cries, sitting up straight. "It's her son! Her son is the dad! So how can she possibly judge you? And anyway, that thing she said? It's not original. She was quoting Jacqueline Kennedy."

"Really?" Somehow this makes Liz feel better. She opens another bottle of wine and, savouring the reckless joy of confession, tells Charlotte about the night she drifted into George Stonechild's yard and ended up drinking with him most of the night. She tells how Mary Magdalene walked over to their house the next day to lecture her.

"When was this? Sylvie was born?"

"Yeah, she was born. She was five or six. It was the same summer as the swing incident. Anyway, the doorbell rings and Mary Magdalene is standing on the veranda. She's obviously been talking to George, and she says, 'Before you get in any deeper, Liz, I feel I should warn you. He's a fake, you know. He doesn't have an ounce of aboriginal blood.' I couldn't believe my ears. She is *such* a fruitcake. *Please*, I said."

"Which was pretty insulting to her."

"Well, yeah. She'd had *a kid* with the guy. And she didn't believe me in any case. She just kept gazing at me with concern and pity. And I know she spread it around. For months afterwards women would look at me earnestly and say, 'So, how are you and Aiden *doing*?'"

Charlotte laughs. "God, she's a piece of work."

Liz drains her glass and reaches for the bottle. "She *is*. But you know, it's weird. She can still make me feel inferior. Like, she's let her hair go grey, and instead of thinking how old she looks, I kind of envy her. For daring to look old. For being more *real*. She affects everyone that way. Once, years ago, we were all trying to cram into a car to go somewhere and one of the women said, 'Mary Magdalene can't ride in the back – her aura's too big.'"

"So is her aura still visible to the naked eye?"

"Not so much."

"Maybe only the young can see it."

"That's it!" Liz cries. "It's like a taste for cherry cola. Everybody grows out of that eventually." But she's not really convinced. Everyone adores Mary Magdalene. It's the way she turns her warm eyes on you and sees you totally. That's what Liz always shrank from, that stifling intimacy that could suck you in like quicksand.

"You know, I'm dying for a smoke," Charlotte murmurs, and gets up to search for her purse.

They end up on the veranda, coats and boots on. And there, leaning against the railing and holding her cigarette high, Charlotte casually gets back to George. It's clear to Liz why she made the effort to move their little party outside. Along with caring for Liz (she does care), she's always been a gossip hound.

"Does Aiden know? About that sordid little neighbourhood drama?"

"Of course not." Liz sticks her hands deep in her pockets. "You think Aiden doesn't keep secrets from me?"

"You think he's had affairs?"

"Affairs? Don't be bourgeois."

"He does kind of act like a free agent at parties."

"Oh, I know. The cool way he swans around. Eat side by side but not from the same plate, yadda, yadda." She thinks of a summer afternoon when two women driving a tiny vintage car rolled into the driveway. They were picking up Aiden for a three-week workshop, and they made a hilarious thing out of cramming his gear into the car. One of them was a long-haired Asian beauty, the other older and shaped like a penguin. The lively, congenial manner Aiden switched on for both of them – it seemed at the time a way of saying *fuck you* to Liz. She was on the veranda and he said as an afterthought, "Oh, this is Liz," and she put it to herself that two could play that game. After they had driven away, she called Jenn's mother and arranged for Sylvie to sleep over at Jenn's, and then she dressed up and went to a party on the river.

A car creeps up the street, snowflakes swimming in the long shafts of its headlights. It turns the corner. Liz leans over the railing and looks out into the yard, trying to see the snow falling invisibly in the dark. Is anybody worth the gift of your desire? You look around a party and all the men are wonderful – effortlessly funny, and tall, with strong, tanned arms, golden hairs glinting on them – and you feel a bitter pang at the tiny portion of this buffet you will ever be able to partake of. And then the next night you look around at the same crowd and see a collection of bloodless wonders, fretting about mould in their basements. Both of these visions are deeply true.

"I'll tell you Aiden's dirty little secret," she says to Char. "It's how very, *very* straight he actually is."

"But that's not what you meant," Charlotte says.

She's not going to let it go. Liz is shivering. It is Aiden's fault, she thinks. All of it. He taught me how to be. He drove me to it. But not in any way she can explain to Charlotte, especially drunk. She shoves her hands up her sleeves and feels the gooseflesh on her bare arms. "Well, for one thing," she says, "he still smokes the odd joint and he won't tell me who his dealer is. I think it might be Sylvie. Can you imagine, him colluding with her like that?" She hears her voice thicken, and out of nowhere she's crying.

Charlotte steps towards her, turning her head to blow away a long trail of smoke. Then she grinds out her cigarette on a patch of ice on the railing, throws the stub into the spirea bushes, and puts her arms around Liz, reaching up to stroke her hair. It feels totally false. *Off*, like their conversation.

Liz moves away. "Oh, there's more to it," she says to Charlotte. Her voice is portentous. God, she's drunk!

"What more?"

Liz shakes her head. Now it seems she's laughing. "If I told you, I'd have to kill you," she hears herself say.

After a two-day visit, Charlotte flies back to Vancouver. Aiden sits downstairs long after Liz has gone to bed. The house is so quiet. He remembers this waiting sensation from Liz's pregnancy – a sense that all the real action is interior. He pours himself three fingers of Glendronach and reads the film reviews and cartoons in the latest *New Yorker*, the radio on low and tuned to a French station. It's a jazz program; he likes it for the host's sexy voice, the way her confiding chat washes meaninglessly over him. "Peenk Floyd," he hears her say at one point.

Around one o'clock he turns on the TV. The U.S. public broadcaster is playing a doc about evangelicals holding something called a "Last Days" convention. Well-dressed white Americans sit around tables in a hotel ballroom, talking complacently about apocalyptic indicators like hundred-pound hailstones and carnage in the Middle East. One of the main interview subjects is a fiftyish blonde, a Republican wife type. "People believe the world will last forever, but God has other plans," she says. "All the floods, the tornadoes, the famines – I'm actually happy when I hear about them on the news. Because these are signs that Jesus is on his way. It's *exciting* to be the generation God has chosen to live out the End Times. I'm excited. Are you excited?" This is directed at the unseen interviewer. They cut to a crane shot of the red-carpeted ballroom, and Aiden flicks off the TV.

Who is he to sneer? Every Saturday morning when he was a kid, he knocked on doors for the Jehovah's Witnesses. He went with his mother and her friend Helen, wearing a clip-on bowtie, his hair plastered to the side with a comb and water. He was the only one of the kids his mother dragged to the Kingdom Hall and proselytizing door to door. Their beat was Wolseley, as it happened, where Aiden and Liz live now. They walked down from the other side of Portage Avenue, badly dressed emissaries from the wrong side of the tracks, carrying urgent news of the end of the world to happy breakfasting families.

The house creaks in the cold: he's hearing the iron gears of things slowing down. He gets up and goes to the bookshelf and pulls out his battered copy of *The New Oxford Book of English Verse*. The summer his MIFT program started, when he went to Otter Lake as sole owner for the first time, he wanted a solitary retreat. And he vowed not to run the generator. No radio, no music, no books except his *Oxford*. He'd just done a lot of emotional work at the group therapy intensive – it was almost a spiritual experience – and he had the idea that he'd paddle up to the dock and a more fully realized self would be waiting for him there, somebody who could live in silent harmony with nature for two weeks.

Early on, taking a hike to the top of the island, he stumbled – on a rough patch of concrete he'd never noticed before, halfway up the climb. Fucking concrete, poured for no purpose he could see, on a ledge where granite broke through the topsoil like a whale breaching. He roamed the island in a rage all afternoon, assaulted by the sight of the rocks along the waterfront that Rupert had painted white, and the flagpole from which Rupert used to fly the Stars and Stripes he'd bought on a celebrated retirement trip to

Chicken, Alaska, and the barbecue pad and the lawn grass and the toilet bowl installed in the lawn grass as a petunia planter, and the tin cans and beer bottles thrown into the bush behind the cabin.

After a supper of cold beans and bread, he sat on the rocks reading Gerard Manley Hopkins. His undefended dissertation was on Hopkins, and his *Oxford* opened on its own to "God's Grandeur." He'd bought the book as an undergraduate, and "God" was circled in ink and annotated in his younger, neater handwriting:

creative life force
eternal pulse of nature
Gaia?

Hopkins, of course, could use the word God straight-up. He'd been born Church of England, and then he'd jeopardized his prospects and broken his parents' hearts by becoming a papist. The Catholic belief that God is in the material world, in the bread and wine: that's why Hopkins had converted, because the symbolism appealed to the poet in him. He was sent to teach in the north of England, where the sheep were black with soot from the factory chimneys. He thought that if you paid enough attention you would see beyond that, you could see God. He swooned looking into a bluebell, and so he ate it as a Eucharist.

Sitting on the rocks in the failing western light, Aiden read the poem over and over. The last lines made his breath catch every time: *"Because the Holy Ghost over the bent / World broods with warm breast and with ah! bright wings."*

The next day he got to work and felled the flagpole like a pine tree, sawing off the stump at its concrete base. After that he took a sledgehammer to the barbecue pad and broke up what he could. He pried up the whitewashed border stones and dismantled the aluminum filleting table his dad had screwed into the rock. Got rid of the things that offended him most, that reeked of his dad, that *wore man's smudge and shared man's smell* – although of course all that was a conceit, the notion that Aiden (tramping the island in shoes assembled by indigent children on three continents) was fundamentally different, that he *deserved* to be there. The real estate deal had filled him with so much private satisfaction (*We own it – it will be here for us when the city burns*), but that was nonsense too, the idea that he, in his nanosecond of time, should have any meaningful claim to a piece of Precambrian rock five hundred million years old.

One time, after the light was scoured from the sky in the black west, he decided he wanted to see the whole night unroll. He carried a sleeping bag and pillow outside and made a nest on the lower ledge with its beautiful lichen, and there he lay while the sun dropped behind the fringe of spruce on the far bank and tiny stars began to prick through the green sky. He watched the water silver over, and then along the shoreline he saw the silver pucker into an arrowhead. A line of arrowheads – an otter, swimming with her young. When they were out of sight, he rolled onto his back and lay looking at the stars in their webs until he fell asleep. The temperature plunged during the night, and in the morning the dew woke him: his hair and his sleeping bag were drenched. It was astonishing being anointed like that by a perfectly cloudless, enamel-blue sky, and lying on that granite slab, he was stoned by wonder at the faithful rotation of the Earth and the perfection of a day washed with light by a sun that hadn't even risen yet.

He's still got the *Oxford* in his hands, and he opens it. In the warm light of a lamp with an amber shade, he turns his eyes to the poem. *His* poem, you might call it: he would acknowledge it as a kind of scripture. "Nature is never spent," he reads aloud. "There lives the dearest freshness deep down things." But it's an old poem, an old consolation, and he finds that he doesn't have the heart to read to the end.

Sylvie was right to try to stay away from Liz: she caused her first-ever fight with Noah. Before Sylvie had a chance to tell him what had gone down with her parents, he called her.

"I was just talking to my mom. Did you decide to keep the baby?"

"What makes you think that?"

"That's what your mother told my mother."

"Oh god." She held the phone away from her for a minute.

"Did you? Did you tell your mother you've decided?" he was saying when she put it back to her ear.

"I got cornered, Noah. They were pushing me, pushing me, and it just kind of came out."

"So you're not really serious about it."

She couldn't link the voice coming out of her phone to his actual face. "I don't know," she said. "I guess I am serious. I don't really see any other way."

Now no sound at all came from the phone.

"Noah, do you want your kid to grow up in a ten-room mansion in Lindenwoods? Do you want her driving an suv when she's sixteen?"

"Nobody will be driving suvs when this kid is sixteen."

"No, all right, but you see what I mean. It's going to be hard, I know. But maybe we have a chance to do it right. With this baby. To show that it can be done."

Again he didn't respond.

"Noah," she said. "Use your words."

More silence.

"Fuck, Noah. I feel like shit when you don't talk."

She hung up and dropped her phone on the bed. In a minute it rang again. In that strange flat voice he said, "You're just going to have to give me time."

Well, they have time. Sylvie has the impression this pregnancy will never be over. Her stomach is huge and her belly button sticks out like the knot in a big balloon. But she's going to classes and turning in her assignments; she's sucking back kale smoothies and eating hummus sandwiches stacked with veggies. Her skin is clear, her hair crackles ("You're a biosphere," her friends all say, "a walking biosphere"), and she tries not to fret, because she knows Noah will come around.

While she's waiting for that to happen, she makes her own plans for the first few months. She'll buy a cradle at Value Village and she'll keep the baby's sleepers and diapers in a drawer of her dresser. If you're breastfeeding, that's all you need – a woman's body is perfectly adapted to feed a baby on nothing. She knows her baby will be the most popular resident of Laurence Hall; her friends will be at the door night and day, begging to take her for walks. It would be unfair to Kajri to have a baby waking her up in the night, though, so she goes to the student housing office and puts her name on a list for a private room.

Laurence Hall does not currently allow children, that's the biggest catch. Sylvie makes an appointment and goes in to speak to the dean. Dean Semple (his actual given name) is a funny guy who thinks the styles of his own university days are cool. "You got lucky," she says. "Spikes are back." He narrows his eyes but basically he likes her – she can say anything. He offers her two pieces of the Kit Kat he has open on his desk and tells her the board of regents is meeting in a few weeks. "But I've got to warn you," Dean the Dean says, "it took them two years to reach a decision on Coke machines."

Most students will sign anything you put under their noses, so Sylvie writes up a petition. She circulates the clipboard in the lecture theatre during her Evo-Devo class, which is huge. It comes back with two names and *Are you nuts?* written across the bottom. Sylvie slides the clipboard into her backpack. People secretly keep cats and dogs in apartments all the time, she thinks darkly. She's not going to panic. Nothing in the universe can make her fall back into her mother's vortex.

But the weeks are passing, so in desperation she takes her petition to the entrance of the university daycare centre. It's late afternoon and the parents, mostly moms, are just arriving to pick up their kids. The first woman she approaches reads the petition and says, "Laurence Hall? Not sure why you'd want to do that." She looks at Sylvie with a curious expression. Sylvie has no idea what she's seeing or thinking, and she hates it, it's like this woman has a strange power over her. She leans against a pillar of the daycare centre. Something is pressing inside her head, as if her brain is too big for her skull, crammed in and hurting. She bends down cautiously for her backpack, swings it on, and heads for Laurence Hall.

It's dark when she wakes with a gasp to see Kajri by her bed with a Thermos mug of teabag chai.

"I didn't mean to scare you."

"It's okay," Sylvie says. "I need to get up." When she reaches for the mug, she discovers that her fingers are swollen like sausages. She can hardly bend them. She puts down the mug and goes to the bathroom to pee. Her feet are puffy too, even the soles – they feel squishy to walk on.

"How are they going to get this thing out of me?" she says when she comes out of the bathroom.

Kajri gives a little shrug. "It's been done before." Her voice is matter-of-fact.

And then both their eyes go to the ghostly sonogram of the seven billionth baby hanging on the wall. Sylvie suddenly sees the true meaning of that picture: it's not that her baby is exceptional, it's that it isn't.

Kajri is gone when Sylvie wakes up in the morning. Her headache is gone too, and the swelling in her hands and feet is down. She goes to her classes, and then at one o'clock she runs into Benedictor in Lockhart Hall. He's on his way to visit a friend who has two tiny kids. "Can I come?" Sylvie asks. He's surprised, but he says sure.

And then his friend isn't home; only the guy's wife is there in their tiny apartment on Carlton. Her name is Asnaku, she's twenty-six and beautiful, and she has incredible micro braids. She makes them lunch, a spicy lentil dish that they eat with injera. One of her babies is sleeping on its tummy in a mesh playpen, and Benedictor sits comfortably at the kitchen table holding the other.

"So, what's the secret to being a good mom?" Sylvie asks, reaching over to run her fingertips along the baby's plump arm. The baby looks at her out of the corner of his amazing eyes – he's flirting with her. What she wants to know from Asnaku is how you raise a baby with very little, the way people do in much of Africa, but she can't think of a tactful way to ask this.

Afterwards she calls Noah to tell him about it. When he picks up, he sounds okay, and she is terribly relieved. "The most important thing, she says, is to carry your baby all the time. Tie it to your body with a big piece of cloth. Parents in North America always drag their babies around in car seats, and the baby never feels the warmth of the mother's body."

"So does she tie both her kids into a carrying cloth?"

"No!" Sylvie laughs. "It's nuts – she gives me this advice, but actually she has all sorts of plastic shit. Mobiles and swings and Jolly Jumpers. She grew up in a refugee camp in Kenya and it makes her happy to be able to buy that kind of stuff. But it doesn't mean we have to do it that way."

We, she hears herself say. She can't see how he's reacting because he's on his cell. She can hear a crowd in the background, as if he's standing in a hallway. Will he be a part of the baby's first summer? He hasn't heard whether he got into the Lake Malawi project. She feels so sad about never seeing him. She felt especially bad in the first prenatal class, where all but one of the other women had their partner there. "I really miss you," she says.

"I miss you too," he says politely. "But I've got to go, my lab is starting. I'll try to call tomorrow."

Well, they have never been part of each other's university life. He stayed in Guelph for reading week. He said he would come home but he's so against flying that Sylvie told him not to. He won't come now until his exams are over and the baby is due.

Not that Sylvie is really into the prenatal classes. In the first class, after they had all introduced themselves, they were asked to do a matching exercise to learn the correct names for reproductive body parts. Sylvie left at the juice-and-cookies break and skipped the next few weeks. She goes back when they're scheduled to start the breathing exercises, because Kajri says her mother says the breathing is the most important part.

Thea ends up coming as her coach. The mothers lie on mats with their coaches sitting cross-legged at their heads. Sylvie lowers herself slowly because bright pinpricks of stars sparkle around the edges of her vision when she moves fast. She's beside Dahlia, the only other mother who doesn't have her partner with her. She is only twenty but she already has a two-year-old at home. Dahlia is clutching a stuffed cloth doll dressed in camouflage gear. When she sees Sylvie looking at the doll, she passes it over.

"Sylvie, meet my husband, Lance. Lance got me through the last delivery and he's going to get me through this one."

"Hi, Lance," Sylvie says. "Wow." She looks closely into his silk-screened face and then steals a glance at Thea, holding Lance so Thea can see the white stuffing leaking out of a hole in his thigh.

"You've never seen these before?" Dahlia says. "You're kidding! They're called Hug-a-Hero dolls. I got this one made in the mall in Fargo. You take in a picture of your guy on a flash drive and they screen it onto the face. My daughter loves it. But I said to her, 'Tonight you'll have to cuddle with Buster Bear because Mommy needs her hero.'"

Dahlia has fine natural blond hair clipped back with aqua plastic barrettes. She has gentle eyes of the palest green. She and Sylvie are lying with their faces six inches apart, keeping their voices low because the teacher is talking.

"You should get one," Dahlia whispers. "It was $29.99, but that includes the uniform, and they have, like, army, navy, air. Although the uniforms are American."

Sylvie passes Lance back, ashamed of her unkindness. The real Lance may be overseas, or he may already have been killed. "My boyfriend's a student," she says softly. "He's doing his master's at the University of Guelph."

"Oh. I thought for sure you were a service wife."

"Why?"

"I don't know. You just look like one."

The breathing has started. Sylvie and Thea are supposed to lock eyes and puff their breath into each other's faces, and right away they start to laugh.

"Remember the pregnant psychic?" Thea gasps. "That George Costanza went to? She was going into labour?" It's true, they're panting just like the pregnant psychic.

By the time they get to the second breathing pattern, in which you go *hee-hee-hoo*, they're both streaming with tears. All around them fat, earnest women in sweatpants huff and puff with their eyes wide and their mouths in slits, concentrating as if it's rocket science.

"Hee-hee-ha," Sylvie laughs helplessly, gripping Thea's hands, trying desperately not to pee. "Ha, ha, ha," she hears Thea reply, and then she slides into the dark.

They keep Sylvie in the hospital overnight. The next day her blood pressure is normal and they discharge her, with the understanding that she will stay on bed rest. Aiden takes Liz's car and picks her up. She's sitting in a wheelchair by the obstetrics ward nursing station, already dressed. She's never been sick, never, since her own birth, been in a hospital.

The resident comes by and leads them into an alcove for a chat. "So, you think you get the picture?"

"Yeah," Sylvie says. "My body is freaking out because it views the placenta as foreign tissue."

"That's about the size of it. So we're just trying to get your body to chill out for a bit longer. Every week you can last is a huge benefit to your baby. That means no more classes, no working at the computer, no going out. You can get up to go to the bathroom, but move slowly. No break dancing. No slasher flicks. No Facebook . . . Well, maybe Facebook."

Aiden interrupts. "We're going to insist that Sylvie move home to her old bedroom, where we can keep a better eye on her."

"Absolutely," says the doctor.

It really is a beautiful room. It was meant to be the master bedroom. It has three wide windows overlooking the street, and it had a walk-in closet before such things were even heard of. Liz redecorated the room when Sylvie was in high school, in an effort to lure her back into it. She bought new furniture, made a tiny-paned quilt in shades that look like wheat and sand and willow branches. On the windows she hung blinds made of some sort of unbleached fabric.

"Your mother did a great job with this room," Aiden says.

"Yeah," Sylvie says. "It's true eco-chic." She walks slowly over to the bed and sits down. After a minute she lies on her side and says into the pillow, "That dresser – it's rainforest teak."

Above the bed hangs a picture Sylvie drew when she was little. Liz had it laminated onto a board. It's a drawing of their family. All three of them have huge, U-shaped smiles that go up past their ears. The mother has spokes radiating from her head, like the Statue of Liberty. Aiden can only assume they are rays of power, from an era when Sylvie worshipped her mother. Doesn't every kid go through a stage like that?

"I'm going to lose my courses," Sylvie says, again into the pillow. "Friday was the last date for voluntary withdrawal. They'll be on my transcript as incompletes. Or failures."

"I'll talk to the dean."

He and Liz bring in their suppers on trays and eat with Sylvie, and then Aiden sets up the old television and DVD player. From the basement he hauls up the two Coke crates of books Sylvie saved from her childhood. "You are so set up, chicken!" he says. "For the next month you can live the life of Riley."

"Who is Riley, anyway?"

"Fucked if I know." He puts in a DVD and sits on the wicker chair while they watch Mr. Bean dash around with a rubber turkey on his head. Tears of laughter run down Sylvie's cheeks. When it's

173

over, he goes downstairs to make her some hot chocolate. She's lying down with her eyes closed when he comes back.

"Thanks, Dad," she says, but she doesn't make any move to sit up and drink it.

"What's up?"

"Oh, nothing."

"Tell me what you were thinking, honey."

She doesn't answer.

"You know," he says, "you're going to get back on track. You'll do the things you always wanted to do. It might just take a little longer."

She opens her eyes. "There's a war going on inside me."

"I guess you could look at it that way. But just lie still, think happy thoughts. The armies are going to call a truce."

Upstairs he and Liz lie three feet apart. "Where the hell were you tonight?" he finally says.

"I was in the basement going through those boxes of old baby things. I am the hewer of wood and drawer of water in this family, if you haven't noticed."

He rolls over, reaches a hand towards her. "You know, this is not normal."

"You got that right."

"I mean this tension between the two of you."

"Your teenage daughter is eight months pregnant," Liz says. "She has pre-eclampsia and she's on bed rest just below us. Would this be a good time for a big, cathartic cry fest? Is that what you're looking for?"

"No, I guess it's not," Aiden says, and forces himself to close his eyes.

Sylvie lasts until the Thursday of week thirty-seven, when her blood pressure goes nuts again and Liz and Aiden take her to the hospital.

Her doctor decides on an emergency C-section. While she's being prepped for surgery, Liz and Aiden sit in a waiting room at the end of the ward.

A nurse comes by and says, "You'll want to be with your daughter through the delivery. I'll be back in a while to get you ready."

"What does *you* mean?" Aiden says after the nurse is gone. "Both of us?"

"I have no idea." Liz fishes her cellphone out of her purse. She walks quickly down the hall towards the elevator to call Maggie.

"So?" he says when she's back.

"She'll try to get Noah on a flight. It probably won't be till tomorrow."

She gets some change from her purse and slips it into the slot of the coffee machine. A Styrofoam cup falls crookedly and rights itself, a stream of chemical whitener trickles out, a stream of coffee. She picks up the cup and swirls it to mix it. She takes a sip. Then she walks up the hall to the drinking fountain to dump it.

Aiden gets up and moves to the window. There's no sill for him to lean against. He tips his forehead against the glass, looking down at the flat roofs of the building next door, where furnace vents and air conditioning units compete for space. His dad is two floors up, in the extended care unit, in a locked ward because of his wandering. They're waiting for a bed in a nursing home. Meanwhile, he'll have these roofs to look at.

The window faces north and he can't gauge the time from the light. Sylvie was lying on her side when they left her room, about to have a catheter inserted. Her face was so puffy he could hardly recognize her. God knows, he doesn't want any part of this. Somewhere in the world there still exist maternity hospitals where families wait outside on the street, clutching flowers and stuffed animals. He read about one not long ago, in Kazakhstan or somewhere. When it's all over, a nurse comes to the window with the baby in a pink or blue blanket and gives them a wave.

He turns back from the window. Liz is sitting on a couch with her legs crossed, one foot swinging. Her face is cold. Everything is hard-edged in the light of his own anxiety – it's clear to him that he's failed to protect. He's always had an ease with Sylvie, he'll give himself that; he's always felt a sort of awe at this separate being who is so much like himself. The best tack, it seemed, was not to impose his own notions on her, not to impinge on the beautiful blossoming of her personality.

In point of fact, he seldom had a clue what was going on. One night at the lake they sat by the firepit all evening, not talking much. Eventually the mosquitoes drove Liz into the cabin, but Aiden and Sylvie sat on in the dark, still mostly in silence, dropping a log onto the fire now and then. There was no moon, and an owl was hooting softly across the narrows. Suddenly, out of nowhere, she dropped her head and began to cry. She sobbed and sobbed and she wouldn't talk. She was tall by then but she still had those wispy bits of hair along her hairline, the most tender hanger-on of childhood, and he was startled by how adult her weeping sounded, how perfectly it voiced what he felt about the end of her childhood. He wanted to carry her piggyback up to the cabin, the way he always did at night. When they got up to go in, he turned his back and stooped, but she just touched his shoulder in a gesture that seemed strangely mature and then walked up the path ahead of him. Still, he came in to tuck her into bed. Right away she curled up with her face away from him. He had to let her go – that's how he felt at the time. Into whatever it was, however much it scared her. But does any parent know for sure how to play something like that?

Four nurses, two on each side, roll Sylvie from her stretcher onto a narrow board. She has a tube up her nose and a tube in her arm and a tube wormed into her bladder or maybe even her kidneys. The operating room they call this place, but it's not a room. It's a sinister bright spaceship, or the inside of a freezer. It's cold, freezing cold, and music is playing. Celine Dion. That's what the baby will hear the instant she's born.

"Turn the fucking radio off!" Sylvie shrieks, and someone does.

She lies on the narrow board and people mill around her, all eyes. They lift her legs and arms, make small adjustments. Everything is known in this vicious light: How she likes to show off. How everything is a game to her. How secretly greedy she is, how hateful, her heart like a cold, hard stone.

Sylvie reaches out with her free hand and grabs a nurse's arm. "My mother," she says. "I want my mother."

8

The Good Life

THERE WOLSELEY LIES IN GOOGLE EARTH, A segment of orange tucked into a curve of the winding Assiniboine. Twenty-four streets, three blocks deep at most, bordered by the river on one side and Portage Avenue on the other, and close enough to downtown that you can walk. Close enough that you can *skate*, now that the city takes a Zamboni down onto the ice in the winter.

The neighbourhood was built more than a hundred years ago, for white-collar workers with aspirations. Its lots are narrow and on some streets the houses are resolutely simple in the Arts and Crafts tradition. But on the east–west avenues you see the money and ambition, the Queen Anne embellishments, like fish-scale patterns on the gables. In the course of things, many of the two- and three-storey houses were divided into suites and the usual atrocities were committed. Liz and Aiden bought into the area in the late eighties, a brick three-storey on a street that was mostly frame houses, a house with a wide veranda and an eyebrow window that surveyed the street from just above the eaves. It had beautiful mature elms in the yard and a brick garage on the back lane. They bought before the market heated up, they paid *nothing* for that house, and then they poured their money into restoring it.

Like it or not, they were part of a wave of gentrification. Everybody on the street was hauling construction materials out of Beaver Lumber on a daily basis, trying to contend with plaster-and-lath walls and galvanized plumbing and knob-and-tube wiring. So they had a lot in common, and some of their neighbours got right into the communal thing, tearing down the fences between those narrow lots, barbecuing bison burgers together on summer evenings, and feeding each other's roaming cats. Collectively, they fought the ugly monoculture of Kentucky bluegrass, transforming the boulevard into an exuberant block-long banner of lupins and poppies and bleeding heart and peonies.

Aiden was cautious. It irked him to think they'd bought a package – real property, lifestyle, friends, politics – all in one transaction, and after growing up in the city's working-class north end, he was embarrassed by Wolseley's earnestness, the bookstore full of crystals and tarot cards and Tibetan prayer flags, the women lying down in the street to stop Malathion trucks from rolling in when the city wanted to fog for mosquitoes, and all the petitions and charity drives and backyard clothing exchanges. They thought of themselves as socialists, but half of them owned cottages on some lake or other. For Christ's sake, they were living in houses built for families of ten and a hired girl.

He and Liz bought in Wolseley for two reasons: because Liz was keen – where else could you get this much character home for that kind of money? – and because the day she spotted the listing and talked Aiden into going to see the house, a strange thing happened. He parked in front of 385 Augusta and was instantly pulled back to the days when he'd been taken door to door witnessing for Jehovah, back when Wolseley seemed exotic to him. He followed the real estate agent up the front steps, and he remembered ringing the doorbell of a house with a veranda, and a woman inviting them in. He stood in a hall much like this one while his mother and her partner launched into their spiel, proffering *The Watchtower*. But all the woman's frowning attention was focused on him. "How old is this boy?" she asked, and then she bent over so she could look Aiden right in the eye. "Your mother should not be using you like this," she said. "It's very wrong. But one day you'll see a chance to get out. Make sure you take it. Run like hell, the minute you get the chance!"

Thirty years later, as the agent led them through the sunlit rooms of 385 Augusta, Aiden found himself thinking, with an agreeable sense of sliding towards the inevitable, This house. It was this house.

All in his mind, no doubt. But he couldn't deny that life in the granola belt was comfortable. On the tree-lined streets of Wolseley, beauty and goodness merged in a most pleasing fashion. He was glad to give his daughter all that, glad to spare her the cold pragmatism of the North End, even gladder she hadn't spent her childhood watching TV in a garage-faced monster home in a treeless suburb with no sidewalks.

And Sylvie was the sort of kid who occupied Wolseley fully. A vivid strawberry blond with a mobile face, rollerblading up the centre of the street, running their old dog Oscar off leash. Handing out brochures on how to lure swifts into your chimney. Tobogganing at the creek, walking with her hoe over her shoulder to the community gardens. Making friends right and left. Wolseley was a gift to a child, a place where people knew and loved her and believed in a better future, with communal beehives and chicken coops. When Aiden grasped (a bit late, he's prepared to admit) the primacy of those early years, he was relieved by how terrific a kid Sylvie had turned out to be, and he gave a lot of credit to the good-hearted countercultural vibe hanging over the neighbourhood, like chords from an acoustic banjo.

And he was right, Wolseley was in Sylvie's bones. The contours of the riverbank at Omand's Creek crept into every picture she drew. The old houses seemed right to her – This is what houses *are* – the garages that were once stables, the chalk-scrawled side-walks dappled with sunlight, tiny footprints where a squirrel had scampered across wet concrete. The neighbourhood was a map of memories, smudged with the colours of all the things she's felt. The Halloween she went out as Princess Furball and a guy in a Cyclops mask pelted towards her and wrenched the pillowcase of candy out of her hands – it's still here on this street, her outrage. Here, in this back lane, the wonder of finding a huge dead pine sawyer beetle (the one she varnished and kept as a scarab in a little round tin). Here's the house she loves best, where the guts of a grand piano lean against the veranda like a huge harp. Here's the Dumpster where one Mother's Day morning she ditched her white patent leather shoes with the bows on the toes so she wouldn't be forced to wear them to Nana Glasgow's. There's the path to the river, where she would crouch in the undergrowth in her secret den, hidden so deep she could believe she was lost. Here's where she saw a run-over squirrel writhing in the street and tried to catch it in a plastic bag to take to the vet. Here's where she was riding her bike when the sun glittered on the leaves of a lilac hedge and she understood about her mother: She doesn't like the kind of kid I am. Here's the park where they all faked epileptic seizures, thrashing around in the weeds, and wouldn't stop until they made Emily cry.

There's the gargoyle crouching on the Callaghans' veranda roof, a wicked face scaring wickedness away.

Thea lived three blocks away. All through grade six they put on plays on Saturday mornings, first in her basement and then in her yard. But by April, the *Buffy the Vampire Slayer* remakes and *Dr. Who* had fallen away. They were going to Gordon Bell High School in the fall. Something old had run its course, something unimaginable beckoned. Sylvie was feeling it and all her friends were too.

From Easter on they did nothing but weddings, building an elaborate set with fairy lights and white sheets draped over lawn chairs, fighting fiercely all week to be the one who stood under the arch with a hand tucked into Nathan's elbow. Sylvie loathed it. It embarrassed her – Jenn or Emily or Thea simpering as they strutted up the aisle, Celine Dion and the plastic flowers and the simulated kiss. Sylvie would only play the minister, who at least had lines that pleased her. The whole thing was childish – that's what she let on, but really what she deplored was the cheap splendour of the ceremony, stripped of the tests that should have come before: the noble prince riding his horse up a glass mountain, the princess hiding her true nature under mud and furs. Their glorious vindication, all wickedness revealed and punished. But how juvenile was that?

Then the summer came, and with relief she moved into another era, out at the old Fort. Even when she wasn't at work she tried to be Rachel McKenzie, the factor's daughter. She marvelled about riding in a car, for example, as if it were a crazy steam-punk invention. In bed at night, she read old books by candlelight. All of this drove her mother crazy, but her father thought it was very cool, and at first so did she. Then she outgrew her button boots and had to wear ballet slippers for the last month. She began to hate walking through the gate of those stone walls, thinking of the Scottish traders who had huddled inside, while outside, on the riverbank, an aboriginal family lived in a beautiful tepee. That family was kept out of the Fort – proof of the fearful, racist attitudes she, as the daughter of the factor, was supposed to share. She was officially sick to death of embroidering, sick of Rachel McKenzie, who, pestered by tourists asking the same boring questions, had less personality as every day went by.

And then that was over too. Sylvie had only a week before she started high school, and she and her mother went on a holiday alone together.

The highway they took was straight and smooth, and the Earth, Sylvie noted, was totally flat: ahead on the horizon, you could see trucks and cars racing along its straight-line edge. Sun shone on the pavement but the sky to the south was dark – it was as if they were driving under a portobello mushroom.

Sylvie had her dad's binoculars. He'd forgotten them the week before, when he hitched a ride up to the marina at Minaki, where he kept his canoe chained to a tree. The binoculars weren't as easy to use as she'd expected. They made *everything* bigger, including the huge, empty sky. You could see a pair of Canada geese perfectly with your bare eyes, but they vanished when you looked through the binoculars. Then suddenly you'd find yourself right up beside one of them, so close you could imagine you heard the creak of its wings.

"Does your dad know you have those?" Liz asked. Sylvie glanced down at her mother's platform sandal on the gas pedal, brown straw and wood. She herself was wearing the one new thing she had for high school: low-slung jeans with a beaded belt. There was to be a shopping trip, at the world's largest mall. If the sort of clothes Sylvie needed for her new life were to be found anywhere, apparently they would be found there, and her mother was the person to find them. Although maybe not. Her mother's slim legs were tanned, not white like Sylvie's, who had her dad's fair skin, and his eyes and body type and hair. Liz's hair was flame-coloured at the moment, and something snappish and hotter than usual radiated from her.

Sylvie lifted the binoculars back to her eyes. "He left them on the boot chest. He meant for me to bring them."

"Yeah, right." Liz was eating an apple. She finished it and opened her window, and the noise of the highway roared into the car.

Sylvie lowered the binoculars. "Hey!"

"It's an apple core."

"Mom! It will attract mice to the side of the road."

"Mice."

"And the mice will attract eagles. And the eagles will get hit by cars."

Eagles. The minute they crossed the border, she began to look carefully for signs of American culture, which, on her father's behalf, she intended to spend the weekend criticizing. Her father had been away most of the summer on his course, or else up at Grandpa's cabin at Otter Lake, which was now theirs. Sylvie's mother had spent the summer painting; she was totally redoing the house, as if hoping he wouldn't recognize it when he came home. When they were together they either walked around in silence or they argued. They fought over money – all the money her dad had spent on the cottage – or mostly they fought because her dad refused to argue about money. They fought because he was dropping out of his Ph.D. program to start again, training for a job her mother said would always be marginal. Even when they were just exercising their wits in the normal way, there was a nasty edge to the way they spoke. For example:

LIZ: I question whether children should be deprived of a happy childhood and its innocent pleasures because of their parents' politics.

AIDEN: Well, really, the question is whether any child would want to go to Disneyland without a lifetime of corporate propaganda.

LIZ: Is there a man alive who would see a Bose sound system as a vital necessity without a lifetime of corporate propaganda?

AIDEN: I have my own critical faculties where music is concerned, thanks. And I exercise them.

LIZ (*folding a leg lithely onto the lawn chair and examining her toenail polish*): I concede she's a little old for Disneyland. I think we should take her to the Renaissance Festival. It's just a day's drive, and she would love it. She deserves a holiday. And we can go to the Mall of America. Get our daughter some great new gear for junior high.

AIDEN: This thing's in Minnesota?

LIZ (*lifting her chin*): Yes.

AIDEN: You'd drive into the States?

LIZ: What do you mean?

AIDEN: Would you enter the borders of North Korea on holiday?

LIZ: It's hardly the same thing.

AIDEN: It was a stolen election and it's an unlawful regime. They're not getting a dollar of my money while that cross-eyed chimp is camped out in the White House.

LIZ: Well, as long as you're happy. Sylvie and I will just look after ourselves then, shall we?

As they drove, Sylvie expanded the lists in her Wonder Woman notebook. Of road kill. Of vanity plates. Of cool clothes she had seen people wearing. She maintained her lists and she worked on colouring an intricate stained-glass window with felt pens. It was a beautiful maiden and a hunter in furs, very challenging, but (she thought, slitting her eyes to blur the colours) it was still colouring; against all her resolve, she had brought along childish occupations.

They passed two trucks of pigs on the way to market, their backs pressed against the bars – Sylvie could see their swinish skin. "They have numbers written right on them," she said to her mother. "In blue ink. Don't you think that's insulting?"

"Mmm," her mother said. Sylvie thought about the fur loft at the Fort, stacked with glossy pelts from plank floor to ceiling, the poignant stolen treasure of beautiful animals, and the horror she'd felt when she spied their dangling tails with *price tags* tied to them.

They passed an old-fashioned gas station with a yellow dog lying on its side on the gravel in front. Sylvie studied the dog, which was not leashed. "That dog is dying," she said. "It must have been hit by a car."

"Mm-hmm," her mother said.

"Mom," she said. "Do you think dogs go to heaven?"

"Mmm."

"Do you?"

"Do I what?"

"Think dogs go to heaven?"

"Heaven? What are you, Sylvie, six?"

Finally she said, "Why don't you read to me." Sylvie fished *Sabriel* out of the mess at her feet and opened it at the beginning. As she read, Liz cruised along with her head tipped against the headrest and a remote expression on her face. A few pages in, Sylvie started weaving some of her own lines into the novel, keeping her voice perfectly even ("especially those new products from Safeway, that you can buy with a coupon and serve to your guests after the theatre, as long as you remember to spray them with insect repellent and keep zombies and vampires out of the fridge"). Liz's listening expression did not change in the least, and Sylvie understood with a deep ache why her mom had asked her to read aloud. She put down the book. That got Liz's attention. "Had enough?" she said. Sylvie didn't answer.

They never actually drove into the storm they'd seen in the morning, but over and over, all day, the sky changed and the mood of the day changed with it. Sleep tugged at Sylvie, and when she opened her eyes again, the prairies and farmland were gone; they'd entered a forest. On either side stood massive trees of verdant green, with red and yellow patches hanging here and there in their upper branches. Not trees with needles, just great, spreading maples or oaks (what were they? she longed to know), each separate tree a towering goddess, and crammed so close together that they made a solid wall of green. She'd never seen such a forest, yet she knew exactly what it would be like to walk into it – the canopy shutting out the sky, the ferns and secretive toadstools in the darkness below, the scampering animals – and she pressed against the window in astonishment as they drove on.

THY PORTRAIT IN RENAISSANCE DRESS WHILE THOU DOST WAIT. Sylvie dragged her mother over to the booth. *Whilst*, it should be, her mother pointed out.

The guy working the booth had tufted red hair and a crooked smile. He was trying to deal with a lot of customers at once, darting back and forth from one group to the next. "If you folks need any high-pressure sales tactics here, you just let me know," he said as he went by.

"No, we don't," Sylvie said quickly to get him to stay. "We already want to do it."

Liz opened her eyes wide with an annoyed and helpless look. The costumes were just fronts with Velcro fasteners at the back, and you put them on over your clothes. Velvet and silk low-necked gowns for women, little-girl dresses. Sylvie found a boy's *veston* and a chain-mail hood that she liked a lot, and the guy let her wear it.

Afterwards, her mother put the folder with the picture in her bag and they continued browsing along the circle of shops. Then they took a wrong turn and ended up where they had started. Liz spied a rough castle called Chateau Vino and said she was going to sit down and have a drink. She gave Sylvie ten dollars to spend, which, added to the money Sylvie already had, meant she was carrying a fortune.

It was better without her mother. There were moments when the dust stirred up by all the soft leather shoes hung in the sunbeams and you really thought you were in a Renaissance market. The costumes were wonderful. Little dogs were dressed like Elizabethan courtiers, with ruffs around their necks. At a snake display, huge cream-coloured pythons writhed around their owners' necks and shoulders, and a contortionist made similar lithe and muscular movements on a stage. The rides were powered by strong men in pantaloons. Water had to be hauled in this world, like at the Fort, and wood had to be chopped, but it was a world full of magic. It was full of adults having fun. What kids there were tended to be fairies – more like *faeries*, which is the way she saw the word when they had garlands of fruit and flowers in their hair and wings made of overlaid transparent leaves.

A beautiful woman with a garlanded head approached two children. She was a faery herself and she couldn't speak, but she beckoned the children away, dancing backwards through the crowd, and their parents followed, exchanging amused glances. Then Sylvie noticed a blindfolded man with hands and feet tied, lying on a cart, and a group of people jeering at him, spitting on him. She began to wish she'd come when she was small, instead of now, when she was almost as tall as her mother. She was too old for the rides and the faeries; she was too young for the adult games.

Then she saw a faun wearing horns, a girl around her age with shoes made like hoofs, being held by the wrist by an adult as though she'd been captured and dragged into this babbling human market. The faun turned her face and met Sylvie's eyes with an expression of wildness and bafflement. Not long after that, Sylvie spied a rack of small horns in a shop, and that's what she spent a chunk of her money on. They were made of clay, glazed greyish white, and they looked exactly like animal horns. Their elastic was hidden by your hair.

When Sylvie got back to Chateau Vino, her mother was sitting on a stool and a minstrel was singing to her – *Catherine, would you do it again, fall in love with an awkward man?* – looking deep into her eyes, and she had a strange, inward expression. Sylvie waited until he'd gone and then she leaned against Liz's shoulder and knee, doing the little girl thing in spite of herself.

"Great horns."

"Thanks."

"Are you tired of it yet?"

"Nope."

"Well, maybe another hour, eh? And then we're going to go see a friend of mine."

Sylvie stood up. "What friend?"

Her mother said something she didn't catch.

"What friend?" Sylvie asked again.

"I said, someone I know through Esme Gwynn. A filmmaker, a really interesting person. Might as well visit while we're so close."

Sylvie wandered back into the market. She saw a shop full of snow domes of fairies. The faery queen she'd seen enticing children into the market was standing flat-footed by the cash register.

"Twenty-nine ninety-five," she was saying to a pissed-off-looking father. "Or I can give you two for fifty dollars. Just 'cause those girls are so adorable. What do you say?"

Sylvie stood at the fence of the play area and looked into the weary eye of the elephant. She drifted through the food kiosks where adults were drinking tankards of ale and chomping on smoked turkey drumsticks. *Legges.* She thought of her father, alone in a silent landscape of rocks and spruce. He was so far away it might be morning where he was; she could see him standing on the step of the cottage with a mug of coffee in his hand. She went back into the market and bought a net bag of chocolate gold sovereigns. Then she bought a pewter pendant, a bat with folded wings, hanging from a twig.

She still had fourteen dollars but she couldn't be bothered to spend it. Finally she wandered back to Chateau Vino and agreed to leave. Liz asked a guy in an information booth where the exit was. "You got any money left?" the guy at the booth said humorously. "Because I'm afraid I can't let you out until you've spent it all."

Liz called her friend from the vast parking lot to get directions. She put on a lively expression as if she thought this friend could actually see her. Leaning against the car, peeling the gold foil from one of her chocolate sovereigns, Sylvie watched women wearing hoop skirts and velvet bustles climb into their suvs. She placed the chocolate coin on her tongue, and as it lost its shape, she saw her mother's face go from excited to tense. A picture rose in her mind of the three of them – Liz, Aiden, and her – sitting in the living room. The blinds closed, the TV turned off. She's crying and her parents lean forward, each of them taking one of her hands. It's not you, it's us, they explain.

Then Liz snapped her phone shut and said they'd go back to the motel for the night and visit her friend the next day. She scrawled directions on the festival program and dropped it into the pocket of the door.

"You know, I wasn't thinking straight," she said as she started the car. "There's no point shopping in the U.S. on Sunday. All the best stores are closed."

Sylvie lifted her bat pendant and pressed it to her chin, daring her mother to dig deeper.

And she did. "Americans go to church," she said. "They still do the Lord's Day thing."

They followed a narrow road to the highway. The sky was clear and the sun was low. Black dogs of shadow bounded along the gravel shoulder, racing neck-and-neck with each vehicle. Sylvie turned the binoculars on one but she couldn't catch it. She was wearing her horns, but she was leaving the festival the same girl who walked in.

9

Goodnight Moon

SPRING'S ARRIVED. THE SNOW'S VANISHED FROM the lawn, leaving behind a ghostly mould like a collapsed parachute. Buds swell on the ornamental plums and raindrops meander down the windowpanes. From the speakers in the Glasgow-Phimister living room, Joni is singing about the crocuses she'll bring to school tomorrow. And on the coffee table, in a nest of eyelet cotton and white wicker, spring's crowning specimen lies. Aiden can hardly look at her petal face for the clamour that starts up in him.

Krzysztof Nowak's mother has been driven over for a formal viewing. No baby-kissing for her – she takes one skeptical look and hobbles straight to a chair. Noah touches a hand to Sylvie's shoulder and walks towards the fireplace, studying the baby from a distance. But Natalie, his half-sister, runs across the carpet and leans over the bassinette, putting her face right next to the baby's.

"She smiled!" she cries.

"It's your smile she can't resist," Maggie says. "From the minute babies are born, they mirror our expressions."

Sylvie's in the Mission chair with an afghan over her lap. She's a mermaid washed up onshore, the flotsam and jetsam of the occasion all around her: a wooden rattle painted pink and cream, a mobile with seven belugas lying jumbled as though caught in a net. Three sleepers, four dresses with matching panties, three squeeze toys. Natalie shyly brings over her gift. A board book, *Goodnight Moon*. Thank you.

Rain thrums against the window and the room goes dim. Can Maggie pick up the baby? Yeah. And can Natalie hold her? Uh-huh. Natalie sits very still, her little arms full to capacity and her feet sticking straight out in fuchsia tights. Her face is like Noah's when they put a pale yellow gown on him at the hospital and he sat in an armchair and held the baby. Grave. Inquiring. Unscathed.

MAGGIE: That's a beautiful little quilt, Liz. Did you make it?

LIZ: Thanks, I did. While Sylvie was on bed rest, those last few weeks. A tiny quilt like that doesn't take long to run up.

The irises Maggie brought have found their way into a vase – Chilean irises, lifting their sharp purple beaks into the northern air. The *baba* sits with both hands on the head of her cane. She's dressed as if she just got off a steamship from Gdansk. A doorbell rings on the sound track in Sylvie's brain, but someone else hears and answers it. More flowers – pink roses and baby's breath – from Auntie Maureen in Toronto. It rings again and Wendy from next door dashes in with an octopus she made for the baby out of purple yarn. She dangles her hand into the bassinette and the baby clasps one finger. The adults smile at each other across the kilim rug. It's a reflex, they say, all babies do it.

Then George Oliphant is in the archway. "Congratulations, little mama." A new George, with short hair and a soul patch and glasses with big black frames. Patti in a yellow slicker. With great ceremony they present a silver baby cup. "We would've had it engraved," Patti says, "but we didn't know her name."

"That's all right," Sylvie says. "Nobody does." She pushes at the pile of gifts to make room, and *Goodnight Moon* falls. She starts to bend for it, but black threads of pain pull at her stomach. She sits back.

"So where did this little critter come from?" George asks.

"We don't know," Aiden says. "We childproofed the house but she got in anyway."

PATTI *(to Noah)*: Were you with Sylvie, dear? When the baby was born?

NOAH: No, I didn't get home in time.

AIDEN: Liz was with Sylvie, holding her hand through the whole thing. I ended up in the triage area, but that was great too. They brought the baby there almost right away.

PATTI: How much does she weigh?

LIZ *(tossing proprietary happiness like fairy dust across the room)*: Six pounds, three ounces. She would have been huge if she had gone full-term. And her APGAR was *seven*, which is amazing under the circumstances.

WENDY: What does APGAR stand for again?

LIZ: Let me see. *(She holds up her fingers, rhymes off some words.)*

AIDEN: Grimace? G for grimace?

LIZ: They like an irritated baby. It's considered a very good sign. And who wouldn't be irritated after going through all that?

MAGGIE *(lifting the baby from Natalie's arms and cradling her like an expert)*: It's kind of telling, isn't it. Hospitals just assume babies have to be traumatized. By a natural process. I had both kids at home. Natalie is a little fish – she was born in the bathtub, and it was lovely! For all of us. So peaceful. Noah was there, weren't you, honey.

WENDY: How many times was she up last night?

SYLVIE: Twice.

LIZ: She wakes up and nurses and goes straight back to sleep. Of course, it's early days.

PATTI: And how are *you*, sweetie?

SYLVIE: I'm fine.

LIZ: She is doing just great. We are so proud of her, the way she is handling everything.

PATTI: I'll tell you the secret, Sylvie. Eat, sleep, poo. Forget everything else. Be a mother grub.

MAGGIE: It's so important, breastfeeding. If you can keep from supplementing, even just a little. They're seeing a lot of necrotizing colitis in preemies, and it's all from using cow's-milk-based formula.

LIZ: This baby is not that premature.

AIDEN: When Sylvie was born, I was reading Rousseau. I had the idea our kid would eat the instant she was hungry, sleep when she was tired, follow the lead of her own desires, and be a happy child of nature.

PATTI: And how did that work out?

AIDEN: Aw, who remembers those early days?

PATTI *(cackling)*: I bet Liz does!

GEORGE: So, kid, when you off to Africa?

NOAH: I'm not going. I'm working at Presley Point again.

GEORGE: Didn't get into the program?

NOAH: I got in but I turned it down.

GEORGE: Hey, dude, that's sweet! You can work my booth at the Folk Fest.

PATTI: You're *pale*, though, darling. Did you lose a lot of blood?

LIZ: It always makes the recovery harder, doesn't it, when the mom has to have a Caesarean. Not every woman can have the luxury of a home birth.

PATTI: At least she didn't have to go through labour first. I was in *hell* for sixteen hours when Troy was born. Back pain – did any of you girls have back pain? Oh god, I practically chewed his daddy's hand off! Turns out I was fully dilated but it wasn't enough – well, look at the size of me – and then all of a sudden they're wheeling me into surgery. And here the suction thing breaks down, and by the time they get that little bugger out of me, the doctors are *wading* through blood. Those cloth booties they wear? They were absolutely soaked.

AIDEN: All right, everybody – time for bubbly!

It's real Champagne for once. He's twisting the muzzle off the first bottle, the flutes are at the ready on a tray, and George Oliphant is up like a shot, snatching the bottle from Aiden, heading for the kitchen. Then he's back in the archway with a butcher knife in hand, he's sabre-slashing the glass neck, and Champagne bursts from the glass throat and splashes wildly over the flutes. They dodge flying glass, they cheer, and George decapitates the second bottle. They lift their flutes to the baby, awake and remote, still half in another world.

Aiden cranks up the music. He's got a mix on: this is Shivaree's big hit, *Goodnight Moon*. Some of them know it and they start to laugh. Aiden turns to the little girl on the couch and puts out a hand. "I believe this is your song, Auntie Natalie," he says. She jumps up to dance and he looks over her head at Sylvie and winks.

Liz and Wendy took belly-dancing classes together long ago, and they raise their arms and undulate. George and Patti start to move with the stoned look of old hippies, and Max scrambles to his feet and barks. Sylvie angles her legs out of the way (*Your stitches are tearing, Sylvie*). Sparky's up – his mother's dragged him up – and Sylvie feels wonder at the sight of him in his clean jeans and worn plaid shirt, still encased in his old life. He looks her way with eyes that beg for rescue, and the sexy voice from *Kill Bill* drips down the windows (*What will I do, I'm just a little baby*), and in the bassinette on the coffee table their own baby lies, her profile perfect and white and her fists waving. Behind her floats the face of the granny, scowling. She's daring Sylvie to pick up the baby. Sylvie stares back. She's beyond me, she says with her eyes. Look at her, she's far beyond my feeble love. Then the doorbell in Sylvie's head rings again, and she hoists herself out of the chair and goes out to the hall.

A man is standing on the veranda, a bulky man with dark greying hair and a shadowed face. Sylvie opens the door. "Krzysztof," he says, in careless impersonation of a total stranger. "Sylvie?" he pretends to guess. He tosses his wet jacket on the banister and runs a hand through his hair. Maggie's in the archway and he drops a kiss on her lips, then steps into the living room, where Liz is at the bassinette fussing with the blue and red quilt. She darts a glance in his direction and then she straightens up and works her way through the crowd to be introduced, a half-smile on her face and Sylvie's sleeping baby as tender camouflage on her shoulder, and all the quiet treachery of the day finds its focus at last.

A party at 385 Augusta . . . how long has it been? For a few years they had a great thing going with Peter Kohut, a guy Aiden knew from high school. What a brilliant guitarist that guy turned out to be. He'd show up with some musician buddies and people would stream in from all over the neighbourhood, and they'd get a bounce going on the hardwood floor. One morning Liz and Aiden came downstairs and found three characters they'd never clapped eyes on before, sleeping in the living room. But then Wendy came to a party and started handing out singalong sheets for "Big Yellow Taxi," and that was the day the music died.

Oh, well, Aiden's got a pretty good ear for a playlist. David Lindley now, doing his California thing with reggae. Aiden's squeezed into a corner of the living room, drinking Corona with Patti. Patti turns to him with liquid eyes and says, "He was the third one to go," and next thing he knows she's vanished and he's been teleported into the hall, where he stands with a welcome-to-summer G and T in hand. The front door is propped open, watery light pours in, and Tracy Chapman is begging them for one more reason to stay. These lovely little folds in time – he only ever has them at parties.

He sips his G and T and watches Noah move along the veranda railing, passing around a box of Cubans in his courteous fashion. The other grandpa brought the cigars: George is all over the chance to show off his prowess with a smoke ring. Lucky Patti's made it outside – there she stands in a clean and sparkling world – and Liz is up at the end, doing her sexy shtick with a cigar. "When Sylvie was born, I was in labour so long they had to shave me twice," she deadpans in Patti's direction. It's an old line she stole from *Ab Fab*, but everybody falls against the rail laughing.

Whereas Aiden's marooned in the entranceway with the brooding Slavic artist, who's standing with his eyes on the Afghan prayer rug, sucking back a tumbler of Glendronach from what Aiden has always considered his secret stash.

"Machine guns," Aiden says. "Helicopters. AK-47s."

Krzysztof does the three-second pause that lets you know your place in the Doric temple of his thought. "Beg your pardon?"

"The designs in the prayer rug. It was apparently made while the Soviets were having a go at Afghanistan."

"Hmm." Krzysztof frowns, looks closer. "How'd you end up with it?"

"Bought it at an auction in the ballroom of the Marlborough

Hotel. I can't say I've quite got my mind around it. You are standing on a symbol of my moral confusion."

Krzysztof barks dryly.

"So, you working on something at the moment?" Aiden asks.

"Yes, of course."

"What's the premise of this one?"

"Um, it's, uh, kind of a post-urban fantasy set in the bush. About a post-tech society."

He's got a slight accent and a modest, almost ingratiating way of speaking, but Aiden's been around, he knows this tone as a further refinement of ego. "What happens?" he asks. Artists hate this question, in his experience.

"Uh, a father takes his kid on a hunting expedition, they're desperate for food, and the kid becomes his prey."

Aiden turns back to gaze out at the veranda, where water drips in a silver chain from the lowest point of the plugged and sagging eaves. "It's a psychological thriller?"

"I'm not really into psychology."

He hasn't shown a flicker of interest in Aiden or what he does. "You think it's plausible," Aiden asks, "on the face of it, for a father to go after his kid with a rifle? However hungry?"

"I'm interested in the anarchy of the post-apocalyptic scene. The aesthetics of anarchy, I guess you could say."

The Road: The Next Generation?"

Krzysztof looks at him with open distaste. Aiden turns to peer towards the kitchen, thinking, Eat something. He can tell that Liz ransacked the place for snacks, though he hasn't laid his hands on as much as a cracker. When she invited people, she said, "Stop by and take a peek," specifying after dinner so they'd arrive fed. But then Maggie showed up with her crew about four-thirty (didn't she purport to know the best hour in a baby's biorhythms?) and they're all starving, and now it's seven-thirty and the second wave has hit – happy partiers who ate at home and are settling in for the night.

Somebody's turned the music right up. The baby's crying. Aiden checks the living room. Still filled with yakking women, women from SERC bonding with women from the neighbourhood. The granny hasn't moved from her chair. The last time he caught sight of Sylvie, she was enduring Wendy's account of making the yarn octopus, and she was white as a ghost. But he can't see her now. Maybe she's changing the baby.

He turns back to Krzysztof. "So what caused the big collapse?"

"Collapse?"

"The apocalypse. In your film."

"Oh. Oh, I don't go there."

Aiden drains his drink, grabs the shard of lime with his teeth, bites into it for its food value. "With all due respect," he says, "I don't grasp a story about human behaviour that's indifferent to the human mind and human feelings. I'm trying to remember a film of yours I saw at Cinematheque a long time ago. A bunch of kids out in the bush being killed off one by one. By animals?"

"No, they offed each other."

Aiden hears the baby's crying torque up. He and Krzysztof have drifted up the hall and he can't see if Liz is still out on the veranda. "So again," he says, "it could have been a psychological thriller."

"Not really. If you recall, they were taken over by totems."

"Some sort of malignant force of nature?"

"I don't like to talk about my work in thematic terms. But yeah, I am interested in notions of wilderness."

"The aesthetics of wilderness?"

"Beg your pardon?"

"You're interested in the aesthetics of anarchy. So I presume you're also into the aesthetics of wilderness."

Krzysztof doesn't deign to answer. He lifts his shoulders wordlessly to withdraw from the conversation. He'll be used to being God in his own little world.

Aiden takes an involuntary step closer. "You know, fear is big. I get why you want to scare the shit out of people. But ever consider making a film about real stuff?"

"What are you talking about?"

"You have to ask me what real stuff is?"

"I'm asking you what you're talking about."

The women from the living room have drifted to the archway. They're hearing a baby in distress; they look around anxiously. Their eyes snag on Krzysztof and Aiden.

"Okay," Aiden says. "For example, what it's going to mean when the arctic ice is gone and the poles start absorbing heat instead of deflecting it."

"You want a film about ice," Krzysztof says, "maybe you should make it yourself."

"Hey, excuse me. I'm asking you a question about your work, seeing you dismissed mine out of hand."

"I'm an artist. I'm not a scientist. I'm not an ideologue." His boyhood in Sevastopol or wherever is seeping into his speech.

"An artist has a vision of the world."

Krzysztof turns to face Aiden, as if he's squaring off. "You want me to tell you what I see?"

"Sure, by all means."

"I see a man who's getting old, who sees his own death staring him in the face, and decides the planet is going down with him. You think the world's coming to an end. Every generation thinks that – a certain type of mind in every generation. It's just not my subject."

"But it is your subject." *Asshole.* "Your film's about the end of the world."

Then Maggie's there and the baby's on her shoulder, her whole tiny body clutched into a spasm of squalling. "This. Infant. Is. Starving. And she needs changing. I can't find a diaper. Sylvie's in the washroom in your kitchen. She's extremely upset."

He goes to the kitchen. Noah's little sister is sitting on the floor outside the pantry, swinging the purple octopus like a pendulum between two of its braided tentacles. "Your baby's crying and you're crying," she says sweetly into the confessional.

Aiden can see Sylvie's bare feet under the half-doors. He waggles the doors: there's a half-inch of play in the sliding bolt. "What's up, sweetheart?"

Sylvie opens the door and falls against him, sobbing.

"Come on, let's get you up to your room," he says, putting an arm around her shoulder. They start up the stairs. Natalie follows, and Max, and Maggie with the screaming baby. Faces in the hall lift to watch their reproachful parade.

At the door of Sylvie's room, Aiden tries to takes the baby from Maggie. "No, I'll settle them," she says. "Why don't you get Sylvie something to eat."

Liz is still out on the veranda. "Our daughter needs attention," he says. She turns a startled face in his direction, follows him inside, and makes a move towards the stairs. "It's okay, Maggie's with her. But she needs to eat. What have we got?"

When he comes back upstairs with a plate from the microwave and a glass of milk, Sylvie is sitting in the rocking chair in her terry robe, nursing the baby. Her face is swollen but her sobs have stilled.

"Terrific," Aiden says to Maggie. "Thank you."

"Oh, no worries," she says, getting up off the bed. "Like they say, it takes a village." She leans over and gives Sylvie a hug. "This was way too much, wasn't it. I know you need quiet. You're going to need lots of time to heal. And lots of support." She's talking tenderly into

Sylvie's face, nose to nose. "And we are here for you. You remember that, eh? We're all just a phone call away." At the door she stands for a minute, including Aiden in her reproving sympathy. "My numbers are there," she says, nodding towards Sylvie's desk. "Work, home, cell. Anytime, eh?" Then she's gone.

The desk is cluttered with baby things, gifts. Aiden shoves them over and perches on it. He picks up a stuffed pig and turns it in his hands, keeping his eyes cast tactfully down, although Sylvie has a shawl draped over her shoulder. Below them, the music turns off. Liz said she would send everyone on their way. The silence is impressive. Maggie is right – it was too much. It's as if Liz was desperately signalling to their friends, We are not at all ambivalent about this baby. And he's ashamed of that pissing match in the hall. He waits for Sylvie to lift her head and meet his eyes, but she won't.

"Did something happen, honey? Was it Noah?"

She shakes her head. "I'm just tired," she says after a minute, in a little voice.

"Why didn't you slip out? You could have come up here with the baby."

"You guys were standing at the stairs."

This is what he and Liz used to call ego disintegration time – they read it in a book. "It's pretty overwhelming, I know," he says. "But look at that baby. She's fine now. It's wonderful, the way you can meet her needs. And she meets yours too. You sit holding her like that and she warms your heart. Literally."

"I wish I could lie in bed and feed her."

"She's a little young for that. And so are you. I know the way you sleep."

"Dad, do you think she can see yet?"

"Sylvie. Honey. Of course she can see. Maybe you're thinking of kittens."

He watches her, shaken. She seems to be coping most of the time, and until now she's been in reasonable spirits. But there have been troubling lapses. The name thing, for one. The whole week at the hospital, Sylvie refused to discuss the name, or she joked about it. Evo-Devo was a big contender. As luck would have it, he was alone with her the night a nurse brought the birth registration forms to the room. Sylvie scrawled something on the form and went back to eating her Jell-O. He picked it up and read it out.

"Whatever," she said. "It's rude, sticking a name on another human being. Especially when you don't know what sort of person she's going to be. When she's old enough, she can name herself. There's a culture that does that. I wish I could remember which one."

"What does Noah think?"

"He doesn't care."

Liz hit the roof when he told her. Well, first she heard it as *Fawn*. "Fawn Phimister?" she said in disbelief.

"Yup."

"You have got to be kidding. That's the worst name I have ever heard, bar none."

"Well, it's a different generation," Aiden said gamely. "I guess it sounds good to her."

Liz had just come in from her meeting and was standing with her coat on. He beckoned for her to come and sit on the arm of his chair, but she stayed on her feet in the archway.

"Is it some sentimental reference to Bambi?"

"I doubt it. Bambi was before *our* time. Anyway, it's not the baby deer. It's F-A-U-N."

"Faun Phimister."

"Yup."

"What's the middle name?"

"No middle name. I'm not sure she took it seriously. She was kind of in a mood."

"Oh, for god's sake." Liz leaned into the frame of the pocket doors and closed her eyes.

In fact they never use the name. They say Pumpkin, or Angel, or they just say "the baby." Sylvie herself does not use it. "I am watching this girl like a hawk for postpartum depression," Liz says to Aiden every day. Well, so is he.

The feeding is almost finished. It looks to Aiden as though the baby is drifting off. Sylvie lifts a finger and gently touches her cheek. That's a good sign.

"Let me take her," he says. "You need to eat your supper."

"I have to burp her."

"I can do that."

He lays the warm little bundle on a towel over his shoulder and pats her back until she pukes up a teaspoon of hot milk. Then he changes her again, and Sylvie eats her warmed-up lasagna and drinks her milk and crawls into bed. It's a piece of cake changing this baby, what with the Velcro tabs. She kicks her white legs vigorously at him. We're fine, he tells himself. We're all fine. The elms have died and the valleys in B.C. have all turned brown, but nature can still do perfection. He picks her up gently and walks her around the room, and she's asleep by the time he lays her in the crib.

"Are you going to be all right, honey?" he asks, his hand on the light switch.

"Oh, who knows?" Sylvie says, but she manages a little smile.

Three o'clock. Sylvie sits up in bed and turns on the lamp and looks at the squalling baby in the bassinette. Her incision hurts like crazy and she feels hollowed out from all her crying. It's cold in her room, so she pulls on her robe and sticks her feet in her slippers. She picks up the baby the way they taught her, as though her head is in danger of falling off, and moves carefully over to the rocking chair.

Bracing herself, she slides up her T-shirt and thrusts her left nipple at the baby's mouth. The baby jerks her head as though Sylvie is tormenting her, but at the second try she grabs on, and Sylvie feels the shock that hits her every time, that her stretched and beat-up and sliced-open body should be used like this by another human being. Everybody takes it for granted. Her own body takes it for granted – her boobs, for example, which are big and hard as rocks. "She drinks it just like it's the real thing," she said to her dad at breakfast, and he looked startled and said, "Sylvie, honey, it is the real thing." Apparently she's no longer allowed to make jokes.

What freaks her out most is the baby's eyes. Just now when the light came on, she didn't as much as flinch. There's never been any evidence that she can see – except, come to think of it, how scared she looked once when Sylvie bent over the bassinette. What Maggie said at the party explained that: the baby was mimicking Sylvie's expression. Her eyes are half-open now, and Sylvie reaches over and turns off the lamp. In the dark the baby settles into her meal, sucking rhythmically, and an ache starts up in Sylvie's abdomen, the way it always does when she nurses. Then she feels a light touch, as though a butterfly has landed on her. The baby has reached up and put a tiny hand on Sylvie's breast, as if to comfort her. Warmth spreads through Sylvie's body, and she bends her head, taking in the baby's smell.

She's just about to make the switch to her other breast when she hears footsteps on the stairs. The door opens all the way, letting in yellow light, and Liz is standing there in her blue silk robe. Sylvie clenches her toes in the sheepskin lining of her slippers.

"Why are you sitting in the dark?" Liz's hand moves towards the light switch.

"Don't!"

"Oh, okay." Liz walks over to the bed and sits on the edge, where a few hours earlier Maggie sat talking in her soft voice. Her black shadow leans against the far wall.

"You don't need to sit with me."

"No, it's all right. I wasn't sleeping anyway."

She's brought the stale nasty smell of cigars into the room. Sylvie puts up her hand like an awning over the baby's face, as though she can filter the air with her fingers.

"I'm sorry tonight was so tough," Liz says. "We should never have had that many people over, or let them stay so long. I don't know what we were thinking." The blue robe she's wearing is the one thing she owns that Sylvie has always secretly loved. In the dim light she can see the red flowers and vines twining over it. "It's so great to have you home. You know, honey, being with you during the delivery was pretty much the most beautiful thing that has happened to me in my adult life. I want to thank you for inviting me to be there."

"Yeah, well, people about to have their stomachs cut open will say anything."

Liz ignores this. She reaches across from the bed and touches the baby's foot, and then she presses damp fingers onto Sylvie's hand. Her robe sags open, showing the shallow channel between her breasts. "I have loved these past few weeks, Sylvie. It's been so special being able to give you support. And tonight I'm scared we're going to lose that. I couldn't get to sleep just now. I guess it was seeing Krzysztof come in that brought back that whole terrible trip to Minneapolis."

Sylvie starts to rock herself in the chair (Fuck off, just fuck off, she breathes), but the smooth, sinuous rope of Liz's voice keeps on winding, tightening around her. "And so I just want to say I really hope we can put it all behind us. The trip, the whole thing. Because I can't help but feel that it changed things for us. You know, you were only ten or eleven. You don't know what happened, and you don't have any idea what it—"

Her voice comes out as a roar. "I know exactly what happened! I know exactly what it meant! But you know what else? I don't give a shit. It has nothing to do with me. So fuck off. Just fuck right off about it. Live your own sick life and leave me out of it."

Liz bends forward on the bed and the black shadow bends over her. Fuck off and play by yourself, loser, the faun whispers in admiration.

Sylvie has stopped rocking. She *is* hollow, she doesn't feel a thing. Just fingers of cold air on her ribs . . . *The baby*, she thinks with a shudder. It's still there, a weight along her arm. It's not moving, its lips are slack around Sylvie's nipple. "Oh god!" she shrieks, jerking it up in horror. The baby's head flops and she starts to cry, and then her mother's bending over her, talking in a low voice, lifting the screaming baby out of her arms.

10

Free Will

THE NEW MOM IS LEARNING TO DRIVE. HER PARents bombard her with arguments and she doesn't have the energy to resist them. She walks into the licence bureau determined to blow the written test, but it's ludicrously simple and she's not smart enough to figure out how to get it wrong. So then she has her learner's and she goes out practice driving with her dad while her mother minds the baby. "You're a natural," Aiden says as she zips down Osborne.

Women are in and out of the house all day – Wendy, Maggie, Genevieve, other women from SERC. They float in with arms full of useless consumer goods and croon over the baby and gush about her poop and the way she sleeps and nurses. And the new mom is doing just great too, after a few wobbles at the beginning. That's what they all say, planting kisses on Sylvie's cheek. She's a plaything for Liz and her cronies (the old crones) and no one, not even her dad, gives a shit. No one gets what's going on – that Sylvie's been turned into the sort of person who drives a carbon-spewing car, for example – not one of them cares enough to intervene. No one gives a shit that she's forced to live in the litter of Liz's material excess, with piles of wet wipes and used Kleenex around her; that she's constantly subjected to hypocrisy and ignorant opinions and the smell of frying bacon; that she has, in other words, totally vanished, leaving in her place the sort of person she and her friends have always despised – a pathetic teenager with shit for brains who worries about her weight and shape and checks her phone every half-hour to see if her boyfriend has texted her. Who sits in the upstairs bathroom devouring her mother's *Elle*. Who filches bacon in a paper towel, standing in the kitchen toilet to eat it. A loser who watches reality television hour after hour. That's to barricade herself from Liz, who rarely goes to work, and whose phony caretaking zeal infiltrates every room of the house, forcing Sylvie to close her door and sprawl on her bed watching *What Not to Wear* reruns, mostly for the moment when the victim (usually overweight and always desperate to be special or even outrageous) is led to a mirror to see her new demure, kitten-heeled self and begins to cry with happiness and relief. Sylvie watches hungrily, turning a deaf ear to the baby's fussing, trying to figure out: is anything left of who these women were?

It's still cold but it's already June. Her girlfriends, everyone but Kajri, come over to the house to visit. They crowd into the hall and hug Sylvie, and their hair gives off the childhood smell of spring from their bike ride over. They hand her a baby outfit they found at Value Village. They sit in the living room and steal curious looks at Sylvie, and they pass the baby around and swoon over her. "She's awesome," they say.

"Yeah," Sylvie says.

"Look at her *eyelashes*," they say.

"I know," Sylvie says.

Somehow, visiting Sylvie gets them talking about *The Sims*. "I had three kids," Thea says. "I gave them free will, because it makes the game more interesting, and they drove me crazy."

"What do you mean, free will?" someone asks.

"They could take snacks from the fridge, that sort of thing, but they didn't really look after themselves. If you didn't take them to the bathroom, they peed on the floor."

"I know, it was gross," Jenn says. "I couldn't deal with it. But I loved that game for all the stuff you could buy and the way you could fix up your house. Let's face it, it was like playing Barbie and Ken. But without the sex, ha ha!"

"They could have sex. My couple had sex." This is Ashley, lounging on the couch with her feet on the coffee table. She starts in on the story but Thea talks over her in her big voice.

"I got rid of my kids."

"How? The game won't let you do it."

"There's ways posted online. If you don't clean their hamster cage, the hamster will get an infection and bite them and they'll die."

"Or you can put them in the swimming pool and take out the ladder," Jenn says. "That's what I did."

"You *drowned* them?"

"Yup. One by one. They flailed around for a long time before their little arms finally sank under the water. It was kind of thrilling, in an evil way."

And then embarrassment covers all their faces, it suddenly clicks with them how insensitive this is. So they jump into another round of elaborate compliments about the baby in the bassinette – Sylvie's surprisingly real baby, who's lying there dozing with her eyelids half closed and flickering.

It's the week botany field school starts, the week Noah would have left for Malawi. But instead of flying off to Africa he's living in a cabin an hour north, monitoring algae growth. He comes into the city on his days off and sits in the living room with Sylvie for an hour, holding the baby when she suggests it. He is a simulacrum of his old self, too, wooden and quiet. Her mother is causing this, glancing through the archway at every opportunity to see how they're getting along. Or the baby is, with her talent for transformation. When other people are around, she's a white doll, perfect and serene, but the second she and Sylvie are alone, she morphs into a furious imp, squalling *waah waah waah waah*, her eyes fixed glassily on nothing.

Sylvie tries to tell Noah about it. "Well, she's growing fast," he says, "and you're her food source." It's a fact that she's hungry every hour of the night and day; she's got the ravenous appetite of all invasive species. With her rough little tongue she's worn the skin off Sylvie's nipples, not that this deters her. Once Sylvie has a tiny white foot in her hand when the baby grabs onto her sore tit like a barracuda, and she digs her fingernails into the sole of it as a warning. Liz hears the ruckus and comes up the stairs. She takes the baby and Sylvie lies face down on the bed.

"It's hard to settle an infant who is this worked up," she says, walking back and forth, patting the baby's back. "Noah needs to take his daughter on his days off. To give you some respite."

"Is Noah going to breastfeed her?" Sylvie asks after a minute.

"Oh, it's true," Liz says with a sigh. "There's always that." The baby's calmed down by then and she hands her back and waits until she starts to feed. Then she forces Sylvie to look at her. "My point is this: you have to work out a more formal agreement with Noah. If you don't want me and Maggie interfering, you have to work it out yourselves. Or we will step in."

She will die if she does not get away from this woman. She will die if she doesn't find someone who sees what's going on and cares. Noah won't be on the boat until August; he's at the research station, where he just has to take readings every six hours. She texts him: CAN WE COME AND SEE YOU? and he answers, SATURDAY?

She goes to find Liz. "Thea's willing to drive me up on Saturday morning," she says. "We'll come back Monday."

Liz looks at her suspiciously. "You plan to take the baby?"

Well, *duh!*

Sylvie extends this phase of the operation until Friday, and then she goes sadly into the kitchen with the baby over her shoulder and announces that Thea was going to borrow her dad's car for the weekend, but now she can't. So can they take Liz's?

Liz, intent on frying mushrooms, acts at first as though she didn't hear. Then she dials down the gas, stooping to peer at the flame as though the knob won't do its job without her supervision. Finally she turns to Sylvie. "You need to spend time together," she says. "I know that."

"So can we have the car?"

"We?"

"Thea and me. Thea will drive. She's had her licence since she was sixteen. You'd only have to use the bus on Monday."

"And Thea will stay for the whole weekend to help you out?"

"Yes." Sylvie doesn't react to this insult. She can see all the issues roiling around in Liz's mind: *a safe crib for baby; contraception after baby is born; when wild animals attack.* "Mom," she finally says, "I'm not asking you whether I can go. I'm an adult, I'm going. I'm just asking if we can take your car or if you prefer that I hitchhike with the baby."

"Oh, Sylvie," her mother says wearily. "Is this the way an adult talks?" She turns back to the mushrooms. "All right," she says after a long minute.

When Thea appears at the door on Saturday morning, it's obvious she hasn't been to bed. Sylvie texted her, BRING JAMMIES, and she's got her backpack with her.

Before either of them can speak, Liz pops up on the front walk. "You travel light," she says.

"I don't have a kid," Thea says, instantly perky. "Not like some lucky people."

Liz has been to the pharmacy; she's dragging a humungous bale of disposable diapers.

Thea peers at the label. "Polypropylene, cellulose, and chemical gel," she reads out in a bright and shiny voice.

Liz turns a shoulder to Thea. "Think about it, honey," she says. "Are you going to schlep stinking cloth diapers back from Presley Point?"

"Actually," Sylvie says, "I'm going to get a carrying board – what are they called? – a tikinagan. You fill them with sphagnum moss. It's crunchy and dry. It absorbs pee."

"Like kitty litter," Thea says.

But nothing can deter Liz from dragging that bale of landfill out to the car. She's already loaded the bassinette. Standing in the driveway after the baby is strapped into the car seat, she tries to get both Sylvie and Thea to lock eyes with her for a lecture about weekend traffic on the cottage highway. "Dear," she says (or possibly *deer*) as she presses the car keys into Thea's hand, "you really need to watch. Don't be out around dusk. And text me when you get there."

"I can't. They're out of cell range at the cabins. Noah can only text from the research station."

Liz turns back to the car. She waves through the window at the baby. "We should get one of those Baby on Board signs," she says.

Thea smiles reassuringly at Liz. "We will be *so* careful." She has a great trustworthy face. Well, actually she looks like a feral child, but all the mothers congratulate themselves that they are smart and open-minded enough to look past that and recognize her true qualities.

"God, I'm glad to be out of there," Sylvie says the instant they're on the street. "You have no idea. They've turned me into such a child. If I hadn't escaped for the weekend, I'd have been about *twelve* by Sunday."

"God," Thea says. "Really." At the stoplight at Broadway she lifts the weight of her caramel-coloured hair in two hands and twists it into a knot, and it's so close to Velcro that it stays in place. "The *deer*! Maybe if you got a Baby on Board sign they'd think twice about running onto the road."

She turns right and barrels up Broadway. "What will she do? If she finds out."

"I can't even feel guilty," Sylvie says. "As if I'd be taking you along. Hey, this is the first time I've got into these jeans since the baby. They're the jeans I wore up at Presley Point last summer. I love having my old clothes again." They're in the left lane, and then Thea crosses Memorial towards downtown. "Where are we going? Aren't we taking you home?"

"No, I'm meeting everyone for breakfast at the Don Deli."

"Shit! I don't want to drive through downtown."

"You'll be fine."

"Yeah, I know. I'll be fine." Two kids were once caught driving a car on the Arlington Bridge. They were *eight*. One of them sat on the floor and worked the pedals while the other steered. "Weird that my dad put the car seat on the right side."

"Why is it weird?"

"Well, I'll be able to see the baby while I'm driving. It's almost as if he knew I'd be alone." She was in the bathroom when he went out this morning. She called goodbye to him through the door, so glad she didn't have to look him in the eye.

Thea lurches to a stop in the loading zone in front of the Don Deli. They both get out. "Come in for a minute," she says.

"Are you having a Fringe meeting?"

"Yeah. We've got a script. A really good one. Benedictor is in now, and he's amazing. Actually, we got the idea from something you said."

"What do you mean?"

"What you said about doing an allegory. We're doing a thing about slavery – about the British ending slavery. Like, it's about changing the whole system to do the right thing, even if you have to rebuild your economy."

"That's cool. It could be awesome."

"Well, come in and we'll tell you about it. Bring the baby."

"No, I want to go and see Noah."

"Yeah!" Thea says. "I bet you do!" She looks at Sylvie with glittering eyes that say *Make it a good one*. Then she slings her backpack and walks away. Sylvie opens the driver's door and sinks into the seat.

It's cold to be out on a terrace, but Aiden and Defrag end up in the courtyard of a café-slash-used-bookstore on Westminster, where, over an exceptionally good cup of coffee, Aiden sits expounding on Jehovah's Witness doctrine regarding the End Times.

Heaven with its golden streets has a capacity of 144,000, Aiden explains, and it's now officially full up. So the Witnesses have had to propose an overflow paradise on planet Earth. In this paradise, children will keep on growing until they reach their prime, and as for old guys like Aiden, the film will flip into reverse – you grow young at the same pace that you grew old.

Aiden takes a sip of his coffee and leans back in his chair. Shit, it's a great thought! One morning he'll wake up to silence: the ringing in his ears will be gone. The day after that he's got full range of motion in his left big toe, the joint that kills him now when he cross-country skis. First thing you know he's having sex twice before breakfast, and outside his window a western meadowlark pours out its astonishing song. Because the earth is going to heal too. The hole in the ozone – mended. The Great Pacific Garbage Patch – vanished. The obscene wounds of the Athabasca tar sands, the Three Gorges Dam – well, some of those things will take a while. But we'll have *eternity*, won't we, here in this beautiful world.

"Pretty cool," Defrag says.

"Well, you know, people scorn the Witnesses," says Aiden. "They're like the trailer trash of Christian cults. But they got all that right. They know where the heart lies: here, in this world, not in some gated community in the sky."

Defrag's in his scruffy old pea coat, and their server, a kid with a white towel tucked into his belt, is wearing a leather jacket. Aiden tries to warm his hands on his coffee mug. This is his second refill; he's having trouble prying himself fully awake. The baby was up a couple of times in the night. Her crying is a comforting sound, though, like hearing a train whistle in the dark.

"You should see our little sweetheart," he says. "You know, I'm not getting a lot of sleep, but I still wake up in the morning feeling like all's right with the world. We'd never have chosen for this to happen, but it's been good for us."

"You know how wasps live?" Defrag laughs. "On sucrose excreted by their larvae."

Defrag's coverage ran out two weeks ago; it was Aiden who phoned and suggested coffee. Technically this is a violation of professional boundaries, but Aiden can hardly start working pro bono, which in any case would embarrass Defrag. Anyway, he tells himself craftily, you've been brewing coffee for the guy in your office, for years.

"So, how you doing?"

Defrag shrugs. "Without."

Aiden can't help but laugh. He resettles himself, trying to get comfortable on the little cast-iron chair. "What's your Saturday usually like?" Actually, he has a pretty good idea. He once lived in the apartment block Defrag lives in now. It's a rambling red and grey edifice at the foot of the Osborne Bridge, with working fireplaces you're not supposed to use and treacherous outdoor corridors that run like scaffolding along the upper storeys. There's something fitting about it for Defrag. It's like a den, or a tree house.

"Saturday," Defrag says. "Oh, you know," and Aiden regrets the way he's been yammering on. Defrag is pale, he's laughing like a hyena. He's got bare feet shoved into his runners and his eyes are red-rimmed. There's a sore on his bottom lip. Malnutrition, Aiden thinks. "Order a muffin," he says.

"Don't believe in the muffin."

"How about a croissant?"

Defrag doesn't answer. It's obvious that the way Aiden usually operates with his clients constitutes being a pain in the ass in a courtyard café.

He cranks his head to scrutinize the limbs of the boulevard trees above. "Ever think about the Wolseley Elm?" he asks. "That tree that grew in the middle of the street and was saved by protestors when the city wanted to take it out?"

"I think about it," Defrag says. "I think about what happened to it."

"I don't actually know what happened."

"An anti-tree-hugger blew the sucker up. In the night. Some pro-development asshole went and shoved dynamite into a knothole."

"God," Aiden says. "After all that."

They sit in silence, mentally tossing that pathetic little vigilante into a pit along with Dick Cheney and the captain of the *Exxon*

Valdez. Then for a while they kick around their thoughts about activism. Aiden learns that Defrag was big in the disarmament movement at one time, the chair of an umbrella organization. Good for Defrag. Aiden's own political efforts were more along the lines of delivering anti-American diatribes at parties. A fellow traveller, you might call him.

"Well, Jake," he says, "they haven't blown us up yet. I think it worked."

"Yeah." Defrag laughs. "We thought the bomb was going to do us in. Turns out it's the eating and the fucking. How do we protest that?"

Aiden hitches his chair a little farther from the table so he can stretch out his legs. "You know," he says, "I had a conversation with a filmmaker a few weeks ago and I think he gave me an out. I made some comment about how every thinking person is scared shitless by climate change, and he just dismissed it – said it was, like, apocalyptic thinking. That people in every age think the world is coming to an end. But actually it's all about us, we're just project-ing our own mortality onto the world. When we were religious, we dreamed up a religious apocalypse. Now that we're into science, we muster up scientific data to freak ourselves out. But it all comes down to the same thing." He rubs his knuckles against his jeans, warming them. "I'm expressing this quite a bit better than he did, actually."

Defrag opens the hatch to let a couple of black-coated chuckles escape. "I think he's on to something," he says. "Just give me a few weeks to wean myself off empirical thought."

Aiden watches him affectionately. He so completely knows the guy. He knows his politics and his music and his drugs. He knows his twenties especially, the squalid apartments and the stoned roommates, the Salvador Dali posters, the stacks of sci-fi paperbacks, the stupid non sequiturs that passed for wit, endless petty defiances against The Man – he can see that history in every gesture, just as he can see the fears that flicker now on the edge of Defrag's vision. When he was training, when they talked about professional boundaries, none of his profs or supervisors ever said, One day a client will walk into your office and you will recognize a true friend.

The kid in the leather jacket comes to refill their coffees. When he's gone, Defrag reaches into the pocket of his coat and pulls out a little shard of paper. "You want to see my first image? It was captured by the pinhole camera in Assiniboine Park." He hands it to Aiden. It's about half the size of a playing card.

"How did you develop it?"

"You don't develop it. It's photographic paper to begin with."

Aiden pulls his reading glasses out of his shirt pocket. The wiry mass that fills the bottom half of the picture will be trees, trees that went bare and moved their branches a million times in various winds, and then leafed out again. Astonishingly, there's a familiar arc in the sky above them. A rainbow – a wonky rainbow, as though each colour in the spectrum had to make its separate lonely effort to scale the sky.

"How long was your camera up?"

"Six months."

"Well, how the hell did you catch a rainbow?"

Defrag chokes on a huge burr of a laugh; it's going to take him a few minutes to cough it up. Aiden sits studying the picture, feeling like an idiot. Finally it clicks. That arc is the tracks of the sun, struggling to rise morning after morning.

He passes the paper back to Defrag. "So where's your old buddy Aiden? I hammed for that camera every time I went by." This gets Defrag laughing again.

Aiden downs his coffee. Then he hears himself say, "Hey, Sexsmith's in town. Did you know?"

"You're kidding."

"He's got new material. He's playing the Walker, and apparently the house is still half-empty. I was thinking about going tonight. Are you up for it?"

After the girls drive away, Liz goes back into the kitchen and stands still, listening to the silence. God help that tiny baby. Well, Noah will be there, and Thea – such a funny girl with her overeager face and her hair like a chenille plant, the tendrils a pale dirty pink as if they've picked up dye from things she's rubbed against. But she was queen of the babysitters' brigade in high school, she practically raised the Callaghan kids across the back lane. Their baby will be all right.

The quiet is wonderful. Aiden is out too; he rode off while Liz was at the drugstore. Before he left, he emptied the dishwasher and cleaned up the kitchen, and he even scrubbed the pots from last night's dinner. Too bad she never saw this sort of effort when his own daughter was born. When Liz was hormonal and almost psychotic from lack of sleep and Sylvie wouldn't latch on properly, and awful women from La Leche League were in the house day and night, not quite prepared to deny a starving baby a bottle of formula but eager to imply that Liz was a total failure for the situation, as she had declined to walk around during pregnancy with her nipples clamped by clothespins to reshape them for a woman's supreme task. And what was that silent shape floating like a blow-up doll over their heads, bumping now and then into the crown moulding? Aiden I'm-too-sexy-for-my-life Phimister, poetry book in hand. Twenty years of parenting have changed him, there's no doubt about it. He's like the foxes she saw in a documentary not long ago. You fed them, you cuddled them, and by the third generation they'd started to change physically. Their ears no longer stood up, their tails were curling, their feverish hatred of humans had been stolen away – they'd turned into dogs.

She starts to put the kettle on for tea and then changes her mind. She'll go for a walk to celebrate her freedom, that's what she'll do. She hasn't made it to yoga in weeks, but at least she can walk. She takes her Rockports out of the boot chest, and in a flash, Max is at the door, wagging his whole back end. His tail thuds against the wall. "Hey, Max," Liz says. "Cool your jets." She lifts his leash off its hook and snags a plastic bag from the bin.

Out on the street, she turns in the direction of the river. It's cool, but she'll warm up if she walks fast. The neighbourhood is finally starting to bloom. The house next to Wendy's has tiny blue flowers naturalized in the front lawn. Those are scillas; they're in the hyacinth family. A great idea for a lawn. She'll plant some in the fall.

Max is panting with his passion to move. Liz glances at her watch and thinks again about the kids in the car heading north. Her prickly, pebble-eyed daughter, no doubt still ranting to Thea about Liz. She's still rocked herself by the shock of what happened the night of the party, the night Krzysztof came to the house and Sylvie was so upset. Liz had finally mustered up the courage to go down to her bedroom, determined to have it out at last, and found Sylvie sitting in her white terry robe with the baby at her breast, looking in the dim light from the hallway like a Catholic icon, and it seemed as though the scene Liz had imagined for so long, the explaining and the pleading and the longed-for reconciliation, would finally take place. But that was not remotely what happened, and now Liz has something new to carry around with her:

a rough little pellet of pain and shame. An end to the thing (please god), a stinging, biting end to the thing. She can hate me if she wants, she says stoutly to herself, fingering the pellet as she strides up the street, but she asked for me, and we will always have that. She knows about Krzysztof, she's always known. And yet, when it mattered, the day of her baby's birth, Sylvie needed her mother.

She's on Wolseley Avenue, where the finest houses are. Always a pleasure to walk along Wolseley. She sticks the plastic bag in her pocket and thinks about a conversation she had when Sylvie was tiny. Somebody (it must have been one of the GAP women) said, "If you pay attention to what your baby is telling you, she will make you into the sort of mother she needs you to be." Liz was overcome with despair, hearing that. People talk about how helpless babies are, how vulnerable, but it never felt that way to her. From the day Sylvie was born, she was a force to contend with. She resisted anything you tried to give her. If you indulged her whims, she'd flip to wanting the exact opposite. If you tried to cuddle her, she'd squirm frantically away. She was not powerless – she had the power to demonstrate to the whole world what a lousy mother Liz was. Well, now she's a mother herself and they'll see how that turns out. This new baby, luckily for Sylvie, has a softer way about her, more of an inquiring presence. You can already see it in the way she opens her round eyes and looks thoughtfully at them.

Liz doubles the leash around her hand. It's cold, a humid sort of cold with no promise of warmth in it, and she walks quickly, darting glances into the gaps between houses where dogwood and saskatoon and high-bush cranberry compete for the sun. Sometimes when the baby opens her eyes, she seems to ask, Who *are* you? Then her eyes glaze over and she falls back to sleep. But the question remains, as though her very appearance in their house asks it. "Who are you?" Liz says to Max as she follows him along the street. The boulevard elms arch, their buds all soft and pale, and the green points of iris poke from the flower beds: everything waiting brightly for its meaning to be revealed.

The summer Aiden started his counselling program, the summer Sylvie worked at the Fort, Liz went to a party at Esme Gwynn's house on Palmerston Avenue. Esme was a maker of experimental films. She was also the director of an artist support organization Liz had freelanced for when Sylvie was small. "I was a bad hire for the Film Group," she said frankly when she offered Liz her first contract. Esme loved film but she didn't have an administrative bone in her body. She praised Liz lavishly for the grant applications and reports she wrote, as you might praise a cleaning lady – all work that was not art she held in contempt.

One night she invited Liz into the editing suite and showed her two versions of a short film she was making. It was about a couple arguing, obviously at the end of things, as they wandered around the old cemetery at St. Boniface Cathedral. The setting was lovely, but a little heavy-handed as a metaphor, Liz thought. Esme showed her the two cuts without sound. In the first, the husband (played by the guy in charge of equipment repairs for the Film Group) was clearly an asshole. In the second, his face was open and pleading, and the wife looked as though she despised all men in general and him in particular. "An editor can make a film say anything she wants," Esme said.

Liz hadn't spoken to Esme for several years, and then that day she saw her in Safeway, picking up plastic cups and mix.

"I'm so glad I ran into you," Esme said. "I'm having a barbecue tomorrow. I'd love it if you came." The whole community was celebrating, she said. Wasn't it thrilling about Krzysztof Nowak?

"Fabulous!" Liz said. "What can I bring?"

Esme crinkled her eyes appreciatively. "Bring a salad. Something for the vegans."

The meaning will be in the details, and Liz remembers them perfectly. Walking over wearing a great linen sundress and a baleful sense of freedom. The sundress was vintage; she'd bought it in a little shop off the Magnificent Mile when she and Aiden had that weekend in Chicago. It had a sweetheart bodice. She was wearing strappy sandals and sporting a lavenderish pedicure. Carrying a dark straw bag she'd bought on Isla Mujeres, in which was wedged a chilled bottle of Chardonnay and a blue covered bowl with her salad (marinated wild rice with currants and slivers of almond and apricot).

It was a tiny house on the river, no doubt once a summer cottage, before Wolseley was Wolseley. The crowd in the narrow backyard spilled onto the neighbours' unfenced property. Liz ran into Esme almost right away, her long, bony feet in buffalo sandals and her hair in a queue down her back. Liz saw in a flash that her own toenail polish was over-coordinated with her sundress. Esme didn't need fashion – she had personal style.

"I've got a press notice I want to show Krzysztof," Esme said. "Come on, I'll introduce you."

Liz followed. She had no clue what the occasion was. Back when she worked for the Film Group, the buzz about Krzysztof Nowak was just starting. She'd never seen his films, but Aiden had. "Those film school grads might know everything about cameras, but they know shit about life" – that's what Aiden had said when he came home.

Krzysztof was squatting beside three classic hibachis full of actual charcoal and approaching a state of readiness. He got up when Esme introduced Liz. He was their age, not a kid at all, and lavishly good-looking. This party was in his honour but he was grilling the steaks; he had also, strangely, provided them. On a folding metal table were huge trays with twenty or thirty strip loins marinating and a tarnished silver boat of glistening sauce. "Taste it," he said, and Liz dipped a finger in and put it to her tongue.

"That's amazing," she managed, so broadsided by the sight of him she could hardly speak. The corners of his mouth tucked in in sexy acknowledgement.

"It's got an espresso base," he said.

"He'll tell you it's his signature sauce," Esme said, "but I happen to have the same cookbook. *New Essentials*, by Alessandro Aquilino." She said the name as if she spoke Italian.

He ignored her. He stood there with the press notice in his hand, not reading it, his eyes on Liz.

"I'm going to have to ask for decaf," she said. It was lame, but it didn't matter. She was still holding her salad. "I'll just take this over to the buffet table," she said.

"Make sure you come back," he said. "I'm going to save my best steak for you."

She smiled and turned and wove her way through the party, almost tipsy from the racket he'd provoked in her. Thinking, All right then, cataloguing his features in her mind: the slightly hooked nose and the green eyes and the heavy beard that meant he would never look clean-shaven. Thinking how European he seemed in a charcoal shirt and pants, the faint accent (marvelling and thinking, I'll have that, the way you might when you see the perfect object on a shelf in an antique store, not that you want it so much as that you're sick with yearning to be the sort of person who would own it). And then she spotted a woman standing gracefully by the buffet table, arranging the bowls and platters, and it was Mary Magdalene.

Well, Liz had the advantage. She got to watch Mary Magdalene lift her head and register Liz – distaste, you'd have to call her expression – and then almost immediately produce a smile. She had one of those unravelling topknots that look so great with thick, wavy hair and classic features. Six or so years since they'd seen each other. Since the summer of the swing accident. Of course she was running with an arty crowd now.

"We're living in Point Douglas," Mary Magdalene said. "I just love it there. It's an old farmhouse from before the Louise Bridge was put in."

"You're back with George?"

"George Stonechild? I haven't seen him in years." Somebody passed her a foil package of supermarket cabbage rolls and she smiled a thank-you that actually looked sincere. "Krzysztof and I bought the house three years ago," she said.

Chris Toff and I, Liz heard, but then Maggie glanced towards the barbecue and she got it. "Oh!"

Mary Magdalene took Liz's salad and pried off the lid. "Wild rice," she said appreciatively, and stuck a spoon in the bowl. Then she asked how Sylvie was.

"She's great. She's got a role at the Fort this summer, as a historical enactor. The daughter of the factor, actually. She's loving it – it's just her thing. She's getting tall."

"Lovely Sylvie," Mary Magdalene said. "She has long bones, that girl."

Liz, of course, was experiencing an insane attack of amnesia regarding the name of the child who'd had his nose broken while under her care. "So is my little guy," Mary Magdalene volunteered unhelpfully. "Getting tall, I mean. He's into tai chi. I have to leave in an hour. He had a class tonight and I have to pick him up."

She reached a hand towards Liz with that sympathetic expression she had perfected. She had a beautiful mouth. Even when she was serious, her mouth carried the memory of her smile.

"Liz, someone who might know about George Stonechild is Peter Biggin. He ran into George on the street in Vancouver about five years ago. He was in really bad shape. Into hard stuff, apparently. It's very sad. Anyway, Pete would be the one to ask."

Liz gave Mary Magdalene a wide berth for the next hour. She talked for a while to Steve Presunka, a guy who knew Aiden. "He's doing an intensive for a master's in counselling," she said.

"Lying on the floor on pillows, re-enacting his birth?" Steve said, and treacherously she laughed. Steve Presunka was always inclined to be dismissive of Aiden, though it was hard to know why: he was a thirty-five-year-old man who worked in a bicycle shop.

She moved on. It wasn't her scene but she knew enough from the Film Group job to fake it, and she worked the yard like a pro. She never actually looked at Krzysztof but she kept her ears tuned – god, how people fawned over him. And then, standing with a plastic tumbler of warmish white wine in her hand, she glanced back and saw that Mary Magdalene was over at the hibachis. She witnessed the tableau of their goodbye kiss. She saw how beautiful and well-matched they were; she saw domesticity, possession in the clasp of Mary Magdalene's hand on his upper arm. But as Mary Magdalene turned away – as she was in the very act of turning – Krzysztof angled his head and scanned the crowd, and Liz knew he was looking for her.

She took her time, but she didn't have the will to wait forever. When she drifted casually over to the hibachis, he pointed to the steak he'd been saving for her, a tenderloin with fine marbling. She turned her full smile on him, not bothering to be coy. He served everyone else and then he grilled their steaks together. Liz went to the buffet table to get salads. Walking back with two plates, she saw him clearly – a man who risked caricature in his perfection – and she felt a sudden euphoria. She hadn't known his provenance when she first caught sight of him, and what she'd felt in that moment, it was like a calling, a command from a gleaming realm where the proportion of things was totally different.

They carried their plates towards the river. A massive cottonwood grew so close to the collapsing bank that you could see it would be threatened by the end of the summer. Esme had made no pretence of landscaping. There was a cement wall halfway down the yard, almost hidden by ragweed and burdock, the foundation of an old building. Liz and Krzysztof sat on that wall with their plates between them, and he handed her the steak knife and fork he was carrying for her in his shirt pocket. He had the wide shoulders of a construction worker. She thought how daring it was for a man to take up work that said, I'll show you a world you've never before imagined. The meat was tender, so delicious that she understood why people would kill for a good steak.

Below them the brown Assiniboine crawled. "It's great to live by water," Krzysztof said. He was off to the States for a few months. He was working on a feature screenplay; he had an artist-in-residence gig at a lake just outside Minneapolis.

"Oh," she said. This was such a clear sign that she was helpless before it. "I'm taking my daughter to Minneapolis at the end of August," she said. "To a festival." There are things you have no idea you are looking for until you find them.

The sunset was behind them but mango-coloured light shone off the trees on the far bank. It seemed it was never going to get dark. The music stopped abruptly at one point and excited cries rose from the yard. Then they heard what everybody else had heard: a loon calling, its wonderful, insane cry floating on the evening air.

"I've never heard a loon in the city," Liz said.

It called again. It was upriver, to the east. "That's the tremolo," Krzysztof said. "It's normally a distress call, although sometimes you hear a pair doing a tremolo duet when they fly over their own territory."

Liz could hear her blood thudding in her ears.

"So, you married?" Krzysztof asked, and she understood that it did not lower her stock with him to say, "Yeah. Sort of."

"Happily?" he asked.

"Most of the time," she said.

Venus started to shine like the point of light at the centre of the TV screen when Liz was a girl. The music had resumed. As they walked back up to the house, a guy appeared on the riverbank to the east. He was holding something up to his mouth, like a harmonica. He came closer and the something was revealed to be a black-and-white plastic bird: a loon whistle shaped like a loon. The crazy tremolo flew out again, over Van Morrison's reedy voice. Everybody laughed and exclaimed.

They stepped into the yellow light of the tiny, crowded house and put their bloody plates on the counter. Krzysztof made his way through the crowd and she followed him. Into Esme's bedroom, full of arty kitsch, a cheap white Mexican blanket spread over the bed. He went over to the bookshelf. He's going to show me something he's written, she thought with a sinking feeling, or an article about his work. Instead he pulled down a novel at random and ripped a page out of it. Then he picked a pen out of the mess on the bedside table and scrawled something on the page.

She didn't look at it when he handed it to her. Like someone who had done this sort of thing before, she just folded the paper twice and tucked it into the sweetheart bodice of her sundress, then followed him back to the kitchen.

There's been a water main break on Evanson, and the street is blocked with ugly piles of river clay. Liz is stepping in muck before she realizes it. The dog ignores the mud, he's fully absorbed in sniffing the hedges. Liz has a plastic bag of his poop in her hand; she hasn't found a place to ditch it. She stands, momentarily disoriented, then pulls Max around and starts to walk back up Wolseley Avenue. When she gets to Augusta, Aiden is riding towards her.

"Hey," he calls. "Where you been?"

"Out for a walk. Where did you go?"

He veers across the street and brakes. "Just grabbed a coffee." In spite of the cold, he's wearing shorts. "Did Sylvie get away all right?"

"Yup. They should be almost there by now."

He's agile, swinging off the bike. But his legs look old, all the mechanics of their tendons and muscles on full display. He's owned these shorts since Sylvie was born. He may even be carrying provisions for his journey in their several saggy pockets: a lunch bag with boiled eggs wrapped in waxed paper, a flashlight, a creased map. His freckles have spread and paled and blurred. They're showing their true nature as sun damage. He's a grandfather, isn't he. Liz thinks about Krzysztof Nowak's stony face when that neighbour walked into the party blowing on the loon whistle. Aiden, if he'd been taken in, would have looked at Liz with comic chagrin. She feels the customary fondness for her husband rising in her chest, and she feels something else – a sense of dismay at the film that's just unspooled in her memory, which failed to reveal anything really.

They walk up their driveway and Aiden rolls open the garage door – it's an old door that opens like an old-fashioned wooden pencil case. He wheels his bike in and she walks towards the garbage can and drops in the dog bag. She turns, and Aiden is right there. "We'll have the day to ourselves," she says, and takes his arm, and they cross the yard and climb the steps of the deck together.

11

All You Need

THERE'S THE LITTLE LANE TO THE COTTAGES AT Presley Point, and there is Noah, grinning in front of cabin eleven. He's tanned and his hair is longer: he looks like his lake self. "Refugees from the city," he says, kissing her lightly.

His cabin is closer to the lake than cabin two, where she stayed with him last year. It's a shack in comparison; it has no glass windows, only screens and shutters hinged at the top and propped up with sticks. "It's fine," Sylvie says as her eyes adjust to the dark and she takes in the peeling linoleum and the sagging bed. "It's all you need."

She'd throw herself at him but the baby is fussing in her arms, tremulous and stinking. So she sits on the old couch to change her and Noah watches attentively. Afterwards she hands the baby to him. He does it right, careful to support her head. While he holds her and looks at her warily, Sylvie wanders around the cabin, still a little shaky from the drive. Getting onto the highway was the worst part. She'd never driven an entrance ramp before, and a truck blasted its air horn at her and roared past in a threatening way. She swerved and her two right tires hit the rumble strip, and then a sports car zoomed by and the driver slowed down as soon as he was past her, flashing his brake lights just to be an asshole. And all this time the baby was screaming her lungs out. But they made it.

This cabin is just one room, with a bathroom built into a corner. Nailed to the wall on the kitchen side is Noah's silver sleeve, the scale armour she always thought was a falconer's sleeve. She touches one of the leaves with a finger.

"It's not silver!"

"It was made from beer cans."

She flips the leaf over and, sure enough, it has a Labatt's Blue logo on the underside. Somebody spent a lot of time making that sleeve, though, cutting the leaves and stapling them onto the fabric so they overlapped perfectly. She pictures a Labatt's-drinking props man bent over a workbench and swearing every time he nicked his fingers.

Noah is holding the baby crookedly and she's letting out little pips of distress. She's hungry and there's no point in his even trying. Sylvie takes her back and arranges a baby blanket over her shoulder so Noah won't be too freaked. To her disappointment, he puts on his cap and picks up his laptop and goes out. To the store at the end of the cabin line, he says, to try to get a wireless connection. And she sits there in the dark and chilly cabin with the baby chomping on her, more alone than if he were a thousand miles away.

When he gets back, they set out for a walk. She doesn't even ask him if he wants to carry the baby; she just straps the sling on herself. They walk up the high trail along the line of cabins, towards a little path that climbs a cliff jutting out into the lake, a lake the grey of the ocean. Last summer when Sylvie was here, grass-green waves lapped the shore like thick paint. It's too early now for algae bloom. A white fishing boat crosses the water towards a line of little white flags. "That's their nets," Noah says. They stand in a cold wind and watch two men haul the first net up and onto the deck and start tossing the fish into the hold. Snatching up the flashing pickerel one at a time, as though they're racing to count them – 26, 27, 28, 29.

"I was talking to a fisher at the dock yesterday," Noah says. "He's harvesting eight hundred pounds a day. He has to lift his nets every six hours."

Sylvie can't take her eyes off the thrashing mass of silver fish gasping in the net, hauled out of an overly fecund lake where all this life is a sign of its dying. "He calls it harvesting?" she says. "Did you ask him if he plants them?"

When the fish are counted and the boat is gone, Sylvie and Noah step back onto the sandy path, the baby hanging face-out in the sling on her front. She's a quiet weight on Sylvie's chest and they're almost back at the cabin. If they can get her out of the sling without waking her up, they'll have a couple of hours to themselves.

"Are her eyes closed?" Sylvie asks Noah.

"Yeah. She looks pissed off."

"Her expressions are funny." She tells him what happened on Main Street that morning, when a cop car pulled up right beside them at a stoplight. "I was really scared. 'Play it cool, baby,' I said, and I looked in the back and she was staring straight ahead, looking totally innocent."

That's a mistake. The penny drops for Noah – she can see it drop. He takes a step away from her as if he needs some distance to see her clearly, and then he's silhouetted against the lake and she can hardly see his face. "You haven't taken your road test. You don't have your licence!"

She gives him an *oh, well* shrug. "I was fine," she says. "What difference does it make? My driving is the same, with that little piece of paper or without it." She was fine once she got up to speed, that part is true. Once she got up into the lake country there were almost no other cars on the road, and she felt as if she were on one of those rides at the Ex, where your little red car whizzes along a track and you rotate a big plastic steering wheel and you couldn't go off the road if you tried.

She rips open the Velcro fastener of the sling. "Take her. If you pick her up gently, we can get her to bed without waking her up."

But he just stands there. "Sylvie, you're not insured without a licence. I just assumed you'd taken your test. If you hit somebody, if they end up paralyzed, they'll *sue* you. For millions of dollars!"

"Good luck," she says, "trying to get money from me."

His whole body reacts to this. "Christ! What about your kid? What about keeping her safe?"

"*My* kid?" She sees his face go red. She's shaken by the way they're staring at each other, how far their eyes have stabbed into their real and baffled selves. "*My* kid," she says again fiercely. "Take her. She's yours. You can look after her from now on."

He takes the baby, pries her out of the sling, and lifts her awkwardly to his chest. He's at the cabin door, he reaches out his free hand to yank it open. Sylvie hears its spring complain and she turns and walks in the other direction. Everything's moving around her, the leaves trembling in the wind and the water pixellated in the light and dark grey clouds racing towards the lake as if they're in a stop-motion film. She lets out a howl of fury. "We were fine!" she yells.

On the overlook there's a crude bench made from a split tree trunk. She walks out to it and sits down. From here she can't hear a thing going on in the cabin. Nothing in front of her except water and sky – she's out on the rim of the known world. She lowers herself onto the bench and lies with her knees up, watching the clouds jostle high above her. Feeling the wind lick at her front where the baby was lying, snatching up the feel of her and carrying it coolly away.

We'll have the day to ourselves. That was code, of course. When they fall onto the bed in the loft, Liz knows she wants it, but her lust is . . . elusive. At first she won't let him take off her panties – sometimes that's best. Then, almost as soon as he's inside her, she feels an orgasm gathering like storm clouds in the distance. When it overtakes her, it's not about sex, it's about Aiden, how hungry his mouth feels, how *taken over* he seems, and tears spring out of the corners of her eyes as she comes. Afterwards she lies sloped along Aiden's warm side, the tears still tickling in her ears and his long, freckled arm holding her. Sex is a miracle, she thinks. "Sex is a fucking miracle," she says, and he lets out a little snort of appreciation.

Although actually she's becoming less and less a fan of daytime sex. Partly because of the skylight, through which the sun pours, gloating at the fishy whiteness of their skin and the way the flesh on the inside of her upper arms has started to crinkle. "Why the hell did we put in that skylight?" she asks.

His shoulder moves under her cheek. "It was a trend at the time."

"Well, it was our one big mistake." The Plexiglas has yellowed; it looks like a window in a trashy mobile home. "I think it was your bright idea, Aiden."

"Mine? I've never had an idea in my life. Not about home renos."

He has an arm up, studying his bent elbow. "You know, I was lying here thinking about my old friend the poet G. M. Hopkins. He used to keep a list of his sins in his journal. They were pretty funny. 'I was strangely aroused by an etching of a crucified arm' – that was one of them. Poor guy. Poor, tormented bastard. Picture the priest on the other side listening to that. Say his confessor was gay. Wouldn't it make a great screenplay?"

"It's been done," Liz says. "The straight version. I've seen it." She pulls up the light duvet. He reaches over and pushes it down.

"You know, Aiden, you were right into decorating in those days. You *were*. You replaced the baseboards. You took off all those layers of wallpaper. I was slaving away with a little scraper and you walked in with that great big steamer. I couldn't believe it." She runs her hand along his ribs. "And it's a good thing," she says. "Other people have engagement rings. They put a notice in the paper and they rent a hall. They send out invitations. All I had to go by was this house. *He's doing it*, I kept telling myself. *He must be in*. The day you installed the crown moulding in the dining room, I ran over to Charlotte's and said to her, 'It's official.'"

"Crown moulding. I don't even know what that is." He pinches her upper arm softly. "I was just trying to score another blow job in the pantry."

She tips her head up and gives him a long kiss. "You can't pretend with me," she says. "Look what happened to Charlotte and Roger. Once their house was gone, it was over." It's true. Charlotte and Roger had a big scheme: they were going to take their kids out of school and travel around Europe until their money ran out. They sold the house and put all their stuff in storage, and then the two of them were standing in the backyard at Charlotte's mom's, arguing about whether to buy their caravan in England or on the Continent, and suddenly they looked at each other and realized there was no reason to bother. All they had to do at that point was pick up their backpacks and walk away. Well, they had to sort the kids out as well. But this is Liz's point about a house – it anchors you. Such a huge joint investment, you can't do anything crazy and impulsive when you hit a bad patch.

Aiden reaches up and yanks at his pillow. "That's one version of things," he says. "But I often wonder what really happened."

"To Charlotte and Roger?"

"Yeah."

"Oh, I'm not sure they were ever that good together. I think they dreamed up the trip to distract themselves from how bad it was. For one thing, Roger could never last longer than a minute. It was always like having sex with a teenage boy."

"God, Liz, how could you possibly know that?"

"I'm just going by the way he was with me."

"No, seriously."

"Charlotte told me, of course."

"She shouldn't have told you. It's not respectful."

"Aiden, we've been best friends for twenty-five years."

"All the same." He pinches her arm again, this time in rebuke. "It's a female thing. I hear it all the time. Women plunder their partner's privacy, they don't give a shit. You share confidences like . . . like they're your currency. Men don't operate that way."

"No? So what do guys use as currency? With their friends."

He thinks for a minute. "They share their drugs."

"Ah."

And then his head rolls in the other direction, and she props herself up on an elbow and watches sleep overtake him. That's the thing about Aiden: you never know what he's thinking. The main miracle of sex is what it does to him – the needy look it brings out on the face of a guy who never really needs anything from anybody. She nestles against him, still savouring the afterglow. Enjoy it. Because, odds are, tomorrow or the day after, he's going to stage one of his big withdrawals. Poor guy, she always says to herself, he's scared of me. I might suck out all his juices, like a lady spider.

She rolls to the side and the granite cotton of the sheet fills her vision. The way she put her hand on Aiden's arm in the backyard just now – was it sex she was wanting? Truthfully? Not exactly. She was in a strangely worked-up state, but it wasn't lust. It was just the fitting thing to do, staging a bit of afternoon delight when the house is empty. Marriage is made up of fitting gestures. If you always do what you feel like doing, you'll never make a relationship work. Of course, you can take that too far. Like Liz's mother, who was, you might say, a perfect collection of fitting gestures. But suddenly Liz feels a rare pulse of sympathy for her mother. Somebody has to pick up the slack, given that men pretty much do what they want. And then she's on a daybed in a house of wood and glass furnished entirely by the forest, with Krzysztof over her. The moment comes back to her whole. Not his perfection (though no doubt he was perfect) but the perfection of her desire, her desire to be made real. What are you supposed to do in such moments?

Aiden sinks into a different plane of sleep. She hears his breathing change and she's hit with a new understanding, a most painful thought: that the way she felt and acted when she wandered into that party on the river was entirely ordinary. She was like somebody out of *Desperate Housewives*. There was nothing profound about it, just her glimpsing the possibility that all she was – all the energy and life and longing (which she sees now like the water in those thin silver cups, fresh and cold, that you get in a Thai restaurant) – that all of that would just dribble away and vanish into the dusty ground.

After Sylvie's fed the baby, somebody thumps on the front wall of the cabin. A skinny guy in a Goldeyes cap grins in the doorway. "Sylvie, hey!" He steps into the cabin hauling a twelve of Kokanee. She's friendly in a cautious way because she doesn't have a clue who he is. He has a friend with him, a large older man in a plaid shirt.

The baby's in her car seat on the table, awake and in her contented phase. The skinny guy spies her. "Hey, Sylvie!" he shouts. "What the fuck? You been busy!" He sets the beer on the table and walks around, looking at the baby from all angles. "Cute. Boy or girl?"

They pull out chairs and sit down. "Gilles," the guy says to his friend, "give the lady a beer," and they all crack cans and lift them over the baby. "Cheers," Sylvie says. "Go, Jets!" says the skinny guy, and Gilles lifts his can silently. He has a broad chest and a kind, alert face, like a woodcutter in a fairy tale. He's taken off his cap and hooked it onto his kneecap, and his thick grey hair is dented in a line all around his big head.

Noah's at the station doing his checks. "We'll talk when I get back, okay?" he said when he was leaving, but he's been gone more than an hour. This is the first beer Sylvie's had in six months, and it tastes fantastic. She asks how the summer's going. "Work sucks," the skinny guy says. "I'd rather be on EI." He was on EI all winter and he got to go ice fishing every day after freeze-up. And he went to Fargo for a Garth Brooks concert and ended up sleeping in his truck. In February. "No shit," Sylvie says.

Noah comes in, looking unimpressed to see them here.

"Hey, Burb!" Sylvie's new best friend yells. "You been busy." He raises his can in Noah's direction.

"You betcha," Noah says. He reaches for a beer.

Tyrone, Sylvie thinks. She met him when she was here last summer. They played horseshoes, and he was wearing the same T-shirt: DON'T HUNT WHAT YOU CAN'T KILL.

"What's with the shorts?" Tyrone says. "It's fuckin' cold! And they try to say it's getting warmer. They must think we're stupid."

Noah ignores him. He pulls out the fourth chair and sits down. Tyrone goes back to studying the baby, who is sucking on a plastic pot scraper from the kitchen drawer.

The cabin fills with the yellowish grey of daytime darkness. Rain starts to come down, hard. "Shit," Noah says. He gets up and runs outside.

Tyrone hands Sylvie another beer. The shutters on the front of the cabin drop with a bang and the darkness deepens. Noah comes back in and takes his chair again; she can sense the damp coming off him. They sit and listen to the rain, the four of them around the little square table the way Sylvie's nana used to sit with her bridge friends. The wind is all from the lake, so Noah has lowered only the front shutters. On either side of them rain falls like a heavy curtain, they can hear it pounding wetly on the ground.

The baby gleams in her white onesie, as if all the light in the dim room is coming from her. Gilles's big face fills with pleasure. He leans over and puts out an index finger, and she wraps her fingers around it and tries to pull it to her mouth. Gilles grins silently and shakes her tiny fist.

Tyrone has shifted from checking out the baby to checking out Sylvie. She takes a long pull on her beer and swings her legs up to the arm of the couch, which is in her corner. She's had to change because the baby puked on her favourite top, but this one is fine, cut low over her breasts – her new, spectacular breasts. The beer is amazing; she feels herself coming back with every swallow. Her parents have been puritans about her having a drink, but alcohol is actually good for nursing mothers, it makes their milk flow.

And here she is at the lake with the guy they call Burb, who almost glows with the intelligence he brings into this tiny cabin. She's amazed by him, as if she's seeing him for the first time, and she longs to know him, to penetrate the secret of his composure. How neat he is – his long cyclist's leg muscles and his T-shirt that looks as though it's been ironed. His fingernails on the beer can clean and trimmed. He looks after himself as a matter of course.

He believes that rules have a purpose; he doesn't see them as a challenge or an attack on his freedom. They are part of the systematic way things work. He's been like this since he was little. When he showed her the mimosa plant, he didn't feel awe at the way it curled its leaves up over your finger. From what she can remember, he knew what was happening, based on plant chemistry. Possibly hydraulics were involved, like a male erection. And he was *seven*. Think what an amazing scientist he will be! But, she thinks, he is somebody who can be broadsided, because there will always be phenomena outside what your systems predict.

Pheno-mena. She takes a long pull on her beer. Phena Mina.

"So, you two go to school together?" Tyrone is looking at Noah.

"No, we met last summer."

"Where'd ya meet?"

"At Zach's cottage."

"Well, actually," Sylvie says to Tyrone, "Noah and I were best friends when we were little. We played together all the time. I almost killed him once. We were at the park, we were swinging really high on these huge swings, and I dared him to jump off. He did it, and the swing came up and smashed him in the face."

He swivels his head and looks at her out of that exact face.

"What," she says. "You don't remember?"

"I had a concussion. I got my nose broken. Of course I remember. I just didn't remember it was you."

"Who did you think it was?"

"I don't know . . . that kid who lived behind the store." He's just pretending, because he's mad at her. He remembers *everything*.

The baby lies with the pot scraper on her chest. They sit with their eyes fixed on her and listen to the rain. She's getting sleepy. Her eyelids start to slide.

"Hey," Tyrone says. "Your kid looks drunk."

Noah's laptop is on the counter behind him. He reaches for it and pulls it down to his lap. He opens a spreadsheet and starts entering data from a little notebook, stroking and tapping the touch pad expertly.

"Hey, Burb," Tyrone says. "Don't you watch the news? You're not supposed to sit with a laptop on your junk. It's bad for you – you're gonna fry your sperm. Ha! Guess it doesn't matter now. Your boys already did their swimming. Your boys already won the goddamn Olympics!"

Noah closes the laptop and puts it on the table. He gets up and goes over to the counter, where his iPod is docked. The clanging of Sister Machine Gun fills the cabin. "Fuck, Burb," Tyrone says. "You trying to drive us out with that shit? You don't got no Garth Brooks?" Thunder rumbles over the music. Gilles crushes his beer can and opens another.

Noah sits back at the table. His face is absolutely blank.

"So," Sylvie says, opening herself another beer. "What's the 'Burb' all about?"

"You can probably figure it out," Noah says.

It seems the rain has mostly stopped. Tyrone stands up. "Well, we'll leave you two lovebirds to it," he says. "We're gonna go see what Wheeler's up to. You can keep the cans. I owe you anyways."

The screen door slams. This startles the baby, who slept through Sister Machine Gun but now starts to fuss. Noah goes to the counter and turns off his iPod. It's colder than ever, and Sylvie puts on her hoodie and sits cross-legged on the couch.

Noah walks restlessly around the cabin. "What's that smell?"

She doesn't answer. He finally discovers the diaper from home that she dropped by the couch earlier. He doesn't say a word, just puts a plastic bag over his hand, picks up the diaper the way you pick up dog poop, and heads for the door.

"By the way," Sylvie calls as the door slams, "I'm starving."

In a minute he comes back in and goes to the sink to wash his hands. "I'll get us some pizza," he says. The grocery store at the end of the lane has takeout. He puts on his cap and sets off, still in his T-shirt and shorts.

The baby is winding up to throw a real fit. Sylvie picks her up and goes to the screen door and watches Noah make his way down the cabin line, head straight up in spite of the wind and the rain. It's only two weeks since she saw him in the city, but he seems taller. He *is* taller, she realizes with a pang – he's still growing.

He walks by cabin two without once looking to the side. Her old self is in cabin two, lying on the bed slim and naked and propped up on one elbow, her hair falling over her face and her whole body rimed with sweat. The room is full of afternoon sun and Noah is naked too, sitting on the edge of the bed gazing at her. They're not talking; they're both stunned by what just happened on the saggy cabin mattress.

She was hungry that night. When they got up, she made black bean dip, which they ate with taco chips. Noah pan-fried some pickerel. They had imperial cookies from the lake bakery – it was a three-course meal – and they lit a candle, sticking it on a saucer with melted wax.

The baby has settled down by the time Noah gets back. They turn on the lights and sit on the couch, picking orange coins of stinking pepperoni off a convenience-store pizza, not talking. The couch is up against two big windows, and Sylvie feels the cool post-rain air on the back of her neck.

When the last soggy piece is finished, Noah digs out a deck of cards and asks Sylvie politely if she would like to play rummy. She decides not to answer, but when he deals her a hand, she picks it up. They use the couch between them as a table. He plays intently, going for the discard pile every chance he gets. He never lays down, so there's nothing for Sylvie to build on. His goal is to cash out big and stick her with a handful of points. And he does. After three hands the score is Noah 345, Sylvie minus 90. This is the conversation he promised her.

He has an open beer on the floor beside him, but Sylvie has stopped drinking. The booze in her system feels like a strong current she has to swim against. She looks around the cabin, not bothering to sort her hand. The baby drops her pot scraper and tips her head to the side with a sharp look that is exactly like Noah. He doesn't give any sign that he sees it – he's too intent on sorting the hundreds of cards in his hand into tiers, searching for a discard so he can go out.

Watching him, she finally gets it, the bitter truth this whole day has been trying to teach her: Noah is an android. This explains everything. How he's never cold, how focused he is on the task at hand. His flat voice and the stiff way he moves, the impersonal look in his eyes. He's an android, no doubt about it. She sits with her unsorted cards in hand, her chest squeezing and her eyes burning. The question is, did he just turn into one because of everything that's happened, or has he always been one?

"Excuse me," she says. "I have to go to the bathroom."

The bathroom is over-lit and has the sort of fake flush toilet you can't put toilet paper down. Noah has burned incense by the sink. She puts her finger to the little cone and watches it crumble into ash. Then she opens the tin medicine cabinet. Everything is lined up and spotless. His razor and his shaving cream. His sunscreen and his inhaler. His toothbrush and toothpaste – he has one of those keys so he can squeeze his toothpaste methodically, without waste. On the top shelf, which she can't see without standing on tiptoes, is a box of Band-Aids. And in the corner, behind the Band-Aids, a stash of condoms. Sylvie crinkles one of the envelopes and feels the perfect flexible ring inside.

The baby is fussing when she comes out. Sylvie sits on the couch and ignores her until Noah finally picks her up. He walks methodically around the perimeter of the cabin, bouncing her up and down, moving her from one shoulder to the other. But she won't settle and Sylvie has to take her. While she sits on the couch and nurses, Noah goes out to do his midnight checks. When he comes back, he lies on the bed with his laptop. He's holding it conscientiously on one thigh, she notes, not on his crotch.

After the baby is burped and changed and sleeping in the portable bassinette, Sylvie stretches out beside him and he pulls up a movie he's downloaded. He seems to be totally engrossed in it, a black-and-white film about workers in a chemical factory gradually turning into lizards. They're at the stage of losing their ears; within another minute they'll have nothing but holes on the sides of their heads.

"Why are you watching this?" she asks.

"It's a cult classic," he says.

They lie fully dressed on the quilt, their heads propped up by pillows that smell of mothballs. He's wearing his five-toe rubber sandals – he looks like he's starting to develop his own exoskeleton. Sylvie doesn't even pretend to be watching the movie. The bare overhead light is still on and she has to close her eyes against it. Why do people ever talk? she thinks. Her legs are strangely heavy. She feels herself sinking into the bed as if it's an air mattress deflating and there's nothing she can do to keep herself afloat.

A loon wakes her and she drifts on the oscillating sound, feeling a deep sense of recognition and relief at being at the lake. It's stopped raining. The waves and the wind in the trees are all one sound. She's alone on the bed – Noah has moved to the couch. From somewhere below comes whimpering. Sylvie's jeans are cutting into her thighs; she gets out of bed and wiggles out of them and drops them on the floor. She has to pee badly. When she gets back from the bathroom, she stands at the end of the couch for a minute. Noah is on his side, still wearing his shorts. His long, strong legs are scissored – likely he's cold. He had a blanket but it's slid off. She sees herself nudging him onto his back, straddling him as he stirs awake and opens his arms for her. Lying over him, dipping in low to find his mouth, her new body moving with all its old joy.

The whimpers from the bassinette are turning into wails. Sylvie stoops and picks up a hot, damp, stinking little bundle. The chemical gel in the diaper is so swollen up it's like holding a roly-poly doll. She sits on the edge of the bed and pulls up her shirt. Her bra is stuck to her where milk leaked and dried; it's like peeling a Band-Aid off a wound. The baby snuffles under her shirt, clamping toothless gums on the soft skin where Sylvie's breast and armpit meet, and starts to suck like a lamprey eel. Sylvie pries her loose and arranges her properly, enduring the first painful chomp on her sore nipple. Then, on a sudden impulse, she levers herself up and tiptoes across the cabin in her T-shirt and panties, holding the baby cradled in both arms.

Outside, the wind and the waves separate into two distinct tracks of sound. The ground is cold and wet under her feet. Bug bulbs drop cones of yellow light in five or six doorways along the cabin line. Sylvie can hear and sense the lake but she can't see it. If she heads in that direction she might walk off the edge. So instead she moves cautiously around the side of the cabin. She makes out the dim shapes of two Adirondack chairs; she puts out her hand

and feels the rough wood of one and lowers herself into it, trying to keep the baby horizontal. The dark wall of cabin ten is just a few feet away. She tips her head back. No moon and no stars. Clouds are hiding the stars.

The baby is making a little squeak with each suck on her nipple. Sylvie pulls her off and makes her latch on again. The longing she feels for Noah is as sharp as a knife – she could cry for how much she wants him. Her breasts are all in lumps because there are little sacs swollen with milk inside them, like the seeds in a pomegranate. She can't bear to think of him seeing her. Noah is one thing, whole; he's like a tree that grew up in the shape it was supposed to have. And Sylvie . . . she's crooked and mangled and grafted together, someone who wants so badly not to be who she is that she is no one at all. And yet, if you'd asked her anytime in the past year, "Does Noah love you?" she would have said yes without a second thought.

A few inches away from her through the screen, he coughs. The door closing must have woken him. She hears the couch squeak as he turns over or sits up.

"Hey, Noah," she says.

He gives a little grunt of surprise. "What are you doing out there?"

"Just getting some fresh air."

"Are you warm enough?" His voice is close, right at her ear.

"Not really. I'll come in in a minute. As soon as the baby finishes feeding."

The loon cries again from the direction of the lake: a different cry, three liquid spurts of sound. "Hey," he says, "we almost never hear loons in the south basin."

She doesn't answer.

"Is there something I can do?"

She runs her hand over the baby's head. There's the dent where the bones haven't closed. The fontanelle. "Sure," she says. "You can tell me why I feel so shitty."

"Yeah," Noah says, "I know. It must suck. Always being on call."

The condoms in Noah's cabinet, they're a kind she's never seen before. Durex Performax, black wrapping with a yellow swirl. Standing in the bathroom earlier, she counted them. Seven.

"You want to know what sucks?" she says. "It's trying to decide which is worse, liking you the way I always have or realizing that I really don't. Like you."

He receives this in silence. Vividly, she sees his face when he was seven. They're in trees, maybe down at Omand's Creek, and he's showing her something – a huge secret, some little stone carvings wrapped up in a cloth. George Stonechild made them. She remembers arrowheads, and tiny figures with four nubs for legs and knobs at each end for the head and tail. "This one's a fox," he said. "This one's a bear."

"What's this one?"

"I don't know, he didn't tell me."

"Why don't you ask him?"

"I'm not allowed to see him anymore."

It was only after Noah moved away from Wolseley that he finally ended up with a dad.

The damp ground is freezing her feet, and she lifts one leg and tucks it up on the chair. "You know," she says, "I have saved you in ways you don't even know."

"Are you really pissed with me about something, Sylvie?"

She hears the loon again and waits until it's finished, and then it's the hurt of the afternoon that washes over her. "You never told those guys about the baby, for one."

"It's not like we talk."

"No, I'm sure you don't." Tears are drilling like nails in the corners of her eyes, but she's determined not to cry. "They all have kids, you know. Their girlfriends all got knocked up. In grade ten. I guess you want to be different from them."

"I am different," he says in a low voice.

"Yeah, well. That's nice for you." In a minute he'll mention the shining example of Einstein's girlfriend. Sylvie's got goosebumps on her thighs and arms. The baby might be cold too. She needs to go in, but first she will say the important things. "Listen, I know what I did was wrong, driving up here without a licence. But I had to see you alone, so I made a bad choice. All I have in front of me right now are less than fabulous choices."

She can read Noah's silence: *I didn't have a choice at all.* She tips her head back. The clouds have shifted; they've opened to disclose one little patch of stars, like another bright scrap of memory. The baby's sucking has slowed, she's almost finished this meal. "Are you going back to Guelph in the fall?"

Noah doesn't answer. Liz is obsessed about their having a written agreement. And why did Sylvie never talk to Noah about it? Because she's been expecting that any minute now this will all be over, they will all wake up from the spell.

"Noah, are you going back to university?"

"I don't know. I don't know what to do. They're paying for everything. And the research I'm doing, it's really important. Not just to me."

She lifts the baby to her shoulder and pats her back. The couch squeaks and a big square of yellow falls on the side of cabin ten. Then it goes black again and the screen door slams and in a minute he comes around the corner of the cabin. He's put on jeans and runners and he's carrying the quilt. Sylvie stands up and he drapes it around her and over the baby. They sit down side by side on the two chairs.

What she needs to say is this: I should not be trusted with this baby. But they just sit listening to the moan of the waves and the rush of the wind, and then he's the one who speaks.

"I guess I wonder, are you trying to prove something?"

"What do you mean?" Even with the quilt over her she's shivering.

"By keeping the baby."

Treetops move above the cabin, a darker black against the black sky. It's a good question, she thinks. They could spend the rest of the night talking about it. But it's not the sort of thing she wants to get into with a stranger, however kind he is.

12

Faun Vision

T HAT WHOLE DAY IN SOUTHERN MINNESOTA
would have had nothing to do with Sylvie except that the
lane winding through the forest was a trail she might once
have followed in a dream. And the red house looked, as she sat in
the front seat of her mother's car with horns growing out of her
head, as though it had grown up in the woods the way the trees
grew. Two vehicles were parked at the end of the lane, a grey car
and a big white van with alligators painted on the side – green alligators levitating on their tails.

"Where's the van from?" Liz asked.

Sylvie read the plate. "Wisconsin," she said. "Haslet Hygiene.
Suppliers of hygiene, cleaning, and paper products."

Then they saw that a table had been set out under the trees, on
ground sprinkled with early-fallen golden coins. People were sitting
around it – two men and two women – with glasses and jugs and
plates of picked-over food, and they lifted their heads, startled and
annoyed by a strange car in the driveway.

"What the hell?" Liz said. "Is it too late to back out?"

"Yes," Sylvie said. "They're looking right at us."

One of the men got up from the table and walked over to greet them. Liz parked properly and they opened their doors. "You found it," the man said.

By the time Liz got out of the car, she had put on an arch manner that Sylvie despised. "We're the only Luddites in the Western world without a GPS," she babbled, letting her door close with its expensive *plunk*. "But I had a great navigator." She introduced Sylvie as her "charming personal assistant."

The man glanced over the roof of the car and gave Sylvie a quick, unsmiling nod, like a celebrity trying not to encourage a fan. He was unshaven but not bearded: the bottom half of his face looked as though it had been shaded in with pencil. He stood close to Liz, talking in her ear, while the three people at the table watched curiously.

"I've still got some hangers-on," he said in a low voice. "Totally unforeseen." And then, obviously afraid his friends might have heard him, he raised his voice. "Drifters," he called. "Riff-raff. Fucking Yankee freeloaders." One of the women at the table cheered and raised her glass.

"Oh, no problem," Liz said, smiling, and the man led her towards the table with a hand on her back.

From somewhere Sylvie could hear children shouting. She hung back. The elastic of the horns she had bought at the festival was starting to call up a halo-shaped headache on her scalp, and the feeling she had grew stronger, that she was in a scene from something else, if she could just figure out what – the trees so stout and tall, thrusting clouds of yellow and green leaves up into a brash blue sky, and the shuttered house, and the table, the people lounging around it with their jugs of wine or cider. And on the edge of the clearing . . . but was it a clearing? It was more that the forest wandered carelessly around the narrow house and tossed flame-filled bushes at a shingle-covered shed, and then, as it gathered into darkness by the woodpile, slyly opened its verge to reveal, beautifully camouflaged from human eyes, a slight, brown, upright creature that Sylvie recognized with a leap of her heart as the faun she had seen at the Festival. Returned now to its natural environment, watching Sylvie with an appealing gaze. No one but Sylvie saw it.

"We're fortifying ourselves for an afternoon of cooking," said the woman who had cheered, indicating two big jugs with home-made labels: *Brookside Cider. 100% Natural.* This woman had silver-ish blond hair cut as short as a man's, and she was lavishly pretty, like the roommate in a sitcom. "Big feast tonight," she said.

"I don't know what I was thinking," Liz said about their empty-handed arrival.

"How could you know what you were walking into?" the woman replied. Her name was Adrienne. "We were supposed to be the hell and gone back to Madison today. Nine o'clock this morning we're all crammed into the van. But we were *so* wrecked from last night, and the kids were fighting like beasts – one of our little monsters threw Liam's *shoes* out the window – and we're out on that maze of roads without a clue how to get back to the highway, and then we come across this awesome farmers' market, and so we stop. It was so cool. They had, like, salads full of *flowers.* Fresh cheese curds. Puffed Wheat cake – do you remember Puffed Wheat cake? We ended up buying everything in sight – a bucket of salad and jugs of cider and wild game! We bought bloody *game,* for crying out loud, and we don't even have a cooler. So then we set off again and we're desperate for a bathroom by that point, and we come to a corner that looks kind of familiar, and Peter looks at me and I look at him and we tool back up the lane. You should have seen Krzysztof's face when we pulled in! But what the hell, we thought, we've got the van until Tuesday and he's got all the room in the world. Well, really, it's because we felt sorry for Krzysztof, out here all on his own. Although, I guess he wouldn't have been . . ."

Her voice was trailing off because everybody was looking in the direction of the faun, who was coming across the yard. She was about Sylvie's size. Her hair was brown, the brown of her body and limbs, and she had grey horns with furry brown and white ears standing up behind them. She walked straight up to Sylvie and stood staring at her as though they were animals in the forest and no one else was around. Her features were pert and her eyes were bold, tilted and golden – an eye colour Sylvie had never seen except in dogs.

"Sylvie, this is Payton," Adrienne said from the table. "Isn't this a nice surprise, Payton? You've got somebody to play with!" And then Adrienne pretended to turn her attention back to the adults, but Sylvie could tell that all of them were holding their breath to see what the faun would do.

She just stood and stared at Sylvie, unabashed. It was clear that the rules of human behaviour did not apply to her. Sylvie knew it was her own horns that had drawn the faun towards her.

"What a gorgeous harvest table," Sylvie's mother said, sitting down and gesturing to Sylvie to take the chair beside her. "I'd kill for one."

"This place is fabulous," Adrienne said. "And you get a very generous stipend. I've applied three times but I've never been lucky. Too much competition from *assholes* to the north. As if you don't have your own retreats. Your whole bloody country is a retreat!"

Krzysztof flipped a chair around and sat on it backwards, ignoring Adrienne.

"This is my new strategy," Adrienne said, shoving her own chair back and swinging her feet up onto the lap of the man beside her. "I'm going to pester Krzysztof so he can't work. Drive up at every opportunity. Keep him pissed and hungover and distracted. He'll never be invited back."

"How do you know each other?" Sylvie's mother asked.

"Oh, artists all know each other. Borders don't mean anything to artists. We're like migrating animals." She leaned forward and poured herself another glass of cider. "Payton, why don't you take Sylvie down to play in the guest house? But take your hoofs off first – you're going to twist an ankle. And drop the mute thing, already. You are creeping Sylvie out."

"Excuse me," Krzysztof said unpleasantly. "The guest house is my goddamn studio."

The faun continued to look at Sylvie with imploring eyes. Sylvie considered getting up in response to her unspoken plea, but she felt confused and abashed by her gaze and she was insulted by Adrienne's term *play*. So she just sat as though she were part of the adult conversation, trying to figure out the meaning of this scene she had found herself in, which was not immediately evident.

The other man at the table wore clip-on sunglasses flipped up, like awnings over his regular glasses. He was nice-looking but totally silent. He was married to Adrienne, Sylvie deduced from the flat tone of her voice when she spoke to him and the fact that her feet were in his lap. The other woman Sylvie judged to be the age of a university student. She had long golden hair and beautiful big eyes and a sad and lifeless air, and she never spoke.

From their seats at the table they could see a tree house where three little boys were playing. One had a rope with a plastic milk jug tied to it; he was dangling it from the platform and the other two were below with sticks, hitting the jug like a piñata. They were slightly different sizes, but from their similar childish behaviour Sylvie judged them all to be about eight. Adrienne explained that the blond kids were hers and the kid up on the platform was

Payton's little brother, Liam. She seemed about to say something else, and then she changed her mind.

"These comely Canadian wenches have been on their own pilgrimage, to the Renaissance Festival," Krzysztof said, pouring Liz some cider and gesturing to ask whether he could give some to Sylvie (Liz shook her head). "That crude commercial rite of Bacchus down the road. Dowagers streaming in by the thousands to show off their goods. The plunging décolletages! The boobs thrust out like howitzers over laced corsets – my god!"

"I beg your pardon," Liz said, putting a hand to the neckline of her top. She had on skinny white capris and a new top, very low-cut, in a pattern that was not quite an animal print. Enlarged tree bark maybe. "You weren't actually there yesterday, were you?" she said.

"Took the kid a while back," he said.

"We were there yesterday," Adrienne said. "It was the longest afternoon of my life."

"I hear you," said Liz. Talking in a bubbly but secretly nervous way, she went on to tell them how she had struck up a conversation with a woman. In the *Chateau Vino*, she said, making fun of the name. "Just this ordinary woman. I mean, she was dressed like Maid Marian and she still managed to look like a soccer mom. I asked her where she was from – I figured she'd say, 'Minnetonka. I'm a clerk at Walmart,' or something – and she says, 'I'm the second daughter of the Earl of Blackmoor. When I was sixteen, my father tried to marry me off to a cruel baron. So I escaped to Bristol in a turnip cart, and then I became the mistress of Captain Kidd.'"

They all laughed. They talked about the cybergoths who were starting to take over the festival, and about the mishmash of costumes you saw there, mythological creatures such as centaurs and unicorns walking around with people in Elizabethan dress. "It's sort of like the Flintstones riding dinosaurs," Liz said. And Krzysztof said, "It's not in the least like that," and Liz put her hand on his arm and laughed flirtatiously into his face.

They talked about the cider and tilted their glasses up to the sun, and Krzysztof and Adrienne argued about whether this cider was cloudier than the cider they had drunk the day before. Adrienne's husband and the university student laughed along with the others, but Adrienne's husband hardly spoke and Melody, the young woman, never did. She was wearing cut-offs and a tiny lacy black top, and she sat tightly, as though she was too cold to move. Sylvie could not figure out who she was connected to, though it was Krzysztof she watched with her big, sad eyes.

And all the while the faun stood by Sylvie's chair, gazing at her with an intense expression of appeal. When Sylvie looked in its direction, it took a step backwards. It was trying to lead her away but it would not make a *Come here* gesture. And so finally Sylvie got up and the faun turned and led her towards the house. They were about the same height, but the faun's hoofs raised it a few inches. The hoofs looked exactly like real hoofs, split and brown and glossy. The faun was wearing brown shorts and light brown tights with fur sewn on them, fur that curled prettily down over its hoofs. It had a tail that grew naturally from the back of its shorts. She – *it* – was perfect.

The door to the house was painted a deep red and had an old-fashioned iron handle. The faun tilted its head and looked at the handle curiously, so Sylvie went ahead and opened the door. The house was dark after the sunshine of the yard. A hunting lodge, it would have to be. Hoofs clicking against the wooden floor, the faun turned mincingly around, as though in wonder at discovering a human abode. It looked with surprise at the big stuffed sofa and chairs, at the tall grandfather clock, and at the fern, into which it buried its face for a moment. Then it tripped around the kitchen, looking shyly at the white appliances, and cunning came into its eyes. Come here, it said by tilting its head. Sylvie walked across the kitchen. There were shelves crowded with bottles of all colours and shapes, and piles of vegetables on the wooden sideboards, and a big old-fashioned stove, and a deep white sink. Where a *body* lay. A long, pinkish brown body with tiny arms, curled piteously to fit into the sink. Headless. The faun smiled over it, enjoying Sylvie's horror.

Sylvie ran outside and sat again on the chair beside her mother. She put her feet on the rung of her mother's chair. Above them the trees breathed and dropped sunlight in patches on the table. A tray of Puffed Wheat cake was brought out and broken into chunks and the little boys ran over from the tree house and grabbed it up. Lemonade was poured for them and cheese was cut. Wasps discovered the table and the boys began to whine.

Sylvie said no to the cake. She felt too sick to eat. What was it in the sink? It was dead and skinned. Bloodless, neat, muscle-bound. It was not the shape of any animal she knew. It was a life form that had fallen from another world and been slaughtered in this one.

Payton had come back outside and taken her spot at the edge of the forest. She also ignored appeals to eat. Sylvie could not look at her. She was appalled by the graceful, innocent way she stood and moved, when in fact she was so knowing and so cruel.

Then there were efforts to get Payton to take Sylvie to the lake. "All of you can go," said Adrienne. The boys hooted and ran to fetch their things. "I guess this is why we pay you the big bucks," she said to Melody, and Melody stood up reluctantly.

"I don't have a bathing suit," Sylvie said, and Adrienne laughed.

"Payton has two," she said. "Payton, you'll lend Sylvie one of your swimsuits, won't you?" and Sylvie understood that what was funny was the word *bathing*.

"Are you coming?" Sylvie asked her mother in a low voice. Liz gave her head a private shake, not meeting Sylvie's eyes. She moved slightly on her chair to shut Sylvie out.

"They're in the canvas bag in the back of the van," Adrienne said, but Payton gave no sign that she'd heard. "Sylvie, come and pick out which one you want," Adrienne said loudly.

So Sylvie got up and followed Adrienne to the alligator van. Adrienne opened the big door at the back and beckoned Sylvie closer. "I just wanted to talk to you for a minute," she said in a low voice. "I wanted to tell you their mother is very sick. Payton and Liam's mother. Well, she's dying, actually. It's harsh to say it that way, but it's the sort of thing that happens, and you're a grown-up girl, I can see how mature you are. She has breast cancer. The poor kids don't have a father. God knows where they're going to end up. We brought them with us to give everybody a breather. I thought I'd tell you in case Payton is a little hard to take. She can be, I know. But will you cut her some slack?"

"Yes," Sylvie said. They were standing under the door, looking through the van windows at Payton, tiny and motionless under a tree, as though they were looking at her through the wrong end of binoculars.

"It's really nice that she has you to hang out with today," Adrienne said. "I hope you can get her to go swimming. I don't know if she'll take that costume off. Her mother made it – her mother was very talented that way. She always intended to take Payton to the festival, and then things got really bad really fast." Adrienne pulled two bathing suits out of a red canvas bag. An orange two-piece and a blue and white striped one-piece. "Just take these upstairs. I bet she'll follow you. You can grab towels from the bathroom."

First Sylvie went to the car and got her overnight bag, and then she walked alone into the cool, dark house. She saw a steep staircase and she climbed it. Upstairs, she went into the first bed-room she saw. It had a large brass bed and a big wooden desk and a round rug made of rags, braided and coiled in a way that Sylvie knew how to do herself. The whole house, with its solid and simple furniture, reminded her of the big house at the Fort. Three or four books were scattered on the desk, and Sylvie picked one up. *The Golden Bough,* with a beautiful thick cover of moulded leather. Inside were old-fashioned illustrations in soft colours, as though hand-painted. In the first, a barefoot woman in an animal-skin dress led a goat away from a forest. She had her head turned back regretfully and she was blowing on a long horn. Sylvie turned the thick pages slowly. She recognized an adult version of the sort of stories she loved, but the text was dense and resisted her.

Also on the desk was a photograph, a family portrait. It had been taken at the booth Sylvie and Liz had visited at the Renaissance Festival. To Sylvie's surprise she knew all three people in it. The woman was Mary Magdalene, who used to come to their house and whom Sylvie loved. Once when she was little, when all the mothers were sitting around talking in the dining room, for no reason Mary Magdalene reached out and lifted Sylvie onto her lap. Then she got up from the table and carried Sylvie to the couch, where she sat and read to her, a story about a mouse dentist who dared to fix the teeth of a fox. It was the only time Sylvie ever heard that story, but she remembered it perfectly. And there in the picture sat Mary Magdalene with her curling dark hair, a happy childhood memory resplendent in a blue velvet gown.

And beside her was her son, Sylvie's old friend Sparky, wear-ing a leather vest laced at the front. He was taller, of course, but it was him, with his hair and eyes exactly the same warm shade of brown and his happy interest in the world showing on his face. He was holding one arm so that it showed off a beautiful sleeve of overlapping silver leaves. He must be thirteen. He looked willing to be in the picture, not sulky and aloof like a teenager. It was a beautiful picture, as though they truly were a family living in a stone house in a valley with mist rising around it and sheep grazing on the hills.

"Krzysztof's family," said the faun, at her elbow. She laughed at how startled Sylvie was. "It's feathered mail," she explained then, as if she could read Sylvie's thoughts. "Falconers wear it so the falcon can land on their arm and not tear the skin."

"They didn't have anything like that at the photo booth," Sylvie said.

"I guess it belongs to the kid, then. He must be a falconer." Then Payton pointed to Krzysztof, the man sitting outside at this moment with her mother. "What a pig. Well, that's an insult to another hoofed beast. What a *human*."

Sylvie put the photograph back on the dresser. "I thought you didn't talk."

"Fauns talk among themselves," Payton said. "What did you think? Did you think we're just what humans see?" Her freckles were perfect little brown ovals drawn on with a makeup pencil. Her breath had a mushroomy smell. "Go and change," she said. "Go into the other room." She picked up the blue and white bathing suit and thrust it at Sylvie. "Take this one. Put it on under your clothes."

As Sylvie walked across the hall, Payton called, "You'll like it. It's got a hole in the crotch."

Adrienne and her husband were in the kitchen working when Sylvie and Payton walked through with all their clothes on. "My, aren't you the modest pair," Adrienne said. "Well, have a fun time *bathing*."

Sylvie did not look over at the harvest table. Melody was standing by the step and they followed her across the yard and onto a path that opened into the woods. She had on a black bikini under a long, see-through shirt of pale yellow, and she was carrying her purse and a big canvas beach bag. Her body was thin but curvy; her breasts looked like two apples rocking on the narrow board of her chest. The trail they followed was covered with fallen leaves and sank gradually lower. The three little boys ran ahead and Sylvie walked silently beside Payton. They had to walk slowly because of Payton, who plodded along in her hoofs, holding her hands in front of her like kangaroo paws.

Sylvie was not wearing a bathing suit and she suspected that Payton was not either. When she went back to the big bedroom after tucking the bathing suit under a pillow in the second bedroom, Payton was still dressed in her faun costume, standing at the window looking through Sylvie's binoculars.

"Cool," she said.

"Are binoculars allowed in your faun act?" Sylvie said.

"Actually, little sucky Canadian girl, binoculars were invented to give faun vision to humans."

She handed them to Sylvie in a sneering, check-it-out-for-yourself way. Sylvie raised them to her face and, without having to refocus, saw the temple of a man's bent head with a vein twisting along it. She located the arm that belonged with this head and followed it down to where Krzysztof's hand, a big, expressive hand with dark hairs on the backs of the fingers, was exploring the white fabric covering a slender thigh. Then she handed back the binoculars.

None of them spoke on that long walk to the beach, except Melody, who called once for the little boys to wait. As she walked, Sylvie thought about Sparky and Mary Magdalene, about how terribly she had missed them since they moved away, without realizing it and without thinking about them very often. But suddenly

her grief blurred her eyes and squeezed her chest, and she understood that she'd been *waiting*, as though they'd promised to come
back for her and were late.

Finally water glinted through the trees and the woods opened
to the lake, a finger lake with a tiny beach and a swimming area
roped off. Three pairs of sunbathers lay on the sand. No one was
swimming – the sun was warm but the air was cool, and the water
would be too. Melody dropped the beach bag. She knelt and pulled
two big deflated beach toys out of it, and the blond boys sprang for
them. "Share with Liam," Melody said as the three of them ran
up the beach. "The pump?" she called after them, and one of the
blond boys came back for it.

In spite of the cold, Melody took off her yellow shirt, spread
out her towel, and lay down in her bikini. "Stay together," she said
to Sylvie and Payton without looking at them. "Don't go outside
the buoys." She fished an MP3 player out of her purse and stuck in
earbuds and closed her eyes.

Sylvie and Payton sank back into the woods. From its edge
they watched the boys blow up the two inflatable floats. One was
a purple turtle and the other was a sort of Jeep or tank with a cord
dangling from each end. It had a label you could read with the
binoculars: Aqua-Hummer. The pump was a foot pump; Payton's
brother, Liam, took it over almost at once and worked it hard, first
with his foot and then with the heel of his hand. He was skinny but
he worked fiercely, leaning his whole body into the job. When both
floats were inflated, he stood up in satisfaction, and in a flash the
two blond boys had yanked them away and were running towards
the water. Liam ran after them and tried to grab onto the floats,
but they managed to kick him off. He fought them, splashed back
and forth from one beach toy to the other, while Adrienne's boys
paddled vigorously away from him.

Sylvie and Payton watched for a while, and then they grew tired of his misery and stepped back into the woods. The game they fell into playing was not to be where humans expected them to be, but always to be watching. They found a spot very close to where a couple was lying and set about spying. Sylvie trained the binoculars on the woman and picked up the skull pendant hanging between her breasts. Then she swivelled towards the man just as he was rolling over, his muscles writhing like the pythons she'd seen the day before. When they stilled, she discovered a big eye tattooed between his shoulder blades.

Then Liam was back, crying across the sand and floundering through the weedy verge towards Payton. Payton froze into one of her faun poses. "They won't share," he wept. Angry tears smeared the dust and sand on his small face. He batted at her arm once or twice. "Payton, it's not fair," he cried. His little tummy went in and out as he sobbed.

Payton stood in a patch of weeds, her face remote. Sylvie was shocked by how alike the two of them were. She knew exactly who they would be at school, both of them hanging around the fringes in their own grades, with their furtive faces and their dark talents that nobody admired, and the awkward yearnings that everybody recognized and mocked.

"Listen," she said to Liam. "Why don't you just play with something else?"

He recoiled from Sylvie. He was old enough to be ashamed of crying in front of a strange girl. He reminded her of a famine victim in the uneven knobs of his backbone and the thin slats of his ribs, and in his knees, which were bigger around than his skinny legs. He turned back to batting at his sister, bleating, "Payton. Payton." He was too thin to hold up his swimming trunks properly, and the crack of his ugly little butt was visible.

Sylvie suddenly loathed him as though he were her own disgusting little brother. "Fuck off and play by yourself, loser," she said in a voice she had never before heard coming out of her chest. She reached over and swatted his butt hard with the back of her hand, and that was what finally drove him away.

With Payton silent beside her, she picked up the binoculars and turned back to her joyless spying. It was an ugly lake, long and marshy. It smelled of rotting snails and of toilets. No cottages were visible on its margins, but rickety docks had been built out into the lake. She checked out the next sunbathing couple, and she began to hate faun vision, which revealed black bristles on the woman's legs and the birdlike dart of the woman's eye down the page of a stupid magazine, and the man's balls (crinkled skin with sparse and piggish hairs) nudging out one leg of his shorts, and the chewed chicken bones he had tossed towards the bush, lying now with sand sticking to them and flies crawling over them.

She lowered the binoculars and turned to look for the boys. Liam was nowhere to be seen, but Adrienne's blond sons were towing the beach toys up onto the sand. Apparently they were leaking. The boys went looking for the pump. While they were retrieving it, Liam appeared out of nowhere at the shoreline. The blond boys spied him and ran down to chase him off. Then screams of outrage rose and the two boys pounded back to where Melody was lying motionless on her towel.

"Liam pissed on our floaters!" they shrieked. "He pissed on the Hummer and then he pissed on the turtle! He did it so we can't play with them! He did it on purpose!"

Melody craned her head. Liam was standing at the edge of the water facing them, a small, malevolent figure with his swimming trunks pulled up crookedly and the corner of a beach toy clutched defiantly in each hand. "Oh Christ," she yelled. "What a little shit!"

"What a shit!" the brothers cried, picking up the theme and dancing to it on the sand. "What a fucker! He's a goddamn fucker! Do something, Melody!"

But instead of getting up and dealing with him, Melody flopped over onto her stomach. She lay absolutely still, ignoring them all. One of the brothers kicked sand at her and she ignored that too, and finally they ran back towards the water, yelling threats at Liam.

Sylvie got up helplessly and began to cut across the beach towards the path. Payton came hobbling along after her. The sun was lower now and fell in visible shafts through the trees, lighting up separate clumps of leaves on the forest floor. The trail was clammy under her feet. At a certain point she became aware that Payton was close behind her. Barefoot now, wearing ordinary footless tights. She no longer had fur; it must have been attached to the hoofs.

The clearing was silent. No one was sitting at the harvest table. Between two trees hung a hammock, and in it Adrienne's husband lay sound asleep. No one was in the kitchen. A pot bubbled on the stove and cooking smells hung in the air. The Puffed Wheat cake sat uncovered on the counter. Sylvie snatched up a piece and shoved it hungrily into her mouth, and Payton did the same.

Then Sylvie crept soundlessly up the stairs and Payton followed. The bedroom doors were open and both bedrooms were empty. They could hear water splashing in the bathroom and the squeak of someone's butt on the floor of the tub. Sylvie swallowed the last of the Puffed Wheat cake and turned to go back down the stairs, and just then a pure, beautiful voice lifted into the hall. "*As I went down in the river to pray,*" someone sang. "*Studyin' about that good ole way.*" It was Adrienne. Sylvie could picture her holding up a sponge, squeezing water onto her white shoulder while she lifted her voice with the careless joy of a song-filled bird. She finished and then she began again, singing more slowly now, her voice filled with longing. They stood listening on the stairs, clutching the smooth banister. *"Good Lord, show me the way,"* Adrienne prayed, and then her voice died out and silence filled the house.

The building Sylvie understood to be the studio was down a path that branched off the trail to the beach. A little stream ran alongside, and the mud of the path was slick and studded with rough-capped acorns that bit viciously into Sylvie's feet. The studio was made almost entirely of glass, and it was so deep in the woods that no sunlight reflected off it. Sylvie stopped when she saw it and stepped away from the path and into the trees. From where she stood, all she could see inside was something small and white.

It was Payton who crept up, who raised her head and looked. Then she ducked, crouching below the window, and turned her small, knowing face in Sylvie's direction. A foot, Sylvie thought. There's a bed up against the window, and someone is bracing themselves against the glass with their foot.

Back at the beach, the sunbathers were gone. Just their outsized footprints left behind, and the immaculate impressions of their towels. Their drink cans and chip bags. Little nests of cigarette butts. Melody was lying on her side, rolled in her towel like a blanket, sound asleep with her blond hair tangled in the sand. The little boys were nowhere in sight.

It was cold now; no one would think of swimming. The wind had started to blow up waves. But two coloured shapes bobbed halfway down the narrow lake. Sylvie lifted the binoculars to her face, and after a minute a curve of purple plastic moved into the frame. It was the inflated turtle. No one was on it. Then she picked up the Aqua-Hummer; the two mattresses seemed to be tied together. And in the Hummer she made out a small human arm. It was Liam's. Liam, who lay with his white face propped against the edge, like a castaway who had been several weeks at sea. He was closer to the far shore than to this one. She saw his arm move, but he did not appear to be paddling.

Sylvie handed the binoculars to Payton. Gooseflesh had come out on her arms and on Payton's too. Payton knelt beside her and lifted the binoculars to her face, which was white now, all its freckles rubbed off. With her turned-up nose and her high little cheeks, it was not a hoofed creature she resembled but a squirrel. Not a real squirrel, Sylvie saw – a Disney one. While she scanned the lake, Sylvie sat on the sand, her head bowed, not looking out at the water. Somewhere in the course of the afternoon she had lost her sandals and her horns, as well as the gift of speech. Her legs were covered with scratches and her bare feet were rimmed with mud from the path. She wrapped her arms around her rib cage and bent over them, digging her feet deep into the dirty sand.

13

A Square Yard of Turf

EVERYTHING IS EASIER WITHOUT A MOTHER, contrary to what the fairy tales say.

She came back at the end of that summer and the neighbourhood appalled her. The sun glinting off the casement windows, the red vines heavy with purple berries. Bronze flowers in their autumn mounds and the ghostly stencils of fallen leaves on the sidewalk. And on the weekend when they raked the yard, her father lurching around the elm trees carrying her mother piggyback, Liz shrieking with laughter, tossing her hair from side to side. It was sinister in the worst way: it covered its wickedness with beauty.

In her second-floor bedroom Sylvie dreamed of a little boy's body in a sink, hands and feet tied with vines. The next night she slept on the futon in the basement, and she never moved back upstairs. It was the year she put away childish books and did not take other books up – nothing as dangerous as stories.

It was the year their dog Oscar came home from roaming the streets and crawled up the veranda steps, vomited, and died. The year she was out walking with her grandfather and he spat in front of the 7-Eleven and said, "Goddamn rug-riders." The year she was sitting eating buttered popcorn and saw, on their flat-screen TV, a sea of skeletal children in Darfur waiting on the ground for the aid trucks. The winter she started slipping out of the house in the night, walking the silent snowy streets (leaning on the railing of the Maryland Bridge and picking out the black line of open water between the snowy riverbank and the ice, thinking for one terrified minute, I'm not really here, until the cloud of her breath on the dark air reassured her). It was the year the polar ice cap shrank to its lowest size yet, the year she had Ms. Lewinski for science and they all went around putting bumper stickers on the teachers' cars and on their parents' cars that said: I'M CHANGING THE CLIMATE. ASK ME HOW. The year her body turned both slim and lush, the year she got sick on vodka-spiked Slurpees down by Omand's Creek, the year of the co-ed sleepover at Jenn's, when a boy from Kelvin squirmed onto the mattress between her and Jenn and in the dark lay a hand sweetly on her right breast. The year she discovered Value Village and never again wore clothes bought by her mother. The year she started calling her mother Liz. The year she realized a rubbery black coating had grown over her heart.

It was the year she untethered herself from Wolseley and started hanging out with the tradespeople on its edges. She got to know Iris, the hoarse-voiced woman who ran the laundromat and lived above it and dressed in clothes people left behind in the dryers. She met three brothers from Vietnam who called themselves "velo engineers," and she sat with them on the back steps of their chop shop on Sara Avenue, chewing sunflower seeds and spitting the hulls on the ground. She made friends with Tat Sing Lee, who owned a convenience store on Portage. He had a plot in the community gardens, and in the spring she started helping him. The next year he was sick and on chemo and she did all the work while he sat on a plastic chair and told her what to do. That winter he died, and she talked the clerk at City Hall into letting her keep the plot, even though there was a waiting list.

All through high school she gardened, as though it might save her. Her garden was a row garden – that's all she knew. She grew carrots, beets, kale, peas, onions, and green beans, and she gave all the produce away. She never grew anything as frivolous as flowers, and she never bought bedding plants, she grew everything from seed. Sprinkling minuscule grains along a trench and then digging up the stout, firm roots in the fall – it made her feel like a wizard. Carrots were her specialty. She loved them for the tininess of the seeds and the feathery tops, and for the fact that wild carrot, also known as Queen Anne's lace, will find garden carrots and breed with them.

She knew enough to leave the carrots to sweeten in the ground until the first frost, and then she dragged her wagon over on a Friday evening, wearing her blue hat with the fat braids. Crickets chirped from the edge of the allotment. Marigolds like knots of yellow yarn were scattered on the cleared plots, and broken tomatoes rotted here and there. She bent over her carrots, the noise of the city around her. The tops lay dead on the ground, marking the rows. She loosened the earth with her spade and then wiggled out each root. In the morning she'd carry a bag to Iris at the laundromat. A bag to Nathan and his mother, and to the Nguyen brothers. That family from Somalia who'd moved onto Spence Street – she'd given vegetables to them before. She'd leave the wagon outside their apartment building while she was inside. If hungry people came along and stole her vegetables, obviously that would be great. But if they didn't, she'd take a bag to her grandfather, who lived on canned soup and bologna.

"Scarlet Nantes" her carrots were called. They were lovely and straight because she had thinned them faithfully, and with their rounded tips they looked like new candles. She nestled them in rows on a blanket in the wagon, and then she shoved the dirt back into the trench and raked her plot. By the time she turned up Westminster Avenue, her wagon wheels squeaking, a harvest moon was lifting itself over the tall trees of Wolseley.

That night at Presley Point, while Sylvie and Noah and their baby sleep, fish flies wriggle out of the muddy bottom of the great lake and swim up through fathoms of black water. At the surface they sense the warmth of the dark air and they cast off their fishy disguises and rise into the starry sky with cellophane wings. Then daylight overtakes them and they spiral helplessly down, glomming onto the asphalt shingles of cabin eleven.

Noah goes outside to do his tai chi and a minute later he's in the doorway, saying, "Come outside for a minute."

Sylvie comes to the door with the baby on her shoulder. It looks as though a frilly curtain has been hung over the front of the cabin.

"They're what I was screening for on the boat last summer," Noah says. "When they were in the nymph stage." He's holding a wriggling worm with wings you can pinch like handles between your thumb and forefinger. So many emerged from Lake Erie a few years ago, the Doppler radar picked them up – Alison, a woman he works with, told him this. They live only a day, just long enough to mate and lay their eggs.

Alison, Sylvie thinks. She shoves his hand away, revolted by the antenna-like hairs sticking out of the fish fly's tail.

Miles away on the horizon, you can see the tufts of waves blown up during the night. Sylvie is bleary from lack of sleep and from the beer, and from the light that lies uneasily over the lake and the bush, bleaching away their nighttime conversation. A cheap red kayak struggles along the shoreline, the kayaker banging his paddle against the plastic sides with every stroke.

Noah turns up the path. "I'll run up and talk to Alison before I do my tai chi. I want to catch her before she hitches a ride with someone else."

Alison has today and tomorrow off. She has a driver's licence, and Noah wants to see if she will ride into the city with Sylvie. Sylvie was eating a bowl of granola when he sprang this news on her. "Today?" she said. "It has to be today," he said. "There's nobody going in on Monday." The baby was sitting in her car seat with a little trail of spit-up on her chin and was indifferent to this news.

"I'll try to talk her into hanging around until noon," he says now. "We can do something this morning. Take the canoe out maybe." He frowns as he says this, hearing how stupid it is.

The minute he's out of sight, Sylvie runs back into the cabin and puts the baby in the car seat and begins to shove her things into her bag. Her clothes from yesterday, the baby's blankets, her hairbrush and makeup bag. She takes the big bale of disposable diapers because she doesn't want Noah looking at it and thinking of her. While she's strapping the car seat into the back, the baby bats impersonally at her face. She looks like a stranger's baby this morning, rounder faced and bigger headed than usual.

Noah is still nowhere in sight. "Bye-bye, Daddy," Sylvie says in the baby's voice as she heads the car up the little trail that runs to the main road.

She can see the sun shining in a wintry way behind thin clouds. A hydro line runs along the lane, and a crazed blue heron is trying to perch on a wire, like a tightrope walker on stilts. When she reaches the main road, she turns the wrong way, she turns north. This is to throw them off. She can picture them chasing her down, this Alison person in wild confederacy with Noah, the two of them skimming over the landscape like the canopy walkers in kung fu movies and throwing themselves on the hood of the car, pressing their accusing faces against the windshield. Sylvie drives quickly, nimbly away from them, taking pleasure in the snap of gravel under her tires. When she can peel her eyes away from the road, she glances in the rear-view mirror. Her eyes meet the baby's, and in an instant the baby is crying. Mile after mile, she cries. In her rage she's worked her way to one side of the baby seat – all Sylvie can see now is a tiny fist shaking.

This is the road they took the night Sylvie met Noah, almost a year ago. Thea was driving her dad's old minivan. It was late – they couldn't leave until Sylvie's shift at Stella's finished – so Sylvie was designated to stay awake and talk to Thea and help her watch for deer. Thea could hardly see over the steering wheel and she drove very strangely, with her right foot on the gas pedal and her left foot ready to hit the brake. It was after two before they got to Zach's road. They had slowed right down, shining Thea's big flashlight out the window, looking for a sign that said MO'S MARINA AND ENGINE REPAIR, and they spied deer – two does, standing still on the gravel edge. The spotlight caught their eyes.

"Holy shit," Thea said, braking.

"I wish I knew what that is," Sylvie said. "In their eyes, that makes them gleam like that."

"They're throwing death rays at us." Thea drove cautiously past them and turned up the lane to the cabin. "Wakey, wakey," she called to their three friends sleeping in the back seat. Nobody moved.

"You know fauns?" Sylvie asked. "Like from mythology?"

"Yeah," Thea said. "Mr. Tumnus. Standing by a streetlight holding an umbrella. That was James McAvoy – did you know? The guy from *X-Men*?"

"It was a *lamppost* in the forest," Sylvie said. "I always think about fauns when I see deer. Because *fawn*, right?"

"Well, duh, fauns *are* deer. Half deer."

"No, they aren't, Thea. They're half *goat*."

The baby's crying is plaintive – it's hard to shut it out. On either side the bush is scrubby, she's driving through a stretch of muskeg. Not like the forests she dreamed about as a kid: the massive trees with their limbs lacing overhead, the forests where you went in as one thing and came out as something else. She sees the faun crouching in the filtered light, talking in an ecstasy of sibling viciousness, unhinged but galvanizing, her eyes golden. Just an ordinary girl whose mother was dying.

She drives on along a highway that bisects the bush in a straight line. She hasn't met a car in miles. For the first time she notices a terrible stink in the car. It's the diaper from yesterday, rotting on the floor of the hatchback. Then she realizes that the screaming has stopped. She tilts the rear-view mirror. The baby is sitting with a look of pure sorrow on her face, but she is alive.

This is Zach's corner. There's the sign: MO'S MARINA AND ENGINE REPAIR. Sylvie could drive up there now and see the old boathouse where she and Noah kissed; she could stand in the echoing darkness and listen for their voices. But the boathouse and the cabin will be covered with fish flies, which seem to follow human settlement like a plague. And Zach or his family might be there.

On impulse she turns left onto a gravel road and follows it for a few miles. Then a trail angles off the road, grass growing up the middle of it. *Drive me*, the trail says, so she turns off and drives into the bush. *Stop here*, the bush says after a little way, so she does. She stops and presses the window down and sits for a minute, listening to insect sounds and the twitter of birds. Then she gets out. She opens the hatchback and picks up the dirty diaper. The baby is asleep. She'll sleep now until noon, and then she'll wake up in a panic as if she's about to starve to death. Sylvie is an expert regarding this baby. She closes the hatch as quietly as possible and looks for a minute at the white dome of her daughter's head, dead to the world on the other side of the tinted glass, before she starts to climb the ridge.

A little way into the bush, five or six young poplars are brownly dying. People have been here, the earth is torn up, exposed as pure golden sand for no reason that she can see. Thistles are growing at the edges of the scar. There's a Cheetos wrapper plastered onto the sand. Cotton takes how long to degrade? But it will, eventually. She crouches, scooping sand with her fingers, feeling how cold it is just under the surface. A crow lifts in disapproval off one of the dead poplars, floating upwards. As she stoops, Sylvie feels how heavy her breasts are. She hadn't really believed she and Noah would make love. She just pictured how he would run his fingers tenderly, sympathetically along her scar.

She has never before worried about his liking other girls. Never once. I had the idea I owned Noah, she thinks. Because I knew him when he was little. I made up a story about him, and now he's stepped out of it. The silver falconer's sleeve – it was armour made from beer cans, as it turns out. At one time it glowed in her mind like a talisman. Not magic exactly. Meaningful. Or *sacred*. Will she ever see that force in things again? Or was it only inside her – some molten underground stream that she crouched beside and dipped things in to make them special?

She buries the diaper and then stands and starts to walk along the ridge. She's wearing flip-flops, she has to watch her footing. There's no path but there is a natural way. She can see the lake lying like fresh cement along the horizon. This is mixed forest, untouched: spruce, oak, aspen, poplar, Manitoba maple, birch with its chalky paper, and lots of scrubby bushes she can't name, rising and falling by a logic of their own. As she walks, her eyes lay squares over it. If she'd gone to botany field school she'd have been given a square metre of this land, and she'd have taken it apart with tweezers and identified every single bit of plant life in it.

She's over a second ridge when she finds what she's looking for. It's a perfect little diorama of bush, a square of permaculture. Her eyes peg it at its corners. It's sunken, as if it may have been a creek bed long ago, or the source of a spring. There are poplars all around, but her square metre is mostly tiny shrubs and lichen. Three shoots of spruce like miniature trees. A single stem of oak with wavy adult-sized leaves. She'd have had a whole summer to spy on the secrets of these plants and how they make a garden for each other, and if she was lucky she'd have discovered some synergism nobody has noticed before.

She crouches by her square metre, taking it in. And then, from over the ridge, she hears her name. A deep voice, a dream voice, like God's. *Syl-vie.* She scrambles to her feet. Now there is sun, as there has not been sun in all these weeks. Now it's hot – she finds herself in a different day, lightheaded from the sun. She goes to brush off her shorts and her hand encounters a small, soft bit of ectoplasm. Panicked, she flings it at the bush – a fish fly. Something flails in the corner of her eye, white, spasmodic, and she leaps in the other direction, startled. It's her hand, it's her fucking hand.

And then she hears it again. Syl-vie. With a yelp she starts to run, clumsy in her flip-flops. Syl-vie, the ridge calls. She turns, slips, and rights herself. Around her the aspens quake and spruce trees clutch the earth with knuckled roots. *Syl-vie,* the voice calls again, and she scrambles in terror up the ridge in the opposite direction.

THREE

14

The Wilds

IZ SLIPS OUT OF BED, LEAVING AIDEN ASLEEP, and goes down to the kitchen. She smells baby in the house – puked-up milk and the diaper pail and the ancient perfume of talc – and she feels more buoyant than she has in ages. She puts on coffee and reaches for her tattered recipe file. She still has a day and a half of quiet ahead of her. She'll get a stew going in the slow cooker for their dinner tonight (they can be carnivores while Sylvie is away), and she'll make a couple of vegetarian casseroles with an eye to restocking the freezer. Then in the afternoon, if it's warm enough, she'll take the phone and a glass of wine out onto the deck and get caught up with Char.

She's at the stove browning cubes of flank steak when Aiden wanders in, looking like death warmed over. "What time did you get home?" she asks.

"Around midnight."

She pours his coffee. "The kids don't have a very nice day at the lake."

"It might be warmer up there."

"How about pancakes?"

"No, I'm okay."

Doctor Jekyll has left the building, she thinks as she sets the coffee pot back on its element. This is our own Mister Hyde, hunched on a stool in his tattered Eric Clapton sweatshirt. Then something wiry inside her asserts itself, and she turns back to Aiden. "So how was the concert?"

"Didn't get in."

"Oh. I thought you had tickets."

"I never said I had tickets."

"So what did you do?"

"Just went for a drink."

"How's Neil?"

"I didn't see Neil."

"Who'd you go with?"

"Jake."

"Jake. You know a Jake?"

"Defrag. My client."

"Since when do you socialize with your clients?"

"It was a one-off."

"Still."

He gets up and opens the bread drawer and drops two slices into the toaster.

"What have you got planned for today?"

"I plan not to plan. That's my plan."

"Well, you need to clean up all that tree debris, for one thing. The grass is never going to come up."

"Okay, I'm on it."

He eats his toast and drinks his coffee, a cone of silence over his head. After that he settles into the armchair in the living room and works his way methodically through the weekend *Globe and Mail*. He does something with a pencil, the crossword or the

Sudoku. Finally he goes upstairs for a shower. Then, when she's chopping vegetables for a peanut stew, she hears him out in the hall, putting his boots on.

"Where you going?" she calls, keeping her voice friendly.

"I thought I might ride over to Don's Photo."

Liz puts down her knife and steps into the hall. "Don's Photo? Whatever for?"

"Oh, just to look around. I'd like to have a video camera. Or at least a webcam. While the baby's tiny like this."

She is truly aghast. "You're planning to buy a video camera. You've got that much spare cash at the moment."

"They're not that expensive, Liz."

"You're not thinking, Aiden."

"What's to think about? It's not that big a deal."

"Everything's a big deal. Do you have any idea how much the diaper service costs? As just one example."

"Oh god, Liz, we could live on half of what we earn now."

"Aiden, you are so full of shit." By then she's too furious to talk.

He's gone several hours, during which she rehearses her arguments and cooks, quickened by her rage. "He's a wanker," she says to Max, slamming the cutlery drawer shut. "He's a total goddamn wanker."

By the time he comes back, the evidence of her industry is lined up and cooling on the counter. She looks over at him when he appears in the doorway but she doesn't speak.

He shrugs. "Don's was closed. I just rode around the park."

"Well, that's five hundred dollars you didn't blow." Her overly-pleasant voice is going to put him on his guard. She drops her dishtowel and lowers herself into a chair. "But you know, we do need to sit down and have a serious talk about finances. Now might be good."

"You think so, eh," he says, opening the fridge, and the danger she senses is a heady foretaste she hasn't encountered in quite some time.

"Yes, I do," she says. "I'm overdrawn at the moment, and I suspect you are too. It's going to be years before Sylvie is on her feet. It's going to be really tough. We'll need a second car, for one thing. My salary is frozen, and your practice is not exactly growing."

He opens the cheese drawer and checks out its contents. At the sight of him rummaging in the fridge, her fury thrums in her chest. "Aiden. Please don't eat now. It's too late for lunch. I've made a wonderful dinner, *boeuf bourguignon*."

He pulls a package of corned beef out of the meat tray and lifts it to his nose.

"You know . . . you won't like what I'm about to say, but you need to start thinking about it. We're going to have to sell the cottage. It's our only disposable asset. And the taxes are ridiculous."

"What?" It's clear this has never once crossed his mind.

"Think about it. You never get up there, and Sylvie and I haven't been in ages. Sell it to some back-to-the-earth types. Some kayaking kids. It's not doing us any good. It's not accessible."

He stands very still. She actually sees his neck thicken. Then he puts the meat back in the fridge and closes the door and turns towards her. "And why am I not up there?"

"Well, I know, this spring has been weird. But even last year — didn't you go just once last year?"

"Yes," he says. "Just once."

Her heart contracts at the venom in his voice and the brutal downturn of his mouth, and for the first time ever she thinks, *He looks like his dad.*

"Congratulations," he says.

"What do you mean?"

"You have finally found a pretext. To get at the one thing that matters to me. It was only a matter of time, I guess. But I never thought you'd stoop to this – using this crisis, our daughter's baby. To take away the one thing, the *one thing* I care about."

She is seeing it; she is finally seeing into the vault. She stands up. "The one thing," she says, taking a step towards him. "We don't matter? Our life together? Our daughter and this tiny baby? Do you *hear* yourself?"

Their voices are low, they're both breathing hard. Max is on high alert between them. "Don't twist things," Aiden says. "You know what I mean." The phone on the counter rings. He swings an open hand and knocks it off its stand and it clatters to the floor.

"What the hell is that?" she says. "You're trying to intimidate me?" She smells the meat in the slow cooker, she feels the cork, cool under her feet. She sees his exhilaration, what it means to him to accuse her like this, his hatred open and undisguised at last, and she feels a dark rush too: she sees he's right, she *has* been waiting for this chance. Their eyes are locked, neither of them is going to look away. She's tasting blood. He has no idea, no idea what he's up against, the carcass of their sorry marriage is well within her sights – and a dial tone drills into her consciousness.

"Pick it up. It could be Sylvie."

He bends for the phone. In his movements, in the angle of his head and the stoop of his back, she sees his regret already setting in and satisfaction warms her. The phone rings again as soon as he sticks it back into the base, and this time she grabs it.

"Elizabeth Glasgow?" It's a man.

"Yes?"

"You're the registered owner of a silver 2012 Jetta SE?"

"Yes."

"Licence MIE 466?"

"*Yes?*"

"It's Constable Glowicki from the Powerview detachment of the RCMP."

"The Powerview RCMP?" she repeats, trying to make the words mean something.

From the ridge Aiden can see the lake, a dark molten body to the left. The sun hovers above it. It's going to be a long, long twilight. Mosquitoes hit at his arms and temples. What do you call this sort of country? It's scrubbier than forest, not as friendly as a wood. It's bush.

He's standing on a rise above a little trail about twenty miles north of Presley Point. On that trail are parked three RCMP cruisers and a couple of trucks belonging to kids from the research station, and the Jetta, of course, sitting crookedly in a big square of police tape.

He and Liz drove up in Rupert's car with Max in the back seat. On the way, as they rolled north out of farmland and into bush, they tried to get their minds around what the police had said on the phone.

"She was not dehydrated – did I tell you that? They said she's absolutely fine."

"She can't have been there long. The kids will be nearby."

It was a man driving a truck who spotted the car and stopped to check it out. He found a tiny baby alone in it and took her to the closest town, to Pine Falls. Was the car locked? Presumably not. Sylvie's things were in it. When the police called, Liz gave them Noah's name, and Thea's.

"They're hiking," Liz said to Aiden as they drove. "Obviously. It's a beautiful day. They're having a great time and they got carried away. 'Come on, one more bend in the trail!' I can just hear Sylvie. I can *hear* her."

"With the baby alone in the car? I'm not seeing it, Liz."

"You're right, of course. It's beyond belief. It's *breathtaking* that anyone could be that stupid and irresponsible, but let's face it, that's what they are. Your cerebral cortex is not fully developed until your late twenties, I've read that. I can see it in Sylvie, I'm sorry to say. And Thea – well, just look at the girl. But I thought Noah might be a little more mature." He was so plucky as a kid, she said, after the swing hit him. He insisted on walking on his own, even though his eyes had pretty much vanished.

She talked nervously until about the time they passed through Brokenhead First Nation, and then she stopped and sat with her arms tightly folded, staring straight ahead. "Well, at least they're together," Aiden said into the silence at one point. She didn't answer.

But in fact, as Aiden and Liz discovered when they got to the site and an RCMP officer walked soberly over to the Caprice, it's just Sylvie who is lost; she is lost alone. After talking to Liz, the police tracked down Noah. Sylvie had spent last night at his place, but then she took off on her own and drove up to this road and left the baby in the car. Noah's in Pine Falls now with the child welfare authorities. Thea? Thea was never there.

When Aiden walks back from the ridge, the police are taking photos of tire marks, hoping to figure out how many vehicles drove up that trail. "I'm going to hike a little further up the escarpment and take a look," he says to a cop with a ponytail.

"No point. We've been back and forth over about five square kilometres in the past few hours." She puts a hand on his arm. "Listen, you'll just make our job harder if you head off in the dark. Would you mind stepping into the cruiser? We'd like to ask you a few questions."

So Aiden and Liz climb into a back seat with no door handles. "Did she have your permission to take the car?" asks the cop in the driver's seat.

"Of course. Did you think she stole it?" Liz stares at them fiercely.

"Well, we see your daughter's not a licensed driver." They've got her purse, her phone, they've gone through everything and they've hatched their theory. That Sylvie, upset because of a fight with her boyfriend, has walked or hitchhiked back to the highway.

"Oh, come on!" Liz cries. "Without her things?"

Aiden asks whether Noah reported an argument. "He says there was tension," the female cop says.

They hear barking and shouts and the police let them out of the cruiser. Max is dancing in an excited circle of young people, Noah's friends from the research station. One of them opened the door of the Caprice and the dog headed straight up the ridge, sniffed around, and started to dig in a spot where the turf has been torn open by ATVs. And he found a diaper! Recently buried, the sand sticking to it. The kids open it, they display the orange smear inside.

"Yes," says Liz, reading the entrails. "Of course it's hers."

Aiden crouches with his hand in Max's ruff. "Sylvie," he says urgently. "Let's find Sylvie! Where's Sylvie, Max?"

Max smiles and butts his head against Aiden's thigh. Play! he barks. Throw something, Aiden! When no tennis ball materializes, he appeals to the cop with the ponytail, pawing flirtatiously at her thigh. You love me, he barks. I can tell.

The male cop from the car is at Aiden's side. "Can I ask you not to bring your dog tomorrow? If we get a sniffer, it will just complicate things."

"Yeah, of course. I'm sorry. We didn't quite have the picture when we left the house."

The Jetta's being towed to the RCMP detachment in Powerview

for a forensic examination. There's a little motel in Pine Falls that will let them stay with the dog. Its stucco walls are covered with the transparent wings of fish flies, and dead fish flies litter the sidewalk. Where people have walked, the separate wormy bodies have been ground into muck. A teenage desk clerk slides a big, flat key across the counter.

Liz opens the door of unit fourteen and then closes it again.

"What?" Aiden says.

"It's an ashtray in there." She walks back to the Chevy and leans against it, pressing her face into her hands. "I can't believe this is happening," she says.

"Come on," Aiden says, putting an arm around her shoulders.

Inside she finds the ice bucket and fills it at the bathtub for Max. She sits on the edge of the bed, making no effort to undress. "They will have to bottle-feed the baby," she says. "Sylvie will be really uncomfortable by now. Oh god, she'll be going crazy."

"She's spent enough time in the wilderness." Aiden's working at lowering a malfunctioning blind. "She'll be sensible. She'll smear mud on herself to keep the bugs off. She'll climb a hill and orient herself."

Liz looks at him mournfully. "You know, when they held up the diaper, that snowy-white cotton diaper with our baby's pumpkin-coloured poop in it, I couldn't help but think, *That diaper is a testimony to a family doing everything right.*"

Finally they undress and crawl into bed. A few minutes later, Liz sits up. "Oh fuck."

"What?"

"I left the slow cooker on."

She turns on the light and finds her cellphone and calls Wendy. "We got detained. It's a long story, I'll tell you tomorrow. You have your key, right?"

"Why didn't you tell her?" Aiden asks when she lies back down. She makes a small distraught sound and doesn't answer.

Ten minutes later she's up again. She fishes a couple of little blue pills out of the zip pocket of her bag and presses one on Aiden. He doesn't want to take it but she makes him. It's not much of a drug – when the digital clock on the bedside table reads 1:00, they're both still wide awake.

Aiden has been trying to tune in to Sylvie's distress, to get the measure of it. All he can feel is Liz's agitation humming in the mattress. He puts a hand on her shoulder. "Anyone who loves the world as much as Sylvie does is not suicidal."

"Thanks for that," she says. "Suicide hadn't actually occurred to me."

They roll to the far sides of the bed. Aiden turns the clock away and it lights up the wall red. Sylvie's all right, he tells himself. We don't have the stature of tragedy victims.

Their orientation into the bush next morning is decided by a dog with more authority than Max, a beautiful classic German shepherd called Damsel, who retires afterwards to her kennel in the back of a van, having led the police to the far side of a second ridge before she admitted defeat. Forty or fifty human searchers, and all they have is sight – no sense of smell to speak of, and anyway they're walking in a fog of bug spray. Aiden is nauseated from it, and from the RCMP coffee and stale doughnuts, and from the drug Liz forced on him, which put him to sleep eventually but left him irritable as hell, robbed of the night journey, as though he'd been blindfolded and driven towards morning in a truck. That's okay, it's better that everything irks him: the billions of leaves in minute motion from here to the treeline, the grasping nettles, the tiny flies like spots in his retina. Nothing's going to slip past him, not a gum wrapper, not a button, not a Kleenex, not the infrared trace of Sylvie's energy zigzagging across the floor of the bush.

And he's got what nobody else has – he knows his daughter. This morning he stepped out of the motel as the sun was colouring the clouds in the east, and he knew what had happened: Sylvie was looking for something. She set out on a quick, impulsive quest and got disoriented, and now she's living the parent's classic nightmare, knowing she's left her baby somewhere and can't get back to her.

This presumes that her state of mind is the sort of thing you can predict. Noah rolled onto the site in a truck with two other guys just after Liz dropped Aiden off, and Aiden headed straight for him.

"How you doing?"

"I'm okay, I guess. I'd like to get started." He was standing at the open door of the truck, stuffing an anorak into a backpack. "Do you have the gear you need?" He glanced down at Aiden's slip-on shoes.

"I'll manage."

"I'll try to find you some boots. What size do you wear?"

His buddies were banging around in the back of the truck, unloading a blue plastic water barrel. Aiden drew him a few steps away. "Listen, how did Sylvie seem all weekend?"

"Not great. She was really upset on Saturday night, and then yesterday morning, before she took off, she was just quiet."

"Were you expecting Thea to come up with her?"

"No."

"So you asked Sylvie up on her own?"

Noah frowned. "I thought she had her licence."

"Okay, fair enough. But what happened? How the hell did she end up out here?"

"I have no idea. I was trying to find somebody to ride back into town with her, and she just took off."

"Did she seem confused? Out of touch with reality? As though some psychosis was setting in?"

"No, she was just stressed out. Upset. Pissed off with me. I was kind of a shithead with her."

Aiden turned abruptly away, happy to let Noah have the last word on that. He went back to the food table and sucked down a second cup of coffee, kissing goodbye to the prospect of borrowing boots. A cop with a bullhorn climbed up on the tailgate of a truck and briefed them. Somebody handed out water bottles and then they were shuffled into crews, and Aiden saw Noah working his way through the crowd to join him. He had a friend from the research station with him, and a pair of mustard-coloured construction boots. "These were in Tyrone's truck." They were rough and cheap, but they fitted and Aiden took them. So, a generous guy, as well as candid.

They're searching side by side now, he and Noah, walking north towards a fire tower, using it as their compass point. The bush is silent. They're forcing the rodents into burrows, herding the ungulates north. The sun is hot. Look for shade, Sylvie, Aiden counsels as he tramps. It's nightmarish country the further they get into it: uneven, marshy, given to burrs and mosquitoes and random ankle-breaking stones. Root balls wrenched up, their black undersides masquerading as bears – a trick the bush plays over and over. It's the sort of marginal land where bodies are found. A hunter stumbles on a simulacrum of clothes and human bones, two-dimensional and plastered onto the ground. Your whole career as a parent, you're rehearsing for that moment; you always know you're a hostage to fortune.

Two or three hours in, it's like they're doing a boot camp drill, he can't bring his daughter up in his mind. "Sylvie!" he calls. Her name ricochets from the ridge, invisible searchers calling in front of him and behind. As the echo dies out, Tyrone takes it up in his eager young voice. Noah. Gilles, who says her name beautifully, in the French way. And then Aiden can see her again, standing alert, turning her head to check out the direction of the sound.

Liz hates getting into Rupert's old boat of a car – the smell of it, the plaid seat covers held in place with wide bands of dirty elastic. It *is* like driving a boat, she thinks as she turns onto the highway. And there's the fact that Aiden's mother died in this car, in the seat where Liz had to ride yesterday. They were driving up Ness Avenue, Rupert and Greta, following a truck with an open box full of junk. Going fast, the truck hit a big bump and some small but heavy engine part was dislodged, sailed through the air, and smashed into Rupert's windshield. A distributor, is that what Aiden said it was? Greta never knew what hit her, as people like to say when they're not prone to imagining the catastrophe of flesh and blood and bone that suddenly materialized in that seat.

What a strange sense of unreality she has this morning. Go home, the police said when they saw her at the site, standing there miserable in her skirt and sandals. Go home and email us a recent photograph. If I was going to go home, I could have gone last night, she said. They ignored this. There should be someone there, they said. Your daughter may call, or she may show up. As soon as you get there, check through the house. See if she came home while you were out and packed up some things.

Max is whining in the back seat. He's starving, poor dog. In their rush yesterday he slipped into the car, and they didn't want to take the time to drag him back into the house. Plus they were in shock, dizzy with adrenaline – they'd been standing in the kitchen tearing each other apart and all the while, life was working up a real tragedy to dangle over them. So they didn't think too much about the dog. Rupert would shit if he saw Max with his paws up on that seat.

His wife died in this car, and Rupert simply had the windshield replaced and kept driving it. She died on a trip out to the bulk stores in what Aiden calls Little America. They were on the road because Greta couldn't resist canned peaches at ten dollars a case. Liz always blamed her for that, as if her passion for discount shopping had led to the accident. You find something to blame people for when bad things happen to them, because then you can say, I'd never do anything like that. So I'll be okay.

The highway is quiet. She takes the car up to 110. It's bleak country she's passing through, trees, and swamp full of last year's ragged bulrushes, and more trees. Dead spruce still holding on to all their rust-coloured needles. But it's June, the nights are warm enough. No one dies from mosquito bites. And how far could Sylvie wander between the lake and the highway? Liz is amazed at her own calm as she considers this. That's because letting yourself feel fear is admitting that something really terrible may have happened.

At home, Max pads into the kitchen and gulps down a heap of kibble and then curls up on his mat and goes to sleep. The ceramic insert from the slow cooker is soaking in the sink and the house smells unpleasantly of desiccating meat. She calls Wendy, who answers from an aisle at Costco. This time she tells her.

"I'll come straight home," Wendy says. Then Liz calls Thea's number.

Against all odds, Thea is at her parents' place and picks up. "Oh god," she says. "Oh, I'm really sorry. She just *so* wanted to go. I didn't know how to say no."

"Well, too bad about that," Liz says, and hangs up without a goodbye.

She has the number for the relevant child welfare worker; the police gave it to her. There's no answer and she has to leave a message. Then she calls the Powerview RCMP detachment. They have close to seventy searchers at the site now. "Feel free to keep calling in. And by the way, does your daughter have a passport? Check whether she took it. Check her bank account, if you can."

Oh, for crying out loud, Liz thinks as she hangs up.

She climbs the stairs of the quiet house and stands in the doorway of Sylvie's room, surveying the crib with its eyelet lace skirt. The mobile of dancing dolphins, the stack of contoured flannel diapers. Calm, she's still calm. Because they've been here before, Liz and Sylvie. Although it may just be wishful thinking to link Sylvie's being lost now with Sylvie lost then, that terrible evening of the missing children in Minnesota. When she and Krzysztof were back at the harvest table and the au pair came trembling up from the beach with just that sad little girl in the goat costume and they had no idea where any of the other children were. The little girl was crying in a raspy way and was totally incoherent.

She remembers them running down a long trail to the lake and staring in bewilderment at its marshy margins and the waves that were blowing up. Back at the house, they went straight to the phone, telling themselves they were calling the sheriff's office out of an excess of caution, and sure enough, just then a man drove into the clearing with two little blond boys he had picked up on the highway. They were trying to hitchhike to the store with money they had stolen from the au pair's bag while she slept on the beach. No doubt Liam had tried to follow them.

But Payton, this child who had been invited along for respite from the spectacle of her mother's dying, would not be consoled. "Nobody ever liked him," she kept sobbing. And later, when the sheriffs went up the cabin line asking questions, someone turned up with the two empty blow-up rafts, tied together with a cord, and of course there were still two children missing at that point. And then a cottager reported the little boy's body floating in the water.

That other time, Sylvie was lost for five hours. Liz finally found her in the car – where she had *not* been earlier: they had searched the cars, including the trunks – so she was clearly playing some sort of game. Almost lightheaded with relief and not knowing what had happened, what Sylvie had seen, it was very hard for Liz to know how to deal with her. She absolutely refused to talk through the rest of that night, when Adrienne and her husband had gone to the sheriff's office and then wherever else one goes (the morgue? the coroner's?) and Krzysztof was wordlessly doing the *I'm not sure what any of this has to do with me* thing, and the au pair, a vulpine-looking girl, like Princess Diana in her bulimic phase, was a weeping mess, and Liz was obliged to look after four upset children, counselling them about the tragedy, trying to sort out beds for them, trying to get them to eat. She knew Sylvie would be morally offended by the rabbit, so she made up a plate of salad and bread and cheese and took it over to the armchair where she was curled up. Sylvie caught her breath sharply and shrank away.

When they left after breakfast the next day, Sylvie would not get into the front seat. She wouldn't put on a seatbelt. She rode kneeling on the back seat and looking out the rear window or lying with her back towards Liz.

They rolled silently past the Mall of America and headed straight north. It was an early autumn day of shattering beauty. From time to time Liz tried to reason with Sylvie, although god knows, she had her own thoughts to occupy her mind that day. "That makes me really uncomfortable," she said about the unattached seatbelt. "But I guess, when I think about it, we never used seatbelts when I was young. We drove out to B.C. almost every year, right through the mountains, Maureen and I rolling back and forth from the front seat to the back. And we survived."

Silence. Liz put it to herself that there was enough trauma in the drowning of that little boy to account for any sort of acting out on the part of a pubescent child. But as she drove, as the forest gradually slumped into browning cornfields, the painful realization that Sylvie *knew* grew upon her like rheumatism settling into her bones. It was impossible to ask. Either way, where could such a conversation go?

By the time they got home she had run out of stamina. In the kitchen, *Aiden Home* was scrawled on the calendar. On Thursday, three days away. She looked up the number of the marina at Rocky Landing. She asked the guy there if he would take a message over to the island. Tell Aiden Phimister they'd be at the landing, noon tomorrow.

Next morning Sylvie sat in the front seat like a sphinx, and Liz drove east into the Shield with the understanding that she might be driving them towards the end of their life as they knew it. Bring it on, she thought furiously. She was desperately thirsty – she'd spent most of the night in the living room with a bottle of wine, and she'd forgotten to bring water. When they got to the marina, Sylvie pitched in to haul their bags down to the landing, and there was Aiden, paddling across the water in his padded vest, and Liz saw him clearly and knew that, whatever was drawing him away from them that summer, it was not the sort of thing she had let herself believe.

Sylvie dashed down the boat ramp, calling for her dad. As he hoisted himself out of the canoe she threw herself at him, burying her face in his vest. Aiden looked questioningly at Liz over her head. "What's all this about? Was the festival a bust?"

"The festival was fine. No, it's something else. I'll tell you when we get there." Her mouth was so dry she could hardly speak.

"Can't you tell me now?"

"Well, something very sad happened." Terror – the sort you feel in childhood – overtook her: she could feel her heart pounding through her entire body. "After the festival we stayed at a little lake because the weather was so nice. And there were some people from Madison, Wisconsin, on the beach, and a little boy drowned. He drifted away on a blow-up raft."

Sylvie was leaning her full weight against Aiden, as though she were six years old. He tried to get her to stand up so he could see her face. "Did you see it, sweetie? Is that why you're so upset?"

"No!" she cried sharply into his vest. "I didn't see it."

He stroked the back of her head and looked at Liz. She raised her shoulders slightly. He bent over Sylvie. "Well, that *is* really sad. It must have kind of taken the fun out of your holiday."

She wouldn't look at him. So it was Liz who said, "Yeah, it did, all right. It was terrible. So I figured your little girl needed her dad. And how has your time at the cabin been?"

Back in the kitchen she goes to the phone and calls three or four friends, recruiting volunteers. She calls her sister, Maureen, in Toronto and finds herself downplaying the situation to the point where Maureen wonders why she's phoned. She calls Charlotte in Vancouver.

"I am so scared," she says. "Although maybe Sylvie's just trying one on. Maybe she was hiding in the trees, watching the car, waiting to be sure the baby was found."

"Liz," Charlotte says, "that's totally crazy. That's like something out of a movie. Why would she do such a thing?"

"Oh, I don't know," Liz says. "I'm just having trouble thinking straight."

"Should I come?"

"No, stay where you are. Just keep answering your phone, okay?"

She hangs up. She makes a pot of coffee. She hasn't eaten a bite since lunch yesterday. She drops some bread into the toaster and stands with her forehead against the cupboard. The toast comes up and then Wendy is at the side door. She taps and comes in without waiting for Liz to answer.

"We haven't heard a thing from Noah's mother," Liz says. "I can't believe it." She pours a mug of coffee for Wendy.

"Why don't you call her?"

"I tried, but there's no answer."

"They've likely gone to Presley Point to be with Noah. To join the search. Are you going back up?"

"As soon as I hear from CFS."

"I'll go with you."

"Would you stay here instead? The police want someone here — they have this crazy theory that Sylvie might come home."

The phone rings. The social worker sounds pleasant enough. "Sorry I took so long. It's been that kind of morning. But I'm happy to say that I've just been to see your little granddaughter and she is fine. A bit of diaper rash, but otherwise she's doing very well, all things considered."

"Is she taking a bottle okay?"

"Yes. Yes, she seems to be."

"Because she's been entirely breastfed up till now. My daughter has been very conscientious about that." She explains that the baby's been living with them since birth, that they've been actively involved in her care. She manages to drop in a mention of their professions. "My husband is out with the search, but I can pick up the baby right away. She will be missing her mother, but she will have us. Of course we all want to make sure she's not traumatized by a long separation."

"I'm sorry, I'm afraid that won't be possible. We've authorized a transfer to an agency in your region." Just for the time being, she explains, until they get a clearer picture of what happened. Apparently this is usual when a child is found alone in a car. Does Liz have a pen handy? She'll give her the number of Faun's new worker.

Liz can hardly believe her ears. "You're keeping this infant in care?"

"As I said, we are for the time being."

"Why in the world would you do that? When she has a stable, loving home? How can that be in the best interest of the child?"

The voice on the phone moves into bureaucratic overdrive. Liz presses the phone to her ear and hunches away from Wendy, who is right in her face, mouthing, What? What?

At the fire tower they're handed sandwiches of mystery meat and Cokes from a soft-sided white cooler. Wind moves the branches of the spruce around them, shaking fresh scent down on them. Eighteen searchers in this crew. Aiden approaches three local guys he hasn't talked to yet, wanting to shake their hands and thank them. They're sharing a joke, but they shut up the second they see him. "Good day for a search," he says, trying to project an air of confidence in defiance of the cap he's wearing: a black Motorola high-dome with mesh vents that Rupert left under the driver's seat of the Caprice.

"So your daughter's a good walker?"

"Great walker. Zero sense of direction, though."

"Wasn't your wife here earlier?"

"She went back to the city. The police wanted somebody at the house."

Noah is sitting at the edge of the clearing, and Aiden lowers himself down beside him. "Liz wanted to get back to call Child and Family Services. She figures the longer this goes on, the more bureaucracy we'll have to deal with."

"I get it," Noah says.

"So you saw the baby last night."

"No, I just met with the worker. She said the baby's with a family in Pine Falls."

"She'll be fine. Listen, I didn't mean to take this out on you before."

"No. I get it."

Aiden watches covertly while he spreads his anorak on the ground and stretches out on it. A guy of few words, a guy who gets it, and a fastidious guy. All this would be so much easier if they really knew him. It strikes Aiden as peculiar they haven't made a bigger effort in that regard. A whole other side to this story has been playing out for Noah and his family, and Aiden hasn't thought too much about it.

Noah lifts an arm and lays his elbow over his face. He's breathing evenly, sinking into a deep rest. He exudes such a calm sense of self, as if he doesn't have anything to prove. Aiden lifts his eyes to follow a crow drifting over the clearing. He has to watch his tendency to idealize people when he first meets them, especially when he's under stress. Think of how he latched onto Edith Wong at the start of their counselling program. Tagging along at coffee breaks, searching out her eyes to share the laugh every time somebody said something funny. She was baffled by it.

On Aiden's other side is Gilles, the baby's rescuer, a francophone from St. Lazare. Gilles was driving up the trail when he spied the car, and he knew who it belonged to. Then he saw the baby fussing in what he called her bucket and he took her out and walked her, calling for Sylvie. Finally he drove to the cabin. But he couldn't find Noah, and by then the baby was crying hard, so he went in to the RCMP detachment at Powerview. He's up on his elbow now, one boot balanced on the rim of the other, plucking at the grass with his big hands, searching for new details he can share.

"Had to put her bucket on the floor of the truck. Seatbelt don't work."

"What were you doing up here, anyway?"

"Checking out the blueberry crop. Should be ripe in three weeks."

"Well, we got lucky yesterday, Gilles. My god."

He finishes his sandwich and lies back beside Noah, angling his cap over his face and closing his eyes against the pinpricks of sun burning through the mesh. He should have taken off Tyrone's boots so his feet could dry. They tramped through a marsh an hour back and he felt the water worming in. The boots weigh a ton and he's beyond exhausted. Two bad nights in a row, because he lay awake Saturday too, full of chagrin about his evening with Defrag.

When they couldn't get into the Sexsmith concert after all, and decided to go for a drink at the Forks, Aiden feeling like a chump, as though he'd lured Defrag out under false pretences. They walked the concrete byways behind the Westin Hotel and out onto Waterfront Drive, where the museum rose like a vision from a grand and permanent world – the city on the hill – and Defrag was dogged and silent, his face pasty white. Across from the museum he veered into a parking lot and sagged against a car, folded himself over, and tried to vomit.

"God, I wish I'd brought the car," Aiden said. "Let's get a cab and get you home." But just as they started walking again a bus pulled up, and without a word to Aiden, Defrag stepped onto it, flashing his pass. Aiden stood and watched Defrag lurch up the brightly lit aisle and slump into a seat. He waited for a goodbye wave, but Defrag's chin was on his chest. As the bus swung up

Waterfront, he saw the number on the back. It was a Salter bus – it wouldn't take Defrag anywhere near where he lived.

Aiden opens his eyes under his cap. Can you love the world and want to leave it? You can, if you see yourself as a blot on it.

"Been in three searches out here."

It's Gilles again. Aiden sits up. How did they turn out? Don't ask.

"We got a good day for this one," Gilles offers, his black eyes fixed on Aiden.

"It's going to be hot."

"Yeah, but it's long."

It's the solstice, Aiden realizes.

They get back to walking. Aiden is belching processed meat. Sylvie steps vividly into his mind, her new soft, bereft look. She seems glazed these days. Like the girls in the group homes where he used to work, although in their case it was sniff and drugs. We failed her, he thinks. It's a fairly new notion. Just being ourselves with her and loving her, it wasn't enough. We needed some sort of method.

They climb a rise and a low vista stretches before them. Ragged spruce, dead aspen. He feels shaken by its indifference, and the band around his diaphragm tightens. Just for a sec (as though his field of vision has expanded, like a camera lens that gives you more than your naked eye can take in), he sees the whole panorama hurtling towards annihilation, shrivelling at the edges as though a match has been put to it, and he tries to look bravely. He has no choice but to look. But already the vision has narrowed – it's something his brain can't sustain – and he's back in the ordinary bush, where chickadees lift out of the scrub as he advances.

The road, when she comes across it in the white light of noon, is straight and wide and empty. She stands on the gravel shoulder with her one torn flip-flop in hand. Almost at once the haze of heat in the distance resolves into a big red truck. Its brakes thud and it looms beside her, diesel fumes and a wall of sound. The door opens. A man leans across the passenger seat, his face shaded by a cap. "Oh, god, thank god," she cries in a voice hoarse from screaming. He doesn't make any move to get out. He's jerking his head, urgently signalling. Are you in or not? She sees a metal hand-grip and clutches it, putting her bare foot on the running board to haul herself up.

He waves her onto the passenger seat. She can't make out what he says. It's cold in the truck and the smell is acrid. He unscrews an aluminum water bottle and holds it out. *Lentamente*, he counsels as she drinks, dribbles running over her chin and onto her T-shirt. He hands her the cap and then he works a gear and the truck is moving again. She screws the cap on and lets the bottle roll to the floor. On either side she sees the bush that called her name when she was crouched by her square metre of earth the day before. Sliding past the dirty windows, already sunk back into itself, low and scrubby, a sea of trees. The bush that rearranged itself as she stumbled through it hour after hour, offering up bewildering ridges, identical and facing in contrary directions. Swamp where silt welcomed and comforted her feet and leeches attached themselves hideously to her ankles. The slopes where light lay in heartless beauty on the aspen as the sun sank, and coyotes prowled yipping in the dark. (Dad, she said. Try to sleep, he said. It's not you they're after).

The cab bounces and pain from her breasts sears through her. Oh, she gasps. The driver's dark eyes turn in her direction. Kind eyes. He notices her arms, how chewed up they are. From the stings and bites of the insects that were her torment in the bush, drilling into her, over, over, and over, the brutal, obscene question:

Did you leave the car window open? *Se terminó, se terminó,* the man says comfortingly and firmly, as though he knows exactly what happened and how to deal with it. With his eyes fixed on the road, he reaches down and fumbles in a leather pouch between the seats, spilling out its contents on the floor, and thrusts a flat tin at her. He means for her to open it and dab what's inside on her bites. A painted medallion lies among his things, a beautiful Virgin in a blue robe sprinkled with golden stars. Her lovely face is cast down, her hands folded in prayer. A howl gathers in Sylvie's throat – the horror is chewing through the lid she's been holding over it. She sees the silent car sitting by the trail, the baby's white face in the narrow frame of the rearview mirror. The man talks on in a rapid mixture of English and Spanish, and she braces her shoulder against the dusty door of the truck, blindly clutching the open tin of sticky brown salve in one hand and the top in the other, breathing in the ammonia stink of chickens, hearing the stream of his words like a radio playing in the distance, seeing what it means to be found.

15

The Light of My Life

SUNLIGHT IS POURING THROUGH THE SKYLIGHT by six a.m. They call it a loft, but of course it's an attic. The attic . . . you think of madwomen. Or Europe's Jews hiding from the Nazis, or flood victims peering in terror at the black water creeping up the stairs. One day we might be glad of the skylight, Aiden thinks, lying in bed while Liz sleeps. I can pry it open when the water rises, we'll be rescued by boat, or helicopter. If there *are* helicopters. Fuel, what fuel do helicopters use? He rolls onto his stomach. If he worked at it he might doze off again, but he doesn't have the concentration. Lying on his stomach puts a strain on his back. And the mattress isolates and magnifies his heartbeats, which seem to be arranged in arrhythmic sets of five.

They started the night with a summer-weight duvet, but it's been trampled down to the footboard. He rolls back over and looks at Liz, lying on her side facing him, masked like a bandit. She has a pillow tucked between her knees and she's wearing black panties and a pale green tank top. Through the fabric he can make out one breast stacked softly on the other. In spite of her thinness, a little pad of fat is forming under her chin. His penis is stirring – it's always been a free agent. Maybe Liz senses him, maybe that's what the panties and T-shirt are about.

Last night Thea called to invite Sylvie to a Fringe party. "Sorry, she's not up to it," Liz said. She didn't even call Sylvie to the phone.

"That's not right," Aiden said.

"Look at her, Aiden. She's *blotto*."

It's true that Sylvie has some sort of time delay happening. You speak to her and she's like a foreign correspondent via satellite from the Middle East, watching you expressionlessly while the message works its way through the mess of synapses. The doctor at the Kenora hospital prescribed Xanax and the hospital gave her a supply to tide her over until she can get in to see her own doctor. She's not taking it. "Is this all about the water?" Liz says to her. "Because, just for a little while, you could decide to make some fish happy."

They have a Tower of Babel thing happening, Liz and Aiden: they've woken up from their nightmare speaking entirely different languages. And yet he's tempted to tease her awake, lie close and run his tongue along her temple. Apparently one of the pseudo-experimental tortures in the concentration camps was to put a naked man and woman in a wintry hut and watch them freeze to death. They always copulated before they died. That's what Ben Rosen claimed: proof of the primary nature of the sex drive. Ben Rosen, Aiden's first and most irritating roommate, wore a yarmulke on a daily basis – how could you challenge him? He had a seduction routine that involved lemon drop martinis, but Holocaust lore was at its heart.

Aiden sits up, reaches for the shorts he dropped by the bed the night before, and eases his working parts into them. He pulls on his jeans and shirt and goes down the stairs to the second floor, where the oak boards squeak and a baby briefly slept and sleeps no longer. He walks past the doorway of his broken-hearted, brave, and troubled daughter. Her door is open about a foot. She's sleeping on her tummy, her hair tousled, her arms thrown up like a saguaro cactus.

He goes into the bathroom and uses the toilet, glances while flushing at his turd, ancient and greenish in this blazing light, possibly mossy. He washes his hands and face, brushes his teeth. He'll shower at work; he's got clothes there. He makes coffee and flax toast and sits at the counter in the kitchen, eating his toast with honey. The air conditioner is already on, at seven-thirty in the morning. It's *so* hot, says the city. And soon it will be fucking cold. Make yourselves comfortable, you suffer enough.

Peas lie near the gas jets on the range, perfect balls of pure black carbon. Sylvie refused dinner last night, and then she came down to the kitchen and made the dish known in this house is as Indian fried rice. Aiden and Liz sat on the deck the whole time, which required no small exercise of will on Aiden's part, because his impulse is to never stop talking to her until he figures this out.

Kenora is a couple of hours east of the lake, just across the Ontario border. Aiden and Noah made the drive there to pick Sylvie up. On the way home she stayed awake. She said she'd been sleeping at the hospital while she waited for them, she would help Aiden watch for deer. She asked him if he knew who was looking after the baby, if he had seen her.

"So, honey, you stopped to bury a diaper?" he said.

"Yeah."

"And then?"

"I walked up the ridge. I just went for a minute. She was sound asleep. I was thinking about field school."

"Could you see the lake?"

"I could see the lake once in a while, and at first I could see the hydro line. But I think I must have followed them in the wrong direction."

"I can see how you might get lost. But I don't get how you ended up so far away."

"Neither do I," she said in a small voice.

"You remember somebody picking you up?"

"Yeah."

"And then?"

"I guess I fainted."

Noah had slept most of the way to Kenora, and from the stillness in the backseat, Aiden wondered if he had fallen asleep again. She'll tell me when we're alone, he said to himself. He was disappointed, because the three of them talking this through together felt like a good idea. He'd felt such a bond with Noah by the end of their long day of walking side by side through the bush. And they shared that moment of exhilaration and relief when the cruiser drove up to the search site, just when they were marshalling for supper, and the ponytailed cop announced that Sylvie had been located. By the time they had picked up the Jetta in Powerview, by the time he'd called Liz with the good news, Aiden was high as a kite. As he was buckling up for the drive to Kenora, he looked over at his passenger and it seemed that Noah was haloed, his even, tanned, unexceptional features edged with the late evening sunlight coming in through the dusty windshield. How moved he was that Noah wanted to come along, that he was giving himself to their confused family. *Son*, he wanted to call him, the way men do on TV.

He gets up and stands at the window, looking at an empty sky never until this year seen from this yard. A few weeks back, Liz hired a man with a grinder to chip the stumps of the elms. He charged them a fortune and drove away in a blue truck, leaving three massive golden pyramids behind. Somebody has to shovel up that sawdust and haul it away. It's too hot; it's been too hot all week. Anyway, Aiden's instincts are to sit still, keep everything the way it was, so that when the baby comes back and opens her wide, dark eyes in this property they call her home, there won't be any continuity errors, nothing she can latch on to as proof that she was ever away.

When he got home from work last night, a police car was parked on the street in front of the house. Sylvie'd already given a statement, but an officer with a blond brush cut wanted to ask her a few questions. He was initially professional and neutral – Aiden noted his efforts to avoid terms such as *hitchhike* and *abandon*. But after they'd gone through the story of how she managed to get herself lost, he said (as if his was the first brain shrewd enough to have picked this up), "Here's what I don't quite get: You stumble out of the woods around noon the next day. You stand on a secondary road until a motorist stops. And you let this individual drive you south and east, out onto Highway 44, *away* from where you left your baby. You let him drive you as far as Kenora."

"East? I didn't know what direction it was. I was just glad somebody picked me up."

"Did you tell him you'd left your baby alone in the car and had to get back?"

Always the pause. "I tried to tell him. He didn't speak English."

"What language did he speak?"

"I don't know."

"What might it have been? Take a guess."

"Indonesian?"

"Can you describe this individual?"

"He was maybe forty." Pause. "He was just ordinary looking."

"He didn't speak English, and yet he had a driver's licence. Frankly, that's another puzzle to me."

"He was driving. That doesn't mean he had a driver's licence." She had a canny look.

"You could be right about that. But he had a truck. A big – what was it? – black truck. He stopped and picked you up in a truck and he drove south on Highway 11, and then he turned east and went out on Highway 44. Did he harm you at all? Make, er, sexual advances?"

"No. *No.*"

"And you stayed with him all the way to Kenora."

"I was waiting for a town. So I could get out and call someone. And then I might have fainted."

"You might have fainted?"

"I had been walking and crying all night. I had nothing to eat. Anyway, what was the hurry?"

"What was the hurry?" The cop repeated this without inflection, but he darted his eyes to the side as if to say, Where is the jury when you need it?

Sylvie, forced to speak the unspeakable, was scarlet. "If my baby was still in the car, it was way too late to help her."

Aiden bikes through the traffic-clotted streets to work, a middle-aged professional man on a hybrid bike. At the office he showers and changes. They're doing a Schubert hour on Classic 107. Christine Tolefson comes in looking alert, a little life in her painted face. Then it's Norman Orlikow, his hair combed as if he's just stepped out of the *Mad Men* dressing room, wearing saddle oxfords and what Aiden would call a bowling shirt. Sylvie would know whether his look is retro or just weird.

Norman is back after a six-month hiatus. He approached Aiden at the coffee kiosk in the lobby of Aiden's building a few days ago.

"I'd like to make an appointment, Doctor Phimister," he said. "But these are my terms." He actually had only one term: they don't go back to "that stuff that happened." Aiden understood that Norman didn't want to pay for the broken window. His eyes were fluttering nervously and Aiden was struck by what a tiny seed willingness is. But it's all you need, really – or all you are likely to get.

"Okay," he said. "Let's do it."

"You know," he says now, "seeing we're making a new start here, I want to clarify a few things. First off, I'm not a doctor. You can call me Aiden. Second, we need to be clear about why you are here. This whole process is about you learning to see yourself. So you can change. Get over certain things, think about yourself differently. It's not about enlisting me to confirm how cruel the world has been to you. You will be in therapy forever if you don't grasp that."

"Wouldn't you like that? At a hundred bucks a shot?"

"No. I'm not using you for my own ends. That's not what this is about."

Norman seems to be taking this in, turning his lips thoughtfully inside out. It's a fascinating display, like watching an octopus emerge from its den. Then, as an illustration of how sincere he is in his efforts to change, he launches into an account of the work picnic he just attended, at which he tried hard to come out of himself by signing up for volleyball, a sport he'd enjoyed in high school. But sadly, he was ostracized during the game. Volleys that should have been his were scooped and tipped towards other, more popular personnel.

Aiden keeps his eyes on Norman through this whole sad saga, but he can't entirely control the voices in his head. *You keep up that crying, I'll give you something to cry about.*

He runs at noon, runs in the punishing heat. Two guys are sitting outside the shack on the riverbank, drinking beer. Aiden feels a lurch of longing as he peers through the trees. Could you subsist on cattails and catfish? Water – could you drink from the river? Not likely. The river is swollen, it's menacing. You used to be able to trust it but you can't anymore. It's chewing at the banks, it's full of phosphorus and spiteful alien species.

And the air is smoky. A hundred miles away, close to Minaki, close to Otter Lake, the forest is burning. Out of nowhere he thinks about his mother, the way she died. Did she see anything as obliteration flew towards her, as it brutally smashed through the windshield? Did she have a split-second of knowing? In a way he hopes she did. She always believed the world would end with a bang; it would have meant something to her to find out she was right.

Back in his office he jumps into cold water, a naked man soaping his balls in the heart of an office building. He pictures a woman in the next office, two feet away. Sitting at a computer entering numbers on a spreadsheet, eating machine-made sushi off a black foam tray. She lifts her head and says, "Is it raining?" The hot water hits and Aiden reaches in her direction, reaches for the shampoo.

Then he's standing at his office window with damp hair, eating his sandwich – red pepper hummus and cucumber. The exercise endorphins have kicked in, his serotonergic system and his noradrenergic system briefly align. "An Indonesian-speaking individual?" he hears Liz say. He shrugs. Does it really matter at this point?

By midafternoon Liz is up on the stepladder, feeding Polyfilla into cracks on the western wall of the dining room. It's thirty-four degrees but she's full of jumpy energy, she's got to do something. She stretches to reach above the window frame, scraping her trowel over a tiny crack like a bolt of forked lightning. Amazing how much shifting a hundred-year-old house will do.

Sylvie sits on the floor below her with a garbage bag, grooming Max. It's strange and lovely to have her barefoot and cross-legged in the archway where she played all the time as a kid. She's twenty now. They had a quiet birthday with an ice-cream log from DQ. She's thinner than she was at this time last year; she's lost her pregnancy weight and more, and her cheekbones add a new, serious character to her face. Her hair is caught up in an elastic and damp, wavy strands are plastered to the back of her neck in this heat.

For two weeks now the baby's been in the foster home. Sylvie doesn't talk about her. This morning they made a list of things she's prepared to do, and she agreed to tackle one job a day, just to get moving. Plant the lupins Liz picked up at the greenhouse – there's enough sun in the yard now for lupins. Organize their digital pictures into files. Go through her boxes of stuff from the dorm. "I miss Kajri," she said when Liz mentioned the dorm. *Call Kajri*, Liz wanted to write on the list, but Sylvie wouldn't let her.

Liz drags the stepladder to the north wall. This at least is a methodical job, a job you know will yield results: just let things dry and sand faithfully between coats. Against the chalky white of the filler, the old paint shows up dull and tired. It was some sort of ecru – although it would have had one of those designer names. *Operation Desert Storm* is the only phrase that comes to mind.

"My mother was so into pastels," Liz says to Sylvie. "Remember? Her lavender room and her aqua room and her pink room? And every room had one wall papered with a floral print in the same colour. The feature wall, she called it. They bought that great big split-level just when Auntie Maureen and I were leaving home. It gave Mom something to do. She spent two years dithering over colours."

You're dithering over colours, Sylvie points out by her silence, and in silent rebuttal, Liz calls up a picture of her mom in her new home, setting a polished cherry-wood table with perfectly matched and aligned china and silverware. Her mom at the kitchen sink, scrubbing at pots with a martyrish zeal while the rest of them sit at the table eating their dessert. Wearing a pastel polyester pant suit with a coordinating floral blouse – she looked like she'd been peeled off one of the walls of her own house. She was my age, Liz thinks with surprise. No. God. She was *younger*. There's a mystery there – she catches a dizzying glimpse of it and wants to go closer, but an iron door clangs shut in her face. She puts a hand on the wall for balance, heedless of the fresh filler.

Just then Sylvie finds a tick on Max's belly, latched on but not engorged. She pulls it off with a Kleenex and holds it up to show Liz.

"Oh, get that away from me!" Liz says. "You know, when I was young, finding a wood tick was a huge deal. We found maybe one a year. Now they're all over the place. Bedbugs – it's the same thing."

Everything is changing, Sylvie seems to say by her silence.

Mom, she says these days, and Liz says, *Yes, honey*. Like the other day, when they were out on the deck, and she said, "Mom? How many condoms in a package?"

"Usually twelve," Liz said. "Why do you ask, honey?"

"There were only seven in Noah's bathroom at the lake."

"He likely gave some to a buddy," Liz said. "Guys do that." It was an opening, and a better mother would have run with it. But, god knows, they all need a little reassurance at the moment.

Sylvie has an appointment to see a psychiatrist next week. The police are waiting to see the report; they want to know whether she fits the profile for postpartum depression before they decide whether they will charge her. "I'll tell them a story and they'll make up their minds," Sylvie said at the table last night. "Is Sylvie okay or is she sick? Is she good or is she evil? Can she be a mom or can't she?"

"Nobody is suggesting you're evil, honey," Liz said. But (though she's been hounding the child welfare authorities) she's stymied by the whole thing. Sitting on the deck night after night, she and Aiden go over it. Is it such a crime, Aiden says, to stroll a few yards away to bury a diaper? Anyone can get lost in the woods. There was no one around who was going to steal the baby. But Kenora? Liz says. How could she end up in Kenora, unless she was running away? Still, Aiden says. You'd think they'd want this infant with her family while they investigate. I agree, Liz says. I don't get it. There is something going on that I can't figure out. And *Maggie*? Where is the beauteous goddess of new-age parenting now that everything's fallen apart?

On the floor now, Sylvie gives one last lick of the brush to Max's haunch. He recognizes her farewell pat and walks stiffly away. She leans against the wall and closes her eyes. Instantly she's back riding in a big white truck that smells like a chicken barn. There's a leather satchel on the floor at her feet. The driver tells her to open it, and directs her to a cardboard folder with a photograph tucked inside, his *hijas queridas*. Two little girls with dark hair pulled back from their blunt faces. They were standing against a cement-block wall, pressed closely together: Anaclaudia, the taller one in the red sweater, eyes wary and her arm tight around her little sister, and Esmeralda, in a bright pink T-shirt and turquoise jacket, looking trustingly at the camera. "*La luz de mi vida*," he says fervently. "*Sí*," Sylvie says. She's never studied Spanish but she's been to Isla Mujeres.

She opens her eyes and sits up, sinking her fingers into the dog brush, gathering up a handful of coarse grey hair, which she drops into the garbage bag. This story has a happy ending. The man is kind, he does not harm her. After some hours of travel, they come to a town and he pulls up in front of a brick building and tells her to go in. She slides awkwardly down from the high seat of the truck and walks up to the door. It opens on its own, revealing a hospital. She goes straight up to the desk and tells someone who she is and what she has done. Then she sits in a chair with her head in her arms until a woman comes back and bends over her and says, "We talked to the police. Your baby is okay, someone found her in time."

She scoots her butt back towards the wall. She feels so light these days. Because her breasts are vanishing . . . well, shrinking. She lays one hand on her scar, where pain blooms. Not the pain from her surgery – that's gone, she's totally recovered. She can do anything now, as long as she can cope with the feelings that grab at her whenever she moves quickly. Your baby is okay, the woman said. Sylvie sees her tiny, grasping hands, takes in the smell of spit-up milk. The light of my life, she says to herself, trying out the words. She stretches out her legs on the cool floorboards and the old panic rises. *La luz de mi vida*, she whispers, leaning her head back against the wall: it's a little easier in Spanish.

If you talk to someone about what happened, you'll get over it faster, her dad pointed out this morning, standing in the doorway of her room. I believe you, she said. But she knows the way she talks, the hateful sound of her voice when (for example) she is forced to answer the questions of the police. A voice she still hears screaming *Baby* into the bush, a bush that had fallen silent, no sound then but her own panting, and her own calling and screaming, which sometimes echoed.

If she could see the nurse from the Kenora hospital again, she would talk to her. The nurse in the aqua jumpsuit, who took Sylvie to a room and started an IV to get her fluids up, and who was standing with a policeman in the doorway when Sylvie woke up. The cop lifted his hand and said, "Bye," and Sylvie said, "Are they leaving me without a guard?" and the nurse said, "Get a grip. He's my boyfriend. He just dropped by on his break." She came over to the bed and set about checking Sylvie's blood pressure and temperature. Sylvie was feeling drugged from her short sleep, and she was filled with wonder at the sight of this woman planted solidly by the bed with her big feet in pink Crocs, larger than life, more fully realized, a heavy metallic zipper straining over her humungous breasts, a fat, bulging frog-throat with a little chin perched high above it, and a red rash on that throat with tiny black dots in it, as though she shaved. "So tell me," the nurse said in a bold voice as she stuck a probe into Sylvie's ear. "How exactly does a tiny baby end up alone in a car in the middle of nowhere?"

Sylvie rubbed her arms, which were chalky now with calamine lotion. "I had to bury a dirty diaper. And I didn't take her with me because if I tried to put her in the sling I'd have woken her up." Her own voice was hoarse from all her screaming. "I just walked a little way into the bush to check something out. Then, when I turned back, I came to the ridge, and I saw the sand where I'd buried the diaper, but the car was gone. So then I was running up and down, looking for the car, and I got all mixed up. I saw something white under some spruce – it was bright, I could see it from far away, and I thought it was the diaper I'd buried, like it had already been dug up by animals and dragged there. I ran all the way over to it, and here it was a disposable diaper somebody else had dumped there. It wasn't even my diaper. And then I was *so* lost." The nurse was watching her closely with little blue eyes. "It felt like hours might have gone by, or days. It was like there's another world behind the world we're in, and suddenly I was in it. Like I'd stepped through a portal."

"You read too much science fiction," the nurse said. "Your car was there. Nobody moved your car. If you'd stopped running around like a chicken with its head cut off, you would have figured it out. But I understand you walked to the road and you hitchhiked here?"

In the cold blue clarity of her gaze lay the things Sylvie was straining to see. "Are people saying I did this on purpose?"

The nurse lifted her big shoulders. "I haven't heard a word on the subject."

She was bundling up the blood pressure cuff, she was getting ready to leave. The terrible possibilities of the night still gripped Sylvie. But the nurse was going to refuse to utter a judgment, although there was judgment in every line of her body.

"I suppose you have children," Sylvie said.

"I've got three."

"Well, I didn't even know I was pregnant until this baby was half-developed."

"Oh, is that right?"

"And you know – I sort of feel like I didn't really *have* her. I didn't go through labour. All over the world, women labour when they give birth. But it's like modern medicine used a shortcut with me." The nurse was peering at her as if she was looking over reading glasses. Sylvie wanted to grab hold of her arm to keep her there, but she didn't have the nerve. "I didn't even learn the breathing. I treated the prenatal classes like a joke."

"So you think that's why you had a C-section?" the nurse said, provoked at last. "Because you didn't learn the breathing?"

"Well, maybe. In some strange way."

The nurse dropped her clipboard on the bed. "Listen, *Sylvia*. I was eighteen when I had my first baby, and I lived behind a gas station in Cochenor, way up in northern Ontario. I'd never *heard* of pain-control breathing. I had contractions for twenty-four hours and I screamed like a stuck pig through most of it. Second time, I was washing dishes and my water broke, and the next thing I know, I've got a little girl sucking on my tit. My third, I had a planned C-section because I've got uterine leiomyoma, also known as fibroids. So, am I going to be a good mother to one of those kids and not to the other two?"

She was practically yelling by the end of this speech, and she snatched up her clipboard and left the room as though she couldn't get away from Sylvie fast enough.

Sylvie turns her head and looks at her mother, who is crouched now, scraping plaster into nicks along the baseboard. How strikingly graceful and slender she is compared to the larger-than-life woman in Sylvie's mind. Close like this, Sylvie feels her anxiety. She tries so hard, Sylvie thinks. At everything. And still she gets it wrong. How can that be?

Sylvie scoots over to make room and their eyes briefly meet. Liz turns back to the wall and reaches to fill another nick. All these marks, she thinks, from the careless way we swing the chairs around. My mother crocheted little booties for her dining room chairs, to avoid exactly this sort of damage. Oh, and marks on her hardwood floor. She smoothes the plaster with deft cross-strokes, and her mind drifts to dinner. To the snow peas in the fridge and the tofu in the freezer. She'll make a stir fry. No, not a good idea to turn on the stove – they'll order from The Bangkok. And tomorrow or the day after, she'll drive to Western Paint and pick up colour chips. She'll ask for a *green* product. To please Sylvie, who's still on the floor in the archway, hugging her knees, deep in thought.

Though Sylvie is not thinking, exactly. She's back to listening for her baby. At five this morning, she woke up when somewhere, in a crib in a stranger's house, the baby started crying for her morning feed. It was around six by the time she let herself fall back to sleep. I made myself stay awake for my baby, she explains to the nurse, who's standing at the counter in the nursing station in her bubblegum Crocs, counting pills. The nurse looks up with those knowing little eyes. Get a grip, she says.

16

Spontaneous Combustion

LATE ONE AFTERNOON, WHILE SYLVIE IS UP IN her room, a worker from Child and Family Services calls and Liz answers. When that conversation is over, Liz stands looking out the kitchen window for a minute, and then she snatches up her keys and goes out to the car.

The Maryland Bridge is already backed up. She inches her way across it, her hand tapping the steering wheel in a furious percussion and her conviction growing with each tap: that since the day Mary Magdalene glided up these steps in a red coat and a cranberry caftan, a systematic *attack* has been going on. And Liz has been too preoccupied to realize it. She's been like someone slumbering in bed, hearing the small sounds of a crime being committed in the dark rooms of the house, and lazily weaving it all into her dream.

It's an old neighbourhood, River Heights, with wider lots than Wolseley and brick houses set back from the street, a smugger attitude to money. The house is not what Liz expects, though. It's an infill property circa 1964, a modest stucco bungalow with that most pathetic of suburban affectations, a fake brick façade on the front. But the concrete steps are painted purple and a batik sunflower banner flutters from the eaves, and on a wrought-iron bench at the edge of the yard, among the goutweed and spent lily-of-the-valley, Liz spies Krzysztof Nowak's mother, her black babushka tied under her chin and her hands stacked on the head of her cane.

"Is Maggie home?" The *baba* glowers and doesn't answer.

Liz climbs the purple steps. She ignores the doorbell and thumps on the aluminum screen door with the side of her fist. She can smell mown grass and grilling meat. Somewhere nearby, little girls are shrieking. She thumps again, staring back boldly at Krzysztof's mother.

Krzysztof opens the door, clearly startled to see her. He launches into a concerned friend routine and she cuts him off. "Stop the fucking act. My daughter's in crisis. She was lost in the bush. And this is what you people think of – running to the social workers to tell lies about her?"

"What are you talking about?"

"CFS just phoned. So Maggie's behind this! Trying to have our daughter declared an unfit parent. Charging her with all sorts of negligence. She's been into the child welfare office. With a list. In *writing*! We were named, Aiden and I. Don't pretend you didn't know."

But he frowns in a lame approximation of surprise and confusion and steps back to invite her into the house. She steps back as well, off the steps and onto the front walk, so he doesn't have much choice but to come out. He's wearing tasselled slippers and dorky-fitting chinos. He's changed in eight years, Liz thinks. In the hard summer light she's seized with a new conviction, that *Mary Magdalene knows everything*. Only the wrath of a wronged wife can account for this. "You've told her," she cries. "About us."

His face hardens. "Us?" he says. He's changed in eight years, but he hasn't changed enough. Back then, when she was in the kitchen of that retreat house in Minnesota making coffee for the searchers, she glanced over her shoulder to see Krzysztof and Melody, the babysitting grad student, together in the hall. She saw Melody reach for Krzysztof's hand and cling to it, trying to lift it to her face, and she saw Krzysztof twist his wrist away with a patronizing smile.

Over at the bench, his mother is hoisting herself to her feet. "Dat man," she calls in a harsh voice. "Cutting bottles over baby! Why you give him knife? Eh, missus?" She lifts her cane, a parody of the granny from central casting. "*Missus!* Why you give him knife?"

"Hush, Mama," Krzysztof says. "I mean it. Sit down. Keep your mouth shut."

A car pulls up behind Liz's, a little red car with two women in it. Liz can see Maggie's grey mop on the passenger side. She and the driver lean into a lingering embrace, and then Maggie straightens up and opens the door, still talking. She steps onto the curb and waves goodbye to her friend, turns, and sees Liz on the front walk.

"Oh, Liz," she cries, "how *are* you?" And instantly Liz can see that she's got it wrong. This is not revenge. It's just Mary Magdalene being Mary Magdalene. "What are you all standing out here for?" she says warmly. "Let's go inside."

Liz takes in her rayon dress with its uneven hemline, her generous breasts in their saggy little hammocks, her tangled silvery hair. "I've just been talking to the CFS worker. I understand you've been into their office trying to have our daughter declared an unfit parent. Feeding them a list of lies to make sure they don't let the baby come home."

Maggie's smile vanishes. "Lies," she says softly. Her face opens in sympathy, as if Liz's outrage is a plea for her help. And Liz recalls with fluorescent clarity that Mary Magdalene will always keep you smaller than she is. It's futile to confront her – it will never register. There's no anger in her world; there's only need, your need for her. "I know this must be terribly upsetting for you," Maggie is saying.

"And I want to assure you, it's not something I did lightly. I'm just thinking of that tiny baby. That's all it is. I'm thinking of the sort of home a baby needs, the order and routines, a family where children are at the centre." She launches into a soft-voiced inventory of her concerns, starting with the diaper rash the foster mother discovered and leaping back to some supposed incident fifteen years ago, the distress she felt when she found little Sylvie three blocks away from home in her pyjamas.

Liz stands on the sidewalk outside Maggie's house, hearing the screams and laughter of little girls in the next yard, and notes the wrinkles running down from the corners of Maggie's mouth and the way her jawline is softening. She hears the righteousness in her voice and she taps into an old and nourishing hatred, like an underground spring, for middle-aged women – the whole cohort of them, the way they twist and knead and pummel and bully life into what they want it to be.

Maggie's moved on to her anguish about the baby being in foster care. "I'm sure you feel the same way," she says and then her words come out in a rush: "You're going to hear it sooner or later, Liz, so I may as well tell you. I've offered to take the baby myself. Just for now. I was in the office again today – I just came from there – to see whether they might consider releasing her to her father's custody. With our support, of course. We'd all pitch in to make a home for that little girl here." With her soft eyes she includes Krzysztof in this touching scenario, and an old impetuousness steps up to Liz like an ally in her time of need – it's there, shining in the street – wreckage and chaos and all its audacious satisfactions. Except that something else has lit up inside her, a loyalty to something she can't name, closer to her heart. She turns impatiently and interrupts.

"Does Noah want this baby?" she asks. She looks at the elm

trees queuing along the street, diminishing like in a perspective drawing. She flicks her car key open and presses the remote to prompt a faithful blink of her headlights. "Has your son ever shown a single sign of interest in his daughter?"

They're in a different kind of waiting now. Liz is desperate to broadcast Maggie's treachery, equally desperate to keep the story quiet. Evenings, she paces the house, ranting. Aiden takes his drink out to the deck and tries to think his way through the thing. He can picture Maggie in the child welfare office, her face radiant with sorrow and resolve as she delivers the infamous list, and he feels some eagerness to see it, to see what light it casts on their whole domestic enterprise. But why didn't she just drop over to the house and talk to them?

Sylvie can't be persuaded to go to the Fringe play and Liz won't leave Sylvie, so he goes on his own. The venue is a narrow warehouse space with hard benches. The nineteenth-century costumes have clearly been cobbled together at Value Village. Yet he's lifted out of himself the way you hope to be at the theatre. Not as much by the play as by Sylvie's friends, by the fearless way they step into a spotlight on a bare stage and declare their ideals. There's Thea striding across the stage with a wonderful judicious demeanour, her pale matted hair arranged like a powdered wig. And that slight, frail, grey-haired kid is wonderful as William Wilberforce, ringingly voicing the abolitionist's resolve: "We will do less, aspire less, to be better men." Aiden jumps up for the ovation and takes the program home so Sylvie can see the acknowledgements on the back. *Thanks to: Sylvie Glasgow-Phimister, for inspiration. Jaspreet Khan, on the generator bike. Faun Phimister, for the future.*

The next day Aiden leaves work at four o'clock and cycles up to the hospital to visit his dad. He finds Rupert dressed and sitting in a chair. They do this in extended care. "You're up," Aiden says. "That's great. Let's go for a walk." It takes a bit of coaxing, but eventually Rupert is out of the chair and shuffling along the corridor. He's beetle-like now in his shape and movements: he's aged ten years in the past few months. How cruel of life to require such change of the very old. They pause by a drinking fountain and Aiden presses the button. Rupert watches with interest, holding a trembling finger towards the silver arc. Purple blotches decorate his hand, bruising from all the anticoagulants they have him on.

Walking out of the hospital lost in thought, Aiden almost bumps into a small man in a grey suit, heading for the same pod of the revolving door. It's Dr. Peter Saurette. Aiden defers to him and then calls hello as their separate glass fins release them into sunlight. Surprise, or something else, flashes across Saurette's face. "Hi, how are you," he says, and keeps walking. Aiden watches until he drops out of sight in the staff-only section of the parking lot. Lowering himself into a new Porsche Boxster, no doubt.

They've only ever had one client in common. He turns back into the hospital. A clerk with black bangs halfway over her eyes sits at the information desk.

"Jake Peloquin." He spells it.

Her fingers are a blur on the keyboard. "6B, room 803."

Saurette, the lousy prick. But 6B is not psychiatry. Aiden asks the clerk.

"It's neurosciences."

He takes the elevator up to the sixth floor, dread perched on his shoulders. In 803 the curtain is pulled around the bed. "Jake," Aiden says. He hears a throat-clearing that he chooses to construe as an invitation, and slides open the curtain.

"God, buddy. What in hell happened?"

Defrag is trapped in a medieval torture device. A metal ring encircles his forehead, and bars descend from it, clamped into brackets on his shoulders. Screws or pins in each quadrant of the ring appear to be drilled into his very head, so that his skull is a part of the vise. Through the bars he stares silently at Aiden.

He has broken several vertebrae in his neck – it takes Aiden six or eight questions to extract this fact. Not too much damage to his spinal cord, so they don't think he's going to have any permanent mobility issues.

Aiden is still standing at the foot of the bed. "But how did it happen?" In his mind he sees the treacherous catwalks in Defrag's building.

"Oh, just one of those things," Defrag says, as if a weakness in his throat makes talking a huge effort. His skin is waxy pale and his forehead is smeared with orange disinfectant. He can't move, clamped into that thing. And so he can't laugh, and without laughter to obfuscate his meaning, he's not going to talk. That's how Aiden reads it.

"You had a fall?"

"Yeah, I guess you could call it that."

A sense of Dr. Saurette lingers in the little cubicle. His expensive suit, his rectitude. Aiden himself is shambling, he's a shambles. He reaches inside, tries to locate his customary professional composure, and comes up empty. Shrinks get to go through psychoanalysis, he reminds himself, as part of their training. It gives them a huge advantage. All that self-awareness, it's a fucking *superpower*.

"Where were you, Jake?"

"I don't entirely recall."

"How did you fall? What did you fall from?" He wants to be closer, but if he moves to the side and sits down, Defrag won't be able to see him. In his iron cage Defrag shows a new proclivity for stillness. "Jake. Talk to me. Were you trying to end it?"

"Yes and no. I guess if I was really trying, I would have found a better way."

If only one in ten feels grief, Aiden thinks, that one carries the grief of ten. An old fantasy washes over him, more seductive than ever: he'll take Defrag up to Otter Lake to recuperate. That wooden recliner his dad built, he'll drag it onto the lichen-covered rock, and Defrag can lie out there with the Hudson's Bay blanket over him and sink into the small events of an afternoon in the northern wilderness. Watch the fish jump, the blue heron lift from the reeds, dragging its long legs after it. What's stopped him inviting Defrag in the past? The rules, or conventions, or principles – he wonders at how slavishly he followed them. But now it's just a matter of a few iron bars.

He's still standing at the end of the bed when a nurse comes in to check Defrag's vitals. Aiden watches her attach the blood pressure machine. She's slender, fortyish, a lovely natural blond wearing yellow scrubs. He tries to judge her level of professionalism, whether she's likely to tell him the whole story if he corners her in the hall. He puts his chances at low to nil.

"That's really something," he says.

"The halo?" says the nurse. "You've never seen one before? They are the cat's ass. We used to keep people with this sort of injury in bed, with sandbags around them to keep them immobile. And then their muscles atrophied and they got pressure sores and pneumonia. But with this brace, Jake can get up and walk around. Soon. You're looking forward to that, aren't you, Jake."

"Terrific," Aiden says.

As though Defrag has spoken, the nurse bends over him with sudden warmth, and it seems to Aiden that the hum and clatter of the hospital quiets. She fiddles with the IV feed in his arm. She straightens his blanket and cranks his bed up a notch. She sweeps a pudding cup and plastic spoon off the bedside table and into the garbage, graceful and quick. Before she leaves, she pours Defrag a fresh glass of water. Resting one hand gently on his shoulder, she holds up the glass so he can drink through a straw, and he lifts his eyes in silent gratitude.

When she's gone, Aiden finally moves to the side of the bed. Close up like that, he feels a visceral shock at the sight of those pins – steel, or maybe titanium – bored mercilessly into Defrag's skull.

"Any idea when you'll get out?" He stands with his fingertips on his friend's hand and adds – because what else is there to do? – "The Tuesday slot is yours. We can work on a pro bono basis for a while."

Defrag says something, but at that moment, a cart crashes in the hallway and a nasal voice blasts, "Dr. Fairfax to Obstetrics, Dr. Fairfax to Obstetrics" and Aiden misses it. He bends over. "Pardon?" he says, but Defrag's drawn his hand away and closed his eyes. He won't respond. Aiden has to give up, he has to say his goodbyes and walk to the door, left to construct what he will from those few low syllables, left with the punishing conviction that what Jake Peloquin said just as the hospital leapt back to life was, "I'm afraid I can't take you on at the moment."

"Sit outside with me," Aiden says to Liz after supper.

"It's too hot."

"Come on. There's a breeze."

"Let me finish putting the food away, then."

He gets a rag from the garage and wipes down the mesh and iron chairs on the deck. The sun glowers from above the Callaghans' garage across the back lane. Just before supper, a valve in the sky opened for about ten minutes and a ton of water was dumped on the city. Water that should rightly have fallen somewhere else, stolen from the poor and given to the rich. Now it's sunny again and silver pools glint in the grass. This whole river city is a bowl of unfired clay – the water's got nowhere to go. Wendy's backyard elms are massive, verdant with all the rain. They look like broccoli. By next year they'll be dead.

He tramps downstairs and drops the rag in the laundry, and then he gets his little cylinder of pot out of the basement freezer. A gift from Defrag the Christmas before last, this is the end of it, and mighty fine weed it was. His papers are in a tin on a rafter. He lifts down the tin and rolls his joint over the freezer, enjoying the taste of the paper on his tongue. An old impulse grips him, a familiar urge: to bottom out, to get a toehold on the lowest rung of his self-contempt so he can kick himself back up.

Out on the deck, Liz waves away the joint. She hitches her chair away from his. She's wearing sunglasses.

"Can I get you a drink, then?" he asks. "How about a G and T?"

"No, I'm okay."

They sit and stare at her flowerbeds, where all the shade plants are drooping, shocky from the sun and the heat.

"Did you go in to the office today?"

"No, I just did my email and calls from here."

"Did you get next week sorted out?"

"Yeah. I'm taking until the twenty-fourth. That's three times I've changed my holidays."

"Oh well, that's the boss's prerogative."

She recrosses her legs, refolds her arms. She's thin, and her mouth is a thin, straight line, like her mother's was for the last two decades. "Have you seen your dad this week?"

At the thought of the hospital, his sorrow heaves in his chest. "I went in today."

"How was he?"

"About the same."

Two kids walk down the lane carrying helium balloons that shine like silver bubbles in the aquarium air. Aiden takes a long toke and goes back to his perusal of the yard. No squirrels, he notes, the squirrels fled after their high-rises were demolished. But night crawlers have arrived: gargantuan earthworms have insinuated their way up from the riverbank and undermined the entire property. Mowing yesterday, Aiden almost broke his ankle – the lawn's as lumpy and trenched as if it has been rototilled.

"If you leave that sawdust much longer," Liz says, "it will spontaneously combust and we will have an L.A.-style fire."

"Liz, the humidity is ninety-eight percent."

"When are you going to take out the tree?" The spruce, she means, the tree the city workers damaged.

"I know," he says. "I'll get to it."

A switch has been thrown, he thinks. Crisis does that to couples. It draws you together or it pulls you apart. They never mention Otter Lake. Let's face it, were they ever fighting about the actual sale of a real property? The cottage has become notional.

A cyclist rides up the lane and brakes at their garage. He jumps off his bike with the timing and balance and strength of a guy at the absolute peak of his powers. It's their putative son-in-law. They call hellos.

Noah bends over his lock and Aiden calls, "Just leave it. I'll keep an eye on it."

"Okay, thanks." He walks across the lawn, pulling off his helmet and wiping his face with his forearm. His hair's in dark, wet furrows. "Sylvie inside?"

"Yup." He's shielding the joint in his right hand, dangling it by his chair. "She's up in her room."

Noah stands on the patio, helmet in hand. He's wearing those ridiculous barefoot sandals. It's unclear whether he wants to talk or just doesn't have the social skills to get away from them.

"She'll be glad to see you," Aiden says, to move him along. "Just go right on up."

"Okay, thanks," Noah says. He crosses the deck and walks into the house, protected by diplomatic immunity. The only thing Aiden and Liz have agreed on in the past few days is never to talk to Noah about what Maggie is up to.

"That went well," Liz says when the door closes behind him.

Aiden plucks the joint out of his burning fingers and lifts it to his face with his left hand. It's awkward and unsatisfying, like jerking off with the wrong hand. "Whatever," he says, exhaling a hot little pip of smoke. "His dad is George Oliphant."

The sun hasn't moved since he sat down. There it hangs, five inches above the Callaghans' garage roof, toying with the possibility of not setting at all. Pulling rude colour from everything . . . Liz's red wheelbarrow, the fluorescent lawn.

"We had a social worker here all afternoon," Liz says. "I forced her to take two bags of baby clothes when she left. She didn't want them. She didn't want to be bothered taking them over to the foster home, but I'm trying to stay in their faces. I sent some things our little girl hasn't grown into yet. I hated doing that."

"Yeah, I bet."

"But she told Sylvie they could go and see the baby tomorrow. Sylvie and Noah."

"At the foster home?"

"They have to go to the CFS office on Stafford and visit with her there. Under supervision."

"How about us? Don't we get to see her?"

She shakes her head.

"Well, this is nuts. All this waiting for the other shoe to drop. There must be something we can do." He drops his roach to the deck, grinds it under his sandal. And he feels weary to the bone of the whole fucking mess, which, if his experience with clients fighting over kids is any indication, is certain to lurch from bad to worse, crushing all good will and common sense in its path. He moves in his chair, prying the skin of his thighs out of the mesh, and then, realizing how thirsty he is, gets up and goes to the kitchen.

Back at the door, he stands with an icy bottle of Keith's in hand and looks out at Liz in her deck chair, and a sense of estrangement descends forcefully upon him. She fed this dispute with her absurd rivalry with Maggie. In the set of her thin shoulders he sees a narrowness he abhors. Her aspirations and her narrowness – they're part of the same thing in a way he can't explain, and suddenly they both appal him. He steps back onto the deck, snapping the cap off his beer, and in that moment a path gleams before him. You always have choices.

He sits down. "You know, it just occurred to me . . . Maggie's asking to look after the baby. What if we just agreed? Would CFS be open to it? Because in one sense she's right: that little girl would be better off with her other grandma than with a total stranger." The idea blossoms into its full, splendid shape in his mind as he talks, but he's careful to keep his voice neutral. "Noah would be there on his days off. Sylvie could probably visit."

Through her sunglasses Liz's eyes are hooded, as though words entirely fail her. "Liz," he says, "it was a shitty thing for Maggie to do, no argument about that. But she must have been freaked out by what happened at the lake. I think she's fundamentally a good person. She's warm, she's competent – she's raised two wonderful kids. And she loves that little girl. If we asked for this we'd be showing that we have the best interests of the baby at heart. It's a wisdom of Solomon kind of thing."

She finally speaks, hardly moving her mouth, as though her jaw is locked. "Aiden, that is so fucking stupid, I can't even respond."

He tips his head back and takes a drink. "It goes against the grain, I agree. But think about it. It's like unilateral disarmament. You do one generous thing, you make a gesture of reason and goodwill, and it breaks an impasse." Her chin lifts; she won't look at him. "Anyway," he says, "I'd like to propose this to the social worker, see what she thinks. Or Sylvie could raise it if she's open to it. What would you think if I talked to Sylvie about it?" This courtesy is bullshit and he knows it. He's going to take this forward. You can only give up so much before you are lost altogether.

And maybe she can tell, because at his words she gets up and walks into the house. Though it's so abrupt, the way she leaves without a single word or glance or gesture, that his brain comes up with the possibility that she might have forgotten something on the stove, or she heard the phone ring.

But of course she doesn't come back. The sun finally capitulates and sinks towards the garage. A dove starts to mourn on the power-line transformer. Wendy comes out onto her deck and stands talking on her phone, staring vacantly at Aiden. She catches herself and waves a little apology, and turns back inside, still talking. Behind him the house hums, cooling itself. Their house, which he holds as insubstantial as a Bedouin tent.

He sits as the sun slides without fanfare into the garage roof, dragging the sky down with it, and then he's out of beer. Liz is in the kitchen, wearing a white cotton nightie he doesn't remember having seen before. She's prying the lid off the yogurt, one of her blue sleeping pills gripped between her thumb and forefinger. Those pills are so bitter she takes them with a spoonful of yogurt to protect her tastebuds.

Below the counter, the dishwasher throbs warmly. "Leave me alone, Aiden," Liz says. By then he's got his beer and he's halfway out the door.

Darkness has blanked out the yard, mosquitoes fret near his ears. But the night's far from over, he's just getting started, sprawled in his deck chair, his feet in their worn sandals braced on the grey boards. Who do you wish you were, Aiden? That man who lost all his words, the one who mistook his wife for a hat.

Lights bob up the lane – three lights in an uneven row – and sink like a UFO landing. The security bulb on the garage leaps into action, revealing three guys down on all fours on the grass. They've got miner's lamps strapped to their foreheads. It's night crawlers they're after, flooded out of their tunnels by the rain – they're picking night crawlers to sell for bait.

"Do you mind?" one of them calls.

"Be my guest," he says.

The beams of their lamps swing earthward. Writhing worms dangle from their fingers, gleaming in the light.

They move on up the lane and the security light goes out. Aiden has to resist the impulse to follow them. Then Defrag is in his mind, his white forehead clamped into a steel halo. All the hours he spent trying to establish common ground with Defrag, trying to get him to join a group. So misguided. It's toxic to Defrag, being with people as afraid as he is.

He polishes off his beer and opens another. Then the young scientist is on the deck, the splendid hope of a terrified world, searching in his pocket for the key to his bike lock.

"You didn't lock it, son. I've been keeping an eye on it." He gets up. "Listen," he says, "can you stay for a beer?"

"Oh." Noah lifts his head. "Okay. Thanks."

"So," Aiden says when they're both settled with an open beer in hand. "Sylvie gone to bed?"

"Yep."

"How long you in town for?"

"Today and tomorrow."

A siren pelts up Portage Avenue. The Doppler effect kicks in. Noah raises his eyes. "It's a year ago tonight. That Sylvie and I met, at the lake."

"Well, congratulations."

"Yeah, well." He grins wryly.

They sit, listening to the insect hum of the streetlight in the back lane. "Has Sylvie talked to you? About what happened?"

"You mean when she was lost? The guy who picked her up?"

"Yeah."

"She didn't tell you?"

"No."

Noah pauses for a minute, no doubt trying to sort out his loyalties. "He was a Mexican migrant worker from a chicken farm in Northwestern Ontario. She said he was a really nice guy. It was his idea to drop her at the hospital in Kenora. He was up by the lake checking on a job. His job in Ontario is running out and he's going to have to leave Canada, so he's trying hard to find something else."

"So he spoke English?"

"Yeah, I guess. Enough."

"Why didn't she just tell the police that?"

"Because he wasn't supposed to have the truck. His boss sent him to Kenora to pick something up, and he drove into Manitoba to check out that job. He was rushing to get back before he got in too much trouble. She was scared she would get him deported."

"Huh, the way that girl thinks. So she didn't tell him she'd left the baby in the car?"

"No."

"You must have asked her why."

"I guess it was just hard for her to face what she thought had happened. But she's getting things figured out now."

Aiden takes a long pull of his beer. "What about you? You going back to Toronto this fall?"

"I've been studying at Guelph, actually. And probably not."

"What is it you're taking again?"

"I'm doing a master's in environmental microbiology and biotechnology."

"Hey," Aiden says, rallying, thinking of all the questions he'd like to put to a guy in this particular field of study, though the mellow alertness he counts on with weed has been hijacked in the last few minutes by a crude, heavy inebriation. "You used to be into electricity. And then you moved to biology."

"Yeah, I went through a lot of stages. But it's *micro*biology I'm studying, actually."

"Maybe you discovered electric eels, ha ha," Aiden says, too thick-limbed to swerve from the joke he was setting up. "Well, I've been through a few stages myself. I was a youth care worker for a long time. It's a futile job, given the way troubled kids move in and out of the system – you get very good at playing pool. And then I did graduate work in English, I wrote a dissertation on a nineteenth-century British poet that is as yet undefeated – well, undefended, most people would put it – and then I did the master's in counselling and set up a practice. Liz is mad at me because I've never been much of a provider. She won't say so, but she is. But we're as rich as I can stand being. I can't deal with the consumerist throughput, I feel guilty enough. And I like what I'm doing. It's political, in its own way."

"Political?"

I share your values, man, Aiden wants to say, but he's not quite that wasted. A black shape darts in the dark sky, impossibly fast. It's a bat, hunting. "Well, you know, for example, I have a lot of female clients who shop constantly. It's all about trying to fill emotional needs in inappropriate ways. I had a client who thought she was entitled to sleep with her own son, for Christ's sake. So, how're you going to remake the world except one person at a time?"

Noah's answer is lost on Aiden. The kid's a low talker.

"Yeah, well," Aiden says, staring into the darkened yard. "As if we have that much time. I realize that. And it's a Western privilege, psychotherapy. I get that too. How many self-actualized capitalists does it take to change a light bulb?" He laughs alone, and a huge surge of grief washes over him, that this too, the work he loves, which has so much of the good and true in it, should have to go by the way. "But do you have a better idea?" he says. "Ralph Nader – think about him for a sec. The fate of the world hung on that dude's ideals." He's launching into his rant on the first Bush election, the egregious theft of the White House from Al Gore, when Noah cuts him off.

"You feel guilty?" he asks. "Is that what you said?"

"Come on, man, that's like asking me if I breathe. I'm white. I'm male. I drive. 'I eat, I fuck,' to quote one of my clients. I live off the avails of capitalism. I bought low and I'll sell high. Don't you? Feel guilty?"

"Not really," Noah says. "It's just, like, a problem we have to solve." Aiden can't see his face now, just the shape of his head lit up by the light falling from the kitchen window. "I think the industrial

economies will collapse for sure. And I'm not really afraid of that."
He tosses back his hair in a way he has. "Capitalism, it's a bad system. For almost everybody, and for the planet. But the Earth has had massive extinctions before, and each one was followed by a huge explosion in evolution. So there'll be new forms."

"True enough," Aiden says. "In a couple hundred million years. Something reptilian, maybe. So I guess that's fine, then. Why be scared? Why be sad?"

He tries to swing his left foot up to his right knee, but his leg feels too bloated to bend. It's the air, the moist air – in his torpor he's soaking it in like a sponge. "Noah," he says, planting his foot back on the deck. "Sparky. In our house we used to play this little game. Say there are two kinds of people in the world. Tell me which side of a particular question they fall on and I'll know everything I need to know about them. So Liz starts it. She says, 'Do they have a real Christmas tree or a fake?' Or she'll have some question about whether they make their own vinaigrette. By then Sylvie's all outraged. She jumps in and asks, 'Are they full or are they hungry? Do they have clean drinking water or are their children dying of dysentery?' So, I'm curious. Say there are two kinds of people in the world. What divides them, in your mind?"

"I don't like to divide the world into two kinds of people," the guy says evenly.

Oh, fuck you, Aiden thinks. He drains his beer and bubbles burn the back of his throat. Fuck you, Sparky. Fuck your perfection. Your teeth innocent of fillings. Your self-esteem that's been nurtured like a household pet. Fuck your risible five-toe sandals made of biofeedback rubber. He sets the empty bottle on the deck and shuffles back into the kitchen to the fridge. There's some fancy imports on the bottom shelf, and he schleps the cardboard six-pack out to the deck.

To his surprise, Noah's still there. He waves off the beer. "I'm good," he says.

Too right, Aiden thinks, settling back into his deck chair. Fuck your goddamn goodness. And fuck your ravishing of my ravishing daughter. He breaks a bottle out of the cardboard sleeve and holds it up close to his nose to read the label. Wood something. The sucker's got a traditional cap. But no flies on Aiden Phimister – he's got a church key in his shorts pocket. "Do you recall," he says, prying the bottle open, "hearing a news item some years back, about a middle-aged guy in one of the northern states imperson-ating a suicidal teenager? Online. To entice depressed kids into suicide pacts. It was all over the news. It worked in a handful of cases. He walked those kids through to the completion of a suc-cessful suicide. That guy was a psychiatric nurse. In real life, that was his profession."

"What are you saying?"

"Oh, I don't know. Maybe it's not to the point." He takes a drink and gags. "It's cat piss! Five bucks a bottle and it's *green*, the sons of bitches." He hitches his chair forward, folds his softened body over, and pours the beer onto the patio. "Actually . . . forget it. I think the point that little story makes is – what's the word – *antithetical*." He grins over his shoulder at Noah, who, backlit by the kitchen window, looks like somebody trying to hide his identity on TV. "To my point, I mean. Antithetical to my point, whatever it was."

"I should go," Noah says. "Sylvie and I are going to see the baby in the morning." One of his knees is juddering.

"So what you doing at the lake these days? You counting fish-fly eggs?"

"Not exactly."

"Well, hey, don't go." Aiden hitches back his chair. "Come on, listen. There's two kinds of people in the world – who are they? I'll play, I'll take a turn. I ask: are they earnest or are they ironic? For me, that's the line. Like, think of those kids that did the Fringe play. Sylvie's friends. 'We're donating the proceeds of the show to the Pembina Institute.' *Come on.* Those kids are going to do something that will change the course of events? They're going to reverse the albedo effect?"

Noah shrugs. "So, you call yourself a cynic?" he says.

"I never said that. Either way. Listen, forget I raised it. I want to ask you about something else. As a scientist. It's been eating at me for a long time. I've been hoping for a chance to talk to some-body who knows this kind of thing." But that's as far as he gets with that line of thought. He's hearing a swishing in his ears, the sound of blood being pumped, up or down.

The security light on the garage is back on, despoiling the dark-ness. "I really have to go," Noah says. But he pauses on the way to his bike and looks back at Aiden. "Don't feel too guilty," he says. "You might not sell high."

Aiden sits on in the darkness, thinking about ladders and rope and his friend in an iron cage. About Gerard Manley Hopkins and *his* friend – what was that guy's name? – a brilliant scholar who man-aged to off himself while enacting the hanging of Trollope. He had a terrific group of intimates at Oxford, Hopkins did, and one by one they died.

Then he's on his feet, walking across the lawn. Between two piles of sawdust he locates his spot, assumes a wide-legged stance, and unzips, and when his stream starts up, he tips his head back to the sky, murky with artificial light and smoke from the fires in the north. Finished, he gives his dick a shake and packs it away, swipes his hands on his shorts. Turns back towards the house, a monolith looming in the dark. A foot catches, and he almost falls.

Ah, who do you wish you were, Aiden? That man, the old man you saw beside a road in Portugal. Spring before last, it was south of Coimbra. You and Liz were driving back to your hotel and a man was on the edge of the narrow, ancient, tree-lined road. An old man in a black jacket and cap. Standing in the evening light, soaking his donkey's sore foot in a bucket.

17

The Base Coat

FRIDAY MORNING, LIZ IS UP AND PROWLING THE house before seven o'clock. She discovers a full can of latex primer in the basement and takes it as a sign, so she carries it upstairs along with an armful of drop sheets. Aiden accuses her of being obsessed with home decor, but they've been in the house for twenty-five years and this is only the third time she's painted this room. She did it during their bad summer, when she was all nerves and prickly heat. It was the era of the faux finishes, and in a decorating magazine she spied the mural of an open window with billowing curtains. *Trompe l'oeil*. She's never called it that, because she can't pronounce it.

Liz hitches the stepladder along the baseboard. The first time she painted this room, she felt so much joy at the prospect of making this house her own. She'd lived before that in rented apartments, and then with Denis Fontaine, who owned a condo on Grant Avenue but was religious about beige. She pours primer into the tray, and in her mind she's schlepping her stuff out of Denis's condo. That last ride down in the elevator after he ditched her, she's carrying an open box with her red kettle in it, and a lampshade and a stupid clock with cartoon hands that she snatched at the last minute because it was one of his particular treasures. She steps out of the doors of the building with the box in her arms, and on the wintry street a shameful truth is waiting for her – that she cannot make her own life. The job thing you can do by yourself, and the house thing, and even the kid thing if you really have guts, but the man – he has to fall into your lap. All her friends were walking around in T-shirts that said: A WOMAN NEEDS A MAN LIKE A FISH NEEDS A BICYCLE, but in that moment Liz knew: *there is nothing else.*

She touches the roller to the primer, trying to take on just the right amount of paint for one strip. She hears Aiden tramp down the stairs. She senses him in the doorway but she doesn't look up. "Bye, Liz," he says, and leaves without waiting for an answer. To cycle, hungover, across town to the little room where he'll sit all this long, hot day, listening to other people's troubles. Aiden, with his wonky ideals, not quite designed for the real world.

She's just made the first bite into the mural when Sylvie appears, moving with more energy than she's shown in months. She's got a bowl of cereal in one hand and the milk carton in the other.

"You're up early."

"I'm going for a ride with Noah. Before we go see the baby."

"That's good, honey." She flips the drop sheet off one end of the table so Sylvie can eat there. Then she gets back to her painting, hoping for silence. She hasn't had breakfast or coffee, and she's well on her way to a full-blown headache. She bends over the paint tray again. Under the uplifted roller, her eyes are caught by the milk carton. It's standing on the oak table in a little pool of milk. "You need to wipe up that milk," she says. "It will take the finish off the table in no time."

"Okay, I will."

When she looks up, Sylvie has finished her cereal and is sitting watching her. Balancing inside the bubble of her precarious composure, her shins pressed against a rung of the stepladder, Liz sees that this morning her daughter is not going to leave her alone. "What, honey?"

"I want to ask you a question. Why did you take me with you when you hooked up with Krzysztof?"

Liz stands still with the roller in her hand. Sweat trickles down below the underwires of her bra. Her eyes are caught by the miasma of fine hairs around Sylvie's head in the sun from the curtainless window. Sylvie is watching her intently. When she doesn't get an answer, she frowns and gets up and goes out through the kitchen, leaving the milk and her cereal bowl on the table.

She's in the garage, over by the bikes, when Liz ducks under the half-open door.

"Sylvie," Liz says, "you're going to see your baby today. Whether or not you get her back will depend on what happens this afternoon and in the next few weeks. You are in a real fix here. Don't make this about me." She's standing still because she can't see for the ivy growing over the windows. Then her eyes are used to the dark, and she notices the vines that have wormed their way into the garage through cracks in the foundation. They're bolting across the concrete floor in their desperation to reach the light. Sylvie lifts her head. "Child and Family Services will insist on getting to the bottom of things." Liz says. "You need to talk. Talk to your dad if you don't want to talk to me."

Sylvie's fiddling with the bike pump. "To Dad? Sure." She laughs. "Dad, come and sit down. Apparently we're supposed to get to the bottom of things. You think I'm nuts for leaving my baby in the car? Well, here's what it is, Dad. That little boy who drowned?

345

When we were in the States? It was my fault. He was really upset and his mother was dying, and instead of trying to help him, I called him a loser. I hit him. It was because of me he went out on the lake."

"*Oh.* Oh. I had no idea." Liz steps over the broken concrete towards her daughter. "Oh, honey."

"Yeah, well," Sylvie says, shrugging. She squats beside her bike and fumbles with the valve stem of her back tire.

"You know," Liz says, "kids do that kind of thing. You were acting the way kids act. I'm not trying to minimize it – it sounds like you were really mean to him – but the fact that he drowned right after . . . Well, that was *bad luck*. For everybody concerned."

"You think that's what it was?"

"Yes, I do!" All this time, she thinks. She's carried this since she was eleven.

When Sylvie doesn't answer, Liz steps closer to the bike.

"Honey, maybe you blew it out of proportion at the time. And brooding over it now will change nothing. You are punishing yourself unnecessarily. You are choosing to be unhappy for no purpose whatsoever."

"I get it," Sylvie says, her head bent. "I totally get it, Mom. Nothing causes anything. We're not the kind of people who are ever guilty of anything."

Liz wants to stamp her feet in frustration. "You haven't listened to a word I've said."

"Anyway," Sylvie continues, still not looking at Liz, "I saw him out on the water when you were in the studio with Krzysztof and I didn't go for help." She starts to work the pump and the garage is filled with the sound of its distress.

Liz has to clamp her arms hard against her chest to stop her sudden shaking. She has to raise her voice. "This was all a really long time ago," she says. "Why are you thinking about it now? When you've got so many other problems."

"It's one of the problems I have right now." Her voice over the laboured panting of the pump is calm. "It's not that easy to live as a fake. Mom, I can't talk about this anymore, because Noah is riding over to pick me up and I don't want him to come in and hear what we're saying. As he seems to respect his stepfather."

Emotion rises like steam in Liz's eyes. She tries hard to focus, tries to pick out the salient thing among all the things pressing on her. And there is her tall and beautiful daughter, so troubled, so resolute, bent over and rhythmically working the bike pump, her persimmon hair glowing in the low light. How lovely she is, and how alien – a human being whose heart and mind Liz will never really comprehend. This is what her years of parenting have come to, she sees, this moment standing in greenish light, being asked to put into words the deepest truth she has, a truth she's foraged by herself, with only her hunger to guide her.

"Sylvie," she says, and something about her voice makes Sylvie stop pumping and lift her eyes. "Sylvie, listen to me. I understand what it is to live with something you really regret. Because I do regret it, more than you can imagine. But things are not black-and-white. You lose a part of yourself if you constantly repress your impulses, if you say no all the time. It's hard enough for us to be true to ourselves – for women, I mean, the way we're constantly expected to please other people and make everything run smoothly. You have to honour what you feel and what you want. And if you do, sometimes there will be a cost."

Sylvie takes this in expressionlessly, and then she drops her eyes and turns back to her bike. She presses her thumb and fingers into the tire to test it. Liz hears the dog barking – Noah must be in the yard. Sylvie feels along the garage floor for the tiny black cap and deftly screws it onto the stem. Then she scrambles to her feet and without a word starts wheeling her bike towards the door. Liz is losing her, she has lost her.

She steps in Sylvie's way and grabs the handlebars. "Well, then, think about this," she cries. "Was it just because of you? Don't you think the people who took that little boy to the lake bear some responsibility? Or that girl who was supposed to be minding him? Or *me*? You could blame it on me."

But Sylvie does not leap on this. Instead, her face under the helmet assumes the passionate shape it had in childhood. "If a lot of people are responsible then nobody is responsible?" she says with sudden emotion. "Is that better? Is that easier? To think that nobody is responsible?"

They stand looking at each other, and then Sylvie ducks under the door and she's gone.

After a minute Liz steps out too, into the blazing yard. She's alone: Sylvie and Noah have ridden away. She walks towards the deck over a lawn so uneven she could be crossing a field of rocks. At the door she kicks off her shoes and crosses the kitchen to the sink, where she gets two J-Cloths, a damp one and a dry one. She's shaky, her wrists and elbows and knees are weak. But she wipes up the milk Sylvie spilt on the dining room table and thoroughly dries the wood. Then she drops the J-Cloths in the sink and picks up her roller and goes back to painting.

She paints methodically, noting the gauzy effect of the primer, the texture of tiny tufts the nap of her roller pulls up. It is strangely beautiful. Art could be anything. You could frame a square of what she's just done, the pattern of which is totally due to happenstance, and it would be just as much art as anything else.

Soon the painted window is a ghostly allusion to what it once was and the dining room is simple and utilitarian. A church rectory, Liz thinks. She'll do the finishing coat white as well. To please Aiden, who likes simple things. Her mind veers to the lake – she sees it vividly, Aiden's paradise of inky water edged with rock. Aiden is trotting down from the cabin in his blue swimming trunks, barefoot on the path. He pounds the length of the dock and dives in clumsily. Surfaces, shaking the water out of his hair, and begins to work his way towards her in the strange vertical motion he calls his breaststroke, with his head half out. He's a dark animal moving through luminous water – she will never be that free. Her love for him flounders in her chest. Speak your heart, she says to herself.

He clambers up onto the dock, water pouring off his thighs and blackening the wood, and she hands him a towel. "Aiden," she says.

18

White Crane Spreads Wings

THE OLD GARAGE WILL ALWAYS BE A SPECIAL place to Sylvie: the dense smells of motor oil and dirt and sheep manure, the windows overgrown with Virginia creeper, her father's motorcycle shrouded by a tarp. They were in a grotto, as if they'd stepped down into it on moss-covered stones. It's not the actual things they said to each other, although she'll always remember what they said. It's that her mother followed her out to the garage. That they met there, in dim green light, and passed secret tokens to each other. This is who I am. This is who *I* am.

The question that started it all – Sylvie had carried that question for years, with no expectation of ever asking it. But then a social worker came to the house and gave her a lesson in the power of questions. She came in the afternoon, the day before they were to go and see the baby, a hot, hot afternoon building towards rain. She was young herself, probably no more than twenty-five or twenty-six. She was wearing a grey skirt and a white blouse and she had a formal way of talking even during the casual part of the visit, as if she was still drawing on her course materials. She wanted to interview

Sylvie alone, so Liz poured them tall glasses of iced tea and they carried them out to the deck.

"Tell me about your baby," the social worker said when they were settled in their chairs. "I know that even tiny babies have personalities. What sort of infant is Faun?" By then a white haze had settled over the baby in Sylvie's mind, so there was really nothing she could recall and describe. "She seemed different at different times," she said finally.

The social worker gazed across the yard to where clouds were growing in the west, and then she turned her eyes back on Sylvie. "What's your experience been like as a mom?" she asked. What came forcefully back to Sylvie was being *touched*, constantly touched, on every square inch of her body, inside and out, the baby's sucking mouth always on her. Then she remembered the way the baby would sometimes lift a tiny hand and lay it lightly on her breast, and grief shook her. How long would her baby have to wait to be loved?

A lawnmower roared to life nearby, and the chance to answer was past. The social worker picked up her iced tea. "I wonder if you feel a bit of relief now, not to have to look after her. It would only be natural. You must feel as though you have your life back."

"No," Sylvie said. "Not really."

The social worker was small and neat and serious. Sylvie loomed beside her, exposed in all her pain to the young woman's thoughtful eyes, and she understood that the guise of childhood that had been draped over her these past few weeks in her parents' house had fallen away.

"Here's the address where you'll go for the visit with your baby," the worker said finally, pulling a card out of her bag. "I won't be the one handling the visit. It will be one of my colleagues, Valerie – this is her card. Will Noah be going with you?"

She stood up to go into the house, and then she turned and said simply, "You know, you just need to tell the truth."

After supper Noah appeared in her bedroom doorway. He was sweaty from his ride over. Sylvie got up and tossed over a flannel baby blanket for him to wipe his face with. He looked different. "Hey, you're trying to grow a beard."

"I'm not trying. It's doing it all on its own."

"I like it."

"Gracias." He threw the blanket into the hamper.

The ceiling fan was on its lowest setting, and the dolphins in the baby's mobile circled slowly in the breeze. "Are my parents outside?"

"Yeah, they're smoking a joint on the deck."

"What time did you get into the city?"

"Around two. Alison's boyfriend was up at the lake and he gave me a ride. He was going to the Eco-Network, so I hung out there for a while. I ran into a lot of people."

Alison's boyfriend, she thought, and one little strand of her anguish snapped, like an elastic breaking.

"Jason Stryker – I ran into him. Do you know him? I got the impression he knows you. He's working on protection for the Seine River. They're doing a public awareness campaign and they need people to write trail guides. I said I'd see if you were interested."

"I might be. I'm not exactly busy at the moment." Under that dark stubble, the planes of his face seemed to be in higher relief. It struck her that this might make it easier to know what he was thinking and feeling. "Is this what we're doing now?" she asked.

"What?"

"Acting like it never happened."

He reached up and waggled one of the little stuffed dolphins, and the rest of the pod leapt around it. "I think people with babies still work as activists," he said. "When they can make the time."

"Are you a person with a baby? Is that the way you see yourself?"

"I'm trying. I'm trying to figure out how to do this. It's hard having so much of your life laid out for you. But I guess you know that. And I guess it's like that for almost everybody." He walked over to the bed and sat down. He never had trouble meeting her eyes. She had made a lot of mistakes, but loving him the way she did was not one of them. "So," he said. "Tomorrow we go to see her. What time?"

"One o'clock."

"Will she be at the foster home?"

"No, it's an office on Stafford."

"Do you want to go for a ride in the morning?"

"Yeah, okay. I haven't been on my bike yet. All year."

"I'll come over and pick you up. Your tires might be shot."

She looked at his tanned face for another long minute, and then she said, "Noah, I'm going to see a psychiatrist next week. It's partly for the police, and for CFS. But also, the day I got lost, I hallucinated. I heard my name. Like *God* was calling me, or something."

"That was Gilles."

"Gilles?"

Noah hitched his way along the bed so he could lean against the headboard. "After he found the baby, he walked around by the car, shouting for you. He has a really deep voice. You would have heard him."

It was as if the light in the room went up. She stepped over to the bed and sat down. At an angle, so she could keep her eyes on him.

"Who was the guy who picked you up?"

"His name was Enrique Mendez," she said. What had really happened with Enrique Mendez had grown so slippery in her mind that she had to bear down hard to get it out.

"Why didn't you just tell the police?"

She started to explain and found she couldn't go on, for how fucking stupid it was. "Although it's weird, you know, that he wasn't curious about me. He never said, 'What are you doing out here? Why are you so upset?' He just picked me up and drove."

"He probably didn't want to get into anything," Noah said. "He had his own problems. But most people would have asked for his help right away."

She ran her finger back and forth along a seam of the quilt, a perfect straight line her mother had sewn. Finally she crawled up the bed and lay down. He swung his legs up and stretched out beside her. They lay side by side on the quilt, watching the ceiling fan wobble above them.

"All the time I was lost, I tried not to think about the baby alone in the car. Because it freaked me out so much. And then, when I got into the truck, it was just there. The baby had been in the car for twenty-four hours, and no one had any idea where I had gone, and right then, I understood that she never could have survived. She had died because of me. And I couldn't say it out loud. I couldn't say it to that man. When we got to Kenora and he let me out at the hospital, well, then I finally said it."

She could feel the sweat along her hairline pricking coldly with each revolution of the fan. A door banged below and footsteps climbed the stairs to the loft.

"Everyone thinks I should be happy because the baby was saved and it all turned out fine."

Noah reached over and took her hand. He lifted it to his chest and held it with both of his.

"But you know, if you realize something that terrible could have happened, it's almost the same as if it did. Like the possibility is still there, you're always going to know that."

She let his hand go and turned onto her side, facing him. She wanted to tell him the whole story of that night, what she saw when she watched the sky clear and the satellites crawling among the stars: how infinitesimal she was, and yet, how one little thing she did could turn the whole world black. How could these things both be true? And she wondered whether Noah also knew this, about himself? Did he live in the same strange flicker?

There was so much she could never tell him. But there was a lot that she could, and they had hardly made a start. Then he rolled over too and lay studying her face. It was not sympathy she saw in his eyes exactly, but interest. He was a person who wanted to know her, and who wanted to know the truth.

"It's not just that she could have died because of me," she said slowly. She paused until she had enough breath for the rest. "It's that, all those weeks I looked after her, I never really knew she was alive. I only started to get it that day in the truck, when I thought she had died."

What theatre or courtroom or temple would be adequate for the ceremony they enact that day? In fact it's a three-storey cement-block office building they go into, a shell that could be torn down and erased from memory in a week.

"Sorry, the air conditioning is nuts," the receptionist says. She leads them to the frigid room where a social worker waits for them and where their baby lies. In a car seat on a table, clutching a teething ring in her perfect starfish hands, trying, with an infant's optimism, to cram it into her mouth. She's wearing a familiar red and purple dress, and Sylvie understands that, like the other strangers she's encountered in the last few weeks, the foster mother is kind, she dressed the baby in one of the outfits Liz sent over.

When she and Noah come back out, they lean against the building for a few minutes, not talking, not touching, just trying to get warm in the sun. Then they get on their bikes and ride through the streets to the Forks. To the point of land where people in deerskin jackets and moccasins met for centuries, paddling in from three directions in birchbark canoes. Cree and Saulteaux traded there and danced and feasted, leaving behind projectile points and pottery shards. One of them left a footprint, a single eight-hundred-year-old footprint in the river clay.

A powwow is going on today. Sylvie and Noah cycle up to the sound of drumming. They can see red regalia and feather headdresses and the stoop and lift of the dancers. But they can't get close for the crowd, so they lock their bikes and run down the limestone steps, out onto the riverside path. The brown surface of the river is dimpled with tiny whirlpools. Boats roar by on the water and cars stream over the midtown bridge, and above the city floats a red and blue RE/MAX balloon, so low they can see the intermittent blasts of its gas jets. To the far-off sound of the drumming they walk quickly along the river, weaving their way among joggers and dogs and bikes and happy families with children.

They pass under the bridge, through a dark and dirty passage stinking of pee. On the other side the path becomes a trail, and they follow it to a secluded spot. A narrow stretch of bush where raccoons and squirrels and foxes and otters and even coyotes live out their wild lives in the heart of the city. Noah drops his backpack and stretches out, using it for a pillow. Sylvie slips off her sandals and eases herself down beside him, lying on her back in the dandelions and wild mustard.

In the Child and Family Services office, she was the one who held their daughter first. In the weeks since she'd seen her, the baby she knew had vanished; their little girl had entered a new stage. She snuffled at them as though snuffling amused her, and she held up her head and pressed her strong little legs into Sylvie's lap, determined to stand. Between her own two hands Sylvie could feel how frail the baby's ribs were, she could feel her breath inflating the tiny balloon of her chest. But this little girl had already set out on her solitary journey through the world; she'd seen things her parents knew nothing about.

"Oh, baby. Hey, baby," Sylvie said shakily. She didn't cry — she'd spent the last six months crying. But Noah did: she saw the skin around his eyes soften and redden as tears surfaced. Once you start crying, it's hard to stop. They were side by side on a couch – in that office they dared to sit like a family for the first time – and she passed their daughter to him. The baby drooled over his shoulder, following Sylvie with her eyes.

"She still knows my voice," Sylvie said.

"I see that," said the social worker, whose name was Valerie Glover.

Valerie Glover's face and voice were kind. She was older than the social worker who had come to the house, and warmer. She'd often worked with young parents struggling with ambivalence, she said, and she took its strands apart with care, stressing what voluntary surrender meant, how open and revocable it was for a few months, and how closed and final after that. She read them the legal definition of adoption and offered three paraphrases.

Sylvie was trembling from the cold. Please, she wanted to say. We're not stupid. But of course Valerie Glover was watching them closely, and no doubt that's exactly what puzzled her. Sylvie reached over and cupped the baby's downy head with her hand. "We never even named her," she finally said.

"Have you talked over your intentions with your parents? No? Well, you need to do that. With your permission, I'd like to meet with them."

"My mother will be glad we're doing this," Noah said. "This is what she wanted all along."

The baby reached up a hand and grabbed Noah's ear, and his eyes filled again. In the end, Sylvie thought, when all their visits were over and the papers were signed, that would be what she remembered best. And the baby's steady eyes (Noah's eyes), which met theirs curiously and neutrally. And her eggshell skin, and the way her lashes were fixed to her eyelids. Sylvie took it all in hungrily, trying to press it deep into her memory. She tried to be a responsible agent for her future self.

At the Forks now, she can feel the baby's phantom weight warm on her chest. As they were following the riverwalk, they saw a massive catfish lying on the ground, black and rubbery, mischievous whiskers drooping from its face. The fisherman turned his head and smiled at them, showing the gaps in his teeth, and she thought of Enrique Mendez, who came from a world where you have to do hard things – complicated, dangerous, ruthless things – because you don't have privilege to insulate you.

She closes her eyes and the smell of weeds and mud rises up around her. She can't hear the drumming now, but if she's very still, she can sense it in the ground. After they left her house this morning they cycled over to Maggie's and went to Noah's room to talk. Animals have babies, Sylvie said, sitting on the little bed where Noah used to sleep in his Astro Boy pyjamas. And they just love them and look after them. It's all natural.

I don't know if we can use other animals as a model for everything, Noah said. Humans have kind of taken it to a different level.

From the living room the television blared – Krzysztof's mother was watching *Judge Judy*. Sylvie didn't realize at first that Noah was crying. He was sitting with his elbow on his knee and his head in his hand, and then she heard the dry sounds of his weeping, and leaned against him, one arm around his waist. They sat there for a long time. It's not a perfect way, they said to each other. There is no perfect way.

When she finally lifts her head from the grass, she's alone. She rolls over and props herself on her elbows. The drums have stopped and the sun is low, slicing in bands through the trees. The river seems to have vanished, having taken in all the green of the day.

Noah is down on the bank, she can see his white shirt. He's standing still under the office towers that give the sunlight back in gold. From the tilt of his head, he seems to be listening. Then, against a screen of trembling leaves, his hands float up. As though the force of gravity is reversed – it's levitating them. Suddenly he pivots. Once, twice, three times he addresses the air, his fingers splayed like white flight feathers. He never quite rises to his full height; he's fighting at a crouch.

But is he fighting or is it a dance, or a prayer? Sylvie lies on her stomach and digs her fingers into the root-woven turf, watching as, over and over, he places his feet on the slippery clay of the river-bank and lunges, palms out, working to get it right. For a long time she watches, and then she scrambles to her feet and walks through the weeds towards him, feeling the clay under her bare soles, feeling it dampen and cool as she steps down the bank.

Acknowledgements

THE EPIGRAPH IS FROM THE POEM "RIVER EDGE:" in the collection *Torch River* by Elizabeth Philips. The koan "No Water, No Moon" is included in *101 Zen Stories* (1919), compiled by Nyogen Senzaki.

My deep appreciation to the team at McClelland and Stewart, especially to my editor, Lara Hinchberger – I am endlessly grateful for your commitment and good judgment. Thanks to Martha Magor Webb and everyone at Anne McDermid and Associates.

Thank you to the Manitoba Arts Council and the Canada Council for the Arts for financial support. I was also privileged to work on this novel in two wonderful residency programs: Berton House in Dawson City, Yukon, with the support of the Writers' Trust of Canada, and the Winnipeg Public Library's Writer-in-Residence program.

For their suggestions and expertise, thank you to Dr. Karen Scott at the Lake Winnipeg Research Consortium, Adelle Yanusyewski, Harry Daase, Mary Lou McGurran, and Winnipeg's Pinhole Artist Collective.

Warmest appreciation to Anita Lahey, Maurice Mierau, Sam

Baardman, and Susan Israel, who generously put their minds to earlier versions of part or all of this novel, and a special thank-you to Sam for the title. Hazel Loewen, your insight enriched this book, as it has enriched my life for decades. Heidi Harms; my father, Ralph Thomas; Caitlin, and Bill – I am so grateful for your support and love.